Young Wives' Tales

ADELE PARKS

LARGE PRINT

Oxford

Copyright © Adele Parks, 2007

First published in Great Britain 2007
by
Michael Joseph
an imprint of Penguin Books Ltd.

Published in Large Print 2008 by ISIS Publishing Ltd.,
7 Centremead, Osney Mead, Oxford OX2 0ES
by arrangement with
Penguin Books Ltd.

British Library Cataloguing in Publication Data
Parks, Adele
    Young wives' tales. – Large print ed.
    1. Married women – Fiction
    2. Single mothers – Fiction
    3. Love stories
    4. Large type books
    I. Title
    823.9'2 [F]

ISBN 978–0–7531–7990–1 (hb)
ISBN 978–0–7531–7991–8 (pb)

Printed and bound in Great Britain by
T. J. International Ltd., Padstow, Cornwall

For Jim

Acknowledgements

Thank you Louise Moore, without whom none of this would have been possible. I totally adore you; you are an inspiring luminary.

Thank you Mari Evans, you are wonderful, encouraging and dedicated. It's so much fun working with you. Thank you to the entire team at Penguin for continuing to work so incredibly hard on my behalf. You are all very important to me and I value every last one of you.

Thank you Jonny Geller, my dear friend, what an astute and wonderful man you are.

Thank you to all at Curtis Brown; especially Carol Jackson and Doug Kean, who are excellent agents and friends.

Thank you to all my readers. Without you this entire exercise would seem rather silly. I do appreciate you.

Thanks to my family for gracefully bearing the embarrassment of being related to someone who insists on writing about sex for a living.

Then there's Jim. Thank you for making the space we share on this planet a wonder.

CHAPTER
ONE

Monday 4 September

Rose

I close the door with a little too much force; the slam reverberates throughout the house. In the instant that the bang disappears I notice the emptiness. A void. Silence. I consider shouting "Hello" but I know there is no one to answer. The blankness shouldn't be a surprise. This is the third September I have returned to an empty home after a long summer break and noticed the all-consuming silence. The calm is partly a relief, partly heartbreaking. This year the hush is particularly distressing because I did not have to cajole, bribe, beg or threaten my boys to get them to surrender their vice-like grips at the school gate. This year, Sebastian ran into the playground without so much as a backward glance, let alone a kiss goodbye, and even Henry (normally the most openly affectionate twin) was only prepared to wave at me. From a distance.

Haven't I done a marvellous job? Excellent. Wonderful. I should be congratulated. I have produced confident, independent and secure boys. Well done me.

I think I'm going to cry.

I briefly consider pouring myself a glass of whisky. But dismiss the silly idea because in reality the only spirit in my cupboard is cooking sherry. I could have a glass of wine. I think there's half a bottle of Chablis in the fridge but I content myself with putting on the kettle. Strong coffee is the more sensible choice and I'm famed for my sensible nature.

The phone rings; its cheerful tring is a Red Cross parcel. I pick up hastily and gratefully.

"It's me."

Me, in this case, is Connie, one of my best and oldest friends. She sounds tearful and I remember that it's her eldest daughter's first day at school.

"How was Fran's drop-off?"

"OK," she mutters; she doesn't sound convinced. "She looked amazing. The uniform is so cute. But . . ."

"But . . .?" I prompt.

"Is it usual for them to cling to your leg and sob? I couldn't pry her off; she was like a tiny monkey. She kept begging to come home with Flora and me. She even offered to tidy up her Barbies — that's unprecedented." Connie is trying to laugh but I'm not fooled.

"Very usual," I assure her. "Do you fancy a coffee?"

"I want vodka, but I'll settle for coffee. I'll be with you in five. I'm just around the corner."

If I round up, Connie and I have known each other for nearly twenty years, which is phenomenal and unbelievable. To have known someone that long must mean I'm a fully fledged adult, and digesting that fact requires a mountain of sugar, not a teaspoon. We originally met through my sister, Daisy. Daisy and

Connie went to university together; they were very tight. Connie and I have only become particularly friendly in the last five or six years. We both have kids and, sadly, Daisy doesn't. I've found that kids pull you towards women that you would never have considered being friends with if you didn't have children in common — it's one of the perks of the job. Besides, Connie was very kind to me when my husband left me for one of our mutual friends.

The situation was officially ugly.

Connie was a great pal of Lucy, *the mistress*, but despite that she's managed to walk a diplomatic line and remain friends with both of us. Sometimes, I think I should have demanded that Connie take a more moralistic stance. I should have asked her to spurn her old buddy and my deceiving ex but I couldn't risk it. Friends were thin on the ground at the time and so few people are prepared to see the world in black and white. Extremism isn't fashionable. Not even extremely nice. People who are extremely nice are mistrusted or taken advantage of. Believe me, I'm talking from experience. So, I make do with knowing that Connie is a great friend to me and I ignore the fact that she's a great friend to Lucy as well.

Since Peter left, I've battled with every instinct when talking to Connie and somehow I've trained myself to make only casual, polite enquiries about Peter and Lucy. I do not allow myself the indulgence of ridiculing or vilifying them, which would embarrass and compromise her. I limit myself to the type of enquiry one makes after an old work colleague two people might have in common — civil, distant, even a little distracted — and I glean the occasional piece of choice information using this covert method.

Sometimes, in the early days, I couldn't help myself; little bits of pain or grief would eke out however tightly I tried to guard my feelings — and I'd mention Peter's name. I might have moaned about him or admitted I missed him. Yet I did this with the absolute certainty that I could trust Connie. She'd never, ever repeat to Lucy anything I say about him. This is a remarkable feat of self-restraint for anyone, but for Connie it's a breathtaking tribute to our friendship. Connie isn't discreet and it must kill her to keep mum. I've never allowed myself to reveal my true feelings about Lucy at all. The thing is I don't have the vocab — I don't like using expletives.

I don't worry that Lucy talks about me to Connie. I know that if she does Connie will be loyal and supportive of me, but I can't imagine the scenario ever arising. I don't think I've ever entered Lucy's consciousness, not even when she was eating Sunday roast at my house and giving my husband a quick blow-job in our cloakroom before I served up the pudding and coffee. She was always too busy giving literal meaning to the words "Let's take an intercourse break" to think about me. I'm not glamorous enough to rank among her friends and I'm not rich enough to be her client. Therefore, I am beneath her notice.

True to her word, Connie arrives at my house within moments. I open the door and see that she's fighting tears.

"There *is* something worse than them clinging to your leg and begging you not to leave, you know," I comment.

Connie plonks Flora, her youngest, on the kitchen floor and sits on a bar stool; she reaches for the biscuit tin.

"What's worse?"

"Sebastian and Henry literally skipped away from me this morning. Not so much as a casual endearment flung my way."

As I'd hoped, Connie puts aside her own upset and grins sympathetically. "I saw them in the playground, they did seem really settled. Running around like crazy. I think it was a good idea to stagger the drop-off on the first day so it wasn't too overwhelming for the new starters."

"You mean new parents, don't you?"

"Yes." She smiles, more relaxed now.

I turn away from Connie and busy myself with making the coffee so I can ask the next question with some dignity. "Did you see Peter and Lucy drop Auriol off this morning?"

Because, here's the thing. In among the several million crimes against me that my bleep bleep ex-husband has committed, this one possibly takes the prize. He and his hussy mistress — oh, OK then, his wife — have decided to send their child to *my* school. My school! Well, of course, when I say *my* school, I mean the boys' school. Hello? Isn't anything sacrosanct? Well, no, obviously not. With her form I can't imagine

Lucy being squeamish about moving in on my school turf.

I thought I'd be safe. I never thought Lucy would choose the state school route for her daughter. Peter and Lucy both work in the City and earn shed-loads. They could easily afford a posh little school with incredible alumni.

Sebastian and Henry's school is gorgeous. It does really well in the league tables and there's a marvellous playground; it's almost impossible to get a school with grass in London, yet this one has enormous trees with preservation orders. I'd carefully researched school catchment areas even before I conceived. I insisted Peter and I bought in a particular road to guarantee that we'd get our kids into Holland House. Then several years later, after Lucy had stolen my husband and destroyed my family, the woman had the cheek to announce that she thought it would be nice for Auriol to go to the same school as her big brothers.

Curse the cow.

This had to be a calculated move to hurt me. And it did hurt me, which is astounding because I'd thought that I was already dead to pain that she could inflict, slain by a thousand cuts. Their house in Holland Park isn't even in catchment, but Lucy visited the school and charmed the pants off Mr Walker, the headmaster (and I may mean literally, who knows with that conniving she-devil?). She spun the tale of how it was such a good idea for Sebastian and Henry because they ought to be close to their sister. Cow, bitch, witch. How dare she? As if she cares about the boys' welfare. If she did, then she wouldn't have slept with my husband, while pretending to be my friend, would she? And Auriol is not their *sister*. She is a *half* sister, which is a very important distinction. They have a father in common and nothing more, and what does that mean really? All Peter had to do to earn the title of father was get me up the duff and that simply wasn't too taxing, whatever he might claim now.

It's not like he's had to mop their tiny bodies with cold flannels to bring down temperatures when they were babies, nor has he once applied calamine lotion to a single chicken-pox spot. He hasn't ever taken them to the dentist, the doctor or the optician. He hasn't yet cut nails or hair. He hasn't packed lunches. He does not do their homework with them. He does not have their friends to his house for tea. He does not sew labels into their uniforms. He does not answer their questions on death or bullies.

He does play football with them on Sunday mornings, he bought them Game Boy Advance and introduced them to their first love — Sonic — and he does take them on holiday to Cornwall once a year. It's not that he's a terrible father, in fact he's quite a good father; I'm just saying being a father isn't that tricky, is it? Least not from where I'm standing.

It's not that I have anything against little Auriol, either. She's actually a fairly sweet child, especially considering she's handicapped with the most evil mother known to the western world since Snow White's stepmother. But really . . . the school! Isn't it enough for the woman that she has my husband and I don't have a husband at all, mine or anyone else's? She has silky blonde hair, pert breasts, long legs, lots of cash and more shoes in her wardrobe than Russell & Bromley stock each season. While I have red frizzy hair, breasts that schoolboys would describe as bazookas and fat legs that have so many varicose veins popping and swelling that I look like I'm wearing the tube map. Lucy is a woman comfortable in her skin (although in my opinion she ought to be wearing sackcloth and ashes and beating herself soundly every day). I'm basically a nice enough person who lacks confidence, marked talents and sometimes even a sense of humour. I guess because I can give such a realistic account of us both I understand why my husband left me for her.

But I did have the school. That was my territory. I am class rep this year. A position I've done my time to earn. I always volunteer to take the kids on trips when the teachers need an extra pair of hands. I was solely responsible for the cake stall at the summer fair and for two years in a row I sold more raffle tickets than any other mother for the Christmas tombola. I'm known and liked at Holland House. The school gate is my social life, my haven in times of need and where I get a buzz. That's important. That's sacred. It should be untouchable.

I say none of this. I take a deep breath, turn to Connie with two full cups of coffee and a wide grin and repeat my question. "So did you happen to see Peter and Lucy at the gate this morning?"

"No. Eva, the latest nanny, dropped Auriol off."

"I hope she settles," I say with a smile.

I can't quite meet Connie's eye so I concentrate on blowing my coffee to cool it off. I do hope the little girl settles. I wouldn't want any kid to be unsettled. But, on the other hand, if she doesn't settle they might move her to another school. I wish her well but mostly I wish her well away.

Connie reaches to squeeze my arm. "Are you OK with Auriol coming to Holland House, Rose? It's not an easy situation."

"Oh, it's fine," I lie.

"I feel a little bit to blame. I always think that Lucy was influenced to move to Holland Park after Luke and I moved to Notting Hill."

Connie is a lovely girl but a bit self-centred, and she does hold a general belief that the whole world revolves around her and that everyone's actions are a result of, or a reaction to, her own. To be fair, she is aware of this trait in herself and, more often than not, fights it.

"Or maybe she just moved here to piss you off," she adds with a grin.

"Maybe, but she hasn't. It's great that the boys are just around the corner from their dad if they ever need him."

I lie convincingly now. I used to be hopeless at telling the littlest white fib but all skills can be developed with practice.

"Yes. I guess he can drop in any time," adds Connie.

I nod and refrain from pointing out that he never has. Instead, I offer her another biscuit and ask if she managed to buy Fran a book bag. They've been hard to get hold of — the school outfitter miscalculated demand.

"Yes, got it. Am I supposed to sew a label on to it or can I just write her name on the flap thing?"

"You need to sew a label on the handle. It should be initial and then surname, in blue. Times New Roman font," I reply confidently. My feet well and truly on *terra firma*.

Connie stays for an hour but I can't persuade her to stay for lunch. She even resists my offer of home-baked bread and soup.

"Are you sure? It's organic. Over six different vegetables in it. I made a huge batch for the boys, too huge as it turned out. We didn't manage to eat it all."

"Rose, you put me to shame. Fran and Flora never get to eat like that. My idea of a healthy meal is a bowl of pasta and some frozen peas," she says. "Can we come round for our tea one day this week so that they get a few veggies and something organic inside them?"

I laugh and we agree to have tea together on Thursday. I assume and hope Connie is exaggerating her lack of skills in the kitchen. It's true that historically cooking has not been one of her talents, but surely she knows that she has a responsibility to the children now. Hasn't every mum converted to organic produce? I start to tell her how simple it is to make soup, but I don't even get as far as explaining the most efficient way to prepare and freeze stock when I see her eyes glaze over.

"You know, I always just buy the cubes," she comments, as she hugs me goodbye and makes for the door.

I remember the day when there was nothing easier on this earth than persuading Connie to waste time. She was the undisputed queen of sloth. Of course, that was when she was pretending to be a management consultant. Now she is a photographer and runs her own business. As yet her photography business isn't making her millions but it's clear that the job satisfaction she gets from her work is priceless. At least she no longer resents her husband for enjoying his work as an architect.

After Connie leaves I wash the breakfast pots and then clean the house from top to bottom. I congratulate myself as I manage to dust on top of wardrobes and vacuum under the beds. I spend over two hours tidying the boys' bedroom. It is extraordinary how time flies when you're sorting Lego bricks into different colours and sizes. I do a basket of ironing and put on two loads of washing. One is drying at the moment. I'll iron that tonight while I'm watching TV. I make a ham quiche and peel the vegetables for tea.

At 3.15p.m. I put on a dab of lipgloss and set off to school. I feel a bit guilty. I should have made more of an effort with my appearance. Some of the mums always arrive at the school gate with full make-up and the latest high-street must-haves. But, then again, they have men over four feet tall to make an effort for. I can't imagine Sebastian or Henry noticing whether I'm wearing the latest fashion statement or an old favourite peach M&S T-shirt; one that's been comfortable in my wardrobe for a decade. I'm more of a slummy mummy than a yummy mummy.

That said, although it is only a short walk to the school (literally two minutes) and it's a sunny afternoon, I don't leave the house without finding a cardigan. The sight of my wobbly, flabby arms is not something I want to share. I'm a size sixteen, or eighteen in the less generous brands. I've been this size since I got pregnant and this doesn't bother me at all. Or at least it doesn't bother me enough to make me want to do anything about it. I hate diets, and the only exercise I enjoy is walking the dog, which I do regularly. I do this more for the good of my heart than my figure, though. I've never been skinny. My wedding dress was a size fourteen and had to be let out a little around the bust. I suppose the difference is in those days my bust made men trip over their tongues, while now my boobs hang so low the only person that's likely to trip on them is me.

It's a very pleasant afternoon; rather more summer than autumn because the seasons no longer know when to change. When I was a girl you were guaranteed golden leaves underfoot almost the moment you pulled your school tie out of the wardrobe but it's not the same now. Everything is topsy-turvy. I saw crocuses sprouting in Hyde Park this August. I sometimes think the whole world is going mad. I hurry along the path worrying whether the boys are likely to have lost their blazers if they've taken them off.

As I approach the school gate I see two or three mums already clustering and my pulse quickens. I like this time of day. In the mornings, at drop-off, none of us have time to chat; we're all a little too harassed. In the afternoons I get my dose of adult company. I notice that all the other mums have younger siblings with them. Some in arms and strollers, others pulling on skirt hems. My arms feel empty and for a moment I don't know what to do with them.

We swap pleasantries; catching up on news about where people have been on their hols, comparing which after-school clubs we've enrolled our children in this term and suggesting dates for tea visits.

"Did you get away this summer, Rose?" asks Lauren Taylor. A mum of three, her eldest daughter is in the twins' year. Her middle one's in reception and the youngest is in the stroller.

"Yes. We hired a *gîte* in the South of France with my sister and her husband."

"Oh, I'm so pleased. I was thinking of you and wondering how you manage over the hols. Six weeks can be a long time on your own."

People often assume I am lonely. Even relative strangers feel compelled to say, "It must be very hard on your own," cue sympathetic look. Pity is something I've become accustomed to. Accustomed to but not anaesthetized. It's meant to make me feel better. It doesn't. The exact words may vary marginally; there might be a seasonal twist — "It must be hard to be on your own during the holidays/Christmas/your birthday" — but the sense that they feel sorry for me is the same.

I'm always stunned by comments such as these. How can I be considered to be on my own when I have twin seven-year-old boys, a dog, a rabbit, two goldfish, a full complement of parents, out-laws (the fond name I give my ex in-laws), friends, a younger sister, a brother-in-law, a large rambling garden and a small crumbling house? All of whom/which depend upon me for sustenance, maintenance, guidance, a ready supply of opinions (if only to reject them), walking, weeding, painting, cleaning, etc.

Although it is worth noting that I haven't had sex for over half a decade. This does niggle me from time to time. I comfort myself that there's no point in lamenting the lack of sex. Even if opportunity knocked, I'm not sure I was ever any good at it and I'm pretty convinced that if I was, I wouldn't be now. I've forgotten what goes where.

Lauren continues. "I was tearing my hair out towards the end of the summer and counting the minutes Mark was at the office. The moment he walked through the door I'd yell at him, 'Your turn, I've had them all day.'" Lauren says this without any intention to be rude or malicious. She's simply stating what every happily married mother thinks. "I can't wait until Chrissie starts nursery school next year. Last one off my hands. The new nirvana is an empty house."

"You shouldn't wish it away," I tell her, sourly.

She looks mildly chastised and I'm pathetic enough to feel chuffed by this; it evens the score after her comment about the certainty of my being lonely. I know motherhood shouldn't be a competition but it often feels as though it is. I do like Lauren a lot, however, so I resist adding that *my* best days are the ones when the boys are around me; days when they are drowning me in their noise and mess, because I know she'll be floored with guilt.

I feel down as I suddenly realize that today has been the strain, not the holidays.

"Maybe you could come over for Sunday lunch one weekend. It's no fun having a Sunday alone," offers Lauren. And maybe I would have accepted except that she adds, "Not this Sunday though, we have Phil and Gail Carpenter and their kids coming over. They have a girl in year one and the boy is in year four. Do you know them? Anyway it might be better if you come one weekend when it's not all couples. I think you'll be more comfortable. Maybe when my Mark is working away? What do you think?"

I think I want to punch her but I smile and lie, "I'm sorry Lauren. I'm booked up every weekend from now till Christmas."

Luckily, at that moment I catch sight of the boys snaking their way out of the classroom and across the playground, so I make my excuses and move forward to collect them.

The boys are mortified that I've picked them up and point out that they can walk home in minutes and I can practically see them from my bedroom window if I choose. I incense them further because I waste (their words) precious minutes that could have been spent watching TV (not if I get my way) by chatting to Mr Walker, the head. He's always visible at dropping-off and picking-up times so that the parents can grab him for a moment's gripe or grovelling. He also asks about our holiday but without the pity Lauren interjected into the conversation. The boys kick the pavement throughout the brief interlude and I whisper threats about confiscating favourite toys unless they are civil. When we do walk home they insist I trail behind them, keeping a distance of at least ten paces so their friends don't think they are babies. But they *are* my babies.

As I mosey behind them I consider my lie to Lauren. I know it was motivated by pique. My one bugbear about being single is that married couples never invite you anywhere. They don't want to draw attention to the fact that you are a spare part, not because it embarrasses the single person but because it embarrasses the cosy couples, who on the whole don't know what to do with unwanted wives. Where, oh where to put them?

Still, I know Lauren well enough to trust that she wasn't trying to be offensive in any way, she's just tactless. I sometimes think I live with shackles of tactlessness. Great iron chains that I lug around with me. These chains grow more hefty, awkward and burdensome as friends, relatives and strangers make unintentionally offensive comments and then I have to live with the emotional weight of their remarks.

But then again maybe I'm just touchy. Maybe I should ring Lauren and tell her that a date has freed up in November. It would be nice to go somewhere different for Sunday lunch. Daisy and Simon come to me about once a fortnight and Connie and Luke invite

me to theirs reasonably frequently. Luckily, Luke is a
far superior cook to Connie. But they have busy lives of
their own and I can't impose myself on them all the
time. The boys are often with Peter on a Sunday and
those Sundays are the worst. Relentless. Evil.

Yes, I'll call Lauren.

CHAPTER
TWO

Monday 4 September

Lucy

I am at my desk by 7.45 a.m. I check the Dow, the FTSE and the Nikkei. I linger on the Bloomberg site to get a measure of what the markets have been doing overnight. The US Stock-Index Futures are little changed ahead of rumours that consumer confidence is down and there'll be a slowing of personal spending. There's always rumours, most of which are initiated by traders. The important thing is to be able to effectively, efficiently and faultlessly separate fact from fiction. I keep reading and soon find what I'm hoping to see.

European stocks advanced, led by semiconductor makers, including Infineon Technologies AG, and Micron Technology Inc. — in the US — unexpectedly posted a fiscal fourth-quarter profit after markets closed.

Unexpectedly for some, maybe, but I'd seen it coming and had taken a punt. I can almost smell my bonus. I calculate that the pleasantly surprising

18

earnings from Micron signal good news for tech stocks, there's demand out there and the companies could perform better than the market had previously thought. I immediately check my clients' portfolios and decide what to sell and what to hold on to.

I feel I'm on rock solid ground in the office. I adore my job, everything about it. I like numbers and I like money, which is a good start. But I also relish the fact that I'm a bloody excellent trader and I wield enormous respect among my colleagues; all the more glorious as it is grudgingly given.

I started as a graduate trainee with Gordon Webster Handle, one of the City's most respected and established institutions. I soon discovered that respected and established are euphemisms for ball-breakingly tough and sexist, but oddly that environment didn't intimidate me, I found it challenging. Eight graduates started together. All, except me, were Oxbridge graduates. All, except me and one other, were men. The other woman trader no longer works. She married one of the few dotcom multi-millionaires who managed to turn his idea into hard cash just before the dotcom dream turned into a nightmare. One of the other guys has had a breakdown and I understand that he spends his time on a Buddhist retreat in India. The other five are all still trading, although I'm the only one still at Gordon Webster Handle. A couple of them live in NY now, which by all accounts is amazing — pure adrenalin the entire time. Sadly, not a rush I'm ever likely to experience. A move abroad isn't an option for me now, as Peter needs to live near his sons. Still, I like it here. They appreciate me.

When we used to keep track of such things I regularly earned the highest bonus among my original gang of trainees. A fact none of us has ever got over.

As Jeremy (the self-appointed cocky bastard in the group) pointed out the first time it happened, "Thing is, Lucy, it's unexpected. You might be the best trader among us but you still have a vag. I thought that alone would cost you twenty or thirty grand."

"It is rare to see a case of best man wins," I laughed, "especially when the best man is a woman."

Although admittedly things have changed. Since I had my daughter, Auriol, my bonuses have regularly been ten to fifteen per cent lower than my *lowest* bonus pre-Auriol. It appears I was able to hide my gender until I actually gave birth, then it became impossible, which is not surprising. However, I clearly remember the days when our bonuses were announced and I was the acknowledged hot-shot. Best days of my life. Up there with meeting Peter, graduating with a first, getting married and rather more special than the day I gave birth.

Sorry, but I simply don't buy into all that crap about the day you drop the sprog being the best in your life. It's a messy, bloody, terrifying and painful day. Even though I had an elective Caesarean with a mobile epidural it was still an uncomfortable and undignified affair. People feed themselves such bullshit. I accept that the day your kid walks or smiles for the first time is pretty special, but the day you give birth? *Pleeease.*

I'm not a mother-earth type. I did not enjoy my enormous belly, giving up alcohol or the wardrobe restrictions of pregnancy. Of course, I did the whole gestating thing beautifully. I ate very little so as to keep my weight down, which infuriated my obstetrician, but I was paying him terrifically so I bought the privilege of ignoring his advice. Besides, Auriol was a healthy 7lb at birth so what harm? Getting my figure back was very easy. I have no patience with these women who grumble that they have no time to drag their lardy asses down to the gym — I have two words to say to them: "Maternity Nurse". OK, so they cost, but what better excuse for returning to work than pleading that all your money is spent on your child? Am I ranting? How unbecoming. I sheepishly look around the office and am relieved to see that my rant has been internal.

I take a few calls, respond to the most urgent e-mails, those from senior bods and those who are in different time zones, and then I turn back to the markets. Shares of chemical makers BASF AG and Bayer AG rose yesterday, as crude oil fell for the first day in three. Good, as I'd hoped. The Dow Jones Stoxx 600 Index added 0.4 per cent to 297.44, with all the benchmark's eighteen industry groups gaining, except the Oil & Gas Index. Just as predicted. I pat myself on the back. I'm so good at what I do it's almost possible to forget how phenomenally risky my work is. Still, if the City is full of gamblers, I'm the addict who can count cards and has a photographic memory. I always leave the casino with pockets full of chips.

At 9.15 a.m. a reminder pops on to my screen drawing me away from my figures. I send Peter an e-mail.

Auriol will be walking through the school gates right now. I wish I was there with her. Love you.

In fact I'm not absolutely certain if she started at quarter to or quarter past nine but Pete will be none the wiser either. It's not that I actually needed to be reminded that my daughter is starting school today; I just didn't want to get caught up in something else and not pause in order to send Pete the e-mail. This show of thoughtfulness is a good move. I sometimes get the impression that he thinks I'm not quite up to scratch with the whole mothering thing. Which is dreadful. I hate not being up to scratch.

Of course, I love my daughter as much as the next woman. I worship her. She's bright, pretty, and largely well-behaved, except when she is being unimaginably horrid. I just don't go in for overly sentimental displays of affection. Because really that's all they are, *displays*. And I'm not big on self-sacrifice either. Or crusty noses. Or endlessly retelling the same story. Or answering non-sequential "why" questions. Or sitting in a circle with other mums singing songs and clapping. Or a number of things that society seems to insist come with motherhood.

Not that Pete's ever actually said that he thinks I'm lacking maternal instinct. He wouldn't dare. He knows he wouldn't live to regret such a comment. Even if it's true, I don't take criticism well. He did get a little tetchy last night when he was filling out various administrative forms for Auriol's new school — forms about allergies and permission to take the children on trips, that sort of thing. I didn't know the name of her doctor and so he threw a mini hissy fit. He flung the pen down on to the table and said impatiently, "For God's sake, Lucy."

I responded by slowly looking up from *Newsweek* and turning to him, pointing out, "You don't know the name of her doctor either."

"But you're her mother."

"And you're her father. I work the same hours you do, often longer. It's Eva's job to know these things, not mine."

Wisely, Pete recognized that the conversation was closed. I'm not a bad mother, I simply have a unique style.

I look up from my desk and say loudly, "I have to go to Starbucks. Can I get anyone a coffee? I can't settle, my little girl starts school today."

"Really? I didn't know you had any kids," says my boss, Ralph.

He just happened to be passing when I made the offer of coffee. He's quite new, sent here from the NY office six weeks ago. I'm still trying to get the measure of him. Normally it would be utterly crazy to make a big issue of being a mum in this office (asking for time off because of kids' ill-health, or similar, is suicidal), but Ralph has been a little bit too friendly on the last couple of occasions that the team has gone for a social and I think it's time to remind him that I'm married and have a family. This is one of the few times when being a mummy comes in useful. Marriage or even motherhood isn't usually much of an obstacle to an affair for most City types, but as my new boss is American he's a little more traditional and hopefully will stop touching my arm and waist when he talks to me now. Of course, there is the risk he'll stop talking to me altogether. Most men think women have lobotomies at the Portland Hospital, not Caesareans.

"Education is the most important heritage we can offer. Which school is she going to?" asks Mick, another trader on my floor. He's childless, so I can't imagine he's really interested, just programmed to have the last word.

"Holland House in Holland Park."

"I don't know that one."

"You wouldn't. It's state."

I must be the only trader in history who has opted to send my kid to a state school. Publicly, I pass this off as a socially responsible decision. I argue, where would the state system be if all the middle-class parents, who care about education, pulled their kids out of the state schools? Of course those schools would sink down the league tables. There's plenty of evidence to back up this viewpoint, and it has a certain "lefty" cachet that's very of the moment and that I rather enjoy. As it happens, I was educated at one of the best independent schools for girls in the country and I had hoped Auriol would be following in my footsteps. The boaters were adorable and Latin comes in useful when you want to slap down jumped-up "lads". But Rose put paid to any designs I had.

Besides paying for Auriol's schooling, Pete and I would happily have funded the twins through independent schools but would Rose have it? No, she would not. It's my belief that she rather likes to play the single mum card. She goes out of her way to make it look as though Pete's not quite doing his duty, not quite coughing up enough cash, or time, or thought. That's why she sold up their family home, even though he'd paid off the mortgage for her. She searched high and low to find the smallest residence in Holland Park (although notably, she didn't give up Holland Park altogether, did she?). All that nonsense she spouts about her planning for a time when she'll have no income at all, once the boys are grown, and needing the capital from the house as a nest-egg, blah blah. My question is why can't she just get a job, like everyone else? I'm a mother and I work. I don't wait for someone else to dole it out to me. Oh blast, just thinking about the woman is enough to bring on a headache.

It was so silly and emotive of her to insist that Pete and I offering to pay school fees was "guilt money". Nonsense. He just wants the best for them. I think at that point in the discussion she said something offensive about not wanting them to grow up to be pompous, social-climbing twits as most public schoolboys are. It doesn't take a genius to guess who she was having a pop at when she said that. She said she believed the children would be just as well educated at the local state school and added that private education is a waste of money and only for parents who splash out cash as a substitute for time or emotion. Easy for her to say as she lives in Holland Park; of course the state schools are terrific there. Pete and I lived in Soho at the time, where education is considered an inconvenient interruption to a life of crime and vandalism. But somehow Rose got the upper hand. The way she told it made it appear virtuous to send your kids to state school and positively evil to educate independently. I feel so terribly out of sync. Spending on education used to be considered wise, a privilege yes, but not a source of shame. Certainly better than spending on handbags or curtains. Now the opposite is true.

Of course I couldn't send Auriol to a private school while Henry and Sebastian were attending the "lovely little state school, just around the corner". If I'd done that I would have played directly into Rose's hands. We'd never have heard the last of the disparity between the children. God, Rose is irritating.

So, we had to move. Somehow Pete persuaded me that it would be a good idea to move nearer to Rose and the boys. "Much friendlier." Again I'm not *à la mode*. I don't want to be so very twenty-first-century about our irregular family. I'm actually happier with the role of wicked stepmother; at least one isn't fettered with annoying expectations. We aren't one great big happy family. He divorced her; that shows a certain amount of dissatisfaction with the relationship, wouldn't you agree? I'm quite keen for us to settle into a state of active dislike bordering on loathsome anger. I don't want to be one step away from polygamy, which is what staying pally with the ex amounts to.

I'm not exactly sure how it happened; I was dealing with a big project in Hong Kong and by the time I got home Pete had made an offer on a house just round the corner from Rose's, instructed a conveyancer and solicitor and all but booked the removal van. Good God, had the man lost his mind? No, I admit I hadn't read his e-mails especially carefully; it was a very busy time. And yes, when I did check his messages I did find a series of increasingly frantic notes forwarding details of the house he'd found us and asking if I was happy for him to progress with buying it. OK, I confess, I might have vaguely mumbled that I agreed it would be sensible for Pete to live near the boys but I hadn't meant it.

I take comfort in the fact that the house he chose for us is enormous. Not quite as enormous as the one he and Rose used to own, but people forget, we do have two families to support now. So, once ensconced in Holland Park, there seemed no reasonable alternative — the children are all now at the same school. Mr Walker, the headmaster, was a poppet. He was eating out of my hand after just one meeting. Auriol leap-frogged the waiting list, even though strictly speaking we are a tiny bit outside the catchment area. Nothing untoward, we just evoked the sibling priority rule.

In fact, Holland Park *is* quite fun. Not so desperately of the moment as Soho, where I lived as a bachelor girl, but I've done the late bars, twenty-four-hour shops and the minimalist home thing — it's very over. Holland Park is unquestionably appropriate for this stage of my life. You can't flick your hair without hitting an organic pâtisserie or a children's yoga centre. And it is a total joy that Connie and Luke are just around the corner in Notting Hill. Despite my reputation as Ice Queen, even I admit that there's nothing sweeter on this earth than watching Connie's daughter, Fran, play with Auriol. Besides, Auriol does adore her big brothers; especially Sebastian, who looks most like his father — he grew out of his red-haired stage. Henry still has Rose's colouring — summers are a curse for him.

I just hope the school does the job. If not, I'll have her out of there before the end of the academic year, but I can't imagine I'll have much to worry about; after all, Auriol's genes are phenomenal — she'll be straight As all the way. I wonder if she'll be Mary or the Angel Gabriel in the school nativity? Mary doesn't get to say much but she is on stage all the time. But the Angel Gabriel normally has a darling costume. I must give that some thought and then put my recommendation to Mr Walker.

Right now I'd better go and buy those double espressos.

CHAPTER
THREE

Monday 4 September

John

Bloody hell — is the Queen in town or something? What's with the traffic round here? I understood from Craig that his school was a sleepy, leafy bit of snooty Holland Park. I finally find a space to park about half a mile from the school and ditch my Z4 series BMW. As I get out of the car, I can't help but caress her wing. She's a beauty. I'd marry her if she had tits. What a ride. I soon ascertain that the gridlock is caused by frantic mothers who drive four-by-fours; I've heard about these women. You know, on the radio some DJ is always taking a pop at this weird breed that drive a four-by-four but loathe the sight of mud and break out in a rash if they leave a London postcode. I'd thought they were an urban myth, not unlike everyone believing they are four snogs away from their fantasy celebrity snog. Turns out they are not just an urban myth, crap to chatter about to fill the airwaves, they do exist. For the record, crap filling the airwaves is fine by me. I'm a simple guy. I accept that crap fillers are a big part of what life's about.

I watch these demon mothers aggressively out-stare one another. They mouth "fuck you" through the window at drivers who nick their parking space and when they get out of their tanks they smile and wave at each other and start to chat about daytime TV. Unbelievable. What a laugh.

I immediately scan the crowd of women clustering at the school gate. Disappointingly, there is a dearth of scrummy mummies. I watch *Desperate Housewives*; I was expecting a plethora of women needing a decent and immediate seeing to. Women who were going to throw their knickers at me as though I was Tom Jones, just as soon as I threw a smile at them. I look round; nothing doing. All these women look like mothers. Unsurprising really, as they all *are* mothers and we are stood at the school gate waiting for their bratty offspring to appear to prove the point. I just thought, hoped maybe, for something a bit more . . . well, Kate Moss is a mum, isn't she? And Liz Hurley and that Kate whatsherface, the actress. I'd do any of them. You can't blame a man for hoping.

I push against the mass of kids charging out of school; I feel like a fish swimming against the tide. Their little squirming bodies create quite a formidable force. I'm not often near kids. My sister has a couple of them — girls — and they are cute enough. They are related to me, right, can't be a bad start in life. When I see them at Christmas, birthdays and other family events they seem good enough, bit spoilt, bit demanding, not my scene but OK on balance.

They weren't at the last family do as it was my uncle Ronny's funeral. My sister's gone all middle-class and wouldn't dream of bringing the kids to the wake in case she caused some deep-seated psychological issue which might manifest itself in years to come. Imagine, the girls might break down and weep uncontrollably whenever they were faced with a glass of sherry or an egg sandwich with its crust cut off, or some such bollocks. I reminded her that when we were kids, from what I can remember, we were at a wake just about every month and it hasn't done us any harm. I haven't got an overly pronounced morbid streak. They know how to do a good funeral in Liverpool, some of the best parties of my childhood. Still, I don't blame my sis too much. Clawing for middle-class respectability is an arduous job. One slip and years of ballet classes and brown-bread-eating are undone in an instant. Besides, I'm not above a bit of reinvention myself. I like the possibilities it offers.

It strikes me that an enormous huddle of kids, like this lot, creates an enormous amount of noise (which is to be expected) and an odd smell (which takes me by surprise). It's not an absolutely gut-churning pig of a smell, like nappies or vomit. Christ, I've got a whiff of those kid offences against mankind just walking down the high street. There should be a law against it. What is it with these mothers? Do they lose their sense of smell along with their sense of style when they have a sprog? Mother Nature needs to revisit the blueprint. But these kids coming out of school don't smell of vomit, crap or even pee; they smell of dust, mud, powder paint and kid sweat. This would be foul except they also smell of freedom, which makes the rest of it vaguely acceptable. You can smell the autumn wind in their hair.

I push past the kids and walk into the school, which seems very different and yet exactly the same as the school I went to three decades ago. My local primary school was a 70s prefab concrete box. This school is ancient by comparison, purpose built in 1908, according to the engraving above the doors. The school has separate entrances for boys and girls and real wood floors and all that. My school had parquet flooring in the hall and lino in the classrooms, which, I dare say, was considered the utmost in modernity at the time. We had blackboards and noticeboards, now they have whiteboards and overhead projectors. I peer into the classrooms and note that the minute chairs and desks are the same, as is the scuzzy carpet in the corner of the room where fidgety bums are forced to rest for the duration of Once Upon A Time until Happily Ever After. The crap we feed the youth of today, eh?

I wander along the corridors, hoping to stumble upon the headmaster's office, when I'm accosted by some middle-aged woman who bossily demands to know why I'm in the school and who I am. It takes short seconds to completely charm her. I explain that I'm Craig Walker's best friend.

"Mr Walker, the headmaster?" she asks.

"He may be Mr Walker, the headmaster, to you, Miss —" I pause.

"Mrs actually, Mrs Foster." She simpers as she says that. I look incredulous and mutter something about all the most beautiful women always being snapped up first. I pretend that I'm musing to myself but of course I ensure I'm plainly audible. To get this straight, I have absolutely no intentions on the very plain Mrs Foster but I can't resist flirting with her. I find women so easy to please that I feel it's almost my duty to do so. God knows there isn't one of them, however ugly, that can't be flattered and convinced that they are God's gift to mankind. And they say men are arrogant.

"He might be Mr Walker to you but he'll always be Wheelie Walker to me. It's a little-known fact, but your Mr Walker was the king of the chopper on our estate; when we were lads Wheelie Walker was a wonder."

It never harms to big-up your mates; women like that too, they see it as magnanimous. In fact Craig was known as Weedie Walker or Weeie Walker and he was scared shitless of riding his chopper, climbing trees, being in bat and just about all other boys-own stuff. But no one is going to look good if I say as much. Christ, I don't want Mrs Foster to think I hung out with saps.

"His is the first door on the left after you walk through the assembly hall. If you get as far as the music room you've gone too far. Do come and find me if you get lost or if there's anything else I can do for you."

She smiles bashfully. This isn't a come-on. I know that women like Mrs Foster (over thirty-five, never been especially hot, hard-working hubby, who she's grateful to and for) are not the type to proposition strange men found wandering through the school corridors, even if they make especially nice comments about the artistic integrity of the Year 2 wall frieze: subject, autumn. She just wants to help me in some innocuous way, if at all possible, because she likes me. Women do.

As I open the door to Craig's office I'm overwhelmed by an enormous jumble of papers and books. His jacket is hung on a hook behind the door and it actually has cord patches on the elbows. It's so funny that everyone has their little affectations, even those who you'd believe to be above (or below) such things. I mean, what is old Weedie Walker trying to say? He's not some don floating around the lofty spires in Oxford, is he? He's a headmaster at a local primary school.

Craig's work environment could not be more dissimilar to my own. His little, cramped, dusty, academic office is diametrically opposed to my spacious, dynamic, bright-young-thing environment. There are wall-to-wall books and files which are occasionally interrupted by a photo of some class or other, lots of identikit kids grinning manically for the camera. His large desk looks like it's been purchased from one of those pointless little magazines that you find stuffed in the back of the Sunday newspapers. I wonder if it came with a pack of video covers that are supposed to look like great classic novels. You can't see much of the offensive fake leather anyway, as the desk is covered with papers, pens, pencils, stamps, elastic bands, paperclips, pencil sharpeners, etc. Hasn't the man heard of the digital age?

In my management consultancy firm no one has a set desk, or even a drawer, let alone an entire office. That sort of ownership is regarded as stultifying; we hotdesk. Which means we are forced to carry our laptops, mobiles and BlackBerrys around with us as though they were second skin. The idea is when you arrive at work each morning you enter the reception (acres of granite and glass) and are checked in to an available desk. The hope is to stop cliques forming, to encourage integration of staff and the dissimilation of new ideas and some other bollocks — I forget. To be honest it's a bit of a pain in the arse. There comes a time, in every man's life, when the need to lay his hat somewhere becomes paramount. I have to admit, Weedie Walker's office, for all the chaos, has a certain charm.

"Mate!"

I stand with my arms wide open, an enthusiastic grin bursting off my face. Craig looks up from the papers he's marking and smiles at me. At first he's unsure, a little shy, and then a big grin cracks across his face. His grin is actually very cool, and he looks much less of a nerd when he's smiling.

Craig stands up, walks towards me and holds out his hand for me to shake. I pump it and pull him into a hug. Thing is, Weedie or Weeie he may have been, but he was my mate. Still is. He's a good bloke. Better than me, which I don't have a problem with. Nearly everyone I know is more principled than me but I take comfort in the fact that few of them are as happy as I am. The two facts are related.

It's been about six months since Craig and I last saw one another. This in boy world causes no problem at all. If two girlies who'd been mates since primary school hadn't seen each other in six months, I swear to you, there would be grief, guilt and recriminations by the bucketful. Both would feel neglected or insulted. It must be crap being a girl, with all that emotional stuff all the time. Whereas being a guy is great. More pay, same work, no childbirth, no glass ceilings, no desire to write thank-you notes. Ace.

"Nice office, mate. But serious lack of totty mummy at the school gate. That's all I came down here for."

"John, if you were expecting totty mummy you should have been pals with a guy who is headmaster at one of the chi-chi schools in Chelsea or somewhere, ideally a fee-paying school. Those mothers tend to have time and money enough to keep up appearances. Largely, here, we specialize in being bothered about the children, and I find the mothers are more concerned about their kids' wardrobe and grades than their own wardrobe and calorie intake," says Craig primly.

I wait until the lecture is over and comment, "Big career black hole, mate. I mean, you're a single man. You should have gone in for the job at the private school if that's the case *and* you'd have a chance at poking the odd nanny then. I bet that lot," I nod through his window towards the school gate, "are all working hubby to an early grave and yet still can't afford a nanny. Disappointing though. I'd thought there would be a few women worth a once over. They can't all be lazy cows."

"John, please." Craig pulls his lower lip into this funny straight line when he's offended or upset. He is easy to read and even easier to wind up. "I don't think it's right to think of my pupils' mothers in those terms."

"No wonder you're still single," I mutter. "They are *women*, mate. How else are you going to think of them? Unless you don't think of them at all. You bender."

Craig isn't homosexual, but as heterosexual mates we are duty bound to accuse each other of dirt-digging on a reasonably frequent basis. At least that's the code I play by.

Craig sighs heavily. I've been a disappointment to him for so long now; you'd think he'd accept it. But he's a teacher, right? He always believes I could try harder. Perhaps I'd improve if only I wanted it badly enough. I'm not a total womanizer. Actually, I am. But I do think of other things and can hold conversations about other things. It's just that we fall into these roles, right, when we are together. Craig is the straight one and I'm the laugh, the lad. He was a virgin until he was twenty-one. Twenty-one. Fuck, man, can you believe it? And we went to a school where some girls would shag you for a bag of chips and a croggy home. Still, Craig never saw opportunity, even when it hammered really loudly on the door, which is why our respective roles were written long ago.

"Come on, Sir. Get your coat. There are pubs serving bitter at this very moment. We have an obligation."

I let Craig lead me to his local watering-hole, which is a shabby pub not old enough to be charming, not new enough to be trendy. It's OK. I don't mind. I didn't expect him to pick one of the millions of cool bars in Notting Hill, even though there's wall-to-wall totty in most of those places. While I have a radar for that sort of thing, Craig is oblivious, possibly even repelled. But this pub serves draught and so serves its purpose. Normally when we meet up Craig comes into town and I choose the venue. This works because I work significantly longer hours than he does (I spit when I think of his holidays, but then he probably spits when he thinks of my pay packet), plus, our mate in common, the third side to our triangle of trust and all that, Tom, works at Wapping so it makes sense to meet in town. But tonight Tom isn't meeting up with us, although he is the reason we have to get together.

"I can't believe Tom jumped," I say as I stare at my pint. I shake my head morosely.

"Well, he has been seeing Jenny for five years now, they do live together, own a flat together, it's not what you'd call out of the blue, is it?" reasons Craig. He's drinking coffee, says it's too early for alcohol.

"I know, but mate, marriage? It's so big."

"You did it."

"That's right, and he should learn from my mistake. It's such a commitment."

Craig laughs. "How is it that you pronounce commitment with the disdain that most of us reserve for, well, the other C word, the one that rhymes with runt?"

I start to laugh. "You really can't say that word, can you, mate?"

"I have no wish or no need to," says Craig calmly. Then he asks, "Don't you like Jenny?"

"She's a fair enough bird. Seems to have her head screwed on. Maybe a bit bossy." I grimace when I think of the numerous occasions she's given me earache because Tom has come home paralytic after a night out with the boys. Like that's my fault? "Nice pair of legs and all that but, he's *marrying* her. I just don't see the point in going the whole nine yards."

"I don't suppose you do," says Craig. I don't really like his tone; it's almost pitying. Twat. Mate. But a twat. Craig goes on. "Anyway, he's marrying her in ten weeks' time so can we stop with the theatrical surprise and the public grieving and can we turn our attention to the stag night? That is why we are here, after all."

"Suppose," I agree. "Soon as I get another pint in. You'll have one this time, won't you buddy?"

When I return from the bar Craig has converted the pub into something that looks a lot like a war room, one of those you see on old black and white movies. He has produced a spreadsheet list of invitees, including postal addresses, e-mail addresses and their most recent contact numbers (mobile, work, home). He's drawn up a list to suggest possible venues for the stag and another list where he's "brainstormed" ideas for entertainment. I notice that many of the venues have already been scored out. In angry red letters he's written "TOO LATE". The words seem to take on a life of their own and are screaming accusingly at me. The big red letters shout panic as they become larger and are accompanied by an increasing number of exclamation marks as you move further down the list. I know this is why Craig has been brought on board.

Tom got engaged six months ago and asked me to be Best Man on the spot. Obviously, I said yes; doesn't being Best Man guarantee that I get to sleep with a bridesmaid, maybe two? But other than picking out some cool cufflinks for me to wear on the day I haven't done a huge amount of prep. Jenny got a bit arsy with me. Said I was in denial. Not true, just idle. Look, I get paid to organize all day, draw up charts, weigh up risks, make tough decisions, etc. I don't enjoy doing it in my free time. So Jenny insisted that Craig should become Co-Best Man. His talents for organization and his particular line in sobriety and reliability offered a yin to my yang. Fine by me. The more the merrier. As I say, petty jealousy and a world full of imagined slights are exclusively girlie domain.

"The way I see it, mate, the split of duties should go something like this. You find the venue, I'll supply the booze. You draw up a list of blokes you think we should invite and I'll call them up."

Craig looks relieved and pushes his glasses up his nose. "That sounds fine. What do you think we should do on the Saturday afternoon? Archery?"

"Paintballing."

"Should we stay at a country hotel?"

"B and B — more cash for booze."

"Absolutely no strippers. Jenny has made that clear. She'd never forgive me."

"Course not, Craig, mate," I say reassuringly and make a mental note to sort out the stripper. Tom would never forgive me if I didn't.

We wade through the detail of the stag weekend, agreeing on a venue, menu, guest list and entertainment. We settle on paintballing during the day and wine-tasting in the evening — clearly that's Craig's suggestion. Wine-tasting sounds a bit up itself but might be a laugh, and anyway I conceded because he agreed to go to a tacky nightclub afterwards. After an hour or so we pretty much knock the event into shape. I type a list of to-dos into my BlackBerry, dictated by Craig, and I relax back on the bar stool. Mentally I sigh with relief. I feel smug. I don't think Tom will be disappointed in any way.

"Good work, Craig, mate. Couldn't have done it without you."

"Oh, no problem," says Craig, blushing. He's not good at handling compliments, doesn't get them often enough.

"Really mate, you've put a lot of effort in. All those lists and things. You're a good bloke."

"Couldn't leave it to you, Could I?"

"No, not really," I admit.

"Responsibility is only a tad less offensive to you than commitment, isn't it?"

"Easy, mate. That's harsh." I laugh, sip my pint, take a drag.

"But true." Suddenly Craig looks stricken with terror. "What about the speech?"

"Speech?" I play innocent.

The thing is, although I'm truly grateful to Craig for digging me out of a hole in terms of bringing a little organization to the stag weekend, I do fancy owning the Best Man's speech. The thing is — I'm funny.

"The thing is you're funny," says Craig.

"Meaning?"

"Well, I'm more earnest than funny."

"The aunts would love to hear what you have to say," I tell him, playing it cool.

"Yes, and they'll probably die of shock when they hear anything you have to say, but even so, the rest of the guests will probably appreciate you more than they'd appreciate me."

This is one of Craig's many qualities. He's decent. He probably knows I'm desperate to make the speech. Still, it wouldn't be gracious to be pushy. "We could split it," I offer.

"Good idea. I'll read the telegrams and cards and you can do the funny man stuff."

"Deal," I agree immediately.

But before we can clink glasses and say cheers, Craig adds, "I'll have to see the speech before you make it, of course. No cursing, no revelations about Tom's ex-shags and *do not* mention the time Jenny was wasted and tried to snog you. It was a long time ago."

"OK, you can trust me," I grin.

"No, John, I can't. Even you don't trust you," says Craig. And he's not smiling as he says it. Funny man.

CHAPTER
FOUR

Monday 4 September

Lucy

I make an enormous effort to get home early from work; I tell my boss I have an off-site meeting and turn down two offers to eat out, one of which is with a client — he doesn't pay for my time twenty-four hours a day but he has bought my soul. Normally we go to dinner together once a week minimum. The man's a bore. He has four jokes which he tells in rotation, on a more or less constant basis. He smokes cigars, which I used to enjoy until I fell pregnant with Auriol, and ever since, the smell of cigar smoke has left me nauseous. He drinks heavily and invariably the evening ends with me having to haul his large carcass into a cab. Still, it's part of my job to feign an intimacy with the man so that he continues to give my company hundreds of thousands of pounds to invest. Usually when he's delivering his predictable punchlines I amuse myself by thinking private and important thoughts.

I think about Pete and me taking Auriol to Tokyo's Disney World last April. Obviously I did not entertain the idea of Disney in Paris (weather too unreliable) or

43

America (cellulite too abundant), but I conceded that if we did Disney in Tokyo and we threw in a couple of temples and some cherry blossom trees, the trip would be bearable. Bearable was my benchmark, as we were between nannies, so it was the first holiday we'd gone on without help. It hadn't been our plan to be between nannies (another one left unexpectedly and unaccountably), so we did not have an itinerary of children's clubs as a back-up. To be honest I was thinking of cancelling. What a surprise. I genuinely had a great week in Tokyo with Pete and Auriol. I mean, who'd have thought going anywhere with a four-year-old could be such fun? Not me, certainly. But it's thoughts of Auriol giggling hysterically at Monster Girls and scrunching up her face as she first tried sushi that get me through tedious dinners with colleagues and clients.

At lunchtime I sent Julia, my PA, to buy a dozen helium balloons for Auriol, so I need to take a cab from the office. As I push open the door to our home I'm hit by the smell of something meaty cooking; a casserole of some description would be my guess. I can hear Radio 4 and Auriol's chatter drift from the basement kitchen. These are good signs. In the past, on the first day home to a new nanny, it has been known for me to be greeted by the nanny already wearing her coat and handing me a letter of resignation. It's not that Auriol is a terrible child to handle, it's just that some of these young girls are not experienced enough to manage her creative temperament.

"Surprise," I call.

Auriol bounds up the stairs towards me and flings her arms around my waist. I try to stop her putting her hands on my skirt (it's Emilio Pucci) but the manoeuvre costs me my grip on the balloons and they drift up through the stairwell and hover two flights above us. Eva, Auriol and I gaze upwards at the bobbing mass of pretty pink balloons. I freeze for a moment and wonder if this is going to cause a problem. I often feel entirely at sea with Auriol and have no idea how she is going to react to anything. It astonishes me that I can predict financial markets throughout the world with pinpoint accuracy, I have a widely respected insight into the characters of most people I happen upon, but when it comes to kids in general, and Auriol in particular — I'm stumped. I mean, they are so irrational and unreasonable. So emotional and mercurial.

The balloons hover, teasingly, Eva takes the initiative and laughs, Auriol squeals with excitement and I shrug. This time disaster is averted, no scene. Marvellous.

"How was school?" I ask.

I try to kneel because I read that children like you to talk to them at eye level. Princess Diana always did that and she had a great way with children. Unfortunately my skirt is too tight and I'm in Sergio Rossi killer heels so it's not going to happen. I usher Auriol back towards the kitchen. She's bouncing off the walls and chattering about the new teacher, Miss Gibson or Gibbon or something, and the fact that Fran is in her class. I tell her to stay with Eva and I go to my bedroom to change.

It takes me about fifteen minutes to decide what to wear because I have resisted going down the lazy mum route which is so depressingly prevalent. I have never been seen in a vomit-sprayed or Weetabix-splodged beige top or baggy leggings. My dry-cleaning bill is enough to buy me a small car every year, but standards have to be maintained. By the time I get to the kitchen I see that Auriol has eaten supper. I'm disappointed.

"I came home early to take you out to a restaurant to eat," I grumble. "I wanted to celebrate your first day of school."

My intention is to reprimand Eva for not reading my mind or at least for not checking my schedule.

"It's not early for Auriol," replies Eva. "It was after six o'clock when you arrived home. After a full day at school she is hungry at four in the afternoon. I have made enough beef casserole for you and Mr Phillips too. It's entirely organic as per your instructions."

"Oh, I don't eat much red meat," I mutter, swallowing my irritation. Irritation seems to be sustaining me quite adequately at the moment, that and decent vitamin supplements.

I'm all dressed up with nowhere to go. I slip on to the bench seat next to Auriol and try to engage her. However, she's more interested in the TV which has replaced Radio 4 and is blaring from the corner of the room. I follow her gaze. Some beautiful twenty-year-old girl, dressed as though she's just walked out of a pop video, is being dunked in a pool of custard. When she manages to slither out of the pool, millions of Coco Pops drop from the sky and stick to her. Throughout the experience she is screaming, "Wicked," and "Totally gross man," in the most awful Birmingham accent. It's unsuitable viewing on every count.

"I don't like the TV on at mealtimes," I tell Eva.

"Why do you have a TV in the kitchen and dining room in that case?" asks Eva. I think she is genuinely curious rather than just insolent; besides, as I interviewed twenty-two nannies to fill this position I don't want to pick a fight at this early stage, so I give her the benefit of the doubt.

"Peter and I need to keep abreast of the markets. The TVs are used for news channels exclusively."

In fact I allow Auriol to watch rather a lot of TV at the weekends, but I don't pay a nanny three pounds per hour over the going rate to allow her the same privilege.

"NOT TRUE," shouts Auriol.

Eva and I both pretend not to hear her and Eva switches off the TV. Auriol bursts into tears and splutters a chorus of "not fairs". Eva says she's tired, Auriol that is, and takes her upstairs for a bath.

When they return forty-five minutes later to say their goodnights, Auriol is looking much calmer and prettier. She's wearing powder-blue pyjamas from Mini Boden. She looks cute enough to eat. She could be a child model, only I object strongly to the entire premise. I doubt I look quite so angelic. I have a cigarette in one hand and a glass of champagne in the other.

"You shouldn't smoke," says Auriol. "You'll die and before that you'll look old and ugly."

"Do as I say, not as I do, Auriol," I instruct.

I shouldn't smoke and I usually try not to in front of Auriol. But besides finding it quite relaxing, I'm a sexy smoker. I keep my finger at an angle and men often comment on how elegant my hands are. When I take a drag, my lips double in size, whereas other people's lips disappear. It's a tough habit to kick when it's so alluring.

"Rose says you shouldn't drink either. She says you'll come to a nasty end."

Auriol repeats the sentence in a tone which suggests she has little understanding of the expression.

"That's just her wishful thinking," I mutter as I stub out the cigarette and slug back the champagne. I really must have a word with Peter. I do my utmost to minimize Auriol's contact with Rose but of course chance encounters do happen. When has she had the opportunity to indoctrinate my daughter with her puritanical thinking? The last thing I need is Auriol joining the thought police. I want my child to be hip and relaxed.

"Come and kiss me goodnight."

Auriol bobs under my arm and I can smell her clean hair. Unexpectedly I get a lump in my throat.

"Will you read to me?" she asks.

"Only if I get to choose the story," I reply.

She laughs and I take her to bed, generously telling Eva that she can go home ten minutes early. It pays to keep the staff happy.

CHAPTER
FIVE

Sunday 10 September

Rose

It's a wet Sunday; thank God the boys are with me because I really struggle to fill wet Sundays without them. I rang Peter this morning and told him that they were too tired, after starting back at school, to play football or even visit him today.

"Bloody hell, Rose, they haven't just started reception class. A school term isn't new to them. I thought you said it was a good thing to sign them up to the boys' under-eights football on a Sunday morning. You agreed to it."

"They're mooching round the house, they're quite pale with exhaustion," I argued.

"They're bored. They need fresh air and a bit of horseplay. You mollycoddle them, Rose."

A few tense and silent minutes pass until Peter accepts that I'm resolute. He sighs.

"Well, what will they be doing instead?"

"They won't be bored; Daisy, Simon, Connie, Luke and the children are coming over for lunch."

I'm small-minded enough to take great pleasure from delivering this choice piece of news. I wonder if

Peter ever hankers after the splendid Sunday lunches that I prepared when we were together. The guests have remained the same, my cooking has got even better, the only thing missing is him. Not that I miss him. Well, at least, not always.

Connie and Luke met one another at my wedding. Luke was an usher; he's been a friend of Peter's since their schooldays. Luke then introduced Simon into our group and he married my sis. We were a tightly knit gang. Very close. Too close as it turned out. Lucy and Peter were too close.

Some women say they didn't see it coming. When their husbands stand up and announce their intention to bugger off with whoever it may be that has caught their eye, wives are often stunned. I never had that arrogance. I saw it coming.

It wasn't just the numerous late nights at the office and the increasingly frequent business trips that dominated our last year together. It wasn't simply his escalating neglect and the distance between us which was notable in the last six months. I saw it coming before I stepped down the aisle. I knew that Peter would leave me almost the moment I started dating him. Peter didn't belong to me. He was always on loan. Peter belonged with a more startling, more beautiful, funnier, wittier, posher, stronger, firmer, blonder someone. He was always out of my league.

Truthfully, no one could have been more surprised than me when he asked me for a date. God, the man was stunning. So, so handsome, charming and determined. Everyone liked him. Every girl wanted to be noticed by him, every guy wanted to be his best buddy. Even his bosses sucked up to him. Some people simply gleam and Peter was one of those gleaming types.

When he first asked me out I thought it was a joke or a bet. I wasn't a complete monster by any stretch. I'd always had my fair share of dates. But largely I dated nice boys — ones that were a little bit gauche or spotty but earnest and kind.

I met Peter through work. My degree is in accountancy and I'd landed a great job working in the accounts department of a merchant bank. Peter, who is a year older than me, had a far more glamorous position; he was a trader. In fact, if the office gossip was to be believed, he was *the* trader. He'd already been identified as having something special, he was already making heads and money spin. I guess it was because he was so busy and in demand that he was often late with his expenses. But one day he was so late with the paperwork it looked like he'd have to forgo a reimbursement, so he came directly to the accounts department to sort it out. He was very smiley and chatty with me but I assumed that he was turning on the charm because he needed me to get him out of a hole. He'd be nearly a grand out of pocket otherwise.

After we'd managed to get his cash signed off and the expenses form back into the process, he asked me if I knew a good place to buy a sandwich for lunch. I hadn't a clue why he was asking me — after all he'd been working there longer than I had — and I assumed it was because I looked like the kind of girl who enjoyed her food. I gave him directions to the nearest deli, which he carefully listened to, and then I thought he'd get on his way. I started to blush when he dawdled at my desk and I mumbled about there being a decent sushi bar near by if sandwiches weren't his thing.

"I'm really more interested in persuading you to join me than I am interested in the menu," he said, smiling.

I stared at him. Gormless. Anxious not to misunderstand. My suit must have been flattering, there's no other explanation. I still have that suit, although not the occasion to wear it. So we had a sandwich and then after work we had a drink, then supper. We didn't stop eating and drinking for another eleven years. Eating, drinking and making love. Because yes, of course, back then in the early days, there was a lot of sex.

I could not believe my luck. I would pinch myself. Literally. I had tiny bruises on my arms. Peter, Greek god, handsome stud muffin and all-round good guy, had chosen me. Me! He could have dated anyone and he chose to date *me*. I considered every day a gift and made the most of having this fab boyfriend. I couldn't wait to show him off. I dragged him home, filed him past all my pals, and I took him to meet Daisy who was still at university. Of course, that's when he first met Lucy. Ironic to think that I introduced them. As expected, he was universally approved of. Mum, Dad, Daisy, my friends, Daisy's friends all liked him and I liked him the most of all. So much so, that I refused to listen to Daisy's gentle and not so gentle warnings that

I was in danger of overestimating his worth and underestimating my own.

Sometimes, if I do have a wet Sunday on my own to fill, I torture myself. I've perfected it. After I've done all the housework and ironing and such like, I sit and wonder if he fell for her straight away, the moment he shook hands with her. He must at least have fancied her, he has a pulse. Lord, there are times when I've fancied her, she's fabulous. To look at, that is. I think she's faulty on a number of other accounts, of course. Was he too much of a gentleman to shake me off there and then? Or I wonder if he started to hanker after her when she arrived at our wedding, *sans* date but with the most enormous hat. She wore lilac and captured everyone's imagination. There was no question, she undoubtedly outshone the bride. Or was it later, when I had the twins and we were too bleary-eyed with sleep deprivation to see one another properly? I've never asked. I don't really think I want to hear the answers. As I said, I never expected to keep him. I like to believe he was mine for the six years we dated, and the five years we were married. I don't want to hear that he wasn't mine for very long at all.

Peter left me when the boys were fifteen months old. I guess my luck had run out. He was recalled. The natural order re-established. I'd had a longer innings than I'd expected. My mistake was getting complacent, allowing a time when I thought maybe it was for real, maybe he was for keeps. I should never have forgotten what I'd first believed, that he'd be with a Lucy in the end. Maybe not Lucy Hewitt-Jones, but someone like her. Someone unlike me.

Lunch is a triumph. The boys actually manage to tear themselves away from their Game Boys and come and make conversation (of sorts) with our guests. Connie's children are too young and the wrong sex to be of much interest to Henry and Sebastian. Connie and I joke about how much that will change when they are teenagers. Fran is four and Flora is eighteen months. The way Luke keeps touching Connie, stroking her thigh, squeezing her hand, etc., I wouldn't be at all surprised if number three wasn't announced in the near future. Sometimes, they behave like newlyweds and when they do it catches me off balance. I have to swallow very hard and very quickly to stop myself . . . I don't know what I'm stopping. Stop myself crying, laughing, calling out and congratulating them.

I know why their open and easy affection affects me with such poignancy. The thing is, Connie and Luke had marital problems at around the same time as Peter and I did. Connie is the epitome of wifely devotion and the ideal mum *now* but she once had an affair. Just like Peter. The difference being, they got through it. I used to look at them and wonder what it was that allowed them to survive infidelity, when my world blew apart. I reasoned that Luke could not have loved Connie more than I loved Peter, it's not possible. It didn't take me long to deduce that the difference was Connie loved Luke more than Peter loved me, Connie didn't want to leave. Quite simple really.

54

Daisy is looking tired and too thin. She's not as happy as she deserves to be. Daisy and Simon have been married for six years and it's an open secret between their nearest and dearest that they've been trying for a baby since their honeymoon. They were OK with their lack of result in the first year of marriage. In fact, back then, Simon used to laugh about how he was so keen on the trying that he thought he might be actively disappointed when they got a result. Simon doesn't joke about fertility any more; neither of them jokes about anything much.

The way I understand it from Daisy, after eighteen months of more or less constant and wonderful sex they introduced thermometers and vitamins. The quality of their sex life, predictably, took a knock. She says that the moment is ruined if immediately after sex you have to lie on the floor with your legs in the air. Besides anything else, they have a tiled floor in their bedroom, it's cold. I suggested that they buy a carpet and keep going for it. A further six months down the line Daisy visited her GP and, three months after that, Simon visited her GP too.

At this point they still had a sense of humour about their predicament because they still had hope. They used to entertain the rest of us with hilarious stories about Daisy calling Simon out of meetings, insisting that he got home within the hour because "the time was right". Connie and I even had a go at practising injecting fruit because Simon is a little squeamish and couldn't face sticking needles into Daisy's bottom, which was a necessary part of one of her treatments. We laughed about that at the time, but a series of invasive tests, with inconclusive results, plus three more years of regularly menstruating, has snuffed out all humour. Last month their second attempt at IVF failed and I've run out of platitudes.

Daisy has always loved children. Perhaps even more than I do. I love my children and the children of my friends and even some of my children's friends, but Daisy isn't so particular. She loves all children. She's a primary school teacher, an ambition she's held since she met her first primary school teacher when she was aged five. She enjoys her work and from what I understand she's respected and liked by the staff, parents and kids alike. The thing that breaks my heart is that whenever Daisy tells anyone she is a teacher one of the plus points she always mentions is that the holidays work well when you have children. And whoever she is talking to will always nod enthusiastically, sometimes unaware that she actually doesn't have children.

It's not Connie and Luke's fault. It's not as though they actively try to flaunt their happily ever after in front of everyone. It just sometimes feels that way. With each ripe, healthy pregnancy that Connie waddles through I can't help but wonder whether I'll ever have sex again, let alone another child, or even someone who is prepared to rub my stockinged feet when I'm exhausted or flat after a busy day. Lord alone knows what Daisy must be thinking.

We don't talk about the failed IVF today and we try to avoid dwelling on the issues of the first week of school. A debate about whether sew-on or iron-on labels are best for naming uniforms is not one Daisy can comfortably fake an interest in. Still, the conversation never falters. Connie has brought along her holiday photos.

"Three weeks in Devon. You are so lucky that you are both self-employed and these idyllic breaks are possible," says Simon.

"You didn't do so bad for hols this year, Simes," says Luke. "Thailand last Christmas, skiing in February. France this summer. Believe me, it's my wife's photography skill that makes our hol look idyllic. Think British summer time and sand in your picnic," he laughs.

Connie hits him, playfully. "It was idyllic. OK, camping was perhaps a little ambitious considering I haven't done it since Girl Guides and you've never camped at all."

"Remind me, how long did you manage in the tent?" asks Daisy.

"One night," squeals Connie.

We all laugh, as we had spent some time trying to dissuade Connie from a camping holiday; it's so clearly not her thing. We pointed out that there's no hot and cold running water in tents, let alone a jacuzzi, but she'd been seduced by a Sunday supplement with a headline claiming camping was the new Barbados.

"Do you remember her arguing it would be an economical holiday?" Luke asks the table. We all nod. "We spent £800 on camping equipment and that makes it the single most expensive night of accommodation I have ever enjoyed. Not that I did enjoy it, what with the rain and the hysterical shrieks that there were wild animals prowling around our tent."

"I saw their shadows," insists Connie; she's still laughing.

"Then we couldn't get a cottage and had to pay through the nose to stay at some flash country house hotel, which was wall-to-wall with stressed Londoners. We could have stayed at home for that."

"I loved it," smiles Connie, unperturbed.

"I know baby, I did too, really," grins Luke affectionately. "Even if my bank manager is hyperventilating."

"Can I get anyone a coffee? I found a lovely Fair Trade store just around the corner. They have a fantastic strong Brazilian blend," I offer.

"No thanks, Rose," says Simon, rubbing his small paunch. "I couldn't swallow another thing. That was a glorious meal."

"Not for me, Rose," says Luke, pushing back his chair.

"I'm off coffee," smiles Connie. She is bouncing Flora on her knee; Fran has trailed outside to try to muscle in on Henry and Sebastian's football game.

"Tea?" I offer.

"No, just sit down, Rose," says Daisy with a slight snap in her voice.

The slight snap catches my attention. Daisy is invariably very polite and patient. This IVF must be bothering her enormously. I look up from clearing the table of the final bits of debris and notice all eyes are on me.

"Rose," says Daisy, and then she stops. She glances towards Connie but Connie is suddenly rapt in tucking Flora's curls behind her ears. Simon coughs. "Rose," Daisy tries again. "I'm sure there's a tactful way into this conversation but I can't think of it right now so I'm just going to have to launch right in. As your sister it's my prerogative, think of it as my using my joker card after thirty odd years of being reasonably supportive and sensitive."

I have no idea what she's going to say to me but as I examine the other three faces around the table, it's clear they all know *exactly* what she is going to say and none of them is relishing the moment.

"What is it, Daisy?" I ask with a cool smile, which is entirely fake and unlikely to convince anyone. I feel my face turning scarlet. "Oh God, you're not ill, are you?" Panic seizes my throat and strangles the words, "the children". I look to Connie in fear.

"No, no, nothing like that," assures Connie sympathetically. She leans towards me and squeezes my arm.

"Don't overreact, sis, you are making this job even harder," says Daisy sharply. "The thing is, we've been talking about it, and we think you are wasting your life."

Connie whips her head around to face Daisy and glares at her crossly; she then mimics the chaps, who are staring at the tablecloth. Daisy is the only one meeting my eye — she's trying to brazen it out.

"Wasting my life?" I mutter, confused.

"Yes, that's what we think," says Daisy. I know she's finding this difficult and that's why she's being so aggressive but, even so, I think what she just said is unforgivable.

"Who is 'we'?"

"All of us. Your friends." My "friends" still can't bring themselves to look at me. My friends are cowards, it appears.

"Not wasting it, exactly," says Connie. "I wouldn't say that. You've done such a fabulous job with the boys, you must be so proud, but we were just wondering what you are going to do next."

"Next?" I'm dumbfounded. "The boys are only seven, they're not about to fly the nest."

"No, but they will, Rose, and they need you less and less," said Luke. "Sebastian confided in me that he didn't want you to pick him up from school any more."

"Since when have you known what is best for my sons? What right do you have to involve yourself to that extent?"

"Well, I am their godfather," says Luke.

"I simply wanted you to buy them decent Christmas presents," I snap.

Simon chips in. "We just wanted to talk to you about your future, Rose. Because we're your friends and we care for you. We can't sit back and watch you devote yourself to the boys and completely neglect yourself. You don't do anything other than play taxi driver to them."

"You have no friends or interests outside the school gates," says Connie.

"You never buy yourself a treat but plough endless time and money into finessing their already near-perfect life," adds Daisy.

"We just think it would be nice if you got out and met some new people," Luke chips in.

"Maybe even go on a couple of dates," adds Simon.

I feel horror and shame as I realize that this conversation is the tip of the iceberg. Clearly, these four have sat around another dinner table and discussed me and pitied me, then decided that as my "friends" they have a right to confront me with their impertinent views. Could they have discussed this with Peter and Lucy too? Canvassed their opinion on my sad little life? Oh God, the humiliation.

"You are forty next birthday," points out Daisy. "What do you think about that?"

"The alternative to ageing is considerably more horrific," I point out.

"It's not right that you think the release of the next Disney DVD is something to look forward to," continues Daisy. "You don't even visit the library unless one of the boys wants a book. Rose, you've all but disappeared," she says, finally.

"That's what being a mother involves, Daisy. But you don't understand that," I reply angrily. I don't even temper my sentence by adding "yet," or "sadly". I want to hurt her as she's hurt me. I watch Daisy recoil. "Now, if you don't mind, I think it's time you all left. Sebastian and Henry have homework and they'll need my help."

I stand up from the table and fold my arms across my chest.

"Don't take it like that," says Connie. "We're worried about you."

Daisy says nothing; she's as white as Bold-washed linen. Simon has a protective arm around her; he's leading her towards the door. Luke is keeping his head down but he has started to gather up the children's toys, cups and books.

"Thank you for your concern, Connie. When I need someone to tell me my life is trivial and pointless I'll know who to call."

"We're not saying that," Connie stands her ground. More sensitive women would have caved in by now and begged forgiveness. "You said that," she clarifies and then heads for the door.

CHAPTER
SIX

Sunday 10 September

Lucy

Oh hell, we have to have sex soon. When did it happen that I started to note the frequency, or rather the lack of frequency, that we have sex? We congratulate ourselves now if we manage once a week. Saturday night usually, but even that's not guaranteed. Nothing happening last night, for example, because there was a decent movie on TV. What's gone wrong? I remember when we used to frantically fuck one another in the boardroom at work and then still find a way to slip in a more luxurious session in a hotel before he had to get home. I can't believe *all* the excitement was provided by the fact that he was married to someone else. No, that can't possibly be right. We had sex often enough when we first got married. Bugger, does this date back to Auriol's birth? Everything uncomfortable or inconvenient in my life tends to.

For the record, I do not have a floppy vagina. I've kept mine taut. And I'm sure Pete has no reason to complain about my physical appearance; I know he must still want me in that way. So many women let themselves go but I still manage to visit the hairdresser once a week, the gym three times a week, and I'm still a regular at the spa. Of course, we both have hectic schedules and we seem to be so much wearier nowadays, but it's horrifying to admit that Peter might value his sleep more than a good session with me. I've tried taking advantage of his morning glory, but there's rarely so much as a morning glimmer, let alone glory. I've tried meeting him for lunch, in the hope of squeezing in a quickie, but we just grab a sandwich and a coffee, not one another's bodies. I've tried the late-night massage and moody music — that was a disaster. He was asleep within minutes and had the cheek to thank me the next morning, assuring me it was the best night's sleep he'd had in months. Do I care about his sleep patterns? No, I don't. I care about my neglected sexuality and his waning libido.

It's rather a good thing that Rose said the boys couldn't come to visit today. Now at least I only have to get Auriol out of the way in order to orchestrate an opportunity for me to have my wicked way. I settle her in front of the TV with a DVD and a bowl of dried apricots. I hesitate and then return to the kitchen to hunt out some Butterkist. The apricots would undoubtedly be better for her teeth and digestive system and provide all the right sort of energy but they are less likely to hold her interest long enough for me to get a decent shag.

I go to the bedroom and unearth some sexy underwear. Not that I have any grey items lurking in my drawers. I don't; there is no need for ugliness, but I do have some sets that are more feminine than sexy and we've gone past the point of hoping that subtle feminine underwear will do the trick. I don't think I have to consider crotchless and a nurse's outfit just yet, but black lace and a suspender belt is the order of the day. The classics become so for a reason. I put on a pair of knee-high Gucci boots with steel heels and plenty of buckles and grab my Burberry trenchcoat. It buttons up to the chin and has military overtones that I'm hoping Pete will find exciting. I find him in his study. He's snoozing with an open paper resting on his chest.

"Peek-a-boo," I purr into his ear. "It's pussy in boots."

He jolts awake. "I wasn't asleep, just resting my eyes."

He sounds like someone's grandfather. Pushing that thought out of my head, I straddle him and sit on his lap. I gently grind my ass into his groin in the hope of encouraging a tangible response.

"Are you going out?" he asks, rubbing his eyes and nodding towards my coat.

I lean in and kiss him. "Just been out, baby. And it's cold out there." I say this in a silly, breathy, quasi Marilyn Monroe voice.

"Did you buy any milk?" he asks.

I lean in and kiss him again. It's a long lingering kiss and somewhere very deep inside me something stirs. It's not an emotion, lust is not an emotion.

Peter gently pulls back from my kiss. "I'm not complaining about Eva, she seems very good, but we are short of a few groceries this weekend. Did she get a chance to go to Waitrose, do you know? We do need milk."

I grind a little harder in his lap and my trenchcoat falls open to reveal my thigh. Peter doesn't seem to notice. "They do a good lunch at the Renaissance Restaurant, don't they? Although I am a little too full now."

We never eat in on a Sunday; in fact we rarely eat in at all if I can help it. Our tradition is to go to a restaurant and whenever possible to pick something from a menu which we've never tried before. It's good for Auriol to learn how to behave in restaurants and to experience a number of cuisines; I can't bear kids who will only eat chicken nuggets and then with their fingers.

I nibble Peter's ear and try to remember what he ate. He had calves' liver and duck, not an ideal dish to have before a steamy sesh. I ought to have steered him towards something lighter, maybe chicken, or an aphrodisiac, maybe asparagus.

I snake my arms around his neck and start to run my fingers through his hair. He doesn't seem to notice.

"I've just been reading this fascinating article about a couple who bought their village pub and converted it into a family home. How weird is that? Can you imagine living in your local?"

"I can't imagine having a local, Peter. It's not my thing, really, is it?" I mumble as I continue my concerted effort to find Peter's erogenous zones. Lost treasure, I fear.

He responds, "No, not unless it was a champagne bar. Still, it's a clever investment. They stand to make a fair chunk on it. It's already valued at 60 per cent more than they paid."

He's oblivious to me.

I am sat spreadeagled on his lap, I'm wearing little more than my birthday suit and I'm nibbling his ear. His hand has fallen on to my bare thigh, which he's rubbing, but I get the impression he's absentmindedly trying to warm me up rather than caressing me.

"Lucy, love, if you're going out could you get me some chocolate too. I fancy something sweet after that delicious lunch." He leans back on his chair, pulling away from me, and slaps his belly. "Milk and chocolate — I don't think we need anything else, do we?" He smiles at me, catapulting me somewhere between fury, frustration and fondness.

I clamber off his knee and make for the door. I suppose I could have dropped my coat on the floor and stood in all my glory, surely that would have been hint enough, even for Peter, but something stops me.

I am humiliated. I feel rejected; worse, I feel invisible. For the first time in my life I feel incapable of articulating what I want. Asking for a bloody good seeing to is a step too far.

I leave the house and dash to Cullen's to buy chocolate and milk, grateful to escape the stuffy disappointing domesticity that has castrated my husband. It's no consolation at all to me that the teenage boy who is serving appears to know that under my trenchcoat I am scantily clad. His eyes linger on my boots and then lasciviously he drags his gaze up and down my body. He nearly traps his fingers in the till and he drops my change as he hands it over. But I find the whole episode seedy, not funny at all.

I rush home, get dressed and spend the rest of the afternoon at my PC. When I consult my "to do" list on Sunday evening I have a neat line of ticks next to all my work-related tasks. I hesitate over the line, "Quality time with Auriol", and wonder if spending twenty minutes translating the menu for her and a further ten minutes helping her select a DVD from the cupboard can be classed as quality time. In the end I carry it over as a task that still needs more attention. I delete, "Have sex" and don't even bother taking it forward to the next week.

CHAPTER
SEVEN

Monday 11 September

John

Cracking weekend, although there were times when I felt a bit like Beelzebub inciting an innocent. What has Craig been doing all his life, I wonder? Last week, when we went for a drink to sort out Tom's stag, Craig admitted he was in the market. I think he said he "wouldn't mind meeting someone special, somebody absolutely wonderful", or some bollocks like that. Jesus, who does he think he is? Even John Lennon couldn't make it acceptable for a bloke to talk soft shit to his mates. I chose to interpret Craig's words to mean he needs to get his leg over. Pronto. This interpretation was partially led by the fact that I'm looking for a new fall guy. What with Tom doing the journey and all, I'll be in need of a bit of company when I'm out and about. So I promised to help Craig in his quest.

"Really?" He looked genuinely excited and hope shone right past his quarter-inch-thick lenses.

"Yup, you can learn from the Grand Master. I'll share my expertise free of charge, just for the pleasure of your company."

I wasn't entirely joking. Craig is a good bloke to hang out with. Square and all that, but bright, very witty and with a thorough understanding of the rules of all games from chess to footie, which makes him good company.

"You could start by ditching the glasses," I suggested.

"I wouldn't be able to see anything."

"Hey mate, that's sometimes an advantage when you're on the pull. There are times when you don't want to have to look at the fireplace while you are poking the fire, if you know what I mean." From the look on Craig's face, he didn't know what I meant. "Maybe you could try contact lenses or have them lasered. That's what I did. Can't recommend it highly enough."

"Maybe." He sounded doubtful.

"Girls don't make passes at guys who wear glasses," I added. He shrugged. Maybe he doesn't care. Maybe he doesn't expect girls to make passes at him. Who knows? "Well, at least a different frame," I encouraged.

Truth is, Craig could do with an entire style makeover. Sort of rebranding, that's how I'd talk about him at work if he was one of my consulting projects. We need to shake off the old image (earnest old fogy, with no sense of style, fun or adventure) and reposition him as a reasonable catch. Luckily, women are very forgiving. They'll look at him and think teddy bear, even as he stands. They'll be thinking decent job, no criminal record, no previous wives, no kids and no body odour. Most women will be grateful.

Even so, he could do with some new clothes and a haircut.

On Saturday Craig met me and the lads at the park for a kickabout. I've been playing footie every Saturday morning since I was able to stand. I have to have a really good reason to miss the kickabout, something bigger than death or even a shag.

"Come on Grandad, I'm clear, kick to me."

"Very fucking funny," I call as I pass the ball. The cheeky bastard who calls me Grandad is a lad I work with. Good bloke. Wouldn't call me Grandad if he thought I really was. It was only the other day he was saying how much he admired my stamina. I haven't even dated his sister. Ha ha.

I'm pleasantly surprised by Craig's performance on the pitch. He's kept in good shape and doesn't embarrass himself (or me) at all. Couple of decent passes. It's just a friendly so I try not to get too competitive.

"Coming to the pub after the game, Craig, mate?"

"Definitely, if we've got time for a quick one." I look confused, so Craig tries to explain. "I thought we were going shopping for new clothes." He looks embarrassed and so he should be. Luckily none of the lads have heard him.

"Mate, we do need to get you some new togs but no self-respecting bloke goes shopping on a Saturday afternoon. The shops are full of women."

"But I thought we wanted to meet women."

"We do. But we want to meet them in bars, pubs and clubs. Ideally when they are half cut and frisky. Not in queues at Top Shop. Besides, there's the game."

"The game?"

"The footie game."

"But we've just played footie."

"The game we *watch*. On the big screen, in the pub, with a pie and a pint. Well, several pints to be accurate. Don't worry, I'll lend you some gear for tonight." Craig looks doubtful.

"It won't be a problem."

"Nothing ever is, according to you," mumbles Craig.

We stayed in the pub until after six, dashed home, quickly showered and then went back out by eight. Some drinking time was lost as my mate Oscar and I spent a good forty minutes trying to persuade Craig that real men do wear pink. In the end he still opted for blue; he can be quite stubborn.

It was a wild night. Pub, bar, club, back to mine. Craig buggered things up a bit for Oscar though. Think Os was pissed off. We'd cracked off with these three birds. All clearly available and gagging for it. Met them at the bar and they came on to the club with us. There'd been lots of drinking, flirting and dancing and it was agreed that we were all going back to mine, where a full on sesh was all but promised, when suddenly Craig refused to get in the cab.

"Er, mate. What are you thinking of? Clearly it's *everyone* back to mine." I nodded to the gaggle behind him, to give him a hint. I know he's not as well practised at this sort of thing as you'd hope. My girl was draped around me, hugging me closer than an Hermès tie. Oscar's bird was doing this flirty bump and grind dance just in front of him, claiming that she was teaching him the steps, when in fact it was obvious that she was demonstrating the pleasures to come. And the other bird, the one that was earmarked for Craig, was hovering nervously in the background. OK, she wasn't quite such a looker as the first two. Funny teeth and she needed to cut back on the pies, but she had great tits and besides, it's a numbers game, isn't it? Three plus three. It doesn't work so well if one drops out.

"Not me, thank you. I'm tired and more than a bit woozy," smiled Craig. "I think I've drunk too much."

"There's no such thing, mate."

"What's going on? Why aren't we getting a cab?" asked Goofy-Pie.

"I've had a lovely evening, thank you," said Craig, turning to her. He held out his hand for her to shake. She stared at it, insulted. "I'm just rather tired now and have lots of work to do tomorrow morning. I need to get to grips with the amendments to the maths curriculum for year sevens."

"What? You can't go home now. The party's just getting started." Goofy-Pie flashed a wide grin; she was trying to be seductive but, as I mentioned, her teeth were not her strong point. Still, the woman could hardly be expected to flash her boobs in the high street, could she? "We'd all miss you so much if you left now. Especially me."

Goofy-Pie had not been particularly interested in Craig up until this moment. But as he was evidently giving her the brush-off, he'd instantly become the most desirable man in the UK. Why do women hunt out hurt?

"Can you give us a minute, Sweetie-Pie?" I pull Craig out of earshot. "Mate, you are on a promise. We all are."

"I'm aware that there is opportunity here," said Craig.

"I thought you were looking to pull."

"No, I'm looking for someone special. Linda is a nice enough girl, but she's clearly not my soulmate." As Craig pointed this out, Goofy-Pie began to yell to her mate that she needed a curry or a kebab. I noticed that she was wearing a leopardskin skirt, how had I missed that? I could see the evening falling apart in front of my eyes.

A cab pulled up beside us.

"After a ride?" yelled the cabbie from an open window.

"I am. He's going home," I replied, giving in to the inevitable. I'd seen how awkward Craig was about the pink T-shirt; I knew I wasn't going to win this one. Besides, if we argued about it for too long in the cold night air, the moment might well be lost for all of us if the girls started to sober up and rediscover their shady morals and consciences.

"I couldn't possibly take the first cab," objected Craig, ever the gentleman.

"Mate, I've got some damage limitation to do here. If you're going, get in the bloody cab and get out of here. Talk later."

The consequences were predictable. Goofy-Pie got stroppy and insisted on going home. Oscar's bird said she couldn't let Linda go home alone. My chick didn't seem to have any scruples on the matter, which boded well — I like a girl with as few scruples as possible. In the end, Oscar got a cab with the other two as he was still hoping to get lucky. Perhaps very lucky — I know he's still waiting to tick off a three-in-a-bed romp. All he got was left with a hefty taxi fare. My bird, Gillian, came back to mine and was as devious and lacking in scruples as I could have hoped. I didn't surface until Sunday teatime. Result.

CHAPTER
EIGHT

Monday 11 September

Lucy

"Good weekend, Lucy?"

"Not especially," I reply with unprecedented honesty. Mick asked the question. He's a rare breed on the trading floor because he is not a total arse. We have worked together for about six months and during that time I have seen evidence of genuine humour and the occasional flash of intelligence. I yawn, "You?"

"Split up with the girlfriend, so it wasn't all bad."

"At least splitting up with someone creates a diversion, some excitement."

"Oh dear, oh dear. Is all not well in the Hewitt-Jones slash Phillips palace? Is Princess Lucy a little bored by chance?"

Princess is his private nickname for me. I don't find it quite as offensive as he intended.

Mick has walked up to my desk and he's now sitting on it so that, despite my efforts to focus on my screen and my e-mail inbox, all I can focus on is his thigh. He's wearing a Paul Smith wool suit. It has a little more kick to it than most suits sported on the trading floor. I suddenly have an inexplicable urge to stroke his thigh. The suit I mean. I want to touch the wool. Must be. I look at Mick; he has green eyes, they are a bit like mine, i.e. arresting. He has very black hair, and for the first time I notice his lips. I can't get carried away, as I note they are on the thin side.

Most of the PAs want to sleep with Mick. The only ones who don't are the ones that have already done so. Which, I understand, is not a reflection on his prowess in the sack, just a realistic appraisal of the situation. Mick is clear; he doesn't want a relationship with anyone who can see which sandwiches he chooses for lunch. Despite his commitment issues, ladies line up, each hoping they'll be the one to change his mind. I suppose I can see what they see in him. Trouble.

"Yes, I'm a little bored." I stare squarely at him as I reply. I'm not in the slightest bit intimidated by or attracted to him, and the clearest way to demonstrate this is by not issuing an official denial that domestic bliss can, at times, be domestic dross. We're both clever enough to know that it is; a denial on my part would be positively flirty. "Still, Pete reads me like a book. Next weekend he'll probably whisk me off on some fabulous break."

"Romantic time in Paris, perhaps?" says Mick.

"I was thinking more of a kinky romp in Amsterdam," I reply, smartly stepping back into the role of hard-nosed bitch with three-inch-thick steel shutters firmly pulled down around my private life. "Can you move your butt? You are sitting on my BlackBerry."

Mick flashes a grin (good teeth, I wonder who his orthodontist is?). He slowly gets up off my desk and saunters back to his own bay. "Nice talking to you, Princess Luce."

"Thrilling," I neatly bounce back.

Before I started my relationship with Pete I had more than my fair share of interludes with sexy, wealthy, good-looking men. One or two of them even managed to be interesting as well. Mick's gentle flirting is nothing new. A man trying his luck with me is as natural as breathing. I don't believe in false modesty, it's tedious. The thing is, I'm one of the most aesthetically appealing women most men ever come into contact with. It's just something I've learnt to get used to. Like all blessings it's mixed, not that I've ever met a woman who would believe me. The issue is my blonde hair disqualifies any gravitas that my first class degree in economics and my immaculate, record-breaking career might afford a plainer woman. I've had to work bloody hard to overcome the allocated role of office totty. Still, can't gripe, I'd die rather than have fat ankles.

Frankly, Mick is overshooting by flirting with me. He's overrated as the office Lothario, particularly by himself. OK, he is rich enough, good-looking enough and bright enough. This means he simply wouldn't ever have been enough of a man for me to date. I always specified that at least one of these attributes was rated "exceptional". Not that there's even the question of my dating now. I'm married. I have Peter. I spent a long time wanting Peter and waiting for Peter.

Peculiar then that my La Perla scanties are fluttering. I send Peter a messenger note, which is safer and more immediate than e-mail.

Sex God,
My La Perla scanties are fluttering thinking of you. Don't be late home tonight.
Kitten

Well, my knickers *are* jumping — it's just a *little* white lie. I do not believe that honesty is always the best policy. Seconds later he replies.

Kitten,
Sadly, I think I do have to work late tonight. Did you manage to call a plumber about that leaky tap in the cloakroom?

For a moment I wonder if I'm missing something coded. Can a leaky tap have a cheeky connotation of which I am ignorant? But sadly, it's not coded; we do need a plumber. I reach for the phone and call my PA to instruct her to deal with this. She waves to me from her desk, which is opposite mine. I note this as the criticism she intended but I'm unmoved. I don't do friendly. Fraternizing with the staff simply confuses things.

It is some relief that the markets are buoyant today and I have to concentrate quite hard so as not to make any mistakes. I do concentrate and I don't make any mistakes, but I do make quite a few killings and I feel somewhat brilliant by the time I close down my computer at the end of the day.

Mick drifts by my desk and asks if I want to join him and some of the other guys for a well-deserved drink. I meet his eyes and search for the spark of chemistry that I felt this morning. Nothing. No flutters or shudders. He does look cute with a six-o'clock shadow but he's once again retired back to his appropriate box, the one labelled "colleague". What a relief.

"Thanks for the offer, Mick, but I think I might have an early night tonight. I have a big presentation to a pissed-off client tomorrow."

"Unlike you to upset clients, Lucy."

"I didn't. I've inherited this mess."

"Who from?"

I check my notes. "Joe Whitehead. Do you know him?"

"Yes. He's a tosser. He's just joined our team, although I have no idea how he got a job here."

"Perhaps he's the Chairman's godson," I suggest.

"Maybe. I'm struggling to find an alternative explanation. He's rather stupid and the most dangerous sort of stupid because he thinks he's a genius."

"Obviously the client is expecting full-on suck-up. I'm going home now but I want to run through the figures again later on tonight."

"Fair enough, see you in the morning, Princess."

His easy acceptance of my rejection of his offer of a drink underlines the fact that Mick has no serious intentions on me. This morning's mild flirtation may not even have registered on his radar. I'm a married mother and a colleague — there are less complicated fish for him to fry. Mick likes his sex to be hot, frequent and self-contained.

The disappointment stings me deep in my gut. How can that be? I don't even want him. Why do I want him to want me? How very ordinary of me.

I get home in time for Auriol's bath but don't interfere as Eva has already drawn it; I don't want to upset their routine. I pour myself a gin and tonic and go to my bedroom where I lie on my bed. I can't be bothered to fire up my laptop just yet, so I pick up *Vogue* and carelessly flick through the pages.

The magazine is a long-term favourite of mine. I've subscribed to it since I was a fresher. As usual, the magazine is crammed with picture after picture of breathtakingly beautiful girls. I jot down the details of a new lingerie brand that is just being noticed and the address of a perfume store that an A-list actress has opened in Covent Garden.

Auriol bursts into my bedroom armed with her teddy and a book. It's remarkable to me that whenever she bursts into my consciousness I am freshly aware of her brilliance, vibrancy and beauty. It takes my breath away every time. It's not that I forget how gorgeous she is in between times, it's just that one's own child is exquisite beyond memory. She rather reminds me of some of the models on the *Vogue* pages. She's probably closer to their age than I am. This thought is brutal.

I read two chapters of *Alice Through the Looking Glass* to Auriol. The illustrations are delightful and, for once, she doesn't keep interrupting me with ridiculous questions about unrelated subjects, like "What's your favourite colour, Mummy?" or "Did you have a pet when you were a little girl?"

I bundle her off to bed as soon as possible. When her light is off I realize I've forgotten to ask her how school is going. Still, she'd tell me if she had any issues, wouldn't she?

Instead of supper I take six different vitamins and drink a glass of green wheatgrass tea. It tastes foul but my homeopathic nutritionalist swears by it. Then I dash back upstairs, flop on to my bed, and turn my attention to the suck-up presentation.

What's needed is a mix between show-and-tell and hand-holding. It will be a doddle. After a while, I check the clock. It's nine thirty. Peter is not home. I consider calling him to ask when he will be back. It might be worth staying awake. But then, it might not.

I fight a yawn. I used to have so much energy, so much buzz. I was known for surviving on four or five hours of sleep per night. I used to say you can sleep when you are dead, and I still believe that. I do . . .

I can hear my mobile screeching somewhere near my ear. Disorientated, my first thought is that I've fallen asleep at my desk. I fight through the fog of deep slumber and as I pick up the phone I remember that I'm not at the office but at home in my bedroom. It's probably Peter telling me he's on his way back.

"Peter!" My expression is a subtle mix of delight and frustration. I want him to know that I'm pleased to hear from him but I don't want to let him off the hook too easily for being late home. I perfected this tone when I was his mistress and spent countless evenings waiting for him to call.

"Sorry, Princess. It's not your husband — it's the man of your dreams."

"Nightmares you mean, Mick." I whip my response back at him. Quite a feat, as I'm barely conscious. It doesn't do to let colleagues push their noses into one's home life. On that subject, what is Mick doing calling me at — I struggle to see my watch; the room's pitch black — at 10.30p.m.?

"How are the numbers?" he asks.

"They add up," I reply coolly.

"Finished with the presentation, then? Put it all to bed?"

"Yes." I don't admit I'm also in bed. Which self-respecting trader admits she's knackered at 10.30p.m.? All the other guys will be just warming up for party time.

"Knew you'd have it licked, Princess, so I'm calling to see if you'll change your mind and want to join us. We're heading over to Notting Hill; that's your neck of the woods, isn't it?"

Yes, but not his. "Why are you coming all this way west?"

"Some of the guys are going on to Hammersmith to that strip joint, Secrets. Do you know it?"

"Yes."

"Not my thing."

"Lap dancers aren't your thing?" My surprise is audible.

"Don't get me wrong, I like a dance as much as the next guy. I just think Secrets is a bit down-market compared to some gentlemen's clubs I go to."

"Right. Well, a man has to have standards," I quip. "Anyway, you didn't call me to give me your list of the top three booty bars in town, did you?"

"No. It was just your name came up in conversation —"

Did it? I want to ask the context but know I can't. Mick wouldn't tell me the truth anyway. It might have been that the guys were talking stocks and shares and saying what a good day I've had, or they might have been discussing strip joints and quite a different set of figures. The sexism is only a problem if you let it be.

"As I said, I thought you might fancy a drink after all your hard work today."

"Peter's not home. The nanny has left for the night, there's no one to look after Auriol," I reply.

"The guys were saying you'd have an excuse and that you never party any more. Oh well. No worries. We didn't really want you here anyway, Princess. Just didn't want you bringing one of those lawsuits against us, crying that all the business is done round the lap table rather than the board table and that you weren't given the chance to join in. See you tomorrow." He hangs up.

His joke, like most jokes, finds its foundation in a basic gripe or grievance. It's accepted that many deals and contacts are made in the bars over a bottle of Bolly. Women *are* pissed-off that after they have children the abundant after-hours networking opportunities are history (mostly they are pissed-off because this says something quite definitive about the men they had children with, who, incidentally, are able to continue their late-night networking). I find it simple enough to pay a babysitter and get my ass to the latest minimalist bar without delay or fuss. If that's what the job takes, you've got to do it. Therefore Mick's comment is unfair. I'm normally holding my own with the letchy guys. I was out with them just last . . . I pause.

I can't quite remember when I was last out with my colleagues on a purely social basis. Last week I had to fly to Berlin and was away two nights. I had a client function on the Thursday and I worked late on the Friday. I grab my diary and flick through it. The last time I agreed to a social was six weeks ago. A lifetime in the City.

I drag myself off the bed and into the bathroom. Splashing water on my face, I consider the possibility of daubing on some fresh lipgloss and grabbing a glittery top. I could call Peter; tell him to get home immediately so that I can go to a strip bar with the other men.

I pause again. Look back into the mirror. When did I become the sort of woman who falls asleep too exhausted to take off her make-up? My face has weird indentations where I've slept heavily on the embroidered pattern on the Egyptian cotton bedlinen. My mascara has gone into the fine lines which run like ebullient tributaries from the corners of my eyes. I lean closer to the mirror. *And* I have lines around my mouth. My skin has started to age; there's a general sagging. Slight, probably undetectable to the average citizen, but if a woman in her twenties were to look at me she'd know I wasn't in her gang. I will soon be the type of woman people categorize as beautiful *for her age*.

I carefully remove my make-up, shower, gently pat myself dry and then apply about a dozen insurance policies (a.k.a. bust-firming gel, anti-cellulite cream, foot and hand moisturizer, neck moisturizer and something a bit special for around my eyes). I get back into bed, turn out the lights and wonder where Peter is. I can't claim that he is out more than he used to be; his job demands a lot of him, it always has. The difference is that when I was his mistress it was Rose waiting at home and I was out at work events right by Peter's side. I'm not suited to inactivity.

Just after we got together Peter was offered a great position in another merchant bank. We decided that it was a good idea for him to take it, not only for the extra money but because we both agreed that a bit of space between us was healthy. It had been fine working together when we lived apart but nobody wants to be together 24/7, do they? I hadn't realized how much time we both spent in the office, way more than we spend at home. By not working together we've lost quite some intimacy and now Peter goes to different parties, client dinners and work conferences. Lots of them. And I stay at home and the most exciting thing that happens to me of an evening is a call from Mick.

I sit up and put on my bedside light once more. I suddenly feel too agitated to sleep. I love Peter so much, I do. More than myself. More than my child. This is more unusual than one would imagine. Most men assume that they are their partner's number one beloved but the majority of mothers secretly love their children far more than they love their men — at least they do until their children become teenagers. Peter charms me. At his best he's clever, fun, interesting, dirty, and essential to me. At his worst he's still essential to me. I am essential to Auriol and I find that responsibility gut-wrenching. I'm sure I must fail in her eyes fifty times a day. I don't like failure, especially my own. Her love is such a responsibility.

I idly flick through my diary to ascertain when Peter and I last went out together and alone. Five weeks ago. We go out often but usually with other couples, colleagues or contacts. I'm not sure when that shift in focus happened either. We used to passionately pursue time to ourselves; now our entertaining friends fill in the conversational gaps over the bread basket. It's not that we are bored with one another, it's just that we've heard all one another's stories over the last seven years.

Wow. I hadn't realized that. I flick through the yearly calendar at the back of my diary two times, just to be sure. I feel tremors of excitement in my stomach and within seconds the tremors flourish into full-blown triumph. A feeling I can now luxuriate in forever. It isn't a difficult sum. After all, I was at their wedding and the cause of their divorce. "I do" to decree absolute was five years and two months. Four months less than my marriage to Peter, as stands. I have been Peter's wife longer than Rose was.

How exciting. How important. I feel something like relief wash over me. Peter has been my husband for five and a half years now, which should be enough, but I've always had a nagging anxiety that he belongs elsewhere. He belongs to Rose. I don't believe they are one another's destiny or intrinsically, indefinitely linked. But I do believe that being with him is akin to wearing someone else's jumper, not that I've ever bought a second-hand garment in my life — not even at university when it was trendy. I don't buy into that vintage angle; besides the hygiene issue, I've always believed some day someone would tap me on the shoulder and say, "Excuse me, I think you are wearing my jumper. I'd like it back." They might strip me in the street as they rightfully reclaimed what was theirs. Sometimes, that's how I feel about Peter. He was second-hand to me and some day, without warning, someone (Rose) could demand him back. Of course my unease is nonsense. Not logical in the slightest. That's the thing with irrational fears — they are unreasonable.

But Peter has been married to *me* for longer than he was married to *her*. He's mine now. He's *mine*.

My God, we have to celebrate. This is fantastic. I flick out the light and anticipate a decent night's sleep.

CHAPTER
NINE

Tuesday 12 September

Rose

I drop the boys off at the school gate and swap a couple of sentences with some other mums. I sign up for library duty on Wednesday afternoon and I catch up with Mr Shaw, the PE teacher, so I can quickly ask about the size of the towel the boys are expected to bring to their swimming lessons on Thursdays.

"Any size you consider reasonable, Mrs Phillips," says Mr Shaw.

Mr Shaw is South African and in his late twenties. He's tall, tanned and blond and all the children adore him. Many of the mothers do too. I look at him and see the kind of man I'd like my boys to turn into: strong, polite, happy and with a reasonable understanding of the rules of cricket. I fear that I've lost the ability to fancy anyone and even if a dozen naked Greek gods were to fight for my favour, I'd be unmoved.

"I'm very impressed with the quality of the tracksuits this year," I comment.

"I'm glad you approve," he says with a wide smile. "I'm sorry, Mrs Phillips, but class is about to start and I really mustn't be late."

"No, of course not." I'm suddenly embarrassed. What must this man think of me? "I've got a lot to get on with too. I shouldn't be standing around chatting," I assure him. "I'm very busy."

"No doubt. If you'll excuse me." He breaks free and starts to dash towards the sports hall, leaving me standing, awkward and alone, on the pathway outside the school.

Suddenly, the street is empty. Car doors slam closed as mothers dash off to work or home and the children's chatter is distant. The school bell rings out and I can just make out Mrs Foster yelling instructions that the children must get into neat lines. I stand still until the footfall ceases altogether.

I start to think about my day and what I should do next. I wasn't fibbing to Mr Shaw, I am very busy. I'm planning to clean the windows. I need to pop to Tesco and I need to call the gym and renew the boys' swimming lessons. Sebastian wants to do tennis lessons this year and Henry has shown some interest in karate, so I'll have to make some inquiries there. I also want to spend some time browsing on the internet. Although it's only September, I want to start scouring for Christmas presents. The boys' birthday is in December, so it's always a hectic time. It doesn't do to leave the planning and purchasing until the last minute.

I sigh.

Unexpectedly, I feel down. Very down. I might even use the word depressed and that's not a word I use lightly. Yesterday, I managed to keep busy and avoided thinking about my treacherous so-called friends. I spent the entire day gardening — energetically raking leaves and weeding — preparing the garden to close down for winter. No one called. I knew they wouldn't. Daisy will keep a low profile for a week and then call me as though nothing has been said, that's her way. It's possible that the men have forgotten anything *was* said, that's their way. It will be left to Connie to mend bridges and make friends, but she had a photography job yesterday in Northampton so she wouldn't have had the opportunity to talk. She'll call today. I won't speak to her. Oh no. Certainly not. Not after their impertinence. Never again.

I sigh heavily once again. Mentally listing my chores for today has not convinced me that I have a busy and full day ahead. The opposite. My day sounds dull and overly familiar. The chore list sounds desperate and contrived. All at once I am sure I cannot spend another moment in a supermarket. I know the layout of every shelf and could probably confidently list all the products that are on special offer. I cleaned the windows only last week and remarkably it hasn't rained in between; they don't need doing again. Christmas really is forever away.

So what shall I do?

I'm tired. I haven't slept at all well since the fracas over Sunday lunch. How dare Daisy! How dare any of them! How rude! And interfering! I would never presume in a similar way. My heartbeat quickens once again. Last night it beat so rapidly I had to get out of bed and walk round the house and drink a glass of water to try to calm down. That would teach them, if I had a heart attack or some sort of seizure. Death by indignation. "Wasting my life." Bloody cheek. What makes Daisy think her life is so worthwhile in comparison? From where I'm standing it's pretty clear that her life's been on hold for the last six years and she knows it. She might maintain that all the travelling she and Simon do, and the job satisfaction they get, means something, but I'd argue it pales into insignificance compared to bringing up a family. She'd have to agree with me or else why is she trying so hard to start a family of her own? As for Connie, well, she's been insufferable since she started her own photography business. Just because she's managed to combine a career and being a mother she thinks she's the Queen of the have-it-all generation. She wasn't always so bloody sorted and she'd do well to remember as much. Ghastly.

My eyes sting and there is a throbbing ache in the back of my head.

Not that I've ever been struck by how ghastly Connie's manner is until Sunday. Normally, she's rather sweet. She's always singing my praises and insisting I put every other mother to shame. And up until Sunday I've felt extremely sorry for Daisy and Simon because yes, they would happily sacrifice their exotic travel for the opportunity to be knee high in nappies.

But how could they be so cruel to me? Why were they so nasty?

I realize that I have walked right past my house and am surprised to find myself outside the local Starbucks. Inside there are a number of busy office workers in smart suits, grabbing a quick double espresso before they tackle the tube. There are a couple of mums with toddlers. The toddlers are crawling around the café floor, which I would never have allowed however beaten I felt after a terrible night's sleep — it's unhygienic. There are two people reading a newspaper. I envy them. They look unruffled, as though time is something to be squandered, not something to be filled or something that flies by; which is my experience.

Could I join them? I haven't had breakfast. I made the boys pancakes but that didn't really leave me much time to sort things out for myself. I am a bit hungry, and after a couple of sleepless nights a latte would probably perk me up. I feel momentarily guilty. After all, there's the lovely Fair Trade Brazilian blend in my cupboard, I could just go home and make a cup. It seems extravagant to sit on my own in a coffee shop. As I'm trying to dismiss the idea I find myself ordering a latte and a cinnamon bun. Then I plonk myself in a window seat.

It is a perfect day for drying clothes, warm and windy. The bright autumnal sunshine splatters across the pavement. I feel a moment of satisfaction as I think that I managed to get a load of washing hung on the line before we left for school this morning. Few mums are so organized. As I sink into the roomy armchair I concentrate on relaxing my shoulders. For nearly two days I've been wearing them around my ears.

I try and think positively. The school term has got off to a successful start — relative tranquillity reigns. Apart from Sebastian's grumbles that I oughtn't still to be collecting him from the school gate (ridiculous in this age when you can't sneeze without hitting a paedophile or a speeding driver). The boys come home from school muddy, smelly and tired. They slouch in front of the TV, eat several rounds of toast, drink large glasses of milk and then I coerce them into doing something productive before I cook a hot meal.

Friday was a little disappointing. I spent several hours putting together our annual autumnal nature table. I collected conkers and drilled holes in them and threaded them on to strings so that we could have a conker tournament. I'd also collected a selection of leaves and nuts, searched out a book on hibernation and another on tractors, as I like the boys to have an understanding of things you don't discover on the Loony Tunes channel. I went to the local art shop and bought paint in browns, orange, red and rust. The table was a shrine to the season of mists and mellow fruitfulness. I managed to contain my excitement while the boys munched their way through their toast and then — with a flourish — I ushered them into the lean-to.

"I thought we could paint these leaves and make print pictures," I said.

Sebastian stared at me with ill-disguised disgust. "Babies do that in reception class, Mum."

"This book has some great pictures."

Both the boys resolutely stared at their feet. My pride in my purchase subsided. It was clear that the twins were not enthusiastic about the table.

"No one really plays conkers *ever*, Mum, and they haven't since like prehistoric times, when you were a girl," commented Sebastian.

My first reaction was to correct his understanding of prehistoric times but I realized that he had a point. I can't remember playing conkers. Some of the boys in my playground might have, but it was never as widespread a form of entertainment as Top Trumps.

"We always do a table and it's boring," added Henry.

I was hurt. Offended by their manners and the sentiment. I took a deep breath and reminded myself that they are seven years old and not as tactful as I'd hope.

It was a relief that my root vegetable stew and stuffed apples with custard were received with more enthusiasm than the season table. I didn't mention to the boys that I'd themed the food. I had a feeling it would have been detrimental to their enjoyment.

After they'd finished their homework, bathed and cleaned their teeth, I read stories and checked that there were clean football strips for the weekend. Then I called Connie for a cheer-up chat. We competitively compared our day's irritations, which was a help and a giggle. That was Friday. On Sunday she smote me with her tongue. Who'd have thought it was possible?

I begin to ponder. "Cruel" and "nasty" are not words I've ever had cause to associate with Daisy and Connie.

At least, not since Daisy and I gave up fighting over Sindy dolls. What did they say exactly? Wasting my life. I remember that *clearly* even through the fuzz of two sleepless nights. I wish I could forget it but I can't. The accusation has stung me like a mosquito bite and I can't help but scratch it. In fairness to Connie, she did point out that I've done a great job with the twins. What did she ask me? What am I going to do next?

The coffee, previously delicious, suddenly tastes bitter. I lunge for the bun and stuff an enormous amount into my mouth, desperate to take away the nasty taste. The bun doesn't help. My throat is too dry to allow me to swallow. I chew and chew and chew. I must look like a huge cow masticating grass.

They wanted to talk to me about my future. Their voices shove their way into my consciousness. Last night, when I was in the darkness of despair and self-pity, I was able to filter out the concern and pity in their words. I ignored the assurances that they were only thinking of me and wanted the best for me. Last night it was easy to be angry and indignant and, most importantly, to continue to avoid what they were shunting into view. But in the daylight, with sun streaming through the window, it's not so easy to feign ignorance.

I don't have a future.

Financially I have made myself reasonably secure, although not flush. Peter paid off the mortgage on our family home when he left. It was a huge pile of a place. I sold it and invested a lump sum in secure saving plans and bought a more modest place for the boys and me.

I don't see myself ending up as a bag lady, holding out a cardboard cup and sleeping in the doorway of Argos. But how do I see myself?

I hope the boys will go to university, stay clear of drugs and find careers that they enjoy. One day I'd like there to be grandchildren. Connie's words beat their way through the flowery privet fence that I have carefully built in my mind. It's a manicured fence, which I prune and nurture; a fence I've carefully constructed to keep me protected from harsh realities. But, like a nasty, invasive weed, the words of my friends hack through. "You have no friends or interests outside the school gates." "We just think it would be nice if you got out and met some new people." "Maybe even go on a couple of dates."

I am not an imbecile. I have, on occasion, thought some very similar things myself. Maybe I should make an effort to get out and meet people beyond the school gate. But how would I go about that? It's not easy finding babysitters that the boys are comfortable with. I've never left them with strangers. I suppose I could ask Daisy and Simon to sit, occasionally. They do offer, regularly. But where would I go?

I pause and reflect. I do have hobbies. I love pottering in my garden. My rose bushes were fabulous this year, quite the talk of the street. I'm a good seamstress, I make my own curtains. I'm a very good cook; I've made my own love handles.

It's other people's stares, not the phone's tring, that alert me to the fact that my mobile is ringing. I see that it's Connie. I pick up immediately, despite my vows to ignore her.

"Sorry, sorry, sorry. We're really sorry. All of us. Very sorry. Are we forgiven?" she gabbles without pausing. I stay silent. I want more. "We were trying to do the right thing." I'm mute. "No one knew how to discuss this with you, Rose." Still silent. "If we didn't care about you so much we wouldn't have said anything. We could have just quietly eaten you out of house and home every Sunday, for the next couple of decades. I mean, to be honest, it's not going to be that convenient for me if you do start dating. Next thing you know, you'll fall in love and then you'll neglect your friends. I'll have to learn to cook and you know that I've spent my adulthood trying to avoid that. Rose, we didn't mean to hurt you," she adds, clearly sincere.

What am I to do? Without Daisy, Simon, Connie and Luke my life is pretty dull. There's no point in sulking. I break into a reluctant grin and I break the silence.

"I know," I mutter. "But I hate it that everyone thinks I'm some sort of victim because I'm on my own. The truth is I think it's a blessed relief not to have a man hanging around losing his rag and the car keys on a more or less continuous basis. I love my life. I really do."

"Right," says Connie, flatly.

"I know no one believes me. Everyone from my mother to the old guy in the corner shop think all my problems would be solved if there was a man in my life. But men don't smell very nice and more often than not they don't act particularly nicely either," I argue.

98

"Right," says Connie again. But she still doesn't sound as though she's wholeheartedly agreeing with me. I know she's just too scared of ruining the freshly formed truce to risk openly disagreeing. I take a sip of my coffee but it's turned cold. The frothy treat has been neglected and now is sour. If I was a more fanciful type, I'd see that as a pertinent metaphor for my life.

"You agree with my mum, don't you?" I ask with a sigh.

"And the guy in the corner shop." Connie risks giggling now, I can hear it in her voice. "No, Rose, not necessarily. I don't think all your problems would be solved if you met a man, you'd just have a new batch to deal with. I think you should meet *people*. Not just *men*. Friends. You should develop a new interest —"

"Take up a night class," I finish the end of her sentence with her.

"Well, yes, why not?"

"I was being facetious. If I had a pound for every time someone's suggested a night class to me I'd be a very rich woman."

"People suggest you going to a night class because it's a good idea. It changed my life."

"You really think I just need a good seeing to, don't you, Connie?"

"One step at a time. Personally I've always had a penchant for professor types; you might kill two birds with one stone."

I sigh and hope my resentment is effectively communicated. I feel bullied.

"How about a part-time job?" she suggests.

"I've tried that. It's impossible to find something that fits around the children."

"The last time you tried they were still in nappies, now they are in football boots and after-school clubs. Things might have changed."

"What would I do?" I wail.

"You're a fully trained accountant. A good one. There must be dozens of people that would benefit from you looking over their books. You could do that through the day, when the boys are at school."

She has this habit of making things sound easy, it's quite annoying.

"Who'd employ me?"

"Me for one," she says.

"You can't employ me. I couldn't accept a wage from you."

"Well, maybe we could do a pro rata thing. I could babysit for you while you go to your night class."

It would be impossible not to see her good intentions. Eventually I summon the grace to mutter, "I suppose I should be grateful that you are just suggesting night classes and not speed-dating."

"We're trying to ease you out of your comfort zone, Rose. We're not asking you to make a Herculean leap."

I'm not clear how it happens but somehow or other, by the time I leave the café, I find that I have agreed to Daisy and Connie drafting up a plan for me to meet new people and I've promised to consider enrolling in a night class.

CHAPTER
TEN

Thursday 14 September

Lucy

I make an effort. A huge effort. I take the day off work to visit a stylist for a blow-dry, my beautician for various polishing, waxing, buffing and plucking, and I buy new underwear; although, strictly speaking, this is more for me than him. He's unlikely to recoil in horror at the sight of last season's frilly knicks. I'm not aware that they are attached to any traumatic incidences. I buy La Perla; tiny and shockingly expensive but sometimes less is more. I book us a table at Fifteen, arrange for Eva to babysit and then I book a car.

My plan is to pick up Peter from work. If I wait until he gets home before setting off on our date, the likelihood is one or the other of us will lose the impetus and decide that we'd prefer to slump; him in front of the TV, me with a bunch of magazines. Besides, even if we both do feel lively enough to venture out, we run the risk of Auriol still being awake when we try to make our escape bid. She'll moan and whine and insist she *needs* us to stay in, she'll say that she hasn't seen us *"forever"* and she misses us. Her tears will guarantee that the fun of the evening will evaporate. The girl would suck our blood if she could.

I've already called Susie, Peter's PA, and given her a heads up on my plan. She knows not to put any meetings in Peter's diary after 5 p.m. and not to allow Peter to skip off to the bar before I arrive.

"OK Lucy, don't worry. I'll make sure he's waiting but suspects nothing." Susie can manage this seemingly tricky task with ease because she's an excellent PA. "Is it an anniversary?" She knows it's not our real anniversary because she sent the lavish bouquet just six months ago.

"Of sorts." I don't offer any more of an explanation.

The cab company sends a shiny slate-grey Mercedes as I'm a good client. The driver is Bob. He's driven me before. As I get into the car I notice him checking out my legs (shown to discreet advantage in a pencil skirt) and my cleavage (shown to unapologetic advantage as my Anna Sui shirt is almost transparent). He pulls his eyes away from the mirror and forces himself to look at the road. I'm not in the least offended. I don't make this sort of effort to be ignored.

When the car pulls up outside Pete's office, no one turns a hair. Mercs with tinted windows are a common sight in the City. Everybody is a somebody or at least a convincing wannabe. Peter is clearly delighted when he spots me in reception. Susie has made up some story about a client wanting a quick word with him and waiting impatiently in the glass foyer.

"My God, Lucy, I was expecting a bollocking from some grey client and instead it's you! Not a bollocking at all, just the dog's bollocks!" Peter kisses me on the lips. I don't pull away or tell him he'll smudge my make-up or crumple my clothes. Instead I push my body into his, reminding him how I feel.

"What's the occasion?" he asks as he gives me an appreciative once-over.

"I'll tell you at dinner. Come on, we're going right now."

"I can't just leave, Lucy. I have to check my diary, let Susie know I'm off, shut down my laptop." Suddenly, he looks agitated, irritated even.

I bite my tongue and resist making any comment about spontaneity or rather the lack of it. Funny, when we were having an affair there was never an occasion that Peter fretted about his diary or shutting down his laptop. He was always available to devote himself to me and to allow me to devote myself to him. Now I am his wife and I should be more important to him, but there seems less room for me in his busy schedule. I take a deep breath.

"Your diary is empty. Susie is in on this. She'll pack away your laptop and keep it under lock and key until tomorrow."

Peter looks at me and I watch the irritation melt away. Admiration and pleasure are allowed to seep back. He's staring at me as though he's just met me on the street and is sure he recognizes me from somewhere; he just can't place where.

"You really have thought of everything, haven't you?"

"I think so."

I watch him and will us to reconnect and stay connected. How come we sometimes seem so far away from one another when all I want is to be his second skin? I want tonight to be perfect. I want tonight to be a turning point; I want to turn back. Because I fear we've travelled too far in the wrong direction.

"Come on. The champagne is on ice." I gently tug at his cuff, reminding myself of the way Auriol pulls at my skirt. Peter doesn't resist but allows me to lead him towards our blissful date.

"I feel wayward leaving the office on the dot at 6.30," he laughs. Everyone knows that clock-watching is for pussies. Our mood is buoyant, expectant and fun. All at once I am deeply in love with my husband and feel assured that he is deeply in love with me. In a rush, I remember just how exhilarating life is when we have fun together.

We arrive at Fifteen. I've been here twice before but with work. It's so much more fun arriving with Peter. We chat about this and that, mostly the menu. We order cocktails and I encourage Peter to plump for a wine that costs more than fifty quid. The cocktails wash away the day's cares for Peter (and the sting of the savage bikini wax for me). We settle down to enjoy the fabulous food.

"So, Lucy, what's the occasion? There clearly is one," asks Peter as he forks up something bloody. His open mouth is so sexy.

I grin but stay mute. I haven't decided whether I will tell him what we are celebrating. I haven't decided if I *can* tell him.

"It's not one of our anniversaries, is it?"

Peter thinks it's funny that we have three. One for the day we met. One for the day we got it together. One for the day we married. It's not that I'm overly sentimental. I just like gifts.

I look at my husband. His face is relaxed, a rare enough occurrence for me to comment on it. He's a handsome man. His eyes are his best feature. They are vivid, intelligent eyes. They used to be set in a chiselled, sharp face; all cheekbones and strong jaw, but he's put on a bit of weight recently. This bothers me ever so slightly although I wish it didn't. I try not to see it as a disrespectful slip in standards and a failing in our relationship. I try to see it more as an acknowledgement of our contentment. I remind myself that angular people are rarely content. They may be focused, ambitious, beautiful or freshly in love but they are often depressed, adulterous or on drugs. Better to deal with love handles.

It's his outward show of contentment that encourages me to share. "How long have we been married?" I ask.

Peter chews vigorously and because he's good with numbers it only takes him a second to reply.

"Five years, six months and oh, ten days."

"Four months longer than you were married to Rose," I grin.

I can't hide my exhilaration. I'm delighted with my victory.

Peter stops chewing. He does not look elated or relieved. He does not appear to be sharing my sense of exhilaration.

"And that's it? That's why we are here tonight? Because of some stupid obsession you hold with Rose?"

"No. It's not stupid. And it's not an obsession. I didn't say that." It's too late. The relaxed, convivial atmosphere vanishes in an instant. "It's just a landmark for me," I stutter.

"You are my wife, the mother of my daughter, I left Rose for you. Isn't that enough?"

It isn't. At least not always. Not consistently. I know it should be. I wish it was but it isn't. I daren't confess as much. Peter glares at me. I fully expect smoke to flare out of his nostrils.

"You are such a nightmare, Lucy. When is it going to be enough for you? I chose you. I live with you. I left Rose and my boys for you. What do I have to do to prove that it is you I love?"

I know he thinks I'm jealous and he thinks that the jealousy is below me; unnecessary and undignified. It would be more reasonable and fitting if I pitied Rose but I don't, I fear her. And I'm angry at her. I'm angry that she met Peter first. That she walked down the aisle with him first. That she bore him children first. Twins, for God's sake. How do you follow that act? I'm angry that she influences my home life, everything from how we spend our Christmas holiday to where we live and which school our daughter attends. I'm angry that I have to look after Rose's kids every Sunday. She probably visits the beautician while I'm ritualistically abused by the twins, undoubtedly at her instruction. I resent her presence and her existence. I wish I could annihilate her.

106

I take a deep breath. This is not something I can, or should, share. Instead I try to explain why being married to Peter for longer than she was does matter to me.

"If I say 'prime minister' to you, who comes to mind?"

"Blair, of course. Where's this going?"

"For years after Margaret Thatcher had lost her mind and office, whenever anyone said 'prime minister' an image of her would flash into my mind. Long after Major had been and gone and even after Blair had served an entire term. It took years before I started to think of him first. It's the same with the word 'wife'. Whenever you say 'my wife' a picture of Rose comes into my head. It takes a nano-second before I adjust that mental picture and realize you mean me. Just a nano-second but it feels like a lifetime. Do you understand what I'm saying?"

Peter looks wearily at his dinner and then drags his eyes back to mine before he admits, "Yes."

I know him so well. Too well. Something flickers in his eyes. A lethal cocktail of regret and resignation.

"You do the same, don't you?" I accuse.

"Yes," he sighs. "When I say 'my wife' it takes a fraction of a second to think of you. Hers is the first image. I do understand what you mean."

I should pick up this understanding and turn it over, examine and mould it into a connection between us. God knows we need one. Rationally speaking, I should be thrilled that he has insight into my demons. Perhaps now I can tell him that since the day we got married things have got harder for me, not easier. I should explain that I'm not finding married life a picnic. That I miss the spontaneity, excitement and challenge involved in being a lover and I'm overwhelmed with the mundane tasks involved in being a wife. I do not much care whether everyone in the family eats enough greens or whether or not I switched the washing machine on before I came out to work, and I resent the fact that this role means I have to care about such banalities.

I thought marrying was about making a public commitment to the person one loved most in the world. I thought it was romantic. It's hilarious that I, of all people — Lucy the pragmatist, Lucy the cynic — got caught up in the big sell and believed that we would attain a higher plane by being married to one another, when in reality all I was doing was downgrading my quality of life. Marrying means taking on more work and sacrificing the best bits of our relationship and myself.

But more devastating than the acceptance of the tangible duties being a wife entails is the fact that something intangible has changed within our relationship since we married. Before we married I felt supremely beautiful, sexy, confident, intelligent and assured. I was a woman who knew what she wanted and knew that she was going to get it. Stupidly, by marrying Peter I voluntarily invaded Rose's territory and chose to fight her on her own ground. Big mistake. She was the ideal wife. I was the perfect mistress. Now I'm always playing catch-up in a game where I don't know the rules and I fail to understand what there is to win.

I could explain all this to Peter and ask him for his love and understanding. Maybe he'd take my hand and guide me through the emotional minefield. Maybe we could stay on course, at least for tonight, so that he'll take me home and make love to me; with him edging down my tiny knickers I'm sure that once again I'd feel supremely confident and assured.

Instead, I throw a glass of wine at him and leave the restaurant alone.

CHAPTER
ELEVEN

Friday 15 September

John

It's her. Fuck me. Is it? What's she doing here, though? Didn't she live in Balham or Clapham, somewhere around there? Suppose she could have moved; it's possible. I get out of my car and thread my way towards the school gate. Despite the mass of heads bobbing in front of me I manage to keep my eye on her head. If it is hers, that is. She's wearing her hair straight now. But then everyone does.

"Greenie?"

She doesn't turn to me instantly, but she freezes, and in that moment, I know it's her. Now I'm close I recognize the shape of her shoulders, which surprises me. I didn't know I knew them. I wonder if she recognizes my voice. I bet she knows it's me. She's probably working out whether she wants to spin and face me or whether she wants to run. Slowly, Greenie turns her head and there we are, face to face, after all this time.

She looks older, of course, but she looks better. Glossier than I remembered. Healthier.

"I thought it was you. How the hell are you, Greenie?"

She's lost her tongue. I have that effect on women. Her hand flutters up to her hair and she tucks a stray strand behind her ear. Sweet, she cares what she looks like. After all these years she still wants to impress.

I had great sex with this woman.

Just fantastic.

Until she turned mental that is.

Shit, I'd forgotten she went la la. When I saw her neat little body dash towards the school gate, all I noticed was the way she flashed that wide, cheeky grin of hers. Not at me, at some woman she was chatting to. Her blue eyes sparkled and I had flashbacks of my holding her hair as she sucked my cock; I just wanted to say hi. It's only now, when she's staring at me with that intense, almost angry look, that I remember. She looks like a cornered convict deciding whether to run or rampage. I remember this woman wanted me too much. This woman confused my hunt for sex with her hunt for a soulmate. This woman thinks I betrayed her. If I'd given it a moment's thought I wouldn't have said hi. But I didn't give it even that long. Rarely do give anything that much thought; I'm an instinct man myself. Life's too short.

I decide the only thing to do now is bluff it out. Make out we were nothing more than old colleagues and that we're now knocked out by the coincidence of seeing one another somewhere unexpected.

"Well, well, well. Fancy bumping into you."

Greenie looks around, she's clearly checking out who can hear us. A fat bird taps her on the arm.

"Are you all right, Connie? You look like you've seen a ghost."

Spot on, fat girl.

"I'm fine, thanks, Rose," replies Greenie.

The fat bird hovers, waiting for Greenie to introduce us. She never was that good at thinking on her feet. I'm not sure how we got away with our affair for as long as we did.

"I'm John Harding. Constance and I were colleagues in a former life." I beam and hold out my hand. I'm charming. I know so.

The fat bird takes my hand and energetically pumps it up and down the way women with no sexuality do.

"Rose. Lovely to meet you." She turns back to Greenie, who still appears to be in shock. "Should I find Fran?"

At this point I notice that Greenie has one hand on a stroller thingy inside which there's a kid. Obviously hers.

"Who's this angel?" I ask. It's one of the lines I use on single mums. It always works a treat. Personally, I'm a big fan of single mums, most of them go like rabbits and they are commitment phobic (once bitten twice shy and all that); my idea of a perfect woman. Of course the line works on Greenie too.

"This is Flora. She's my youngest." She smiles as she says her kid's name and looks genuinely relaxed for the first time since she clapped eyes on me. Then she absentmindedly fondles the kid's head. Quite touching.

112

It's a cute kid. As you'd expect. She looks like her mother. "I'm here picking up my eldest. She's just started school. Reception class. And you? Are you . . ."

"Jesus, no, Greenie."

I bat aside her presumption that I'm a dad on the school run. Relief flickers over her face. I wonder if she's relieved that I don't have a brat at the same school as her brat or whether she's relieved that I don't have a kid at all. A kid would demonstrate a commitment to someone. A commitment I was unprepared to give her.

"So, what are you doing here?" She's not making a polite enquiry. Her question has an edgy, impertinent tone. Strangely, I find it exciting.

"Doing a consulting job at the BBC, up in Shepherd's Bush. Although now I've told you that, I'll have to kill you."

I glance at Connie to see if she's recognized the old joke. She says nothing and there's no sign of a playful smile flickering across her mouth. I move on.

"I knocked off early and my mate, Craig Walker, works here so I thought I'd catch him and we'd go for a beer."

"Mr Walker is a friend of yours?"

Greenie is no longer a grey colour; she's turned so white she's almost transparent. I bet she's reinvented herself as someone quite proper and the last thing she needs is her torrid past tripping her up. I enjoy the moment, let her suffer — it serves her right for not being friendlier.

"Oh yes, Craig and I go back years. We were at primary school together. In fact the reason we are meeting for a beer is that we are planning a stag weekend together."

"Yours?" Is she curious, hopeful or fearful?

I pause and then shake my head. "Been there, done that, read the book, got the T-shirt and the decree absolute."

"Oh, I'm sorry to hear that." She doesn't sound sorry. Her tone suggests that I've met her every expectation and every one of them was as low as a snake in the grass.

At that moment a tiny blonde kid flings herself at Greenie's legs.

"Mummy, Mummy, Mummy, guess what we did today."

Greenie crouches down so that she's eye level with her daughter and beams. She doesn't let the kid tell the exciting news because she swoops in for dozens of unselfconscious smackers. Greenie and her kid smile and kiss and chatter for some minutes and I'm forgotten. They mirror one another's expressions of delight, surprise and wonderment and they both laugh at the same time as the child delivers what must be the punchline to the story. They are beautiful.

Greenie catches my eye and appears startled to see I'm still standing in the same spot. Had she thought I was a figment of her imagination? She manoeuvres the stroller around me and hordes of others and makes to leave. "If you'll excuse me," she says formally. "I have to go now."

"'Bye then," I mutter.

She nods.

"See you again," I add.

This time she hesitates as she searches for the correct response. We lock our gaze and I see regret. I wonder if she is regretting that we can't spend longer together or whether she is regretting we ever spent any time together at all.

I watch the threesome disappear along the busy tree-lined avenue until they fade into a dot.

CHAPTER
TWELVE

Monday 18 September

Rose

Annoyingly my friends and relatives have timed their big push to reacclimatize me into society rather well. It's mid-September and I soon discover that there are thousands of classes I could enrol for, all beginning in a week or two. I also discover that most of the classes are inexpensive, as I'm entitled to a single person's allowance or, if I chose something vocational, I'd benefit from a back-to-work freebie. I learn this much from the dozens of brochures which Connie and Daisy have had sent to my house. When I am sure that an entire forest has been lopped just to provide me with a selection of prospectuses, Simon arrives out of the blue and insists that we sit down for three hours, searching on the internet for yet more appropriate courses. I work hard at not feeling pressurized or patronized and remind myself, on an almost hourly basis, that they mean well.

I start my search for a new hobby by flicking through the fattest prospectus. Some of the courses are intimidating, irrelevant or boring. But some, I have to admit, seem interesting. There is a large gap in my general knowledge of history and literature, for example. I find I am a little bit tempted to enrol for a course entitled *Sorcery, Starvation and Sex: a study of sixteenth-century women*, if only because it's a respectable way to reminisce about the days when sex was part of my life, which seems as long ago as the sixteenth century, ha ha.

Bell ringing? Something to do with computers? I'm not a technophobe. I use e-mail all the time, I shop on the internet, I research white goods (and now further education courses) on the internet and I'm a wiz with Excel. But I don't wish to learn how to build a computer from scratch, so I flick past the section on computers. Dog training? No. Our Labrador is too old to learn new tricks. I relate to him but the dog doesn't have a bossy sister insisting otherwise. Flower arranging? Now that might be pleasant. H for horticulture. Well, I do like gardening. I read the small print and discover that I'm being overly ambitious. There are options to specialize in milking goats or dry stone walling. I have a modest London garden, not a farm.

I draw up a shortlist of half a dozen courses that don't actively worry or offend me and I pin the list to the noticeboard in the kitchen. I hope that the list, and the entire idea, will soon be forgotten; lost behind bits of paper advertising organic vegetable delivery and birthday party invites. I see that this is not to be when Luke arrives on my doorstep one evening. He's carrying a bottle of wine and some papers which are later revealed to be application forms. I comment that it seems to be the case that the whole world is conspiring against me.

"*For* you!" insists Luke. "Should I open this wine?"

Luke has been chosen as the one most likely to get me to sign on the dotted line because he's an interesting blend of qualities (infinite patience and yet an ability to be decisive). It's a powerful combination. Besides, I have a soft spot for him and everyone knows that I find it difficult to refuse him anything, which is why I'm so often making chocolate bread and butter pudding, his favourite.

Luke and I rarely have time alone and I decide at least to enjoy the novelty of male company. We chat about the kids. Fran is settling well at Holland House; she's going to dress up as a Hungry Caterpillar for Readers' Day. I tell Luke that the boys are quibbling over the difference between a poem and a nursery rhyme.

When we are seated, with full glasses and a bowl of peanuts, he cuts to the chase and asks the same question all the others have asked.

"So which course piques your interest?" If he's feeling frustrated, he manages to hide the fact. But then he lives with Connie's whimsical nature and appears to delight in it. "I gather you've narrowed down the field a little. Let's see what we have here," he says, spreading out the application forms on the floor, like tarot cards. "Flower arranging, pastry making, first aid, calligraphy, a study of etymology. I might as well confess I have a note here from Connie to steer you away from flower arranging and pastry making."

"Why?" I ask. I know the answer but I'm testing Luke's honesty.

"Well, her notes say I ought to point out that you already have those skills and you wouldn't be stretching yourself."

"But in reality she doesn't think I'll meet any men on those courses, at least not straight ones, and therefore thinks they'll be a waste of time."

"That might have crossed her mind." He grins. "How about learning an instrument?" I shrug. "Something must appeal?"

The truth is they all terrify me. Not the actual learning. Historically, I was a girly swot and something like that never leaves you. I have no fear of practising a skill at home or having to write essays and hand them in on time. I have every confidence that I will be able to understand and retain all that is taught. My fears are more basic.

I'm dreading finding the place of higher education. Driving or catching a tube to somewhere unfamiliar seems a ghastly idea. I'll have to set off hours in advance because I can't bear being late, but I'm not great with maps. Even if I find the institution I'll then have to find the actual classroom, and these places are notorious for having warren-like corridors. *And*, assuming that by some miracle I do get there on time, then, horror of horrors, I'll have to walk in on my own. It will be dreadful.

Everyone will look at me and they'll size me up. Judge my clothes, my manner, my size. They'll categorize me (it's simple, I look like an archetypal daft, bored housewife) and then they'll dismiss me. The other students will be younger than me, or brighter, or fitter, or at least more confident. That much is guaranteed. I will then be required to do one of those dreadful introductions. Who I am and why I'm here? Good questions, dumb answers only required. I remember those hideous intros from training days when I worked in a corporate environment. Worse yet, if the tutor is "wacky" and wants to "shake things up", we'll be asked to reveal something no one else knows about us in order to break the ice. Why would I want to share something with a room full of complete strangers that I've kept from my nearest and dearest? I'm not even sure I have any secrets. Certainly not interesting ones. How lame is that? Would anyone care that my secret recipe for a moist Christmas cake is adding a cold cup of tea?

I might be asked to answer other questions. In the classroom, this is bearable. As I say, I'm reasonably academic; I can usually think of something not entirely stupid to contribute. But answering questions in the coffee break, which will almost certainly be required, is a terrifying prospect. Someone, a bubbly blonde no doubt, will pounce on me as I slosh milk into my cup of instant coffee, and she'll insist on asking about my family. I see it now. Her cheery disposition will be tested as I reveal that I'm a divorcee. She'll try to think of something to say; something kind, conciliatory or witty depending on how nice she is. She'll pity me but dismiss me. I'll never make a dinner party guest; I'll screw up the seating plan.

I tell Luke all of this.

"I see," he says, in a way which suggests he does. This is to his credit because of course he can't possibly see. He has no idea what it's like to be a single, prematurely middle-aged, under-confident woman.

"I think you should do a course in mechanics," he says.

"What?"

"It's useful. You struggle to find anything on your car beyond the ignition and the headlights. Connie and Daisy will get off your back because they'll think by going to a course on mechanics you'll meet men. But in reality the only people you'll meet on a mechanics course are teenage boys, who are often astoundingly shy, perhaps even more so than yourself, and at least unthreatening. No offence, Rose, but they'll think of you as a mother figure."

"None taken. At least I have practice at being a mother. If someone hit on me, I'd be at sea."

Luke smiles, kindly. "Teenage boys will be great. And then there will be other women in the same position as you."

"Women in the same position as me." I echo the sentence because the sentiment has never crossed my mind before.

"Yes. Independent women. Let's face it, as sexist as it is to admit, the truth is there aren't many women in this world who are prepared to change a tyre or check water and oil in their car if they think someone else will do it for them. If there are women on this course the chances are that they will be in a similar position to you. They won't pity you, Rose. They'll admire you. They'll understand you."

I've never considered the possibility that there are other single mums out there. I've never attended those support groups, full of angry dungaree-wearing women sipping black coffee. It seemed somehow indulgent. Besides, I had enough anger of my own to deal with; the last thing I needed was to shoulder other people's. At Holland House everyone is respectably married; even a second, third or fourth marriage seems respectable in comparison to being on one's own. Maybe Luke is on to something. Maybe I've been looking in the wrong places.

"OK," I say quietly.

"OK, you'll do it?" asks Luke, unable to hide his surprise and excitement. He was obviously expecting a longer battle.

"Yes, I think it's a good idea. What day is the course on?"

"Wednesdays from 7.30p.m. till 9. Starts this week."

"Tell Connie she's booked for babysitting and that I'll do her VAT returns if she brings over her files of receipts and invoices."

"You mean the shoebox she keeps under the bed?" asks Luke. "You know how disorganized she can be."

We smile and I pour us both another glass of wine.

"I think I need this," I observe.

"I think you deserve it," says Luke with a fat grin. And he clinks my glass.

CHAPTER
THIRTEEN

Tuesday 19 September

John

There's a woman at work that I would do if I didn't have to work with her for the next three months. In truth, there are dozens of women at work that I would do if I didn't have to see them again, but the one I'm on about is especially hot. Mandy's her name. I like that. Like the fact that she hasn't upgraded her name to Amanda but stuck with the childish derivative that her mam and dad probably use. She's smart and beautiful and in her late twenties. She likes me too, it's obvious. She's always hanging around my desk. There's no doubt about it, I would do her if we didn't work together. But no way. The stakes are too high and there's always totty. I've only ever broken that rule once with, as you'd expect, disastrous results.

Greenie. Connie. What was it about her that made me break my own rules? And of course the old adage *is* true, you should never, ever crap on your own doorstep. If she taught me anything, it was that. Funny, I haven't given Greenie a thought in years but since I bumped into her on Friday she keeps popping into my head pretty much constantly.

Last time I gave her any mind-share must have been about two years ago when I came across her work at a tiny photographic exhibition. Artsy-fartsy galleries aren't normally my thing. But my then Mrs was quite into that sort of stuff and we'd been rowing (situation normal) and I thought I'd try and do something nice with her. For her. So I got a copy of the *Guide* from the *Guardian*. Working from a position of ignorance I had no reason to select one exhibit over another and there were dozens to choose from. I saw this advert for a photographic exhibition of new up-and-coming talent, and it was near to a tube station on our line, so I plumped for that one.

There were six photographers exhibiting. All pretty good, I suppose, but it was only the third set of photos that I found genuinely arresting.

The pictures were showing under a headline "The Bedroom", which was an attention-grabbing title to a man like me. The pics were of women in various states of dress and undress, lying in bed. The women were always alone but you got the sense from the photos that they had all either just been entertaining or were waiting to be enjoyed. The girls were dozing, or snuggling pillows, or wide awake and expectantly preening, and in one photo the woman was having a fag; it was unquestionably post-coital. The ladies were not models. One was breathtakingly beautiful but the others were just normal women like you see in the high street every day, and yet the photographer captured them in a way that made them all look sexy and stunning, or at least peaceful and content. I scanned the leaflet I'd picked up at the door, interested enough to want to remember the photographer's name. I had money on the photographer being a man, but it wasn't. Constance Baker. She'd chosen to use her married name.

It gave me a jolt. I considered the possibility that it was just a coincidence that the photographer had the same name as my old mistress, but then hadn't I heard she'd left Peterson Windlooper to retrain as a photographer? There was no pic of the artist in the leaflet but there were a couple of lines of biog that confirmed that the photographer and my Greenie were one and the same. Good for her, I thought. She'd gone and done it. She'd always said she wanted to be a photographer and, bloody hell, she'd gone and done it. Weirdly and irrationally I felt a huge surge of pride in what she'd achieved. Her work was good. I was glad for her. Even if she was a fucking nutter.

Arty types often are though, aren't they?

I re-examined all the photos. There were about nine in total. Each one of them was moving, intimate and deeply, deeply sensual. One of them stood out as it was the filthiest. Not that this was the kind of exhibition where full frontals and open-leg shots were likely to be displayed, but on one of the photos there was a suggestion that the model was masturbating. Gently, not manically, but circling her vag under the sheet. You couldn't see her face or the upper part of her body. Just the outline of her legs and one foot was tangled in the sheet. Exhibit number 9 was entitled "Self-portrait".

Fuck. The intimacy sent shivers through my body. That was Connie. There, lying exposed for everyone to see. For me to enjoy, privately. Because irrational as it sounds, I believe I had something to do with those photos, in fact I think I can take quite a lot of the credit for Greenie finally becoming a photographer.

We used to talk about it, you see, her ambition to be a photographer, and I told her, way back then, that she could do it if she wanted. I believed in her, see. It ended messy and everything. But all endings are messy, aren't they? It started magnificently. I looked at the self-portrait for about ten minutes, until my Mrs called me a perve and dragged me away for lunch at the local pub.

From time to time someone from Peterson Windlooper mentions Greenie. They've seen her work used in an advert or read a review of some exhibition or other. But I don't dwell. I'm not the type to dwell. Besides, I've had quite a bit going on in my life over the last half a dozen years. Married, divorced, promoted, new car, new home, travelled a bit, more notches on the bedpost. Life flies on.

Funny that she's a mother, though. To someone big enough to go to school. Not a tiny cute baby that you can wear in a sling as a fashion accessory but the real deal, a person. Greenie's all woman. The girl I knew has disappeared.

Girls keep doing that. It's a boring habit.

I call Tom to ask if he wants to meet for a drink. He says he can't. He and Jenny are going to brief their wedding photographer tonight. It's not just the girls that are disappearing. I sigh and have a dig.

"Mate, isn't that woman's work? You didn't catch me doing all that wedding planning stuff."

"No mate, but you're hardly a role model when it comes to the happily ever after, are you?"

"S'pose not. But buddy, will you ever be allowed out for a drink again? A man can die of thirst, you know."

There's silence on the line for a moment or two. Tom knows he has a real laugh coming out with me on the lash. We don't chase skirt together, we haven't for some time. Tom is the faithful type, bless him, so since he got together with Jenny he's simply been an innocent bystander to my antics, but Jenny doesn't believe that. She pronounces him guilty by association and is sure that when we are together we do nothing but pull totty. The truth is we often just play darts, have a chat and a laugh. True, more often than not I go home with some lovely or other, but Tom limits his womanizing to the odd flirty wink. It's harmless fun.

Tom is clearly weighing up the laugh he'd have with me versus the earache that he'd no doubt have to endure because he's been out with me.

"Craig could come along too. We'll tell you what we're planning for the stag," I tempt him.

"Well . . ."

"Craig's on the pull. He needs a date for your wedding. It's our duty to help him out."

"OK. I'll ask Jen if we can get together for a bevvy on Saturday," he says finally.

"Mate, don't ask her, tell her."

Where's his self-respect?

CHAPTER
FOURTEEN

Thursday 21 September

Lucy

Things are not great between Peter and me. It's boring that so much of my time is taken up with this sort of nonsense. Surely if I have to bear the burden of wrinkles at least I ought not to have to worry about the status of my love life. I'm too old for it.

Peter and I never discussed my hasty exit from the restaurant or any aspect of the evening. On the one hand, I am disappointed that the incident was so thoroughly brushed under the carpet; after all, we both said some monumental things and I believe things said in anger, jest or when drunk are often the things that are true. Most of the conversation we make when we are our rational selves is self-preserving bullshit. On the other hand, I look back at the evening with an overwhelming sense of shame and think it's best that we forget the whole messy business.

Bloody Rose.

Peter arrived home about forty minutes after I did. I feigned sleep. He feigned a belief in my pretence. The next morning we cautiously edged around one another.

We showered, dressed and ate breakfast as though we were opposing sides in the early part of a game of chess. We skirted, danced and carefully avoided any genuine interaction. I politely offered him coffee. He courteously accepted it, and civilly offered me the financial pages of his newspaper. I graciously declined, knowing that he doesn't really like to split the paper. He went to the tube station by foot. I made an excuse to set off a little later, rather than walk with him. I said I needed to polish Auriol's shoes, a transparent excuse, of course, as this is not the sort of thing I normally concern myself with. It's Eva who sees to it that our daughter is well turned out for school. Peter civilly accepted my excuse. "That's sweet," he said as he kissed me on the forehead and scurried off with ill-disguised relief, keen to leave the omnipresent doom that filled the house.

And so on and so forth, for a week now. We are two polite strangers living together. We are using the same bathrooms, washing our dirty clothes in the same machine, sleeping in the same bed, eating from the same crockery, but the intimacy is fading, it's all but disappeared.

Still, there is nothing better than lots of work, culminating in a Club Class flight to New York, to allow domestic issues to slip to the back of one's mind. Mick and I have found ourselves working together on a pitch for some new business. A multinational, based in New York, looking to spread the risk with their employee pension fund. We're talking big bucks but it's a straightforward proposal. Frankly, I think we're an over-qualified team. Either one of us could have handled this with the aid of a decent new boy. Indeed, it was Mick's business pitch initially and then Ralph discovered that the client had specified that they preferred "an ethical approach to business".

"Who doesn't?" I quipped.

But I knew that this piece of information was only being brought to my attention because, roughly translated, "an ethical approach to business" means they want to see diversity within the European Team managers; this sort of thing often makes companies feel better about exploiting minorities in places which are further afield. Gordon Webster Handle does not have a disabled black lesbian on their staff (the preferred choice for an ethical approach), so the most diversity they could rustle up in the white male C. of E. environment was me. At least I have to sit down to pee.

"We wouldn't ask you, but that chink guy in Ed's team is already working on something really big," said Mick.

"You mean Ral, he's Malaysian," I replied. I know the City isn't a politically correct place; I'm shocked to discover it isn't geographically correct either. "I'm busy," I objected.

"If you have to get something done, give it to a busy person. Isn't that what they say? What can I do to persuade you to surrender four working days to this pitch, plus find the time for a trip to NY?" Mick beams at me, suggesting that he doesn't think it will take much to persuade me. This disturbs me. Why would he assume I want to spend time with him? Can it be simple arrogance? "Come on, Princess. You never know, you might have some fun."

I agreed to help out. Long hours in the office or long silences at home. It's not such a tough choice. Besides, Mick was right, it pains me to admit it, but it has been fun working on the pitch with him. The way I tell it is that Mick schmoozes the client and I crunch the numbers. As expected, the pitch gives me a valid excuse to avoid Auriol's bathtime and Peter's sulky silence (it's extraordinary how many times one can run through the same set of numbers), and it is while I'm working late at night that I discover Mick is very amusing (which I knew) and reasonably thoughtful (a surprise). He always remembers to order me a veggie pizza because the local delivery place only offers three types of pizza and two of them have salami as the staple. I hate salami with a passion. And he is clever. He may not lead but he keeps up; many men I've met failed to do this much. Besides, he has the occasional flash of brilliance which is exciting. When we ran through the deck with Ralph, he beamed and commented, "You two make a good team, possibly the best team in Gordon Webster Handle. Therefore the client would be crazy not to give us the business."

"They are not crazy, Sir," said Mick. He always calls Ralph "Sir", which would be really creepy except that Ralph is American and in America waitresses call rednecks "Sir", so it's almost become cheeky. "This business is in the bag."

"We can't afford to be cocky, Mick. The client is a deeply efficient, multinational blue chip and we need to give them the best show. We can't let up," I add.

Mick winked at me, and as soon as Ralph was out of earshot he added, "Admit it. This trip to NY is not much more than a courtesy call. We're going to win the business, the fat bonus and the cred."

"Absolutely," I grinned. "Not much more than a bit of handshaking."

We both see it as a jolly. Mick is thinking strip bars. I'm thinking room service and Bloomingdales. And maybe the odd cocktail. Mick and I could nip to the W Hotel Whiskey bar and I've just been told about this amazing downtown eatery called Novel. Everyone goes. There's a waiting list, obviously, but I've never had any trouble with waiting lists. And then we could go to Bar Seine, it's just had a refit — I stop myself.

Where is this train of thought leading? I'm no innocent. I know which station this train pulls in at. First, one admires his suit. Next, his smile and then his humour. Then, his thoughtfulness and flashes of brilliance. Next thing, flies are unzipped and lacy underwear is hanging from the chandeliers. I take a deep breath. Things are moving too quickly and in a hazardous direction. Only a few weeks ago I considered Mick to be nothing more than the office Casanova: a cliché and not of any real interest. I steal a glance at Mick. He is tall, dark and handsome, in a very obvious sort of way. This is exactly the sort of way a chap ought to be handsome. I'm not a fan of quirky. But he is *not*

Peter. Not a patch on him. Not my husband. I need to keep that in mind.

Yes, we're good together. We are a team. Colleagues. That's it. The sparring, the banter, the late-night chats about politics, bars and cars are not significant. Mick has been openly enthusiastic about my being dragged on board his project, even though this will inevitably mean that his bonus is split, but that doesn't mean anything. He's a business guy at the final count and he knows half of something is better than all of nothing, which was the probable outcome of the pitch if Gordon Webster Handle hadn't responded to the brief of a diverse team. So he saw the sense of having a woman on board. What were his exact words? "There's always room for a pretty little lady." This vaguely flirty remark is barely worth noticing, it's just his way. Still, I am grateful that he didn't resent my presence and try to make me feel uncomfortable, as so many of the traders do. He even went so far as to let Ralph know that I'd come up with an entirely new way of looking at the portfolio which is set to be a winner. He can be charming. *Stop.*

Peter. Peter. Peter. Just keep saying his name, I tell myself as I buckle up and relax into the Club Class seat. Problem is, when I say his name I think of the hurried, dry and painful sex that we executed this morning. We're both superstitious about flying without making up and so we made an effort. Effort being the operative word. I have to be very careful. Only minutes ago Mick and I were laughing like drains about the cartoons in *Punch*. If I'm aware that we are becoming a little too familiar and pally, the odds are Mick has projected as far as simultaneous multiple orgasms. I mentioned he was confident. I used to do a great Ice Queen. I think I need to step back into that character.

"Drink, Madame?" The smiley air steward proffers a tray with glasses of champagne and glasses of freshly squeezed orange juice, all neatly lined up like soldiers.

Mick reaches across me and takes two glasses of champagne. He offers one to me and the steward moves on.

"I wanted orange juice," I say stiffly. *Peter*.

"Why? It's free. And it's champagne. Why would you drink orange juice?" he asks reasonably.

Peter. "I'm at work. It's office hours."

Mick snorts his disgust and downs both glasses of champagne. I stare my amazement.

"What? They are only tiny glasses. You didn't want any. You said so."

Sometimes it's easy to forget that Mick is my age. He looks and acts much younger. I wonder if the casual observer would think we were the same age. I wish I could stop obsessing about ageing, it's undignified. But recently I've been unable to ignore the fact that everything is sinking, slowing down or scrunching up. And yesterday's incident at the hairstylist's didn't help. Three months ago, with no prior discussion or warning, my hairstylist of eight years announced he was emigrating. I am bereft. I suppose I ought to have been thrilled for him, as he had finally met the man of his dreams (extremely rich, extremely beautiful and extremely dumb). Stephen and his lover plan to hop from beach to beach and follow the sun all year round. I often find myself feeling jealous of gay couples, who have no expectations foisted upon them regarding producing offspring. They can freely follow the hedonistic lifestyle that I grieve for.

I used to visit Stephen with obscene regularity. I like my hair to be trimmed every four weeks and I like a blow-dry at least once a week, often more frequently. Over the years he has acted as a confidant, a tonic and, of course, a credible style guru. It was Stephen who promised me that he'd tell me when I needed to lose the length on my hair. Brave man. I've always worn my hair long; I do not believe a change is as good as a rest. I believe that you ought to find out what suits you and stick with it. While I nod towards hair fashions, in so much as I introduce, and then grow out, a fringe from time to time, I am not a slave to them. I never sported a perm; I am the only woman who can look back at photos of myself in the eighties with any self-respect.

However, I always knew a day would come when I needed to have my hair chopped. I have a great figure and stunning clothes, so from behind I could be a teenager; long hair helps the illusion for a certain period of time and then long hair becomes ridiculous. But how would I know when the moment had arrived? Would I have the required self-awareness to realize that my long locks were more old hag than fairy princess? I was not sure I would. So Stephen had stepped up to the mic and bravely agreed to assume the role of the person who would tell me when I needed to lose the locks. He loved me that much.

Without him my chances of arriving at middle age with my dignity are significantly reduced.

Since his departure, I have simply avoided having my hair cut, constraining myself to regular blow-dries instead. I did not believe there was a hairdresser in all of London who could fill Stephen's size elevens. But after three months it has become clear that the policy cannot go on indefinitely. I have split ends, for God's sake.

Shaun picked up the mantle, or at least the scissors. I've been on nodding terms with Shaun for several years now, as he apprenticed at Stephen's salon. I reasoned that he'd have a similar technique and would have been trained equally thoroughly. But it transpires that Stephen and Shaun went to completely different schools of charm.

"Lucy, it's time for a change, don't you think? This style is for kids," he said the moment the gown was tied around my neck.

I was too stunned to reply. At first. I remained mute as I processed the fact that Shaun had just broken the news that I'm too old for long hair. Is this the reason Stephen eloped with Marco? Could it be that he isn't as courageous as I'd thought? Shaun interpreted my shocked silence as approval and started to cut.

Wordlessly, I watched my blondeness fall into my lap.

I fingered my glossiness, already longing to glue it back on to my head, but I knew this was not possible. The time is past.

The cut is . . . fine. I cannot find fault and I've tried. It's sharp, sleek, smart, *short*. I tipped Shaun, because if I didn't he would sense my resistance and what I'm resisting is beyond his control.

I rushed home, opened the front door and ran upstairs without allowing Eva or Auriol to see me. I locked my bedroom door and only then did I dare look in the mirror. I didn't recognize myself. I looked like someone else. I looked older, there's no getting away from it. I am older. This morning I noticed veins in my thighs. What's that about? The onset of varicose veins? I still look great when I'm "done" but I've noticed that it's taking longer and longer to be "done". I have more moisturizers to apply; the idea of forgoing foundation is impossible.

The air steward walks past with another tray of drinks and tiny bowls of Bombay mix. Mick reaches past me and confidently helps himself to two more champagnes and two bowls of Bombay mix. This time he doesn't offer me a thing.

"Can I have water, please," I ask the steward.

Mick points to the in-flight magazine. "I'm reading about NY spas — looks like a con to me," he says.

In fact I'd been reading the intricacies of the treatment with interest and had decided that breathing pure oxygen was exactly what my skin needed to fight the stagnation, the droopiness and drabness. I shrug.

"Well, it's good enough for Gwyneth P. and Kate Moss et al. Or, at least, they are named as regular clients of the spa. Of course, they might prefer hot stones being laid on their legs and back." As I say it, I smile. It's not easy to believe in these treatments if you deconstruct them too aggressively. Nor is it easy to play Ice Queen with Mick.

"But Lucy, you don't need any of this crap," Mick says, handing the magazine back to me. "You are beautiful."

Apparently, there's evidence to suggest you generally feel sexier and more emotional in the sky. Flying releases certain endorphins, the ones that you get when you eat chocolate, exercise or have sex, I think. I can't remember the exact science behind the theory, but I guess it does account for the crazy number of people who join the Mile High Club. Something odd must happen to the brain for anyone to consider shagging in tiny, smelly public loos. Especially as getting in and out of the loo with your partner without being detected by any of the staff requires precision planning. I'm talking from experience. Peter and I have managed it twice. Before I became Mrs Phillips, obviously.

So it must be the altitude, mustn't it? That's the reason why the moment when Mick said I was beautiful was so spectacular. The altitude. I take the champagne off him and we clink glasses. He beams at me. I've never been the type of woman to kid myself about men. I know when they want *want* me and when they just want me around. In the past most men fell into the first category; only a humble few admitted that I was out of their league and they would opt for the second category because being my friend or even associate isn't a bad second prize. However, since I married and became a mother with all that it entails, reading male desire has become a more ambiguous and hazardous process. I might be getting it wrong, but if I'm not then I'd say more and more men that I meet are opting for category B. I wonder where Mick is to be categorized?

Accepting the champagne was impulsive and no doubt gives the wrong signal. Although it does taste delicious. What signal do I want to give anyway? I'm only being friendly. We'll arrive in the afternoon. We haven't got any work to do until tomorrow. I don't need a clear head.

Do I?

"Good haircut, by the way, Princess. Very cute."

No, I don't.

CHAPTER
FIFTEEN

Monday 25 September

Rose

Luke was right about the night class, as is often the case with Luke. The car maintenance course was an almost entirely man-free zone and all the more comfortable for that. There were a few youngsters — teenagers whose parents had made it a condition of car ownership — and the rest of the attendees were women like me.

Single, responsible and nervous.

When I got home the boys were in bed and Connie was smiling expectantly. I delayed the inevitable by asking whether the boys had been good. Did they clean their teeth? Did they finish their homework? Connie answered in the affirmative.

"And they were asleep by eight thirty. It's been a doddle. But now, tell me about the class," said Connie.

"We learnt how to change a tyre this week and it will no doubt be extremely useful."

"Good, and what were the other students like? Did you meet anyone like-minded?" Connie is trying and failing to sound casual. Neither of us believes that she wants me to further my education or skill base. She wants me to find a boyfriend.

I decide to tease her for a moment. "I gave my telephone number to two people and even arranged to meet one of them for coffee," I told her as I flashed a wide grin.

"Tell me more," she squealed, excitedly.

"Well, Susanne is a hairdresser and divorced eight years ago. She has three daughters. And Helen works in ad sales for the Yellow Pages; she has a long-term partner but he works away a lot and she has no kids so has quite a bit of time on her hands."

"Women?" Connie could barely hide the disgust in her voice.

"Yes," I replied calmly. "New friends. Potentially. Isn't that what this exercise is about?"

"Well, yes," she admitted reluctantly. "But weren't there any men there?"

"No."

"None?"

"A few boys and the teacher is a chap," I replied honestly.

"What's he like?"

"Married."

Connie left, rather deflated, which was a shame because I'd had a great evening. It was fun learning something new and meeting different people. Connie and Daisy's campaign might have merit.

I should have noted the grim determination in her goodbye. I was crazy to think she'd accept the slight widening of my social circle as a win.

So now a date. Oh, heavens above. How did I ever get talked into this? No, not talked into it — bullied into it. I was nagged, harangued, threatened and cajoled. There ought to be laws to protect people like me from people like Daisy and Connie.

"You said the purpose of this exercise was for me to meet people," I argued.

"It is," said Daisy.

"You said it wasn't all about finding a man."

Daisy and Connie exchanged guilty glances. We all know what their ultimate aim is.

"I've started a night class, per your suggestion, and I have met people there. Why do I have to go on this date?"

"Don't think of this as a date," said Daisy, "just think of it as expanding your social life in exactly the same way as going for a coffee with Helen is expanding your social life."

"Except I don't know this man."

"We are trying to remedy that."

"And it's not coffee, it's a drink, perhaps a meal."

"Yes."

"And it's in the evening."

"Yes, but a Monday evening, which is barely an evening. More of an afternoon in date terms." I stare at her mystified. "Rose, just look at it as doing him a favour."

"I don't want to do him a favour."

"I think you are still operating within your comfort zones," said Connie.

142

"Once a management consultant, always a management consultant," I muttered to myself.

After a couple of days of constant haranguing I realized that they wouldn't let up and it would be easier to simply get the bloody date over with. Of course it was going to be awful but I began to view the date in the same way as I view a dentist appointment, something that has to be endured but only for a limited period of time.

My date is with Kevin Morrow. A brother-in-law of a friend of Connie's. It has come to this — blind dating. The concept is entirely alien to me and yet somehow I knew that one day I would find myself in this place. Kevin, I ask you — does he sound like a sex god, a charmer, a soulmate or even the life and soul of the party? He does not. I walk to my fate like a woman condemned to death. I'm expecting the same amount of fun.

It surprises me that the concerns I have about dating, now, in my late thirties, are exactly the same as those I had in my early twenties. It's depressing how little progress I've made. I can't actively dislike this guy because I haven't met him but I can't like him for the same reason. In my teens and twenties I often went out with guys I wasn't sure I liked. It was usually the case that I dated boys who my friends thought were "sweet" or my mum thought were suitable. Peter was the only guy I dated because he made my heart race.

Plus, all these years on, I discover that I am still anxious that I'll run out of conversation. Other ancient concerns include the fact that I'd rather stay in (as there are good things to watch on TV) and, *of course*, that my bum looks big in everything. My wardrobe was a disaster before I divorced and the passage of time has done nothing to improve matters. Connie tried to be kind. Daisy was more sisterly, therefore ruthless.

"Look, this is funky. This is one of those jersey dresses, right? Eighties fashions are all coming back," said Connie.

"That's so old-fashioned, and even when it was fashionable it must still have been awful," said Daisy in despair.

"I did not buy that in the eighties," I snapped, grabbing the dress and bundling it to the back of my wardrobe before they could see the label, which would have revealed that the dress was in fact maternity wear. Probably the last time I bought new clothes was when I was pregnant.

Naturally the dissection of my wardrobe and the diagnosis — "sadly lacking" — led to an obligatory shopping trip where the girls dragged me from store to store and we argued over what suited me and what didn't. Connie shops at trendy retailers that cater for women the size of Barbie dolls, stores all too terrifying for me to even consider entering. Daisy's tastes are a little more akin to mine and she understands the issues of red hair, but she doesn't understand the issues of being totally without self-confidence or motivation to shop. I don't want to go on a date so how could I possibly begin to get excited about what to wear?

"What look are you going for, Rose? Sexy? Understated? Glamorous?"

I stared at Connie and stayed mute. It wasn't that I was awkwardly refusing to answer; I simply didn't know the answer. What am I? The twins' mum. What do I want to say about myself? Very little, except perhaps I could wear one of those signs they hang on hotel room doors: "Do not disturb."

No one was especially delighted with the fruits of our shopping trip. The cream wool dress reeks of compromise. Connie thinks it's shapeless but at least it doesn't expose too much flesh or make me feel as though I'm mutton dressing as lamb. Many of the outfits I tried on made me feel like an impostor — the reverse of a child dressing up in her mother's clothes. I didn't look cute, just out of place and faintly ridiculous. Connie accepted the outfit, after the addition of a sparkly scarf and high shoes, and Daisy accepted it because her feet were sore and she couldn't face traipsing into "even one more bloody shop".

I am going through the motions. I have been to the hairdresser's per Daisy's diktat. I don't really have a regular hairdresser. I go so infrequently I find that the hairdressers have often moved on in between my visits. So I was "looked after" (and I use the term loosely) by a surly-looking teenager who stared at my hair in despair. She cut it too short, insisted I needed a "lift", and then coloured it to a funny horse-chestnut colour and charged me an outrageous £150 for the pleasure. I have bathed in some of the lovely oil that Connie bought me for Christmas last year. I can't remember the brand name but it came in one of those posh cardboard bags so it must be good stuff. I've covered my body with moisturizer (not that I'm expecting my body to get touched). I'm wearing chastity-guaranteeing tummy-tuck knickers and bottom-lifting tights. My new outfit is freshly pressed and lying on the bed, waiting for me. I stare at it and know that it is all wrong.

It's drab. I should have bought the cerise cardigan in Monsoon.

Kevin and I are to meet at a pub local to me, the Lamb and Flag. The telephone conversation, where we agreed this much, was brief and perfunctory. We did not bother to ask one another's star signs or favourite colours. We did not make jokes about carrying a copy of the *Times* newspaper and wearing a carnation.

The tacit agreement is that if things go well between us we might grab a pizza at the nearby Italian restaurant; if they don't, I'll leave after a swift spritzer and neither of us will have wasted much time or money. I am relieved that at least the parameters of the date are so familiar. If TV is to be believed, first dates are now exercises in imagination which often culminate in excessive humiliation rather than achieving the goal of getting to know someone a little better. I am more inclined to tolerate Kevin because he did not suggest bowling, ice-skating, paintballing or a visit to a new gallery where I would be expected to have a view-point on whether an unmade bed is art. I do not have the emotional energy, let alone the physical energy, to do anything more demanding than eat pizza and make small talk. That much will require a superhuman effort.

The moment I walk into the pub is possibly the worst. At least, I hope it is. I can't bear to think that I might feel more miserable, isolated or vulnerable this evening. We've agreed to meet at 8p.m. I chose 8p.m. because if everything goes horribly wrong and it's all over in an hour, being in bed (alone) by 9.30 is almost respectable. If we met at 7p.m. and it all went wrong, I'd be in bed (alone) by 8.30. A disaster by anyone's standards.

I can't see him. Or maybe I can but I don't know it yet. The pub's pretty crowded; mostly there are gregarious groups of people who all seem to live full and meaningful lives. Even so, they pause their conversations and watch me with undisguised curiosity. I feel so self-conscious that I am sure there is an enormous billboard floating above my head announcing my blind-date status. Cautiously, and as discreetly as possible, I try to size up the room. I'm hoping to identify him, judge him and if necessary abandon him before he even spots me. That said, I'll hate it if I've arrived first and have to wait for him. What if he doesn't show at all? The ultimate humiliation. I make my way towards the bar, trying to look purposeful and at home. I order an orange juice (a clear head is vital and if he no-shows at least I won't look like a lonely lush). I pause, take a deep breath, gather my courage and then look around the pub.

I can make out three men who appear to be alone. One is a spotty boy in his twenties. He's lolling against the end of the bar and must be very drunk even though he appears to be drinking a half pint of lager and lime.

Oh dear God, Connie wouldn't do that to me, would she? I am not a Mrs Robinson and any guy crazy enough to want to be a toy boy would be sorely disappointed in me. But it can't be him — Connie said Kevin was in his late thirties.

There is another chap. A wiry, mean-looking fellow, drinking alone in the corner. He looks like a failed actor, someone who never even got a bit part in *The Bill*. It only takes a moment to work out that this guy is desperately disappointed in the world. He has a thin mouth, angry, alert, flashing eyes and an unkempt appearance. He can't be Kevin. I couldn't think of anyone with whom I'd have less in common and I'm sure Connie said that we'd have a lot in common.

The third and final single man is a stocky, sweating guy sitting at a table near the open fire. I watch as he pulls a handkerchief from his trouser pocket. He blows his nose and then mops his brow. Charming. He must be Kevin. He's chosen the table near the open fire because he'll have thought that was the most romantic thing to do on a blind date. He'll have been too anxious to consider that it's a mild night and the proximity to the fire, or perhaps his nervousness, will cause him to sweat profusely. Not a great blind-date look. It takes a mere moment for me to understand what Connie must have meant when she said we had lots in common. His stomach falls over his belt. His suit is strained across shoulders and arms and not because he has bulging muscles, but because he has a fondness for puddings and pints. I feel something near to pity for him which I find a comfort. Better the chubby guy whose aim is to please than the scowling thesp in the corner, who undoubtedly has an ego inversely proportional to his CV achievements. Emboldened — here goes nothing — I hop off my bar stool, grab my orange juice and start to saunter towards the open fire.

"You must be Kevin," I assert with a bright smile.

At that moment a pretty brunette appears from nowhere. She launches herself on to "Kevin". They kiss in an energetic and comfortable way. I'd guess they've been dating about six months. Long enough to be cosy; short enough to still want lots of sex. I mumble something about needing to borrow an ashtray, even though I don't smoke. But the couple don't hear me anyway, thank God, too engrossed in one another to give the weird lady any attention. I grab the ashtray and fleetingly consider whether I should return to my bar stool or just leave. This whole idea of blind dating is ridiculous. I bet Kevin is going to stand me up and, even if he does arrive, he is bound to be unsuitable in every way. Let's face it, how can he possibly be a suitable boyfriend? I don't want a boyfriend.

"Over here, lady. I'm your man."

What? I look around and see that the mean-looking, egotistical guy is talking to me. He has an amused look on his face, clearly having watched my spectacle with the impostor "Kevin". I gawk at him, unbecomingly.

"You're Kevin?" The name doesn't suit him. I'd have guessed him to be a Hugh or a Lance.

"Aren't you delighted?" He's laughing to himself. He's slouched in the Dralon chair and doesn't even extend me the courtesy of straightening up. He casts a sharp glance at tubby "Kevin" and I see the contempt in his face. He's skinny therefore thinks he's better than the other guy. He despises the tubby "Kevin" on the spot and therefore he must despise me too, because despite my M & S reinforced underwear it's still obvious I've never been svelte. I dislike him for judging me. I dislike him for not seeing that the other "Kevin" must have something wonderful. He has, after all, a pretty brunette clasped to his lips. He's not the one on the blind date. I know for certain that there is no way on this earth I am ever going to be able to like this angry, judgemental, lanky Kevin. He's not my type. This assessment of the status quo takes moments. I wonder how long it will be before I can make a dignified exit.

"While you're on your feet, mine's a bitter," says Kevin.

I bite my lip to avoid prompting him to say "please", the way I have to with the boys. I trot towards the bar and I add "rude" and "tight" to his list of faults.

CHAPTER
SIXTEEN

Tuesday 26 September

John

Jenny didn't allow Tom to meet up with Craig and me this weekend, but we've managed to meet up today because she's working late or something, and she's only let him off his leash on the condition that he is home before midnight.

"Why, mate? What happens then? Do you turn into a pumpkin?" I ask.

Tom shrugs but doesn't answer. He knows he's pussy-whipped and there isn't an admirable way to manage the situation except to stay silent and hope I don't go on about it for too long.

"She must be a great fuck, mate. To justify this loss of independence, self-respect and various totty."

He glares at me, then tries to change the subject. "Where's Craig?"

"Some sort of meeting at the school. I think he said Parents' Association."

"Does he get paid extra for staying late?"

"Don't think so," I shrug.

"Then what can he be thinking?"

"Search me. Should I get us another drink in?"

By the time I get back to the table with the fresh round, Craig has arrived.

"You've had a haircut, mate," I comment. "Looks good."

Craig puts his hand up to his hair and blushes like a girl. "Thanks, John. I went to that salon you recommended."

"Keep it down, mate." I take a mock-shifty, swift look around the pub. "People will think we're benders."

"You two *are* getting very close," says Tom, with a laugh.

"I'd be proud to have Craig as a wife. He's clean-cut, has a respectable job, he's good to his mum and dad."

"Piss off, John," laughs Craig.

It feels good, all this joshing about. Truth is Tom, Craig and I would take a bullet for each other, if the need arose; which is unlikely, admittedly. But the point is we are good buddies. Great ones, in fact. We know each other in the true and proper sense, the way only old friends do. We don't have to impress one another; sometimes we can go out for an evening and we don't even have to talk to each other and we'd still class it as a good night. The lads know where I came from and they came from the same heap. They know where I'm going and how I've got this far. They hauled their asses up parallel greasy poles. Sometimes I feel ashamed of what I've come from but mostly I feel ashamed about being ashamed of what I've come from. Good honest working-class stock, my family. I come from bad wallpaper, cheap nylon sheets, crap tinned food, but not bad people.

The lads get that. Not many people do.

Connie did.

Jesus. What's that woman doing in my head again? I boot her out by offering to go to the bar to get Craig's drink.

At the bar I make eye-contact with a cutie. I tell the barman I'll pay for her round. When he lets cutie know that I've footed her bill she is predictably gushy and grinning. I don't bother to talk to her at this early stage of the evening. By buying the drink I've stated an interest and got her attention; I can afford to spend a bit of time with my mates before I move in for the kill. It does the ladies good to wait.

When I get back to my seat Craig is boring Tom with details of the meeting he's just chaired. Tom is such a decent bloke that he manages not to look fed up and even asks questions at the appropriate time, making a laudable attempt at appearing genuinely interested.

"The mothers are amazing," gushes Craig. "So committed to the school and to their kids' education. We raised just short of two thousand pounds at the summer fair at the end of the last term. Isn't that fantastic? Principally, that's what tonight's meeting was about. We wanted to decide what to spend the funds on."

"I don't get all this fund-raising and committees and stuff," says Tom. "In my day your mother only went up to school twice a year, sports day and nativity play. Any more frequently and it was because you'd done something wrong and were due a clip round the ear."

"Who is on the committee?" I ask.

"Couple of teachers, a parent representative from each class, the local vicar and the odd businessman." Craig pushes his glasses up his nose and smiles. He's touched that I'm taking an interest.

"Remind me, what are the tiny kids called?"

"Year One."

"No, not those ones, before that. The youngest?"

"The youngest ones are the reception class."

"Is there a parent on this committee to represent the reception class?" I try to sound casual but it's not a casual question.

"Yes. One from every year group. Why?"

"Who is it this year?"

"A Mrs Finch. Why?"

"Nothing." I look round for a distraction. "Anyone fancy a game of darts or cards?"

"Why did you want to know who was on the committee?" probes Craig.

"Do you fancy one of the mothers?" asks Tom. He smells a story.

"Not likely; he was bewailing the fact that the yummy mummy counter is pretty low," says Craig.

I ignore them. I plan to go on ignoring them but it's hard because they are both staring expectantly at me.

"It's nothing much. Just that the other night when I was meeting you, Craig, I bumped into someone I used to know. That's all."

"Ex shag?" asks Tom.

"Ancient history," I confirm.

"Jesus, John. Is there anywhere that we can go in this world and we won't find souvenirs from your past?" He's grinning. He enjoys hamming up my Jack-the-lad image. "So, how ancient is this ancient history?"

I pause. An image of Connie's nervous face flashes in front of my eyes. She would not want her kids' headmaster to know that she consorted with me while she was a married woman. I feel a strange urge to protect her.

"Well, she has a kid that's four years old or something. So that must mean we had a fling about eight or nine years ago," I lie. "Before she got it together with the guy she's now married to."

In a way this version of the events is true. Connie was married when I met her but she didn't really get it together with her husband until way after she said "I do".

"So who is it? Do I know her?" asks Tom.

"I don't think I want to know," says Craig. "It will be hard to shake hands with the woman at parents' evening if I know she's had a history with you."

"I knew her as Constance Green. I don't know her married name," I lie, again to protect her.

Tom recognizes the name immediately. "Greenie? That's what you called her, wasn't it?" I can see he is scrabbling round his mind trying to recall details. He raises his eyebrows as the facts start to slip into place. No doubt he has remembered that the affair didn't take place as long ago as I've made out and that she was married. "Wasn't she" — I shoot him a warning look.

155

Tom clocks it and perhaps he considers his alternative question less disruptive. "Wasn't she mad?"

"About me. Probably, she's just a woman," I quip.

"She became a photographer, didn't she?"

"That's right."

"You must be talking about Mrs Baker," says Craig. "She's a lovely lady. Wonderful family. She's married to a great guy."

"That's nice," I comment.

"Did you break her heart?" Craig sounds fed up with me.

"Who knows, mate? I broke her willpower and her moral code. At the time that's all I was aiming for."

Craig looks irritated. I wonder if he's going to tell me that Greenie was too good for me. He often says that about women I date or shag; he repeatedly said it about the one I married.

"Look, I didn't deflower her, if that's what you're thinking." I try to defend myself. "Most women want their first date in a coffee shop and their first sex in the missionary position, it's safe and comfortable. Connie was the kind of woman who favoured cocktail bars and swinging from chandeliers. Believe me, we were evenly matched."

"I can't imagine Mrs Baker being that way," says Craig. He's blushing and I feel I've just told a kid Santa doesn't exist.

"Well, she was." I take a gulp of my pint.

"Yes, she was," confirms Tom; he's grinning.

"Oh God, not you too?" It used to be the case that Tom would sometimes have my sloppy seconds.

156

"No, I don't mean I know from personal experience — just the stuff John told me at the time."

As is always the case between me and Tom, I shared all the grimy details. Tom knew that I met Greenie at work. She was a strange contradiction from the onset. On the one hand all prim and proper and constantly protesting, "I'm married, leave me alone." On the other, she spelt out that she was gagging for it. It was fun while it lasted. Tom knows that we shagged in parks, across desks, at my flat and in hotel rooms. I've told him all that. He might even know that for a time I found her fascinating, although I've never told him that bit. But we are good mates and he might have picked up on it. Tom is watching me very carefully. I feel uncomfortable under his observation.

"Is it me or is it hot in here?" I ask.

"It's you," says Craig.

"Greenie was the last bird before you married Andrea, wasn't she?" asks Tom.

"No, mate, I shagged loads of birds between Greenie and taking the fall with Andrea."

"Yeah, you shagged them but Greenie was the last one that, you know —"

I do know but I'm not expecting him to probe. I'm depending on his Northern-ness and his Y-chromosome to make him shut up.

"Was she The One That Got Away?" asks Craig. He can't hide his excitement. He's a bit of an old romantic, is our Craig. He believes in all that "The One" stuff, which girls believe. He's such an innocent.

I laugh into my pint. "Mate, towards the end I was shoving her away."

"Why?" He looks disappointed.

"It all got a bit intense." It really is hot in here. I scratch my ear and take off my jacket. Tom, the bastard, doesn't say a word but doesn't take his eyes off me.

"Did you love her?" asks Craig.

I laugh again, which means I splutter beer on to the table. Which is a bit embarrassing and a bit of a waste. What a stupid bloody question to ask a mate.

"Love? Love?" I ask with incredulity. "I never gave it a moment's thought."

"I see," he says. Although I have no idea what he thinks he sees. "And did she love you?"

"It wasn't that sort of gig," I mutter. "Now if you'll excuse me, lads, as pleasant as this wander down Memory Lane is, I have a very current lead I need to follow at the bar."

I saunter over to the cutie who I bought a drink for earlier. She's sitting with a group of giggling mates.

"Ladies, I think you ought to know, presently, I'm officially single, but don't tell the girlfriend." I wink.

Three of the girlies collapse into helpless giggles, one rolls her eyes and the fifth is too pissed to have heard me. I pull up a seat. I think the odds suggest it's going to be my lucky night.

CHAPTER
SEVENTEEN

Tuesday 26 September

Lucy

I call Connie to more or less demand that she meets me for dinner. Before we had kids Connie and I used to meet for supper on a regular basis. We made it a matter of honour that we ate at restaurants reviewed in the *Evening Standard*, almost before the ink dried on the newspaper. We'd frequently treat ourselves to champagne, oysters, *foie gras* or truffles. In those days we were cash and time rich. Nowadays, more often than not, Connie comes up with an excuse as to why we can't splurge. She doesn't earn as much as she used to; besides, Luke often works until late and she seems to find it unusually difficult to secure a reliable babysitter. Privately, I've started to refer to Connie as "Little Miss Blow-Out", and whenever I write her name in my diary I do so with pencil as there's always about an eighty per cent chance we won't meet up. This time she surprises me by immediately agreeing to dinner.

Did she notice the urgency in my voice?

We meet at a terribly trendy new-style Indian restaurant in Westbourne Grove. The food is sensational and the turquoise and silver décor works well with my colouring. I'm only half-kidding; even in times of crisis it doesn't do to let standards drop.

Connie hugs me and plants a huge kiss on my cheek. I'd normally disengage and only allow her to air-kiss me in the appropriate way but tonight I find her warmth is comforting.

"So how was New York?" she asks with a huge grin.

"Tiring," I reply automatically. "I was rushed off my feet. The client turned out to be very demanding. He never let up." I've claimed the same to Peter. I put a Small Brown Bag from Bloomingdales on to the table. "I bought you a gift."

Connie dives on to the package and is clearly delighted to find a selection of Mac make-up inside. She gushes her thanks for a few minutes and then asks, suspiciously, "So, if you were so busy, how come you had time to shop?"

I signal to the waiter and choose a wine before I answer her question.

"I lied. It was a total jolly. We barely did any work," I confess in a rush. "We arrived there Thursday afternoon. We went to PM Lounge until late. It was the coolest bar I've been to in a long time. Do you know it?"

Connie shakes her head. Of course not, we're mothers now — neither of us knows what's hot and what's not. I'd have been lost in New York if I hadn't been with Mick.

"It's a cathedral-like temple, set under high vaulted ceilings with skylights. It's worth seeing." She doesn't look interested. "The next day we had a breakfast meeting with the client and he signed off the contract before 10.30a.m."

"We?"

"Mick Harrison, he was there too. Didn't I mention that to you?"

"No." Connie takes a sip of water and studies the menu, then she asks, "So why did you stay all weekend?"

"Well, we had expected to have to handhold the client for a little longer so we had tickets for the big soccer game on the Saturday afternoon. It seemed a shame to waste them."

"You don't like soccer."

"No, but Mick does. And we'd managed to secure a reservation at Bungalow 8 for Sunday brunch. I couldn't let that go to waste. I thought, why not?" Connie is silent. A low trick, as she knows I'll fill in the conversational gap. "I just needed a bit of time to myself," I shrug. "It's not as though there was anything to rush home for."

"Your family."

I resist laughing outright. "Peter and Auriol are always fine without me. Besides, the twins were visiting. I always feel like a spare part when they are about."

We place our order and the wine arrives. I can almost hear the cogs in Connie's mind whirling. Good. I'm glad. I want her to challenge me and cross-examine. I need the discipline. I'm not disappointed.

Connie thoughtfully sips her wine and then asks, "Are you and Peter OK at the moment?"

"No. Not really."

Historically, I haven't been the type to indulge in confidences. It's not a luxury open to mistresses, especially as in my particular case I was sleeping with the husband of a friend of Connie's. But I'm the wife now; I have every right to complain and grumble and exhaust my friend's patience. Maybe I should be talking to Peter. I would, except I can't. Or he won't. Or he can't. Whatever.

I start vague. "It just isn't quite what I thought it would be."

"What isn't?"

"Being married."

Connie gasps. I shoot her a warning look. Good God, it's not like I'm the first to discover this. She clamps her mouth closed and I continue.

"Being married makes me feel so . . ." I want to say old but I can't spit out the word. I try another angle. "Married life is so . . ." I don't want to say boring. Pete isn't boring, exactly. Normally I'm eloquent but I have to settle on an inaccurate explanation. "It's just that I hadn't anticipated how unsexy living with someone is?" I grin and try to joke. "The endless sock washing."

"You don't do your own washing. Eva does your washing."

"I have to see the cycle through, don't I? Cycle after cycle of cooking, cleaning and clearing."

I know Connie is not convinced. My house staff is proportional to the Queen's. I have Eva, a cleaner, a gardener, not to mention the handyman who sees to the odd jobs whenever the need arises and the lady who

162

specializes in polishing silver. I realize that I'm not being clear.

"We had this . . . incident." I avoid confessing to a row. It seems so vulgar, so emotional. "I've been married to Peter for five and a half years now. He was married to Rose for less, yet I'm still eternally second place."

"Well, they were a couple for six years before they married, Lucy."

I glare at Connie but don't dignify her observation with direct comment.

"I was thrilled to note that our marriage had already out-lasted hers. It was, as far as I was concerned, a day of national celebration — there ought to have been bunting in the street, a public holiday. But when I mentioned it to Pete he practically accused me of being immature and said that life and love weren't a competition. Toss! Everything's a competition, especially life and most certainly love."

I realize that despite having verbal diarrhoea, I'm still being economical with the truth. I don't tell Connie about my storming out of the restaurant. I'm beginning to see the episode as ill-considered. I pause and look at Connie. She's full of concern and sympathy. Irrationally, I have an urge to gouge her sad little eyes out. I don't want her sympathy. I don't want anyone's sympathy. So what do I want?

"When I left for New York Peter and I were barely speaking, whereas —"

"This Mick guy has the gift of the gob."

I flinch slightly at her crude choice of expression but have to acknowledge its accuracy. Mick is chatty, funny and full of discreet compliments.

"Where's the crime in having a little fun?" I demand. "I felt careless and carefree in New York. I didn't see the rush to get back to a routine where every day is the same as the next."

"What are your days like exactly, Lucy?"

"Endless effort in the office and then home to plastic toys and long silences."

"Are you having an affair with this Mick?" she asks.

She stares straight at me, a brave move. Most would lack the nerve to launch such a direct missile. We've been friends forever. There's nothing either one of us could say to the other that would shock. Still, there's plenty that would sadden.

"No." I hear her breathe a sigh of relief.

New York had been enormous fun. Fifth Avenue alone is guaranteed to put a smile on my face. And, as expected, Mick was good company — great company, there's no denying it. He was amusing and charming and I flirted with him but only in the most careful way — almost indiscernible — and he flattered me back. I did not allow anything serious to develop. I let him go. That's what one has to do once one is married. Let other opportunities slide.

I've always been extremely clinical about sex and relationships. With the exception of Peter I've viewed every man who has drifted or plunged into my life as a commodity. Something I could buy or sell and use at my convenience. Life is simple once you accept that looks, money, intelligence and sex are only bartering tools, to be used to attain mutually satisfying relationships. Peter changed my view. He found a way to make me believe in love, commitment, regard, passion and loyalty. The magic stuff. Despite myself I was delighted. At least for a time. But there hasn't been much magic for a while now, has there? Perhaps all Peter did was introduce a more complex set of commodities.

As I flew over the Atlantic towards the glittering skyscrapers, I had considered the possibility that Mick would be able to shove me back along my old path and my old way of thinking. In the past if I was not getting enough sex and attention, either quality or quantity, at home, I would have felt completely justified in looking for it elsewhere. Yet this was not the case in New York. I did not want things to develop between Mick and me. Mick turned out to be nothing more than a great travelling buddy. Big sigh of relief.

Followed by big sigh of frustration.

Because if Peter can't make me feel fabulous any more and I don't want anyone else to, does that mean my days of feeling fabulous are over? Is that it? *Was that it?*

Our starters arrive. Fried red pumpkin, it looks delightful. I fear neither of us will pay the chef the compliments he deserves. I push my plate away. Connie doesn't pick up her knife and fork. We fall silent and wait while the waiter fusses. I can barely remember what I ordered for my main course. It hardly matters.

"Mick makes me feel girlish, triumphant and wanted, for the first time in what seems like years." Even as I hear myself utter these words I know I'm the worst of all things, I'm a cliché. "But the feeling was only fleeting. I know enough not to regard the relationship as anything more serious than an ego booster. Spending time with him equates with going to the spa for a pick-me-up facial. Don't worry, Con, I am not going to have an affair with Mick. The flirting, flattering and flippancy over an extremely dry Martini were intoxicating in their own way but I'm not genuinely interested. He was a distraction. A plaything."

"You're too old for playthings," she says, grumpily.

"Thank you very much," I mutter. "It is precisely because this truth hurts so much that I felt I needed to flirt with Mick. Can't you see that?"

Apparently not. Connie stares at me with undisguised astonishment. "You're worried about getting old?"

"No." Yes.

"But Lucy, you're so beautiful, especially for —"

"My age." I glare at her but don't stab her with my fork, which proves I can be mature.

"Ageing is a privilege," she says primly.

"Really. It seems more like a punishment to me. Why is it that everyone puts so much emphasis on maturity nowadays? I don't get it. I enjoyed the hedonistic culture when youth was the 'must have' quality."

"Everybody has to grow up eventually, Lucy. Even you. You married Peter Phillips, not Peter Pan. You are thirty-seven."

I cannot understand her need to say the number out loud. I steal a furtive glance around the restaurant and pray she hasn't been overheard.

"You both have to accept your responsibilities now," says Connie with unbearable smugness.

"Don't talk to me about responsibilities. I work with hundreds of thousands of pounds on a daily basis. I have responsibilities towards mega conglomerates and international governments," I point out tartly.

"But it's an entirely selfish responsibility. Your career is like cooking or bathing yourself. It's about your need."

"Which responsibilities are you referring to then?"

"Auriol."

I stare at her blankly. Auriol? What does she have to do with Mick?

"If you have an affair you are putting her at great risk. You must see that."

"Yes, I do see that." Auriol is a spoilsport. I chew my food rapidly and angrily. "It's so maddening that it's Auriol and all the associated that I needed to have a break from but it was Auriol's face that forced its way into my consciousness in the PM Lounge and at Bungalow 8 too. Hers or Peter's. They are the reasons I would not dream of having a fling. But they are also the reasons I need some space."

"What do you mean, 'all the associated'?" asks Connie with perception.

"You said it, the responsibilities. The endless car runs to the appropriate extracurricular activities. The constant consideration that must be given to feeding a child. I mean, when *are* they going to invent something to eat that is free of artificial colours and flavours, gluten free, low in sugar and sodium but tasty too? Answering non-sequential questions is a bore. So is reading books with pictures and dull, overly moral story lines. In short, I'm exhausted by the constant thinking that necessarily goes with being a parent."

"But Eva does a large percentage of that, doesn't she?" points out Connie.

"Which only makes me a failure."

"By whose standards?"

"Rose's," I sigh.

This is the crux. At last, I've said it. This is what I want to talk about. Will Connie enter into the discussion with me? When I gained Peter I lost the former intimacy that Connie and I had enjoyed. Naturally he came with a price, doesn't everything? But right now, I need Con to throw in her chips with me, just for the evening. I might not be worthy but I'm in need.

"Is there any other standard of parenting? Rose, the gold-medallist, the matriarch supreme. She sets the bar, doesn't she?" I demand.

"Oh," says Connie.

"Oh indeed."

Connie pauses and then finally admits, "I do know what you mean." Music to my ears. "But you two are very different. Since when did you worry about what Rose is up to?" For longer than Connie could imagine, but I don't admit as much, I stay silent. "OK, so the truth is you work so hard that you outsource all the

168

arrangements of your daughter's birthday party. That's not so terrible. Mind you, I think you'd have outsourced giving birth too, if you could have."

"And that is terrible, right?" I query tetchily.

"Rose, on the other hand, does not have a single interest other than the boys. That's not healthy either. Wow, who would have thought I'd turn out the balanced one?" Connie grins broadly. I can't share her joy. Her observation is fair.

"Connie, do you think I'm a terrible mother?"

"No. You just have your inimitable own style."

We grin at each other. Friends again. We can't resolve my dilemma. We both know that, and indeed I knew that before we even began the conversation and nibbled on the wholemeal rolls. I just needed to air a couple of things.

"Have you tried talking to Peter?" Connie asks.

"Not since we got married," I quip back, and then I flash a look that communicates I deem the conversation closed.

We try to chat about other things. I ask Connie if she has any interesting commissions lined up but her answers are brief and perfunctory. I'm not desperately interested in Fran's first few weeks at school or Flora's expanding vocabulary. Connie doesn't even ask me where I bought my new handbag; normally she shows a proper interest. Conversation all but dries up by the time we order pudding and I begin to wonder whether I have over-shared with Connie. Then I discover the reason for her distracted air. It appears she has to do some sharing of her own. She waits until pudding arrives. She's having poached pears swimming in alcohol and cream and a cappuccino on the side. I'm having a double espresso and a cigarette.

"Guess who I met at the school gates?" she asks.

"Obviously, I have no idea who hangs out at the school gates, Connie. Nor do I ever want to."

"You'd be surprised. It's really quite good fun. The mums are all lovely. Anyway, you'll never guess."

"No, I said as much."

"John Harding."

"What?"

I've heard Connie bounce this particular name across various restaurant tables in the past. I've heard her sing out his name with joy and scream out his name with agony that truly seemed unbearable. The last time I heard his name was six years ago and I never expected to hear it again. I never wanted to.

"John Harding the sleazeball bastard ex-lover?"

"One and the same."

"What was he doing there? Does he have kids at the school? Oh. My God."

"No. He's a friend of the Head's."

"He's a friend of Mr Walker's? I can't see the match." Mr Walker is a sweetie. Mr Harding is a rat. "So, what did you think when you met him? First thought," I demand.

Connie blushes. "I was glad I'd been to the hairdresser's and my hair was blow-dried straight. I regretted my lack of mascara."

I see. "Did you talk to him?"

"Yes."

170

"And was he —"

"The same."

"Now I understand why you think the school gates are fun," I joke.

"This isn't a laughing matter," says Connie with irritation. "Now you know why I was so down on you with Mick. I don't want you to make the same mistakes as I did."

I decide to cut to the chase. "So are you going to sleep with him?"

"Jesus, Lucy, what do you take me for?" She looks outraged.

"There's a precedent here," I point out; besides, I didn't take offence when she assumed the worst of me.

Connie had a brief affair with this man within the first year of her marriage. She made me into her confessor at the time. She didn't know anyone else who would reserve judgement so she chose to confide every morbid detail to me. What she doesn't know to this day is that I *did* judge the situation; I just withheld sharing my views. Connie believed that the affair was a monumental, seminal part of her adulthood. She believed that John Harding was a spectacular romantic who was sent from wherever with the express purpose of changing her life. As her closest friend and the person privy to every single conversation and nuance between them, I think that their affair was simply about forbidden sex.

Connie turns scarlet; she's probably recollecting the same as I am. "That was ages ago, before the children, before the photography. God, I can't even remember the person I was then. I certainly can't relate to her. We've all grown up since then," she says sincerely.

"I thought we'd just established that I haven't. And I don't suppose John Harding has either. He doesn't seem the type. You'll have to be careful, Connie."

"And you too, Lucy. You too."

CHAPTER
EIGHTEEN

Wednesday 27 September

Rose

"So? Tell all." Connie flings herself on to my sofa and beams expectantly. Daisy is sitting on a beanbag and she's looking at me with the same glee.

"There's really very little to tell," I reply stonily. I pass around a plate of biscuits.

I know I'm not playing the game. It's been years since any of us dated but I still remember the rules. I ought to supply a bottle of wine and a stack of gruesome, intimate details. Daisy and Connie's gleaming eyes tell me that they won't settle for less. But it's extremely difficult to parade your hopes and the contents of your heart for general entertainment, especially when I haven't even provided wine because this debrief is slipped in on a Wednesday afternoon. Daisy is supposed to be lesson planning, Connie is balancing a hot cup of tea and a clambering toddler; they've found time in their busy schedules to give me their attention and yet I feel horribly uncomfortable with this confessional situation.

"Details!" the girls chorus in unison. I give in to the inevitability of the situation as gracelessly as possible.

"What do you want to know?"

"Is he fit?" asks Connie.

"Not to my tastes but I can see that some women would consider him attractive," I admit carefully.

"Is he funny?" asks Daisy.

"No, unless you mean funny as in odd."

The girls are not deterred. "In what way odd?"

"A satirical, verging on the nasty, sense of humour. A mistaken belief that I'd be interested in *Lord of the Rings* — anything from the collection of the plastic toys to the director's cut — and a total disinterest in everything other than himself. He never asked anything *at all* about me."

"He's shy," insists Connie.

"Arrogant and egotistical," I reply firmly.

"How long did you stay?"

"We had two drinks."

"Well, it's good that you didn't leave after the first drink as you'd threatened," says my sister, ever the optimist.

I crush her iota of hope. "I was waiting to see if he'd buy me a drink, as I'd got the first round in."

"Did he?" asks Connie.

"No."

We all sigh. None of us can forgive meanness. "He talked about his ex-girlfriend a lot — almost as much as he talked about Grimley and Gandor. He's currently between jobs and thinking of changing direction. He no longer wants to be an insurance broker — he wants to write a novel, although he doesn't read any current fiction as he thinks it's all junk. He's saving money to

174

buy a quad bike, so he's just moved back in with his mother who cooks the best Sunday roast anyone has ever tasted."

The girls look devastated. Connie rallies first. "Well, we never expected you to fall in love on the first date. We just have to keep at it."

I stare at her with imploring eyes. I wish she'd drop this. I've never been convinced that I want to meet anyone anyway. She refuses to acknowledge my silent pleas.

"I think we need to approach this more scientifically. Have you thought of internet dating?" she asks.

"Truly, never," I reply.

"But it's the obvious next step," she insists. "Much more controlled. You are able to see a picture of the guy before you commit and you are able to vet interests, etc. You won't have to waste an evening discovering that he has a passion for quad bikes and an Oedipal complex." Connie can always make her ideas sound like good ideas, even when they are the opposite. "Have you got broadband?"

I'm tempted to deny it.

"Yes, she has," says Daisy. "She got it to help the boys with their homework." Traitor.

Connie clearly has a mental list of sites she wants to take me to; she's done her research. At first I feel a slight flush of excitement and optimism as the home page shows a number of beautiful couples all smiling adoringly at one another. Maybe it would be nice to meet someone. The couples are eating lobster in candlelit restaurants; they're flushed with exercise and standing outside ski chalets or picnicking in open fields bursting with poppies; it would take a harder woman than me not to feel squelchy. However, the momentary illusion vanishes when I recognize one of the images.

"Hey, isn't that the picture they use on that optician's advert, the one that's on the side of buses at the moment? It must be a stock shot."

Connie ignores me and starts to read aloud from the homepage.

"Find your perfect partner, browse from over two million singles."

I don't think it is a cheering statistic. So many lonely people. Not that I am lonely. I have a full life. But these people must be lonely if they are prepared to put themselves up for public sale (and ridicule). Besides, I'm not good in crowds and two million sounds like a crowded market.

"OK, let's do a search. You are a woman looking for . . ."

I hurriedly grab the mouse from Connie and tick the box "Looking for a man".

"In the age range?"

"Forty to forty-five," suggests Daisy.

"Too narrow," says Connie with a tut. She types in 30 — 50. Once again I lunge for the mouse and click on 35 — 45.

"I don't want a pensioner. I'd end up polishing his Zimmer frame, just as the boys get off my hands."

"Meeting for?"

"Friendship," I insist.

"And romance," Daisy and Connie counter. I allow them to click the relevant box. We limit the geographical search and then click the bar labelled "Looking for love".

It takes a few seconds before a red heart, almost covering the screen, pops up announcing:

Your search of 120 MILES around LONDON for a MAN aged between 35 and 45 has resulted in 489 MATCHES.

"Wow," says Daisy. "So much choice."

Only eight matches include pictures. One of them is a picture of Austen Powers, so it doesn't count. The guy admits to being five foot one, describes his hair as "thin" and his figure as "stocky". I think of Peter, tall, dark and handsome, and feel sad.

Connie scrolls to the next candidate.

"He's gorgeous," she says, delightedly. In fairness, candidate number two is very fine-looking. I conclude he must be dull or insolvent because why else would he be using this method to find a date? I read his profile.

A couple of things about myself: love travelling, B-ing sociable, food out, family and friends are important 2 me, yoga daily, gym B4 work, self employed in media industry, happy 2 go out or stay home, movies, theatre (plays + musical). In winter like 2 ski/snowboard, summer like places that amongst other things have gr8 swimming/beaches (St John

USVI), play tennis. Happy with life. happy 2 share.
Nearly 4got — I like 2 learn about & drink wine.

It takes me a moment to decipher the trendy
shorthand and get over his appalling grammar. When I
do, my first thought is, I don't believe him. My problem
is I can't remember having that much time to myself
and so I struggle with the concept that anyone else has
enough leisure time to be this interesting. I don't dwell
on the profile. Frankly, any man who makes daily visits
to the gym is going to recoil in horror at my body,
which fails to attend the gym so much as annually. I
consider myself lucky if I carve out enough "me time"
to visit the loo daily. Connie must conclude the same,
as she points to the picture of guy number three.

"What about him?"

He doesn't look like an axe murderer. In fact if he
committed a crime he'd be impossible to identify in a
line-up because he looks like two-thirds of the male
population: five foot ten, short, brown, slightly receding
hair, solid but not overweight, with brown eyes. He's
not especially handsome nor is he particularly ugly.
He's bland. Almost invisible. I see why she thinks we
might be suited.

I read his profile. "He says that in another life he
might have been a golden eagle or Christopher Columbus."

"Whereas in this life he's a wanker," comments Daisy.

I'm relieved that she's also offended by his
over-inflated ego. The guy simply doesn't look the type
to have discovered continents.

178

Connie scours a number of dating sites. I reject sites if registration is free (candidates lack commitment). I reject sites unless photos are included (candidates lack self-confidence). And I reject sites that don't offer an identification check (candidates lack honesty). She perseveres and finds a fee-paying site with a large number of candidates, with checked IDs, photos and detailed profiles.

Next, I rule out anyone who has read *Harry Potter*.

"But you've read *Harry Potter*," Daisy points out. She sounds ever so slightly weary.

"Yes, to the boys. It's a kids' book. None of these candidates have kids therefore they must be kids themselves."

I rule out anyone who has read Bill Bryson's *Small Island*.

"But you liked that too," argues Connie.

"It's on ninety per cent of the lists. I want someone a little more independently minded."

Connie starts to speed-read the candidates' profiles. "Mad on sport, does Iron man triathlon, etc."

I stop her there. "Next."

"Would have been Paul McCartney in a past life."

"Paul McCartney is still alive — you can't be a reincarnation of someone who is still living. Next."

"A suitable person would speak English as a first language and would be white."

We all gasp at the bigotry and chorus, "Next."

"I'm half Irish, so if you hailed from the Emerald Isle that wouldn't be a bad thing."

"Next," I call.

179

"Why?" demands Daisy. "Mum's Irish. You fit the profile. Keep reading, Connie."

". . . And solvent in your own right but not a career-minded power-person."

"Sounds sexist," I mumble. "Next."

"It is important that you don't smoke, as it is a rather disgusting habit — if you don't agree then you're not for me." I do agree so I stay silent. "Weird body piercing and tattoos are also a big no-no!"

I don't have either but am tempted to rush out and have a job lot done. Nipple, tummy button, eyebrow, lip and tongue and that's just the tattoos.

"He ought to respect freedom of expression. Next."

"I like to play with computer technology, hi-fi and home theatre."

"Boring. Next."

We continue in this vein for quite some time. I start to clean the boys' trainers while Connie reads the profiles out loud and Daisy assesses my suitability. I interrupt to point out the obvious shortcomings of the candidates. I wonder how long it will take to tire them.

"This one is perfect," squeals Connie, suddenly. "Listen. The candidate will have depth of character."

"Tick," says Daisy.

"You must be sociable and enjoy entertaining."

"Tick."

"Family and friends are important to you, as I have good relationships with my extended family, friends from childhood, university, etc."

"Tick."

"Might speak two languages."

"Rose speaks three!" cries Daisy excitedly. "So double tick."

Connie continues to read the liturgy of demands. "Overall health is important."

I decode. "He wants a thin girl."

"You would enjoy your work or have a passion."

"I'm passionate about being a mum. But somehow I can't believe that's a passion that will pass muster. He's looking for a woman who runs her own phenomenally successful cottage industry or has an illustrious career in the City." Anger at his arrogance is blistering and bubbling inside of me.

"We could put him on a shortlist," suggests Daisy.

"Not if he was the last man on earth."

"It's a good thing that populating the planet isn't dependent on you," says Connie.

"He's totally unsuitable."

"Why? You ticked nearly all of the boxes!" pleads Daisy.

"He's too demanding."

"Takes one to know one," mutters Connie.

"What does that mean?" She nearly always means something, only she doesn't always say so.

"Well, I just wonder if you should open your mind a little more. You're being very dismissive."

"I'm simply being efficient at sorting the wheat from the chaff. A babysitter costs upwards of forty quid a night. I'm not planning on going on countless pointless dates. I can't afford it."

"But you are planning on going on the odd date, aren't you? Besides, I keep telling you I'll babysit," says

Daisy, reasonably. How is it that on some occasions someone's reasonableness is just as annoying as anger or unreasonableness? "Look, maybe he's not quite right but there are dozens to choose from," she says with a patient smile. "Don't any of them appeal?"

"No. They don't and I can't imagine who will." I feel pathetic and past it. "You have to go, now," I say finally.

I start gathering up coffee cups. They see I'm not kidding and Daisy assembles her bag and coat while Connie scoops Flora into her padded jacket. I bundle them out of my home without much ceremony. I manage to fling a hazy promise to see them soon and I slam the door closed. I turn from the door, lean on it and then slide to the floor.

It's too horrible.

How come Peter walks away from our relationship and ends up with a beautiful new wife, a stunning home and another child? I'm left standing still and alone. I hadn't felt alone until Connie and Daisy started this campaign of theirs. Now whenever I look in the mirror I see what they see. A forlorn, hopeless case. Reading through the profiles of other singletons hasn't helped me to believe that there's a great big community out there, just waiting for me to burst on to their scene — it's left me feeling desolate and inadequate. I wander back into the sitting room. In her haste to leave Connie has failed to close down the computer. I fight the urge to throw my coffee cup at the screen. What would be the point? I'd have to clear up the broken pieces and mop up the dregs. I'd have to buy a replacement computer.

182

There is no one to look after me, other than me. What a vile thought. I slump into the computer chair, still warm from Connie, and I fight tears.

The face on the screen belongs to Chris from SW London. He tells me that:

It would be good if you wanted to do similar things to me — restaurant, a movie, a walk in the country, stately home, sitting in watching a DVD, touring the UK and Ireland, bbq with friends when our weather allows it, beer gardens in the summer, a drive to the coast.

It dawns on me — of course I want to do those things with Chris or someone or other. Who doesn't like movies, walks, beer gardens and drives to the coast? Only lunatics, presumably. But the words on the screen don't seem real. This guy might be a married man looking for a bit of extracurricular. And even if the words are real and he is telling the truth, how do I make the drives to the coast *my* reality? I don't know if Chris is worth that effort or even if I'm capable of that effort.

Why am I here? Chris asks himself. Good question.

A recent visit to my 2-year-old godson and his parents helped me decide that it's time to meet someone special. Am now out of sync with my friends who all seem to have got married and have kids. I've been too busy working and travelling the world to settle down. An attempt to join the single scene by going out the other night made me feel there has to be a better way than shouting over music in smoky dark bars — I hope this is it.

Well, I agree with him there.

A bit about me — lucky enough to have a great family and friends — and a wide range of interests: love exploring new places — whether it's countries, restaurants or places in the UK and London but also very happy to stay at home to watch a good film with some nice wine. Don't like snobbery or stuffiness in any form and value honesty, loyalty, humour and those with question-ing minds.

Too good to be true. Surely.

If that sounds like you I'd love to meet you!

The house is gleaming. I once read on a fridge magnet that a clean house was the sign of a wasted life and I think the pithy slogan might be true; my ironing basket and life are empty.

The boys take, and then take, and then take some more. They give but they are like cruel dictators, they give at random and unexpected moments and they only allow you to bathe in their love for a few precious moments before they demand again. Yet when they go I'll have nothing. What sort of life is that?

184

Blow it. What have I got to lose? A sobering question. I press the reply button and fill out a return profile card.

CHAPTER
NINETEEN

Thursday 28 September

John

I spot her immediately. She's wearing a long leather coat and boots. They are flat boots, which is a shame, but it's not a bad look for the school gate. She's chatting happily with a small gaggle of other mothers and is absentmindedly pushing and pulling her youngest sprog's stroller. The kid is dressed in a fairy costume and is playing with a soft toy in the shape of a rabbit.

They make an attractive tableau.

As I approach, her kid drops the rabbit and it rolls a metre from the stroller. None of the mothers notices. Opportunity has knocked. I swoop in and retrieve the toy, give it a quick rub and present it, with a flourish, back to the little girl.

Of course, by now, the conversation has drawn to a close and all eyes are on me. Greenie mumbles a thank-you but it's not what you'd call heartfelt.

"Aren't you going to introduce your friend?" asks one of the women.

Excepting Greenie, this woman is best in show. She beams at me, which is perhaps a mistake as her teeth are crooked and a bit yellow. Good bod though. She's in a tracksuit and is clearly a dedicated gym bunny. Decent haircut and colour; she looks expensive and groomed but still not a great beauty. Greenie is also wearing make-up but even without it she could knock spots off the other mother.

"This is an old colleague of mine, John Harding," says Greenie, without much enthusiasm. The other women proffer their hands for me to shake; they are notably more eager to engage than Greenie is. They introduce themselves by telling me whose mother they are.

"Ted's mum, Year Two."

"Clara's mummy, Year One."

"Jake and Josh, reception and Year Two respectively."

"Mr Harding isn't a daddy," says Greenie. She might think this Mr Harding thing is distancing; personally I'm finding the formality a turn-on and I'm fighting an erection. "He's a pal of Mr Walker's. Isn't that right?"

Connie has refused to meet my eye so far. She directs her question to my right shoulder. I see that as a good sign. She's been thinking about me. The ladies are excited at the idea that Craig has a life outside the school and they start firing questions at me about whether he has a girlfriend or not. They comment that I must have a tale or two to tell them. Before I get a chance to reply fully the conversation turns.

"Look, they're coming out," says Clara's mummy, Year One.

Connie busies herself waving to her daughter and ignoring me. I lean into her ear and whisper, "Will you meet me?"

"No." She sounds shocked.

"I'd like to talk to you."

"You are six years too late for a chat," she snaps. This time she does turn to face me. I'm aware that the full force of her fury has yet to be unleashed. I can see she is keeping her disquiet in check. Even that excites me. She really is looking lovely.

"I'm not taking no for an answer," I tell her.

"I realize it's the first time you've ever heard the word from me but you'd be wise to accept it."

She bends down to kiss her kid. See, I like her sense of humour. Even with a kid hanging round her legs and all her mumsie mates in earshot she couldn't resist a snappy retort. I've always liked that in her. I grin but can't seem to thaw her.

"I'm deadly serious. I wish you'd stop hanging around here. If it's for my benefit, forget it. I don't want you in my life. Go away," she says firmly.

With that she pushes the stroller away from the school. Her eldest child looks a bit startled and she is only just managing to keep up with her mum's determined, long strides. I follow them down the street.

"There's a lot that wasn't said." I'm forced into skipping alongside her, which looks a bit pathetic but women sometimes go for breathless desperation. It might work.

"Too much was said," she mutters grimly.

Or it might not.

I try another tack. "Nothing heavy. Just a quick catch-up drink for old times' sake." She stops abruptly and I think I've engaged her but I realize she's just trying to cross the road. She acts out an elaborate version of the Green Cross Code.

"You might as well agree, because I'm not going to go away and the other mums will start to talk if I keep turning up at the school gate."

She glares at me. "Why is it that you are only this persistent in the early parts of the game and so distant at the end?"

"Ah, so we are playing a game again." I can't hide my satisfaction at this small victory.

She blushes, it might be embarrassment, it might be anger. Either way it suits her. "We most certainly are not. Nor will we ever be. Go away."

"No."

"Please."

"No."

"You are a bully."

"That's not true."

Greenie looks around the street. There are dozens of mums, nannies and even the occasional dad shepherding their children into cars or trying to rush them home on foot. The kids all squirm and wriggle constantly. Their coats hang off their little bodies and some step on their own scarves which trail behind them. It looks exhausting. Greenie seems to be looking for someone to rescue her or at least help her decide what to do next. There's no one to do that.

189

"I'm very persistent," I remind her. "Just one drink. What harm can it do?"

"None," she says, looking at me with uncut defiance. "You can't reach me this time."

Neither of us believes her and she listens as I give her the address of the pub.

CHAPTER
TWENTY

Wednesday 4 October

Rose

When I heard Chris's voice on the phone my first thought was that he sounded younger than I was expecting. I didn't have the nerve to ask him exactly how old he is. I've checked back on his profile but he hasn't revealed his age there either. On the upside he sounded pleasant, polite and well educated. It appears that he comes from a home country but it's rather difficult to tell people's origin nowadays. Prep-school boys want to cultivate a street accent; northerners speak in the Queen's received. We chatted about the weather (understandably, it has been a glorious and mild autumn, it *is* notable) and we tried to think of somewhere suitable to meet.

He didn't offer to take me to a movie or a show, it wasn't the season for a barbecue with friends, and anyway I always feel hungry after barbecues. Both a walk in the country to visit a stately home and cosying up to watch a DVD required more commitment and assurance of intimacy than either of us were prepared to give at this stage — as did touring the UK and

191

Ireland. In the end we settled on meeting in a restaurant. I had seen a photo of Chris online and so there would be no chance of my walking up to the wrong man this time. Chris asked if I would e-mail a recent photo of myself to him and I agreed, even though I had no intention of doing so. I was not prepared to give up the advantage.

We settled on a Thai restaurant in Notting Hill. He suggested an Indian but I didn't want to turn pink and sweaty at an inconvenient moment. I arrive ten minutes late and spot him immediately. He is seated in the corner; he has a book on the table but he's not reading it. I boldly stride forth.

"You look exactly like your photo," I say.

Chris seems confused for a moment. Unsure of where he is or why. Then he remembers his manners and gets to his feet. He staggers rather than springs. He's clearly had a glass or two to steady any pre-date nerves.

"Is that a good thing?" he asks.

"Certainly." He's tall, blond and all his features are set more or less where they should be. He has a big, easy grin which he's keen to flash. It's all I require. And more.

"I never received your picture," he says.

"Is that a good thing?" I ask jokily.

He doesn't reply, but I assume that's because the waiter is busily taking my coat, encouraging us to sit down and telling us about specials — rather than because he thinks I'm a shocker. I'm rather pleased with how I'm turned out tonight. Not supermodel, I never will be, but I did treat myself to the cerise cardigan in Monsoon and it is quite fetching. The waiter is becoming increasingly irate as we haven't taken our seats. Thai restaurants are always extremely neat. Chris and I are making things appear untidy.

Chris orders a carafe of wine by shaking an empty one. He must have arrived early. He then sends the waiter away, saying that we need some time before we order. In fact I'd like to order right away. I've hardly eaten today. I had genuine first date nerves, which Daisy and Connie were thrilled about. While I still waver about whether or not I want to be out on the scene again, I have felt more comfortable with the idea of dating Chris than I did Kevin. At least I chose to spend time with Chris. The wine arrives and the waiter pours two generous beakers. The glassware is exactly like that used at school when I was a girl, which no doubt is trendy now and I'm simply not in the know. I miss the traditional wineglasses with a delicate stem. Chris has knocked his drink back before I've even had time to suggest a toast.

I see.

Chris starts to talk. He's amusing but not hilarious. His anecdotes are mostly about his amazing group of friends, who really do sound wonderful. From what I glean, each and every one of them is witty, sporty and successful. He tells tales where he appears ridiculous, which is endearing and, in this case, a show of confidence. He even remembers to ask me the odd question and, more often than not, he waits for the answer before he carries on. I have to admit, I'm having a perfectly pleasant time. Chris is amusing and charming. If not a little manic. But, after a while, I find it impossible to ignore the fact that some of the stories don't quite fit together. I'm not certain of the sequencing of events, or the names of his "best friends"; the same name never pops up twice. Besides this, Chris purports to have lived in several foreign countries. If he is to be believed, he must be about ninety-four now.

I think of the empty ironing basket and tell myself I don't care. So he stretches the truth a bit; the artistic licence no doubt has something to do with the fact that he's drunk enough to sink a ship. He's entertaining and I've always allowed charming people more liberties than is sensible. However, after forty-five minutes I'm so hungry that the orchid in the vase on the table is beginning to seem a tempting *hors d'oeuvre*.

"Should we order?" I suggest. "I've been watching other diners enjoy their dishes and everything looks mouth-watering."

"Can do."

Chris doesn't seem to share my keenness for food although he's clearly partial to the odd glass. He asks for yet another carafe, joking that they appear small (they're not), and then he orders food for both of us. I don't tend to object when someone does this, if they are more familiar with the restaurant than I am and have something in particular which they want to recommend. However, Chris's manner suggests he's chosen our meals carelessly. He asked for two of the first starters listed on the menu and two of the first

194

main courses. The waiter suggests some accompanying dishes. Chris agrees without thought and, once again, abruptly shoos the man away. I'd like to think it's because he wants to be alone with me but I'm too much of a realist.

There's a rare gap in conversation so I take the opportunity to ask, "What do you do, Chris?"

"Do?"

"For a living."

"Oh. This and that," he replies vaguely.

I'm not the sort of girl to demand a 75K salary from a date but I would rather Chris was a little more specific.

"Where do you do this and that?"

"In an office."

"Right." I'm unsure how to probe further without appearing rude.

"I'm the guy that times the sequences on traffic lights," says Chris as he pours himself another tumbler of wine. My glass is still full.

"So you are a town planner. You work for the council?"

"I suppose," replies Chris with a shrug and another big smile.

His casual attitude seems a little out of whack with his carefully crafted profile. I wonder if one of his witty friends helped him write it. It doesn't matter, but I remember that he claimed his reason for not meeting Ms Right was that he was too busy working and travelling, which suggests a more serious approach to his career than the one he's displaying now. Then again, maybe I've projected my ideas on to his profile. He hasn't *lied* to me. Chris nods towards my full glass and says, "Keep up."

This conversational track clearly bores him so I try another approach. "Have you had much response to your internet ad?" I ask boldly.

"Quite a lot. You are my third date, Rose."

"How am I faring?" I ask with a giggle. As I make the joke, the last thing I expect is a serious response. For a start, Chris hasn't been serious or considered about anything tonight, and secondly, who would really want to know where they stack up in this type of pageantry. But Chris chooses to take me at my word.

"You're doing fine, Rose. You're a bit uptight, but that's nerves, right? Nothing that a couple of glasses can't cure." I'm beginning to get the sense that Chris thinks there isn't anything that can't be cured by a couple of glasses, from common colds to murderous psychotic tendencies. "I bet we can have a few laughs. Hey? You're up for it, aren't you? I can tell. I'm good at reading people and you strike me as a bit of a goer underneath it all."

I want to laugh out loud. Never have I been so badly misjudged. I could take offence, and normally I would, but there is something liberating about Chris's careless attitude to life and I find I can't get cross with him.

Chris pours more drinks and starts to entertain me with stories about his last holiday to Canada. The conversation becomes increasingly difficult to follow. I'm no longer certain if Chris went to Canada last month or last year. Or if he travelled with friends or went to visit family. He's slurring his words and when the food arrives he can't scoop the rice into his mouth without dropping most of it on his lap. The experience is not dissimilar to eating with the twins.

Eventually he decides that coordinating chat, food and alcohol is too much. He's finding it difficult to focus on anything — a train of thought or a khao soy. He surrenders.

"Tell me about yourself, Rose," he says with another slack and charming smile.

I realize that it hardly matters what I say. The guy is one step away from comatose and not poorer company for the fact. He's not an aggressive drunk or a violent, obnoxious or angry drunk. He's more of a sleepy drunk. His eyelids seem to be lead weights. I feel motherly towards him. I also know that our relationship, such as it is, is going nowhere. I'm not planning on seeing Chris again. Although I imagine if I did we could have another perfectly pleasant evening, perhaps even the same perfectly pleasant evening because he is unlikely to remember much about tonight and we could do exactly the same thing all over again. No harm done. But not much progress either. This evening, or a repeat of it, does not take me far enough away from the empty ironing basket.

And isn't that what it's all about? Progress. Oughtn't tonight to be about us getting to know one another a smidgen better? Obviously it's not going to be. Chris isn't giving much away, and even if I spilled the entire contents of my heart he would not keep the facts in mind and might very well pass me on the street tomorrow and fail to recall me at all. He's clearly a nice enough guy; nice enough for his friends to take the trouble to write a convincing profile and post it on the internet in an attempt to find him someone who'll care for him. But he's a drunk, and as such not someone I would ever consider bringing into my life or the life of my boys.

"Come on, Rose. Don't hold back on me. Tell me all about yourself." Chris has a blob of green curry sauce on his chin. It's a little distracting.

All about me.

"I'm divorced. I have twin boys, they are seven, eight in December. My husband left when they were fifteen months."

I normally say my husband and I split up when the boys were . . . etc. etc. It's much more sanitized. It doesn't blame Peter quite so much. But I dispense with the nicety. Chris is too drunk to notice the distinction.

"Must have been tough," slurs Chris.

This is the stock response, because of course everyone knows that it's not an ideal situation. Normally I comment that these things are often for the best and that we are all managing marvellously, that we all get on very well, etc. etc. Tonight I can't be bothered.

"Yes," I admit. "It was. It is."

"Did he meet someone else?"

Chris asks this question in a way which gives the impression that he could not care less about the answer. No doubt he's dated a number of divorcees in

198

the past and he knows the script. I find his indifference strangely inviting; less threatening than the probing sincerity of the women who used to invite me for coffee and wave a box of tissues. I felt confiding in them was an imposition. They cared too much.

"Yes, he did."

"Of course."

"She was a close friend of mine. Although I never really liked her."

Chris is drinking when I make this observation and he splutters his wine as he laughs. "That sort of female friendship. I see."

I have the good grace to grin and then I try to explain. "She was a friend of my sister's, really. Someone in our gang. She used to have Christmas lunch at our house but I've always found her intimidating. Everyone does. She's beautiful, wealthy, well connected and clever."

"Sounds awful," mumbles Chris.

I smile that he's generous enough to joke. Most men would have asked for her telephone number. "Once she decided she wanted him I guess it was inevitable. Just a matter of time."

"You blame it all on her."

"No, I blame him too. I think he's a spineless, opportunistic, selfish bastard."

I cannot believe I have just said that. It's so against the party line. When Peter first left everyone was angry with him. I couldn't bear to hear the things people wanted to say about him. I excused Peter. I said that he was better suited to Lucy and that I was wrong for him.

199

I've always tried to be fair and nice. But God, it's *such* a strain. I find describing him in such derogatory terms quite refreshing.

"The assaults on my dignity didn't stop when he left. Next I had to endure their lavish white wedding. A church wedding! The same vows repeated! Then they called their daughter Auriol. Can you believe that?"

"Awful name," mumbles Chris.

"Lovely name!"

"Oh right. Then, sorry, but what was the problem exactly?"

"It was my name! The name Peter and I had settled on if I had ever had a daughter. I seethed, but there have been so many occasions since the divorce when I felt I might implode with anger."

"So you told them you were bothered, right?"

"No. I reminded myself of that Aesop's fable about the sun and wind arguing to see who was the strongest. The matter was settled when the wind could not blow the cloak off a stubborn traveller but the sun shone and the guy voluntarily disrobed."

"Er, sorry, who were you trying to get to undress?"

Chris is trying to listen but he's struggling to understand. The best part of three litres of wine tends to have that effect. It doesn't matter, he's just the sort of audience I need right now.

"I heard the story as a child and it's remained with me. Maybe I'd have benefited from a good blow now and again. I didn't show my anger, I just smiled at my ex-husband, who was now intimately acquainted with another woman's gynaecology, and said, 'Lovely name.' I played with the idea of adding, 'I've always liked that name,' because Lucy would know exactly what that meant. After all, Lucy is a woman (among other things). But I held my tongue. More wine?"

Chris turns out to be the perfect companion. He doesn't mind that I skitter from one story to the next or that I get frustrated, wistful or weepy. I assume this is because as a drunk he's used to helter-skeltering from one emotion to another. I talk about Peter and Lucy for most of the evening. I talk about how resentful I feel. How betrayed. How put-upon. I realize that I am breaking a golden date rule by ranting about my ex but I don't care. For once I have the courage to dismiss the rule book.

At eleven-thirty we stagger out of the restaurant. Chris is barely in a fit state to remember his address, let alone invite me back for "coffee". This suits me, I'd have declined anyway. I help him into a cab, smile fondly and wave as he pulls away. He manages to wave back, in a rather limp fashion, before he passes out. I hail another cab and as I settle into my seat I mentally assess the evening. I give it a six out of ten, maybe even a seven. My date with Kevin had not scored at all. Tonight was progress. Walking out of that restaurant tonight, I felt two stone lighter. It was so wonderful to be able to talk freely, honestly and without interruption. I've never been able to talk to Connie or Daisy that truthfully; my pain would have upset them too much.

I enjoyed the freefall of speaking my mind and I make a note that I must recommend Susanne goes on a date with Chris. It's much cheaper than seeing a therapist.

CHAPTER
TWENTY-ONE

Wednesday 4 October

John

I chose to meet on a Wednesday as there's no pressure attached to a Wednesday. Thursdays and Fridays are clearly date days. Mondays and Tuesdays are the days you use up putting in a bit of extra time at work or seeing someone you're not that bothered about. Wednesdays are neutral.

I arrive in good time. I have money on the fact that she'll be late but if she arrives before me she'll turn around immediately. I know she'll turn up. Once, at the very beginning, she ran away from me. After that she always ran towards.

I watch her stride into the pub. She's wearing her leather coat again but this time with heels. Good girl. She's in full make-up and looks great. Chin up, she scans the room; when she spots me, she frowns a little but heads straight over.

"Jesus, Greenie, of all the bars in all the world," I say as I lean to kiss her cheek. There's a moment where I think she might pull away but she doesn't.

"You've misquoted."

"I'm not one for detail."

"You never were."

It's great that we fall straight back into the sparring. I think I liked her mind just as much as her body. Before she turned psycho, that is. Then all I was interested in was her tits and bits.

"But us bumping into each other at the school gate is like something out of a film, isn't it?" I comment. "Like one of those great old black-and-white films where the protagonists' lives criss-cross over and over again. Like they were fated, or destined, or something." She looks sceptical, or at least wary. I'm warming to my theme. "It's fate, Greenie, that Craig is the headmaster at your kid's school."

"That or a horrible coincidence and a vile inconvenience. I guess it depends upon your viewpoint."

"Don't be like that. We were supposed to meet again." She always believed in fate. Despite her cool words I see her mentally struggling. She undoes her coat and sits down on the bar stool next to me. "You still believe in fate, don't you, babe? You always did in the past."

"As somebody once said, 'The past is a foreign country, they do things differently there.'"

Connie orders an orange juice and asks me what I want. I order a pint and a whisky chaser but insist on paying. I'd have preferred it if she'd ordered alcohol too. I was counting on her needing a drink. Her new confidence is somewhat disconcerting. Jesus, I hope she's not teetotal now. I mean, I like a challenge but that would be off-putting.

"Greenie, I have to say it, and don't take this the wrong way, you are looking hot, babe." I lean forward and let my knee nudge hers. I feel a jolt of sexual tension, which is cheering because I believe those things are always two-way.

Connie looks uncomfortable. She gets off her bar stool and drags it a few centimetres away from mine. I see the point she is making. Stevie Wonder would be able to see the point she's making.

"I'm not Greenie. I'm Constance Baker," she says primly. "You know, I was even when we met for the very first time."

"Not to me, you were always Greenie, always will be." This isn't true. I often think of her as Connie, or even Constance, but I've rarely called her that. Funny that first names appeared overly intimate back then, considering the other intimacies we shared.

"Could you call me Connie? Everybody does."

"But I'm not everybody, baby."

She stares at me coolly. I study her face and try to discern whether it's dislike I can see festering there. Or anger? Or disappointment? They are all a possibility.

"You're right, you're nobody," she says.

"No, darling, I'm your somebody and we both know it," I grin, unperturbed.

She looks indignant and snaps, "I don't know why I'm here."

"Yes, you do." I wink at her.

"No, I don't," she counters, firmly.

"Where else would you be?"

This question offers Greenie a choice. She can choose to interpret it at a purely basic level — a genuine enquiry about her busy schedule — thus breaking the obvious tension between us. Or she could choose to interpret it as a more metaphysical question. Where else should Greenie be except by the side of her Hardie? If she wants to flirt she'll opt for the latter.

"I have a million things I should be doing. Invoicing, watching *The Bill*, ironing."

OK, if that's the way she wants to play it, I won't push her. I interrupt her before she lists darning socks as an essential must do.

"Oh yeah, you're a mother now. How's all that working out for you? What have you got? A girl and a boy? The set?"

"Two girls. You met them, remember?" I do remember but I want to give the impression of disinterest. "We might try for a third soon," she adds.

Women say this sort of thing as code for, "We are happy. My husband and I have a healthy sex life. Back off." It's not always true.

"Bloody hell, Greenie. What's the plan? Are you trying to single-handedly populate West London?"

She's looking good on it though, motherhood suits her.

Connie has a thinner face now than before. Age does that to some women. Her skin is almost transparent, she looks delicate. Age has not withered her, etc. etc. She's a regular Cleopatra, more stunning with the years that pass. She used to be cocky and flirty and that was irresistible then. Now, she's deeper. More complete, and it shows in her face. And I find her oddly compelling. I could look at her for hours.

"Let me buy you a proper drink, Connie. A bottle of champagne. For old times' sake."

She looks at her orange juice with something approaching despair, certainly boredom — an expression that regularly used to flash across Connie's face.

"Go on then. I'll have one glass. But it's not for old times' sake. It's to celebrate the fact you've just called me Connie."

I ignore her request for a glass and order a bottle. She used to be known as "Green the Champagne Queen". She can't resist champagne. In fact, Connie is pretty hopeless at resisting anything much at all.

She takes a sip of champagne and then she's off. Like a horse out of the traps, she gallops on; I'm barely able to keep up. She starts to chat about motherhood, as she's taken my casual enquiry to be a genuine request for insight. She talks about her photography. She fills me in on what a couple of her mates are doing, ones I came across way-back-when. She mentions her husband from time to time, quite naturally, as though she does not remember that between us we made him a cuckold. She doesn't ask me anything at all. Can she be that disinterested?

I used to be a bit afraid of her. Can you imagine that? Me afraid? Problem was I saw her for exactly what she was. Too like me. Too wild and selfish. She used me just as much as I used her, although she'd never admit it. It doesn't sit with her romantic image of herself. I wanted to possess her firm ass and tiny tits. Like I want to possess most firm asses and tiny titties that I come across — it doesn't mean anything — I'm programmed that way. She wanted something to perk up her middle-class existence. The early days of her marriage were stultifying and she wanted to shake up her dope of a husband, who had lost sight of her. I often thought that's all I was to her, a big yellow warning card issued to her husband.

And yeah, we had the laughs. She was funny, in a mental sort of way, and that really can be a turn-on. And Jesus, wow, she really was fairly unique with her happy confidence to do just about anything in the sack. Or out of the sack, for that matter. She was far braver than I. Happy to drop to her knees in a back alley if I expressed a whim to wear my trousers around my ankles. I don't usually have the balls for that sort of stuff unless I'm drunk. But then, we were often drunk. Thing is, I'm a victim of slum prudery. The old-school working classes have quite high morals on public sex and that sort of stuff. We don't take that type of personal risk. We prefer our porn in the privacy of our own pad. It's only total louts and chavs that fuck in bars in Ibiza. But Connie isn't a chav. Never was. It wasn't sleazy, it was necessary. Instinctual. Animalistic.

But did she ever love me? I keep returning to that. Bloody Craig. I'd never thought about it. Not really. What bloke does? But now I can't get his question out of my head. And I want to know. I want to know if Connie ever loved me. I *need* to know. What the fuck's that about?

It doesn't matter. It really doesn't. What difference does it make if she fell for me with her head *and* her heart, too? I got a free pass to her wet and willing vag, didn't I? But recently I've found myself wondering, could I have tamed a woman like her? That's what women try (and fail) to do all the time, isn't it? They find a bad boy, fall for him (because he is intrinsically bad) and then spend forever convincing themselves that they alone can hammer out the deviant and turn him into some pussy-whipped shadow. I know loads of birds have tried that game on me, including my ex-wife. I've always thought it was the ultimate in stupidity. I've always pitied and been disgusted by their clingy, crappy wish to be normal, to settle down, but now I'm finding myself understanding it a little more.

Connie is a bright woman, creative, fiery, difficult to please, and now I see her oozing contentment and genuine shiny, bloody happiness and I wonder could I have ever brought that to her? Could I have made her give up the flirting and the risk-taking, the way Luke did? I always think of him as some big sap. But maybe he is the better man. Maybe she chose him.

I dumped Connie, right. I want that noted in our history. She was all clingy and addicted and messy. Too messy actually, which is why I had to say enough is enough. One night she rang me eight times. I'd said I'd see her, told her to meet me at my place and she couldn't find my flat or something. She'd never written down my address and she'd never arrived there sober. Jesus, the messages she left on my phone — a madwoman. In one message she accused me of shagging someone else while I waited for her, like I'd have the energy for that! In another message she sounded close to tears. In another she was shouting hysterically, yelling that she wouldn't be avoided; insisting that I had to call her back and tell her where the flat was. In her eighth message she changed tack and said coolly that although I was a good fuck, I wasn't that good (which is a lie) and she wasn't prepared to drive around East London all evening trying to track me down.

Silly cow.

She'd managed to have a full row with me, go through the entire spectrum of emotions, without my actually picking up the phone.

Yet there were times when I sent her texts, flirty, jokey ones or ones asking her to meet up, and she never even replied. Cool cucumber or mad as a hatter? Thin line.

We had big talks. Some of the things she said to me will stay with me forever. They were so precise. They caught the essence of me, so there were times when I thought she knew me better than anyone in this world has ever known me. Even myself. She seemed to be able to mine a direct line to my deepest insecurities, my strongest passions, the moments I am intensely proud of and those that make me squirm in shame.

I felt known. And liked.

And then other times she didn't have a clue.

After about an hour of her constant chatter and my odd interjection where I bring her up to date about the things in my life, I note that we've drunk the entire bottle of champagne. Now seems as good a time as any.

"Were you in love with me, Connie?" I ask.

She immediately pulls away from me and is wearing an expression I'd expect if I'd just spat at her.

I've been thinking about how to phrase this question all week. I considered asking, "Did you love me?" But dismissed that approach as too vague. It would then be so easy for her to spit out the standard response, "I loved you but I wasn't *in love* with you." A great loophole, which means shit. I know I've used it on more than one occasion. I could have asked, "Were you *ever* in love with me?" But that sounds a bit desperate. Or a statement: "I know you were in love with me." Too arrogant, and it doesn't specifically necessitate a response. She sighs. Her face is full of fear (who is she afraid of, me, herself, Luke?) and regret (Oh so many regrets, rammed cheek by jowl, where to start?) but if I look carefully her face also shines with opportunity. Has she waited six years for me to ask that question? Probably.

We never talked about love. We talked about sex, desire, experience, films, families, dreams, all the stuff that is used as consolations and props and avoidance techniques as we live our lives and especially when we lie in strangers' beds. Tangled in sheets and sweat, we screamed "fuck me", "shag me", "shit that's good". But we never said the really filthy four-letter word. Love.

She does not meet my gaze. People often say liars can't meet your gaze. In the company I keep it's telling the truth that often shames us the most.

"My friends think I was in lust," she says. Her voice sounds unfamiliar, she's breathing too shallowly.

"You've never been one to bend to peer pressure," I point out, digging deeper and complimenting her independence of spirit at the same time. Connie is vain and responds as I hoped.

"No, I'm not."

"So?"

She waits and waits. About a million years, then, "Yes. I was in love with you."

Now she can meet my eye. The words are out. The truth is out. She's staring at me now, challenging. Waiting for my response. I don't say anything, so she goes on.

"I was deeply in love with you for a very short time. I experienced the whole shebang. I could not sleep, or eat, or work." She says these things very slowly. Normally she speaks too quickly, gabbling her words. But she wants to be as plain and clear as possible. Her chest rises and falls. "You were my waking thought, my last thought; you filled all the moments in between and my dreams. For a brief time there was nothing I would not have done for you, including perhaps leaving my husband." I believe her. "You talked about fate earlier, John, and you are right, I do believe in fate. You were supposed to come into my life. You changed everything. You woke me up. I was sleepwalking until Paris. I was living a half life. Not seeing what I had. Not knowing what I wanted."

I've heard it all before, but never from these lips and as I watch her lips (pink, plump and wet) tip out this confession my cock stirs, almost shudders. And more unusual yet, there's a tightening in my chest. I wonder whether I should kiss her. I watch her lips move. Temptingly. Tauntingly? What's she saying now?

"But that was then and this is now. You completely destroyed what I felt. I'm not in love with you any more and I never will be again."

She stares at me with the gaze of one who owns an uncomplicated soul. Where has her tortured soul gone? When did she work everything out? When did she still the longings and find the answers? Why haven't I yet? A wave of excitement begins to slosh over me. It starts at my toes and seems to swell and build until, by the time it rises to my chest, it overpowers me.

I watch Connie gather up her bag. She fishes out some notes from her purse and leaves them on the bar, insisting that this bottle of champers is on her. She walks out of the bar with the jaunty step of a free woman. She thinks she has just closed a chapter. She's finally had the opportunity to say her piece after it festering for years. She thinks she's just got even. She's generous enough to be happy that she's paid me the compliment and I'm that bit closer to knowing and understanding her. Women have complicated thoughts like that. And she's thrilled that now it's all over.

But she's wrong.

By admitting she was in love with me, she has not slammed shut the door and drawn the bolt, as was her intention. Instead, she's just pushed the door ajar. Opportunity scuttles in like a determined cockroach.

If she was once in love with me, she can be in love with me again. And now, for the first time in a long time, I know what I want. What I need. What I must have. Connie.

CHAPTER
TWENTY-TWO

Thursday 5 October

Lucy

"We should go on holiday," says Peter.

There, that's why I love him. He knows me so well. He's always with me. No, he's a step ahead of me. A holiday is just what we need.

"Alone," I say. I'm trying to remember when we last got away alone and I mean truly alone, without nannies or Auriol, or the twins or even a BlackBerry. Peter has wandered through to the bathroom and is splashing water on his face to remove the day's grime. He clearly hasn't heard me.

He says, "Auriol will love it."

Fuck what Auriol will love. Auriol would love staying at home with Eva if we left her enough DVDs and Smarties. I realize that this would be a terrible thing to say to Peter so I try another tack.

"Do you remember the Maldives?" I call through to the bathroom.

"Oh God, yes, it was beautiful there. I loved the Maldives."

We went a year before Auriol was born. We stayed at the Banyan Tree. It was beautiful, relaxed, spoiling and sophisticated. I spent the entire holiday wearing skimpy bikini bottoms and not much else. That was when cellulite was still something that only other women had to worry about.

Peter re-emerges from the en-suite, sits on the edge of the bed and takes off his socks; he starts to cut his toenails. I hate it when he does this in the bedroom. I've spent a great deal of time and effort creating a love haven but no amount of chocolate velvet throws, walnut floorboards and slate-grey lacquer consoles can battle against the reality of treading on toenail clippings. It's a passion-killer, no questions. Before we married I never saw him cut his toenails. Or sniff his armpits. Or scratch his bollocks. Or check for dandruff. He had standards. I push this extremely irritating line of thought to the back of my head and try to concentrate on wangling the holiday I desire. At all costs I must avoid a week at the middle-class equivalent of Butlins, an all-inclusive break at Center Parcs *en famille*.

I kneel behind him on the bed and wrap my arms around his neck. I'm wearing matching Agent Provocateur bra and pants and a short silk wrap — he must have noticed. If he hasn't, he certainly will when the Visa statement arrives.

"It was so hot in the Maldives, I hardly had to pack a thing," I whisper into his ear.

Peter thinks about it and then a slow smile stretches across his face. He's taken the bait and chosen a jaunt down Memory Lane. No doubt he is remembering

216

undoing the side ties of my bikini bottoms with his teeth, as we made love on the private beach our rooms backed on to. Men are very simple.

I start to nibble his ear. I can almost hear the sea lapping the shore as I remember his kisses. Back then, they still varied in intensity, hastening from dreamy to devilish. Nowadays kissing stays pretty neutral; I sometimes have to remind him to use his tongue. And we didn't worry about the sand getting in uncomfortable places, or being spotted, or being bitten by mosquitoes. In those days we never worried about anything much. If I close my eyes now I can almost feel his careful caress, the exciting frisson. In the Maldives we made love on the beach, in the hotel room and on the veranda and we made honest love. We honestly made love.

I clearly remember Peter confidently and expertly easing me from one position to the next, leaving me feeling fragile and cherished, while making him appear vigorous and robust; a cliché but a delicious one. Of course he was stronger then, no sign of a paunch. In those days he dared to confidently drag his T-shirt over his head in one, swift, practised movement. Now he's more likely to want to turn off the light; he often sleeps in pyjamas.

God, I feel hot just thinking about how it used to be. Remembering him and how he used to be. I wish he'd stop cutting his toenails and just turn to me and cup my breast in the cool, confident way he used to. I wouldn't even make him wash his hands, despite the fact that he's been touching his feet. I just long for his fingers to wander over my body again, to find the hottest place between my legs and to push upwards to reclaim me, to reignite me.

I start to kiss his neck. Sod the holiday; we can talk about that later. What I need now is Peter. My Peter, the one who anticipates where I'd like to be touched next and knows the exact pressure I'd like him to apply. I need him to make me grunt, and growl, and moan.

Suddenly Peter is kissing my lips. And I mean kissing. He pushes hard, sensing my urgency and the fact that, in this instance, I want a certain amount of authority from him. He pushes me back on to the bed and climbs astride me. He pulls my robe apart and sits back to admire the view.

"You are so sexy," he mutters.

Finally, the penny has dropped. Yes, I am. He'd do well to remember as much and I don't just mean once a fortnight. I pull his face back down to mine and start to kiss him again. I gently chew his lips and probe with my tongue. I feel his cock solid against my body. He's clearly eager to go. I'm tempted to ask him to simply ride me hard and now. I so want to feel him inside me again, it's been far too long, but I resist. I tantalize to increase his longing and mine. I want to please. To be desired. To desire and then to fuck.

His kisses sear my lips — each one dissolves a jot of resentment or tension between us. I feel myself falling into the moment and it's a glorious moment. I close my eyes and my mind and open my legs. I feel my limbs stretch and flex, ready to push and pull and fuel desire. I can smell my own cum. It smells fantastic. Raw and brave and young. It smells like chances and our history and the future.

He licks, strokes and eventually strikes with the exact precision to leave me gasping, grateful, powerless, powerful. Sex, when executed correctly, can be the most complex contradiction; a daily mystery. We ride firm and fast and then change gear to luxuriate in the lust. I cling to him. Like a monkey, I wrap my legs tightly around his waist. We roll on our sheets, over and over and over again. Our limbs become tangled as we grab and grasp at one another, desperate to consume one another, to gorge and to satiate. Sweat runs down his back and slips between his buttocks, making his skin look like the luminous treasure I know it to be. I chase the stream with my pointed tongue. I come again and again. And with each delicious wave of ecstasy the weeks of frustration are forgotten and the gap between us is washed away.

He howls and then falls off me.

See, we can still do it with style and meaning.

I wish this hadn't been my first thought.

Peter beams at me. I try to focus, something I struggle with if I orgasm violently. "So I should book us all a holiday?"

"Yes," I agree, with a broad grin. Men are so simple.

CHAPTER
TWENTY-THREE

Thursday 5 October

Rose

The school hall is, as usual, horribly cold and draughty. There are six mothers gathered in the hall; as we chat to one another our breath billows in the air. Lyn Finch jokes that we look like a gang of dragons. We, the class reps who make up the Parents' Association, always arrive earlier than the governors. I suppose the businessmen and the vicar are busier with more important things to attend to, or at least they like to give that impression. The majority of class reps are the type of mums that have not been able or not wanted to go out of the home to work and can no longer remember when something could be considered more important than these meetings and all that they represent.

Mr Walker, bless him, always tries to be on time, preferring to throw his lot in with the mums, rather than the men, on the committee. We're all particularly fond of him because of this consideration and many others. Today when he bustles into the freezing hall, clapping his hands together in an attempt to keep warm, I hardly recognize him. He's had his hair cut. He now wears a style which suits him and adds to his attractiveness, whereas before his hair fulfilled a more functional role — it gave his hat a target.

"Mr Walker's wearing new clothes," whispers Lyn Finch.

He's got rid of his hacking jacket with the patches on the elbows and has ditched the brown cords. He's wearing French Connection trousers and a Ted Baker top.

"He must have a girlfriend," she adds.

"Why do you say that?" I ask. I'm irritated. How come Mr Walker can just waltz out and get himself a new partner when I'm failing miserably? Life is easier for men. Fact.

"Well, he's rather lovely, isn't he? Very kind, great smile. I'd imagine lots of women would class him as quite a catch, except his dress sense used to be dire and gave the impression that he collected model aeroplanes. Some bright young woman has spotted his potential and realized that clothes do make the man — all she had to do to upgrade him was pop to High Street Kensington."

I don't like Lyn Finch's line of thinking. Mr Walker's girlfriend shouldn't be trying to alter him — he's perfectly lovely as he is. Why do people have to go around changing things? Haircuts? Clothes? Marital status? Why can't people leave well alone?

"Is it just me, or is it cold in here?" asks Mr Walker.

"It is a bit nippy," I confirm.

"How old do you think he is?" whispers Lyn.

"I don't know — thirty-three, thirty-five at tops."

"He always sounds like someone's dad. 'Is it me or is it cold in here?' " she mimics. "I bet he's the sort of man who always asks about parking before he goes anywhere and he probably has a shed."

I always ask about parking before I go anywhere and I have a shed, so I don't understand Lyn's point.

"The Vicar, Mr Jones and Mr Watkinson have all sent their apologies. I wonder, without them, can we squeeze into my office? It's much warmer there," says Mr Walker.

"Are you being rude about the size of the gentlemen's girths, Mr Walker?" asks Lyn. She can't resist teasing him.

I think she ought to have more respect. He's young, yes, but he is the headmaster. Besides, with this new haircut he finally looks more manly. It's not that the haircut has aged him — it's more that it's unearthed a new presence that presumably was there all along but hidden under the bowl-cut, circa 1979.

Presence aside, Mr Walker blushes. "No, no, of course not."

The governors are extraordinarily fat. They look like characters from a Charles Dickens novel; the sort who run orphanages on a shoestring and gobble the profits.

"You must call me Craig, at these meetings. Mr Walker is so formal."

"Righto, Craig," laughs Lyn. "You can call me Mrs Finch."

Poor Mr Walker. He blushes again but marches us all out of the hall towards his office, with something akin to grim determination. He *is* young to hold such a position. When he was appointed a number of parents tested his resolve. They questioned his decisions on everything from uniform, to timetable changes, to the shape of the sports day trophy. The general belief was that he had to show he could keep the parents in check, because if not, how could he be expected to handle the children's backchat? It was all rather exhausting and depressing to watch until it became clear that somehow Mr Walker does manage everything quite nicely. And now the parents are all fond and proud of him.

The Head's office is a far more pleasant venue for a school governors' meeting, although in the absence of external governors this meeting now ought to really be described as a Parents' Association meeting. Today we are meeting to discuss whether it's practical to introduce cooked school lunches, an issue which needs the attention of the governors but grips the heart of the parents, on or off the association. As such we are unlikely to find a resolution today but it doesn't stop us chewing over the issue.

"The question is can we afford the significant investment required to employ outside caterers?"

"We must find the money. The advantage of the children having a hot meal in cold weather can't be overvalued," says Lesley Downes, mother of Joe, Year Two.

"And mums wouldn't be challenged daily to come up with something creative for the lunchbox," says Lyn. "Anything that means a job less for me gets my vote."

223

"Yes, but at least if you pack their lunch you know what they are eating. School meals receive such bad press, and unless we get Jamie Oliver to pop to Holland Park every lunchtime to check nutritional content, few of us have much faith in the quality of food made by external caterers," I point out.

"True, I don't like the idea of my Katie and Tim eating chicken's claws and bollocks and such," says Wendy Pickering.

I shuffle uncomfortably. Why does Wendy Pickering always have to lower the tone? I don't think there's any need for that sort of language, especially in front of the headmaster. It'll embarrass him.

"No, Wendy, of course not. None of us want to see the children eating bollocks, since it will only serve as an excuse for why so many of them spout it," says Mr Walker, with a grin.

Wendy smiles back. She thinks he's a bit stuck up and she's still testing him. I think he's just passed.

"Now without the governors we can't definitively resolve this one. But it's an important issue and I feel we ought to progress it. I think we ought to allow a number of catering companies to pitch to us. Say three or four? We could ask them to present menus and costing plans and if we are impressed by any of them, we can meet them and test the food."

"Are you suggesting taking us six women out for lunch?" laughs Wendy. "There'll be talk. I can see the headline now: orgies at Holland House, womanizing headmaster caught spanking mothers who put their elbows on the table at mealtimes."

224

Really, she's too much.

"Six women, and the Vicar and good Mr Watkinson and Mr Jones," laughs Mr Walker. "Let them talk. Print and we'll sue."

"I think we should follow Mr Walker's suggestion. Nothing ventured, nothing gained," I say, trying to drag the meeting back on to a more formal note. Clearly the lack of outside influence has had a detrimental effect on the proceedings and I don't like things to be slapdash.

We move on to the subjects of the firework display and the Christmas party. The firework party is organized, as there is an extremely efficient subcommittee dealing with it (I'm on that committee). Today we just have to hand out schedules detailing everyone's duties for the evening. However, the Christmas party is looking shambolic; nothing is booked, not the venue, the DJ, the caterer or even glass hire. I'm panicked about this and think we should have addressed the issue on the first day of term. No doubt all the decent venues will be taken now, and yet it's impossible to get the committee to see the urgency of making a decision.

"Why don't we have it at school? It will save spending money on hiring a venue and then we can spend a bit extra on the food and drink."

"We can't get a licence to serve alcohol on the premises; we've tried before," I point out.

"We should hire a hall," suggests Lyn Finch.

"Halls are too impersonal. It would remind me of being a teenager again and going to the local youth club disco," says Lesley Downes with a mock shiver of horror.

"I don't know that that's a bad thing. I'd quite like someone to try to stuff their hand down my bra and for me to get a high from half a pint of cider," says Wendy Pickering. "It takes so much more nowadays."

How did this woman ever get voted to be class rep? I cough, embarrassed for Mr Walker, but he's grinning. Such a good sport.

"What about a restaurant?"

"It gets costly and no one is ever happy with the way the bill is divided."

"How about hosting it in one of our homes?"

"Well, whose house is big enough?"

Lucy's might be but they'd have to drag out my fingernails before I'd admit as much. There is no way I'm allowing her to become the hostess with the mostest. The last thing I want is for her to have a reputation for generosity stretching across the school. And she would go to town, embrace the whole school Christmas party as though she were entertaining the Queen, just to spite me.

The debate regarding venue flows for about forty minutes. Every time somewhere appears to be agreed upon, someone or other comes up with an objection.

"I got food poisoning last time I ate there."

"They don't have a late licence."

"I'd like somewhere with a dance floor."

"The loos are filthy."

"How about we hire the upstairs of the Ship pub? You know, on Lottfield Road," I suggest. "The food is decent and reasonably priced. There's a small dance floor. We'd be able to let out hair down. We can buy our own drinks, so that personal budgets can be managed."

I realize that I've come up with a decent idea when no one says a word. No doubt everyone is searching for an objection (more fun than searching for a solution, often as not) but they can't uncover one.

"I take that silence to be agreement," says Mr Walker. "Good. Brilliant idea, Mrs Phillips."

I feel extremely pleased to be praised by Mr Walker. This must date back to my being a girly swot, when I lived for the praise of my teachers. However, I can't help feeling a little offended that Mr Walker called me Mrs Phillips. Not Rose. He calls Wendy, Wendy and Lyn, Lyn. But he maintains a formality with me. Does he think I'm some sort of geriatric and therefore I command the respect of a title? How infuriating.

We agree some action points regarding who should book the venue, hire the DJ and communicate with the parents, and then the meeting draws to a close. Lyn and Lesley rush off, as they do Pilates on a Thursday night. Wendy Pickering says she needs to dash because she wants to get to Tesco's. The other two mums are going to the cinema as they've got a late pass. They invite me along but I don't want to take advantage of Daisy.

Mr Walker and I find ourselves left alone to wash cups and return the chairs to the classrooms we borrowed them from.

"Good of you to stay behind and help, Mrs Phillips."

"No problem. I have a few minutes and many hands make light work." I carefully replace the mugs in the staffroom cupboard. Despite a thorough wash they are all stained with years of tea drinking. They need to be soaked in Steradent.

"You came up with some great suggestions at that meeting. There were moments I thought we'd still be debating the venue for the Christmas party until past the Lent term."

I smile. "The same thought passed my mind."

"Thanks for backing me up on the school meals, too. I appreciate your support."

"No problem."

"You are always so much help, Mrs Phillips. If there is anything I can ever do for you in return, don't hesitate to let me know."

I look at the beaming young man. It's past six and I'm surprised to note his chin is shadowed with whiskers. In this light he looks quite rugged. Noting this comes as a bit of a surprise, as the image I have of him is eternally boyish.

"You could do something for me."

"Name it."

"You could stop calling me Mrs Phillips."

"But you call me Mr Walker, even though I'm always asking you to call me Craig." He blushes. Poor man, it must be a curse to be a man that blushes, particularly when you're faced with 250 kids every morning. Although a bit of colour suits him. It shows up his sparkly blue eyes to quite an advantage. I wonder what he looks like with a tan. I can't remember. He must have had one last summer, I just never noticed.

"OK, I'll call you Craig, if you call me Rose."

"I'd love to. Great name. I've always liked it."

"Was it your mother's?" I ask.

"No." Craig looks confused.

I laugh. "Sorry. I think I'm getting paranoid. Yesterday I was pulled over by the traffic police because one of my brake lights was broken. The younger policeman was so thoroughly polite and charming. He clearly took a shine to me. It struck me that I must have reminded him of his mum."

"He probably fancied you, Rose." Now it's my turn to blush. Craig notices and is mortified. "Sorry. I shouldn't have said that. None of my business. I'm clearly mixing with Wendy Pickering too much." He's trying to joke but he's still scarlet. "I just meant if a guy is nice to you it doesn't necessarily mean that you remind him of his mother." Craig turns away and starts to gather up the papers that are scattered on his desk. He knows that he's been a little over-familiar and he's nervous that he's offended me.

"Actually, I went on a date with a younger man recently." I bravely offer this fact to let him know I'm not offended. We're both adults after all. The school bell rang long ago, surely we can have a grown-up conversation after hours?

"Really? Was it fun?"

"Not especially. Kevin swore a lot and was rude to me. If I'd wanted that I could have gone cycling in rush hour."

Craig laughs and I'm encouraged beyond my normal strict boundaries. "It was a blind date. Then I met an alcoholic through internet dating. It's my friends' idea. They are worried about me."

And so they should be. I seem to have lost my mind. What on earth made me tell Mr Walker — Craig — that? I don't want him to think I'm the sort of mother who desperately trails the net looking for sex, like some porn addict.

"I see." He nods, and there's something about him that suggests that I have not shocked him and that he really does understand. But how could he? He's male and young. He's just got himself a new girlfriend. It's unlikely that his friends are desperate for him.

"It appears that if there's a man in his thirties who lives in London and is single, it's for a very good reason. He's too fond of a drink or he's psychotic, boring, a loser, a loony or a combination of all of the above," I announce.

"Oh, right," says Craig. Unaccountably he's blushing again.

"Still, in some ways it's better than sitting in on my own."

"Quite."

"And I've discovered the comfort of strangers is rather liberating." I hope this explains my verbal incontinence.

"Really."

"I'd better get going; my sister's babysitting the boys."

"Yes, yes, I mustn't keep you. It's been nice talking to you, Rose."

230

I smile and leave the headmaster's office. Over the years I've visited various headmasters' offices to be awarded gold stars and merits, which was always a thrill, but I've never left feeling quite as spectacular as I do this evening.

Peculiar.

CHAPTER
TWENTY-FOUR

Monday 9 October

Rose

"Where are you going?" Henry is standing in the doorway of my bedroom. Notably he's still not wearing his pyjamas, even though bathtime was over forty minutes ago and I've repeated my request that he gets into his pyjamas about a dozen times. He is dressed in an assortment of costumes including Woody's boots (the Sheriff, rather than the film director), Buzz's trousers, a policeman's jacket, a builder's tabard and, finally, Darth Vader's mask, which is propped at a jaunty angle on top of his head. He looks like a contender for a Village People tribute band.

Although the question is seemingly innocent enough, I know it's full of resentment and simmering anger so I choose to go on the attack, instead of responding directly.

"Why aren't you in your pyjamas? It's getting late."

In turn, Henry chooses to ignore my question and follows his own line of enquiry. I've noticed that our family can communicate for hours like this.

"Are you going out *again*?" He sounds like my father and he's rolling his eyes with a frightening similarity of manner. "You're *always* out." He's hanging on to the door handle with his full weight. I tell him not to loll and consider my defence.

It isn't true that I'm always out and yet, undoubtedly, my social life has been a veritable whirl since I started my mechanics course. I have been "out" on seven occasions in twenty days. Previous to that, on average, I'd manage seven trips out approximately every two and a half years. I've attended the mechanics course three times, twice staying late to have a coffee with Susanne and Helen, I've been "out" to a Parents' Association meeting, twice, and I've been on two dates. Tonight is my third date. I'm due to meet Ian. Ian was the only one of the eighteen responses to my internet profile that I was prepared to take seriously. Approximately sixteen of them contacted me to say "Get a life," although not always in such polite terms, one suggested I needed sex (ideally with him and specifically on Wednesday afternoons between two and three o'clock), and the final response was from Ian, who said he also has an interest in antiques.

Yes, this weekend I took the plunge and posted my own profile on to that webpage Connie found. What was it called? *www.youtoocanfindloveifyoulookhardenough.com*, or something like that. Connie insisted that it was the next logical step after responding to Chris's profile. Daisy pointed out that I had in fact found the date with Chris rather helpful. Luke reasoned that I would be in control if I placed a profile. Simon mumbled that I didn't have to answer any of them anyhow. It was Simon's argument that swung it for me.

Writing the profile was very difficult. Chris had told me that he'd found it tricky to reduce his life to a couple of paragraphs, but my problem was the opposite. I struggled to fill more than a couple of lines. Of course, it turned into a group effort so my dignity wasn't spared.

"I think you could pass for thirty-five which is practically early thirties so you should probably tick the 25–30-year-old box," said Connie, slicing more than a decade of my life away in one untruthful click.

Daisy bristled. "I think she should tell the truth. What sort of relationship can she have with anyone if it starts off with a deception?"

"There won't be any relationship if she admits to pushing forty," muttered Connie ominously. "At least not with a sexy man. She said she didn't want to be giving bed baths and pushing wheelchairs around Bournemouth, didn't she?"

"*She* did. Can you just remember I'm here?" I pointed out. "Look, I don't mind knocking a couple of years off my age if it helps," I said, surprising myself and the others.

"You'll only attract shallow men," warned Daisy. I don't believe there is any other kind so I'm not perturbed.

"OK, so what do you want to say about yourself?" asked Con. Bitter and twisted from Holland Park is accurate, but not, I fear, what she was after. I stayed silent. "OK then, what are you looking for in your ideal man?"

"I don't want a womanizer."

234

"They are unlikely to admit to that," Luke pointed out.

"I don't want a drinker, or a smoker or an actor." Connie started to type. "I don't want him to have too much baggage — no children or divorces. I don't want any ambivalence when it comes to sexuality. I so don't want to be the lifebuoy for a closet homosexual who can't tell his parents the score."

"You watch too much TV," said Daisy.

"I don't want anyone with food allergies, it's boring. I don't want anyone who still lives at home. I don't —"

"Are you sure a list of 'don't wants' is the best way to go about this?" asked Luke.

"All the men's profiles were quite specific about what they didn't want," I pointed out. "I don't want anyone who lives miles away; I can't bear long-distance relationships. I don't —"

Simon interrupted. "Isn't this supposed to be about you putting your personality forward?"

"She is putting her personality forward," said Daisy glumly. "Why don't you just cut to the chase and write, 'intolerant, judgemental thirty-something looking for an unrealistic ideal'?"

"That is so nasty," I countered with little passion or vehemence, because she was spot on and I don't tend to argue when I agree with a point. I leave that up to men.

Simon, Connie and Luke looked a little startled, no doubt wondering if a row was about to kick off, but Daisy is my sister and we've said much worse to one another over the years. Believe it or not, I know she means well.

"Perhaps it would help if we read some of the other female profiles, to give us an idea of the competition," suggested Connie.

It sounded like a good idea but, oh God, the women's profiles were heartbreaking. Unlike the men, who had largely gone down the overly demanding, offensively brash and boastful route, the women's profiles were self-deprecating, touching, desperate. The women had all included a photo. We are intelligent enough to know that no man will take a punt on a blind profile. Besides, it's better they know about the extra couple of pounds or the frizzy hair up front, rather than have to see the disappointment in their face if it gets as far as a date. They were all sorts of shapes and sizes. Many of the women were actively pretty; all were attractive, more attractive than the men on the site. The average age was thirty-two. This didn't bother me too much because I felt sure lots of the women were being forced into playing the numbers game; most looked as though they had once danced to Nick Kershaw and Paul Young. My guess was that they were on average four years older than they admitted to. Without exception each woman said she was cheerful and looking for honesty. Their incessant hunt for this quality suggested it was rarer than black diamonds and harder to mine.

There appeared to be two different types. Nervous, shy women who looked as though they wouldn't say boo to a goose (these women professed to be outgoing and humorous) and women who tried too hard — they struck semi-provocative poses or madcap I'm-a-wacky-girl poses (these women professed to be intelligent and sincere). None of the women seemed confident enough to say what they really were. Irrespective of the photo style all women claimed to be happy, which seemed unlikely to me.

The five of us silently read the profiles.

"You don't have to do it if you don't want to, Rose," said Connie. She was clearly uncomfortable grouping me in with their hopeful but hopeless cases. Articulating what we all know — that I'm just like them — was extremely painful.

"I want to do it," I said. And suddenly I was sure I did want to post up a profile.

"You do?" asked Daisy, not bothering to hide her disbelief.

"Yes." I didn't elaborate.

It was not that I was suddenly and miraculously desperately interested in attracting a man through this site (or indeed by any means, if push came to shove), but I had an overwhelming urge to show solidarity with these women. These brave and optimistic, wonderful, spirited women who still believed in honesty and still hunted for love deserved my support. I decided to put an absolutely truthful account of myself on the website and see what happened. Of course, I realized that an absolutely truthful account of myself was unlikely to attract anyone at all, but I would be doing the other women a favour. Even the weepy-looking lady from Wiltshire — who rather misguidedly described herself as "funny, decent and good" — looked like a sparkly offer by comparison.

"Why are you always leaving us?" asks Henry. As inaccurate and unfair as this observation is, it stings.

I crouch down next to him and steal a quick kiss. Open affection from the boys is now limited. They are growing up and away whether I like it or not. I have to accept it.

"Darling, Mummy hardly ever goes out. Practically never in seven years, that's why it seems as though I'm out a lot recently, but when you compare it with how often you are out at sports clubs or on play dates, it's really not so often."

I return to my seat at my dressingtable wondering how much make-up to apply. If I choose to go on the date wearing just lipstick will it give the impression that I'm über-confident or just lazy and lacking in self-respect? That's the horror of dating — nothing is simple, everything has meaning and significance, even down to how much lipstick I wear. I carefully apply a pale lipstick and mascara. I'll do. I turn to Henry, hoping he'll tell me I look pretty, as he sometimes does. He glares at me, still angry that I'm about to abandon him.

I hold my arms wide open to invite Henry in for a cuddle. He hesitates for a moment and then capitulates and throws his little body at me. The idea is for me to comfort him, but as he nuzzles into my shoulder I am calmed and reassured by the feel of his breath on my neck. I wonder whether I should bother with this date at all. Is it worth disrupting the boys? Is it worth hauling Daisy over from north London to babysit? Is it worth the effort of finding unladdered hosiery? Surely I could date in another ten years or so, when the boys are grown. That way I'd catch the freshly widowed market, a very respectable market to be in, much better than the tired divorcee market.

"Don't go," whispers Henry. "I'll miss you."

"But Auntie Daisy is coming to look after you."

"I know, but I want you to look after me."

I remember this scenario from over five years ago when I first attempted to date. The twins were less articulate in those days but they were able to clearly communicate their desire to have me around twenty-four/seven by screaming at full throttle whenever I left them with a sitter. If I was ever foolish enough to try to make a dash for the door they would cling to my skirt hem like leeches. They were so all-consuming and so needy I began to concede the battle before it was even fought, cancelling arrangements almost the minute I made them, rather than upset the boys by leaving them. The truth was I enjoyed being needed. And with Peter having made it so damn transparent that I was the last thing on earth he needed, I found the boys' clingy ways rather delightful. But a child is for life and not just for Christmas.

"OK, sweetheart. Mummy will stay in with you and Sebastian. Don't worry," I say, finally.

"Really?" Henry instantly brightens. "And can we watch Pop TV, pleeeese?"

I nod and sigh and pick up the phone. Ian sounds mildly disappointed when I explain I have babysitting problems. He mentions that he's been looking forward to showing me his antique pen nibs and old Rupert Bear annuals. I cannot bear Daisy's anger or irritation so I tell her that Ian cancelled. Her disappointment is acute, and while the boys and I have a very pleasant evening playing battleships and building Meccano models I can't help but share some of her regret.

CHAPTER
TWENTY-FIVE

Tuesday 10 October

John

I arrive at the school gate before eight o'clock, which is a damn awful time of day to be awake but a particularly sodding terrible time when you have a day's holiday. Normally it's my rule on holiday not to surface before midday. But I'm not sure what time kids go to school and as the school gate is the only form of contact I can guarantee with Connie, I make an effort. It would have been easier if I could have just rung her but I never kept her number. I can't even remember deleting it. She was that unimportant by the end. It's funny how casual we are with our pasts. I consider the hundreds of telephone numbers that have been passed to me and the times I have given out my number and yet there are only a couple of dozen friends' names that have actually made it into my address book. At Christmas I send fewer than ten cards.

I sit in my car and watch the harassed mothers come and go. Some of them are managing to keep up appearances and beam and wave to one another. A few look grim but determined as they drag reluctant kids through the gate. Others are out and out furious and are yelling at their kids to get a move on/pick up their bag/gloves/feet/stop hitting their sibling. One or two look distinctly anxious as their kid totters out of sight. The vast majority look as though they dream of a good night's sleep. I thank God I'm a man.

I mean one day I'll want to go in for all that having kids business. Jesus, it's pretty much my duty to pass on these fantastic genes. There was a time I thought I might have a kid with Andrea, but it wasn't to be — good thing as it happened. Connie no doubt thinks it's my destiny to be a Sunday father but that's not what I'm after. One day, when I'm ready for the kid thing, I'll do it and I'll be doing it for keeps.

Finally, I see Connie. I bide my time. I allow her to take her daughter into the school and then when she re-emerges I get out of the car and block her path.

"Hi," I beam.

She looks confused, as though for a moment she doesn't know who I am.

"Hello." Curt.

"Where's the little one?"

"Flora goes to nursery on Tuesdays and Wednesdays so I can work."

Lucky break. I'd wondered how we'd factor in the brat. "Fancy a coffee?"

"No." Connie starts to walk away.

This is becoming part of our ritual now and I'm not in the least bit fazed by it. We've said all we have to say to one another, right? No, we haven't, not by half but she's not expected to know this. I have twenty minutes left in the parking bay before I have to move the car. I know I can persuade her to have a coffee with me within ten. Maybe five.

"How about a croissant? I bet you haven't had breakfast, rushing mum and all that."

"Ha!" Connie's exclamation escapes her mouth, surprising us both by the look of her.

"What?" I ask.

She stops dead in her tracks. "Do you know how much I used to long to hear you say something like that? To invite me for a coffee. To say something, *anything*, that meant you were interested in a chat rather than just a shag."

That's the thing with Connie, she is totally incapable of keeping her cool and playing her cards close to her chest. She's so emotional, passionate, some would probably say volatile. I'm depending on this character flaw of hers.

I hold my arms open in a gesture of conciliation and I shrug, boyishly. It's a good look, I've used it countless times and it's always worked, even when dismissing misdemeanours far more grave than being tardy with an invite to breakfast.

"Well, they say good things come to those who wait."

She scowls. She starts to walk away again but this time her pace is slower, less determined.

"I've had breakfast, thank you. I never leave the house without having it, no matter how rushed things are. Luke always sees to it that I eat something because he knows I get ratty otherwise."

243

I realize that she's trying to make a point here. I don't know her as well as her husband. I don't know something I should know or I've forgotten something she told me about a million years ago, blah, blah, blah. Some girl-point. It's irrelevant. I'm encouraged by the fact that she's prepared to row with me; it shows a level of engagement that I can exploit.

"Well, you never used to eat breakfast." The sentence, innocent enough, is of course explosively loaded.

Connie turns scarlet. "I was always in too much of a hurry to leave your scuzzy flat," she argues unconvincingly.

"I've sold that now. Got myself a place in Marlow. Nice place. Doesn't smell," I laugh. "I even had one of those interior decorator women in to do it up nicely."

"That's such a waste of money," she says tartly. "Couldn't you come up with the ideas yourself?"

"Not the ideas, no."

She shoots me a look. Somehow, she's sensed that I had sex with the interior decorator. Spooky. I pretend not to notice the tension.

"There's lots of space. It's on the river," I add casually. Message is — I've grown up, I'm solvent. I'm not asking her to marry me, I just want her to know that I'm the sort of man women do want to marry.

"Do you suffer from floods?"

See, that is so typical of a woman. Professes to hate me, wants me out of her life, now, right now, but is interested enough to want to know if my gaff floods.

"No, I put all the anti-flood measures in place." Message is — I'm a responsible adult. She gets it. I see that she's relaxed a little.

"It's a long commute," she observes.

"I get sent all over the country. It doesn't really matter where I'm based. At the moment the company are paying for a flat just off High Street Kensington while I do this job with the BBC."

"Very nice."

"It is."

The domestic chat has done its job. Momentarily she's forgotten to be afraid of me and she's inched down her guard. "So about that coffee?" I ask.

I've done my research. I didn't want to blow this opportunity by taking her to a cookie-cut chain, where we'd drink insipid coffee. There is a convincing "Parisian" bar in Notting Hill that's always been cool in its own right, but it's recently been discovered by the trendy media luvvies who live round there and so it's crawling with journos who work for the gossip mags. Although no one is papping this morning (too early) it has a certain cachet, a bohemian luxury, which I know Connie will pick up on.

Bonus is, the café is pretending to be one you'd find on the arty Left Bank in Paris. Total result. Connie and I first got it together in Paris. We shared a magical night and day there once. Christ, if I've remembered, she certainly will have. She probably knows what we ate and what I was wearing.

"Nice place," she says as she nods around the café. It's decked with small glass tables, wicker chairs and adverts for hot chocolate.

"Worth the drive?" We could have walked but I wanted her to smell the leather interior of my car.

245

Women say they are not impressed by cars and that might be true, but I know new leather is a certifiable aphrodisiac. Who doesn't like the smell of wealth?

We sit down and Connie fiddles with the menu. We wait an age for the waiter to come and take our order. He's French and has his mind on higher things than serving his customers. I ask for croissant, yogurt, fresh juice and hot chocolate; I want to string this meal out. Connie orders a black coffee.

"They have extended hours. I can order you a glass of champagne," I offer.

"Don't be crazy, it's not nine o'clock yet."

"It could be like an anniversary glass to celebrate, or commiserate or just to, you know, mark the occasion."

"What occasion?" She looks bemused.

"It's eight years this month since we met."

"No, it's seven years." I hear the impatience in her voice.

"I knew that."

"*Last* month."

"Clocks are different in France."

"By an hour, not a month."

"Oh, don't split hairs, Con."

She sighs and looks momentarily weary. "Look, we should change the subject, the whole discussion is totally inappropriate. I can only be here with you as a friend. Not, you know —"

"As an ex-lover."

She scowls. "I'm offering friendship."

"And I'm accepting." I offer my hand for her to shake to close the deal that I intend to break. She doesn't shake anyway, just nods because then she doesn't have to touch me. She looks around the café. She might be looking for inspiration or an exit.

"Shouldn't you be at work?"

"Playing hooky."

"How mature."

"It's legal, signed holiday form and everything," I assure her. She scowls. I'm not sure what disappoints her the most; her belief that I haven't changed or the evidence that I have. The sulky waiter slams down my hot chocolate and Connie's coffee; some of it slops on to the table.

"He's authentic," she grins, relenting a little.

"I fucking love Paris, it's still my favourite city," I comment.

"Bullshit," she says with a laugh. "You're just saying that. If we'd . . . you know . . . in Bognor Regis you'd be sat there now telling me it's your favourite city."

"Paris *is*," I plead, but I'm laughing too. I'm glad she sees through me. I'd have been disappointed if she'd gone blunt.

"Well, my favourite city is Las Vegas," she states.

"Really, I'm surprised. I'd have thought you'd hate all the tack and glitz. Isn't it sort of shallow?"

"It's anything you want it to be. I like the freedom it represents. Luke and I renewed our vows there. It was extremely romantic."

She looks at me from under her lashes, it's a good look. But what does she want? My congratulations? Her first set of vows were pledged in front of a couple of hundred of her nearest and dearest but they meant sweet FA when push came to shove. She can't imagine I'm going to be intimidated by a quick memory jog in Nevada, can she? I stay silent for a minute then I up the ante.

"So, did you mention to Luke that you bumped into me?"

In an instant she turns the most vivid shade of red. The shame flushes across her neck and chest. Yes, result. The thing about talking to an ex-lover, especially one who was prepared to be unfaithful for you, is that there's no way you can lie to one another about something like this. You both know the depths the other is prepared to sink to. You've taken each other there. We've torn at each other's clothes then bathed in each other's immorality. She's broken standards and promises; I've broken hearts and heads. We've scratched, clawed, spat at one another's sex. There's something quite comforting about sinking so low that you hit the bottom with someone; at least you both know you can't fall any further. You know the worst there is to know about one another. Possibly that's all you know.

She shakes her head, ever so slightly.

"You should be careful, Connie. The sin of omission is very dangerous."

"I didn't want to upset him unnecessarily," she says primly and unconvincingly.

"You never did."

She shoots me an angry look. "We don't need to put him through this."

No, but we will. We're not very nice people, you see. I don't add this bit. She'd bolt for the door. She's not quite as daring as she used to be. That's motherhood for you. The moment is brought to a civilized close by the arrival of my breakfast. I tuck in and she stirs lots of sugar into her black coffee.

I don't believe in love. Well, at least not for me. I believe in chemistry. People do stupid things for chemistry, not love, but it doesn't sound as good, so they kid themselves. The chemistry between us is blatant. You can almost touch it, smell it, taste it. She plays with her hair and lips, perhaps self-consciously, perhaps subconsciously. Who knows? Who cares? The effect, whether studied or not, is that I have a raging hard-on — as in times of old. My banter is sparkling. She's in peals. My eyes are laughing. She meets them every time. When I wink at her she almost gasps out loud. The thing is — we are funny together. We get on. We're both gregarious, motivated, exciting and scurrilous. Besides, we have a shared cloak-and-dagger past and there's nothing more seductive than a dirty secret, particularly your own.

We chat throughout breakfast. There are no awkward pauses. We are both careful not to delve too deeply. We don't talk about anything more personal than horoscopes, but we become reacquainted in a very modern way by asking one another who is our favourite competitor on the latest reality TV show, and why. We laugh about the latest celeb wife-swapping scandal. We exchange views on which high-profile film stars are still hanging out in the closet. There is a definite warmness that I didn't feel in the bar the other night or at the school gate. I like our familiarity. It's relaxing and exciting at the same time.

When I finish my breakfast, I open a fresh packet of fags and offer her one.

"No thanks, I don't smoke."

"You used to."

"Not really, only in front of you, so that I looked cool."

She throws her head back and laughs out loud at this confession, attracting the curiosity of everyone in the café. You can't overestimate the size and appeal of her laugh.

"How stupid was that?" she asks. I'm not thrilled that she thinks trying to impress me is up there with square tyres as far as stupid ideas go. I'm grateful when she asks, "So what are you doing with the rest of your day's holiday?"

"Spending it with you," I reply calmly. I take a drag on my cigarette and wait for her response.

"No way. You are out of your mind." I'd have been disappointed if she'd acquiesced immediately. "I can't spend a day with you." She looks at me and her eyes plead for understanding. I bet she's hoping I'll walk away from this, from her. She needs me to take away the temptation but she can't really be expecting any compassion. She must know it's not my thing.

"Can't or won't?" I ask. I bet her vag is jumping.

"Does it matter? Is there a difference?"

"Obviously there is."

"Why would I want to spend a day with you?"

250

"I'm irresistible." To you. Especially to you.

She pauses. She picks up her handbag and starts to play with the strap. She's weighing it up. I signal to the waiter to bring me the bill. I leave cash on the table, heavily over-tipping, and I lead her to my car.

CHAPTER
TWENTY-SIX

Thursday 12 October

Lucy

I hate it that a night out with Connie has now deteriorated to the point where it means hauling my cookies over to her house so that we can share an average bottle of wine, while she keeps one ear on our conversation and the other on the baby monitor. Then, after we've eaten a middling takeaway meal, I get a cab home. It's hardly fast-track glamour, is it? Still, I guess I'm lucky that Little Miss Blow Out is available at all. What's my alternative? I certainly can't stand the idea of a night in with Peter. I am screamingly angry with him at the moment — more of that anon. Mick is away in Brussels on business or I think I might have finally taken him up on his regular offer of a drink after hours.

Connie used to live in a fairly spacious Victorian terrace in Clapham but they sold up when Fran was tiny and moved to Notting Hill. It was a combination of factors. Certainly Luke and Connie, as successful architect and budding photographer, felt that Notting Hill was a bit more "where it's at" than Clapham; both of them are admirably image aware. Besides which,

Connie wanted to be nearer Rose, not that she'd ever admit as much to me. I'm not sure if Connie saw living near Rose as some sort of penance (it was just after her tawdry but rather exciting affair had been exposed and she made a few random decisions) or whether she thought Rose would be a reliable on-tap babysitter. I can't think that she genuinely likes Rose's company enough to have upped sticks. So now they live in a beautiful but fairly bijou terrace on the Notting Hill/Holland Park border.

"I've mixed strong Martinis," she says as she opens the door to me. "What's up?" At times like this I know why we've been friends for half our lives.

I'd called her this morning; choked with fury, I just managed to spit out enough sense for her to realize that I was furious with Peter. She knows I can't talk about private issues in a voice louder than a hissed whisper while I'm in the office so she insisted I come straight round to her place after work.

I throw my coat aside, barely paying any attention to how it lands.

"Must be serious, isn't that your Roland Mouret mac?" comments Connie. I follow her through to the sitting room and note with relief that both the ankle-biters are in bed.

"Peter has booked a holiday."

"Fantastic! You wanted to get away."

"With Auriol and the boys, for all of half-term."

Connie is holding her expression in neutral, waiting for the bombshell. Doesn't she get it? I've just delivered the bombshell. "Can't you get leave from work?" she asks politely.

"I don't want bloody leave from work to go away with Auriol and the boys," I snap. I'm doing my best not to raise my voice.

"But I thought you wanted a holiday."

"I did, for Peter and me *alone*. I thought I'd made that clear to him. He argues that he distinctly asked if he should book a holiday for *all* of us and that I agreed."

"Did he?"

"Possibly. We'd just had sex. I was in the throes of post-orgasmic glow. Believe me, Connie, I'm not as familiar with that state as I used to be. Maybe I slipped up. Maybe I wasn't concentrating on what he was saying."

Connie cackles. I glare at her.

"What's funny?"

"Isn't that traditionally a woman's trick? Great sex, immediately followed up by a previously unreasonable request, so that you are guaranteed a positive response."

"Yes, Connie, it is," I say with impatience. "I think that's what's annoying me the most. I thought that's what I was doing."

I fill in the details on the night in question. Connie is almost rolling on the floor with the hilarity of the situation. I'm glad I can amuse her. "Oh, come on, Luce. It's not that bad. Where's he booked?"

"Center Parcs."

Connie is going to split in two. She laughs manically. I glare at her for a number of minutes, becoming increasingly irritated. Connie and Luke have holidayed at Center Parcs twice. On both occasions they asked Peter and me to join them and I made it perfectly clear that I'd rather chew off my own arm. She loved both holidays, which just goes to show you never really know anyone.

"I truly can't think of anything worse," I tell her.

"Actually, it's a lot of fun." I look unconvinced. "Don't worry, Rose will probably veto you taking the boys away for a week."

"No, no, she hasn't. I thought she would but she hasn't. She's dating, can you believe that? And trying to get some freelance work doing VAT records or something. She said that she could do with the time to herself and that it was time Peter was more actively involved with the boys. Bitch."

Connie can't see anything other than the funny side. She tries to cheer me up. "Come on, Luce. It will be good for you and Auriol to have a bit of bonding time. And the boys are good kids. I bet you'll love it."

"Did you hear me? He's booked Center Parcs. The modern family's Butlins. I just can't do it."

"Will you take Eva?"

"No, I can't. She's booked a flight home. I agreed to her holiday before she would accept the job back in September. If I make her cancel her trip back to Poland to come away with us, she'll quit."

"It will be OK," says Connie. She squeezes my hand and then goes to refill our glasses.

No, it won't be OK. I'm massively disappointed with Connie; I thought she'd see how unreasonable Peter is being.

"I don't want to play happy families for a week. I don't have a maternal bone in my body."

"But you are a mother. Why'd you have her?"

"It's expected."

"You've never been pulled in by expectations in the past, least not other people's."

"Society, my family, Peter, they all expected me to have a child. Even you did. Besides, I needed to even things up."

Connie sighs elaborately. "Is this about Rose again?"

"No. Yes. How is it, Connie, that I'm still competing against her?"

"Beats me, Lucy. Look, I know you've been, well —" She can't find the words, or daren't. "Not yourself recently. And feeling a bit —" Again she falters. "I had a thought, hear me out. Have you considered having another baby? Babies keep you young."

I stare at Connie amazed. I'm trying to tell her how much I'm struggling with the children already in my life. Auriol stole my youth. How can she suggest anything so ridiculous and inappropriate as having a second?

"No. Peter and I really believe that the world's resources are thinly stretched as it is. The western society is such a greedy consuming one, we take out so much more than we are prepared or capable of giving back. I only have to think of landfills of disposable nappies rotting and I can't bring myself to conceive. People ought to be more aware."

I shake my head sadly. Connie eyes me reproachfully. She's not sure how seriously she ought to take my response. She picks up a handful of nuts and chews silently and carefully. She's irritating me. She looks like a hamster. Connie has let me down, she's changed, she's insisted on popping out a baby every five minutes and she's insisted on loving it. I've lost her. I don't belong, I've never belonged. Connie is the closest I've ever had to a proper friend and she doesn't understand me. Who cares? I don't even aspire to belong. I am a very independent woman. Not a loner, not unsociable, just independent.

Maybe I'm a bit lonely at the moment — alternately lonely or angry. I opt to be angry, it's not as pathetic. Right now Connie is closest to me physically and psychologically, so I lash out at her.

"You all have that holier-than-thou thing going."

"What?"

"The attitude mothers of more than one child have. I'm not sanctimonious when I see a childless woman, I'm jealous of her or I pity her, depending on what sort of day I'm having with Auriol, but mothers of multiples are so sanctimonious. No sooner did I have Auriol than people started to ask me when we'd have another. Any time on the third of neverary."

Connie looks sad for me. What the hell is that about? How have we ended up in such different places?

On Monday Mick will be back in the office. I'll talk to him about Peter's underhand tricks and the

257

unfairness of me having to use precious holiday allowance on a week's break in Center Parcs. He'll understand where I'm coming from.

Connie flops back on to her couch. I notice that the grey buckskin is mottled with spillages and stains. Clearly Connie has lost the plot. She used to be fanatical about keeping her Conran furniture absolutely just so. I rather liked it about her.

"I've had a rollercoaster week myself," she says.

Given her lack of concern for my problem I'm tempted to be uncooperative and refuse to show a polite amount of interest; however, I was brought up to have impeccable manners, they've always seen me through when I had to give morals the big heave-ho.

"Really? Why's that?"

Connie stands up and closes the door of the room.

"I saw John Harding again," she whispers.

"Really? Why's that?" I repeat, deadpan.

"He came to the school. He'd taken the day off work to be with me."

"Well, it goes to show, there's a first for everything."

"The scary thing is I realize that I've started to wear make-up to drop off or pick up Fran from school. Just in case he's at the gate."

"Oh dear."

"Indeed."

I stare at her in amazement while she tells me that she did not go to her studio (hired at great expense twice a week) to work on her photos and instead she spent the day with him. I cannot believe she wants to follow that same road to nowhere.

"Was it fun?"

"Yes," she says with a beam.

"As much fun as it used to be?" I ask.

She pauses for great effect and then beams again, "No."

That's a relief.

Her smile is triumphant. She is utterly thrilled with herself. "Something has changed. I've changed. I'm older and wiser. He's certainly still gorgeous to look at. He's amusing, bright, quirky, but no longer irresistible."

"How sad," I comment.

She looks me in the eye and nods slowly. "Yes, in a way it was. The fact that I found it genuinely simple to resist him was a clear indication I'm getting older. I mean, not habitually chasing a destructive fantasy is more of a sign that I'm approaching middle age than wrinkles or cellulite," she says with a laugh.

"Connie! You are not approaching middle age. For God's sake." I am unspeakably angry with her. If Connie is approaching middle age, then so am I. "You are thirty-six," I remind her. "Middle age is fifty."

"Do you know many people who make their centenary?" she asks with a grin. Why doesn't it bother her more? "Still, the important thing is I've de-mystified him. The way we'd left it before was so uneven. It was rather satisfying letting him know that I don't want him."

I stare at her amazed. "So you told him that?"

"In as many words."

"Wasn't there any sexual tension between the pair of you?"

"He tried to flirt. I'd just bounce back with a story about Flora or Fran. Mostly, I'd recount the less glamorous mothering moments. You know, anxiety about which injections to go for, the tedium of getting into the school you want, the issues around toilet training. You know the sort of thing."

I hold a hand up in front of me indicating that Connie ought to shut up. No, I do not know about the sort of things she is talking about, and even if I did it would never cross my mind that I'd discuss them in public and least of all with an ex-lover. I sigh, rather depressed. There was a time when Connie thought as I did. I've lost that Connie. She's gone. I like Luke. I have enormous respect for him and despite Connie's personality shift I still consider her my best friend, so I am genuinely thrilled for them that Connie feels so unattracted to her ex-lover. Life will be simpler all round and I won't be forced into the rather tedious role of confessor once again, so this is a good result.

And yet.

As Connie said, there is nothing like kicking a destructive habit, particularly a sexual obsession that's likely to threaten your marriage and family stability, to indicate that you have well and truly grown up. She's left me behind. I always used to be the one up front.

A thought occurs to me. I wonder if she is lying to me. Maybe she secretly shagged him until she was raw and she's just holding out on me. In one way this would be awful, on the other hand I'd approve enormously. I do not want to be approaching middle age.

"But you spent the whole day with him?" I ask.

"Yes."

"Why?"

"I wanted some answers to questions I've waited six years to ask."

"Did you get them?"

"No, of course not. When I started to approach any potentially difficult subject John would clam up. Eventually he said, 'You don't want to ask those questions, babe. You won't like the answers.'"

Connie is using a silly voice to represent John. She really doesn't fancy him. She's prepared to laugh at him. That is much more final than hating him.

"It seems that some people really can't grow up," she says with a sigh.

For the first time I see what she finds attractive about this John Harding, a guy that won't grow up. Hurrah, a man after my own heart. I'm only kidding. Sort of.

Connie suggests we order a takeaway but I decline. I make an excuse about having to do some work tonight. I gather my coat and head for the door as quickly as I can without appearing openly rude. Quite some intimacy between us has died tonight. I fear that Connie and I are no longer on the same path and I feel sick with sadness. I can't imagine the time our paths will merge again. I cannot find the same pleasure she does from the domestic necessities that clutter our lives. She'll never care how much money I make company X in a single day. I'm not sure she ever did. I need to go home to quietly grieve for us.

CHAPTER
TWENTY-SEVEN

Thursday 19 October

Rose

It has been very useful learning about replacing spark-plugs and such but, as Luke predicted, the best thing about the course has been meeting Susanne and Helen. Helen is confident, bright and chatty. I was surprised to discover that she's three years older than me, as she appears at least eight years younger. She dresses well and has a social life, which can be misleading. One of her nicest qualities is that she assumes I am like her. It's a compliment. She seems to believe I have just as much right as the next lady to go to the cinema or visit a fancy new restaurant. She often suggests we meet up for a drink or tries to interest me in going to see a show. I intend to accept these invitations at some point — the only fly in the ointment is that Helen issues the invites at the last minute. She calls me at seven and asks if I'd like to meet that night at eight. I've tried to explain the impossibility of getting babysitters at short notice and the impracticality of dropping everything in a moment — but she doesn't get it. So, to date, our social interaction has been

262

limited to a coffee after class, which is always extremely pleasant so I'm not grumbling.

Susanne and I have more in common, even though she is nearly ten years older than I am. Her girls are eighteen, sixteen and nine years old. Chloe was a surprise and the unacknowledged straw that broke the back of the camel called Susanne's marriage. She doesn't resent Chloe's arrival at all. In fact, she says Chloe was the best thing that ever happened to her; a new lease of life when she felt she was getting staid and set in her ways. She realizes that a man who looked upon the third daughter as nothing more than an inconvenience to retirement plans was not much of a loss. She's been divorced for eight years now and is comfortable with her lot.

Susanne owns a tiny hair salon, on a small road off Queensway. She works hard and makes a reasonable living. She has three staff, including the Saturday girl, and she has a regular clientele who have all been visiting her for years and years. Her busiest day is a Tuesday because she does a pensioner special — half-price cut and blow-dry (which she refers to as a set). On production of a bus pass she throws in a cup of tea and a chocolate biscuit. Susanne is always laughing. When I pointed this out she stared at me as though I was insane. "Why wouldn't I be laughing?" she asked. "I'm one of the world's lucky ladies." And of course she is, because she believes it to be so.

This morning Susanne has kindly offered to blow-dry my hair for today's date. With much humour she manages my expectations about the level of chrome, leather and black marble I am to encounter at her salon. But as her hair is always impeccably cut and shiny to the point of looking like she's wearing a halo, I am confident that I can live without the intimidating décor and staff (normally part and parcel of a trip to the hairdresser's).

"So who do we have this afternoon?" asks Susanne.

"This afternoon I'm having tea with a chap called . . ." I pause and quickly reach for my diary. "David Clark," I tell her.

Susanne hoots with laughter. "You forgot his name," she accuses.

"Only his surname." I slip into the nylon gown. It smells clean even though it is stained with splashes of bleach. I follow Susanne to the sink. This establishment is distinctly old-fashioned and down-market. There are no copies of *Vogue* for clients to read, although the customers can scan dog-eared copies of the cheaper weekly mags and are encouraged to do the crosswords on the back page. The tea is strong and hot and served in mismatched mugs, but none of the mugs is chipped. The chair at the basin does not flip into a flat bed, nor is the basin cushioned. But Susanne wraps a couple of towels around my neck in an effort to make me feel comfortable and she tests the water before spraying it on my hair so that I'm neither frozen nor scalded. Most importantly, Susanne does not feel compelled to ritualistically humiliate me by insisting that my hair is thin or split beyond repair. Instead she starts to give me a head massage and it feels sensational.

"You are certainly racking up the numbers, no wonder you are getting confused."

"There really haven't been that many," I defend.

"Hey girl, I'm not criticizing. I'm enjoying living out my romantic notions through you. If I was ten years younger I'd be hooked up for broadband and doing the same thing myself."

"There's no reason you can't date at your age," I say. "Although the internet suitors are an unforgiving bunch. I'm glad I placed that ad in *Time Out*," I add.

Susanne laughs loudly. "Can you believe we live in a time when placing a personal ad is seen as a traditional approach?" she asks.

"No," I sigh. "I can't."

We both remember when it was only losers who felt they had to sell themselves through an ad. Normal people met their boyfriends in normal ways — at a party or through mutual friends — but that world has disappeared. The belief now is that the losers are the ones who are not proactively searching out a partner through blind dates, personal columns, internet or speed-dating. I'd still love to meet someone the old-fashioned way. You know — eyes across a crowded room and fall instantly in love, or at least meet someone, like him, respect him and slowly fall in love with him. Now that would suit me.

"Well, as long as you are careful," warns Susanne.

She's not talking about unprotected sex. We both know that she means I ought to be careful about who I'm meeting. Sex, ha. Despite my numerous dates sex is still a dim and distant memory. I'm not keen to rush anything but even if I was I haven't found anyone remotely attractive in that way. The most physical contact I've had is a couple of air kisses and even those seemed intrusive.

"I am careful. I only ever meet in the afternoons and in public places. I tell someone where I am going and I don't drink alcohol. I follow all the recommended procedures."

"And you still manage to have fun?" asks Susanne with another laugh. She towel-dries my hair and then slathers on generous amounts of conditioner.

"So, meeting for tea. Is tea the new black or is he just after a cheap date?"

"It works for me because the boys aren't disrupted. The twins have music practice after school today. I can go on the date and then be at the school gate for five and they are none the wiser."

"How come these guys are available for tea? Don't any of them have jobs?"

"Not many of them, no. Not what you'd class as a proper job."

I have noticed that the type of man I seem to be attracting wants to be looked after in some way, either financially, emotionally or practically. One guy suggested we had a date at Marks & Spencer so that I could help him pick out a shirt! I conclude that my profile, or my picture, reveals that I'm a top-notch mummy. And everyone is looking for a mummy.

"How did it go with that Ian?"

"He was very persistent, which I thought was a point in his favour. When I cancelled the Monday night date

I didn't expect to hear from him again. But he called the next morning and insisted we met for lunch on the Tuesday."

"That's a good sign."

"Yes, I thought so too, but when we met he was the most terminally dull person I have ever come across. The horror was that after lunch he shook my hand and said that he thought we had lots in common and we should certainly do it again some time. If I have a lot in common with a man who collects antique pen nibs and old Rupert Bear annuals then I'm in deep trouble."

"But Rose, you collect stamps — some might say that's not a million miles away from collecting annuals."

"Well, they'd be wrong."

"And you collect 1950s crockery."

"OK, OK, conversation closed. I see your point, I need new hobbies." Susanne lets another huge laugh explode into the world. I grin back at her; it's quite impossible to take offence because it's clear none is intended. "I am doing rather well in terms of numbers and the variety itself is quite exciting. I haven't done much dating in my time and never expected to. It's interesting meeting new people but I'm afraid there hasn't been a single one that I want to see again."

"What about the guy you had lunch with on Sunday?"

"Jonathan. He was very charming and . . ." I search for the word, ". . . practised. He worked in one of those companies that run corporate training courses. He talked to me as though he was conducting a seminar —

full of high fives and spectacular clichés. *The world's waiting for you, Rosie* and *You only have one life.*"

"I'd rather like that," says Susanne. "There's a whole lot of truth in a cliché."

"I'll give you his number if you want." I couldn't help but wonder how many dozens of first dates he must have been on, to be quite so drilled.

"Well, you never know, Rose. This David Clark might be The One."

"Yes," I agree, although I don't believe it for a moment.

Sometimes I wonder how long I'll have to keep up this pretence of searching for the perfect man before Connie and Daisy accept that there simply isn't such a thing for me.

"At the very least you'll have lovely hair when you pick up the boys from music practice," says Susanne. "Is that your phone?"

"Hello, this is Craig." For a moment I am confused. I can't remember a Craig dropping a response into my e-mail or post office box. The man at the end of the phone coughs and then adds, "Mr Walker."

"Oh, gosh, yes. Craig as in Mr Walker Craig," I gabble. "Are the boys OK?" I demand anxiously.

"Absolutely, yes. Sorry to alarm you, Rose. It's nothing like that. I'm calling on PA business."

"Oh." I sit back comfortably in Susanne's chair.

"I realize it's short notice and quite an imposition, but I cast an eye around the hall this morning and I'm afraid I have to admit that while the harvest festival displays the children made do have a certain authentic charm, I feel we could do a little more in terms of decoration for the service tomorrow. I wouldn't normally care but the local paper is coming to our assembly to see the children hand over their donations to the Salvation Army," he says.

I wonder if Mr Walker has been running, he sounds breathless. It's unusual for a man to be in a hurry, they are rarely busy enough. I'm impressed.

"I'm happy to help in any way. What were you thinking of?"

"I remembered that wonderful floral display you made for the top of the piano for the orchestra's concert last summer and I wondered if you could do something festive with cobs of corn and apples."

"What?"

"Like in a department store."

Craig isn't being especially clear but I understand. I've also seen arty displays of straw, greenery and fruit and veg, rather than flowers. I think I could have a go at that. My hand reaches up to my throat and I realize I am blushing. Fancy Mr Walker — Craig — the *headmaster*, noticing my flower arranging. I'm thrilled.

"I'll happily do whatever I can but we'll have to buy some supplies and ribbon and such."

Craig has caught his breath. Authority is creeping back into his voice, it suits him.

"No fear on that point. We can raid Ms Kelly's art box for ribbons and the parents have been very generous; we have more than enough fresh produce."

I can imagine. Despite the newsletter requesting each child bring in one item to donate to the Salvation Army by way of marking harvest festival, I've seen offerings fit for a king brought to the school gate all week — ours included.

"When do you want me?"

"Would it be too inconvenient to say after school? I know the twins have music practice then. The hall is used for PE, lunch and drama during the daytime."

I'm aware of the demands made upon space in Holland House but I'm also aware that at 3p.m. David Clark (Might Be The One) is expecting to meet me at Nora's Café, the place that sells the yummiest chocolate and orange cake in West London and possibly Western Europe. I do not like cancelling arrangements at the last minute, it's rude. Yet suddenly I feel a rush of excitement when I contemplate seeing Mr Walker, Craig. He's such easy company; very interesting and kind. He's one of those people whose smile physically eases the stresses and worries of the recipient. I want to help him. Besides, it's for the boys. Indirectly but certainly. I alight on the solution.

"I could come later this evening, if you could arrange to get a set of keys to me. I'll get my sister to sit for the boys."

"I was thinking of helping you. I'm not busy this evening and I'd never expect you to work alone. I'm not artistic but I can hold the ladder."

"Fine." I beam to myself. I wonder if my legs need a shave? It's just that if Craig is going to be holding the ladder I don't want to leave the impression that I'm the abominable snowman's rather more hairy sister. Although I doubt Craig would look at my legs as he holds the ladder; he's far too proper for anything like that.

"Would seven thirty suit?" I ask.

"It's a date," he says.

"A date," I repeat automatically.

"Well, more of an appointment," he adds formally.

"An appointment," I clarify.

When I hang up I notice that Susanne is staring at me with a fat grin on her face.

"Who was that?" she demands.

"The boys' headmaster."

"You're kidding me. You never mentioned that he's cute."

"He isn't — well, he is. But what makes you say that?"

"Well, you were all blushy and giggly and hair-touchy. It's clear you have the hots for him."

"For Mr Walker? Don't be ridiculous."

Daisy agrees to babysit, although she is notably less enthusiastic about babysitting so that I can deck the school halls with corn dollies and onions than when I date.

When I arrive at the hall Craig has made a start. He's separated the huge piles of food into type. He's cut several lengths of brown and green ribbon. His efforts are a little random but well-intentioned. We make a solid team. I quickly arrange the food, threading straw and ribbons to great effect. Craig has no artistic flair; he wasn't being modest. But he is a whiz with the hammer and efficiently hangs my garlands to advantage.

Initially our conversation is stilted. Craig focuses on the children.

"Who is looking after the boys tonight?"

"My sister. She's a great help."

Craig looks pleased to hear this but his face clouds as he adds, "Even so, it can't be easy, managing everything on your own."

I'm more honest about this since my "therapy date" with Chris, but that said, I'm not sure how comfortable I am discussing my single mum status with the headmaster. Of course he's aware of the situation but I don't want to be indiscreet; Lucy and Peter are parents at the school too. I answer as briefly as possible.

"Not always. Can you pass me the gingham?"

"But it must be getting easier, now the children are getting older," he prompts.

I wonder whether I ought to agree and leave it at that. After all, that's the simplest and most polite option. But maybe, just maybe, Craig is genuinely interested in what it's like to be a single mum. What it's like for me, at least. The thought cheers me. I plump for that.

"Do you know, in some ways I think things are getting harder."

"What do you mean?"

"When Peter first left I was thirty-three and things appeared possible. Thirty-three is quite young still."

Inwardly I cringe. What on earth made me reveal my age to Craig? Oh well, it hardly matters. He's unlikely to have thought I was younger than thirty-nine. Indeed, it's unlikely that he's given my age any thought at all. I'm embarrassed, so I do what I always do when I'm embarrassed, I babble on and make things worse. "That's your age, isn't it?"

"I'm thirty-five."

"Really, well, that's young. Anyway, I told myself if I dressed in enough bright clothes that I'd muddle through the humiliation and the loneliness and I'd survive. In fact I'd thrive. But over time my certainty slipped."

I fall silent and wait to see if Craig is really listening. He proves he is. "What do you think made the confidence dissolve?"

"I'm not sure, a combination of things. Miserable dates, failed job applications. I wasn't after a world-dominating career, just something to get me out of the house. Mostly I applied to do part-time accounting work that I could've done blindfolded, but every time I had an interview, disaster would strike."

"In what form?"

"My babysitter would fail to show up. Or the car would break down. Or I'd miss my bus. If I did make it to an interview I was invariably late and I found it difficult to concentrate if the interview overran. I'd start to wonder if my mum would defrost the casseroles in the freezer. Besides, I did the maths and realized that the cost of childcare outweighed the income I could generate. So I gave up."

"Have you thought of getting a job now that the boys are in full-time school?"

"I always thought I'd re-enter the workforce around about now, but they finish at half three and have a third of the year off on holiday — what sort of job accommodates those hours? Very few. I considered pyramid selling. But I discovered that I am the literal opposite of the guy who can sell snowballs to Eskimos. I could not give away reindeer skins fashioned into neat little jackets to Eskimos. They'd already have another supplier."

Craig is laughing, which is a relief; I don't want to come across as maudlin or self-pitying.

"Besides, I like being around the children. I'd miss them too much if I went back to work. Being around your kids is a privilege and I think I'm doing a good job. Sebastian needed a lot of extra help with his reading in reception year; would a nanny have been bothered enough to sit for hours repeating the 'magic e' rule? Maybe but maybe not."

"Well, you've done a fine job. The boys are great kids."

I'm so thrilled with Craig's compliment that I nearly cut my finger off with round-ended scissors, quite a feat. I am a praise junkie and my class A drug is being praised about my children; it's an unprecedented hit.

It takes two hours to transform the hall. Turns out that I have quite a flair for this sort of decorating; the years of putting together an autumnal table have not been wasted. The end result is marvellous. Craig and I repeatedly congratulate ourselves.

"You've made the place look sensational, Rose. Can I take you for a drink to say thank you, properly?" asks Craig.

I'm so taken aback that I literally step away from Craig. He notices and blushes profusely.

"Do you mean a coffee?"

"Well, yes, if you like. Or a glass of wine, if you can bear it," he says with a shy smile.

"Don't you have to be somewhere?"

"No," he says firmly.

I don't know what to do. Craig is undoubtedly the nicest man I've met in a long while. He's far better company than any of the men I've endured dates with over the last month. I really would like to spend some more time chatting to him. And a glass of wine in a grown-up place like a wine bar sounds appealing, far better than a date at M&S.

But.

Lots of objections rush into my head. Craig is not asking me on a date. He's simply being polite. The drink is to say thank you for the work I've done. He feels he owes me. I mustn't get carried away. Craig is young and handsome; I'm getting to the age when well-mannered boys will toy with the idea of offering up their seat on crowded tubes.

Mr Walker is the headmaster at my children's school. I can't risk getting drunk and silly in front of him. Not that I'm known for getting drunk and silly but wouldn't it be a terrible first? Besides, while we've chatted pleasantly enough within the confines of the school hall, will we be able to keep up the cordial atmosphere away from our known environment? I wouldn't want to bore the man. And won't his girlfriend be expecting him back? He's probably itching to get back to her and

I bet she's counting the seconds until he returns. I can't allow him to get into trouble just because he feels he owes me the courtesy of a drink.

Although there was a moment back there, or maybe two, when Craig and I were chatting about this and that, and I allowed myself to forget who I was and who he was, and I allowed myself the indulgence of imagining he *was* a date.

Silly, I know.

Totally pathetic.

I'm probably seeing too much of Connie, the Queen of Romantic Notions. She's slowly managing to brainwash me and I have started to think maybe, just maybe, there's someone out there for me. It's not David Clark, that's for certain. What a nightmare the tea date was today. The man was so pompous. He approached the date as though he was interviewing me. My romantic CV was dissected over a period of an hour and a half, and it appears I was found sadly lacking. Finally, he insisted that we split the bill but he paid 40 pence less as he drank tea and I'd had coffee. This cannot be the route to true love.

If only someone like Craig had answered my personal ad. Someone kind and considerate. Someone thoughtful and thought-provoking. I push this nonsense out of my head.

"No thank you. I'd better not. My sister mentioned she had somewhere to go later tonight. I have to get home so she can be on her way."

His smile collapses. It must be the poor lighting in here but for a fraction of a second I thought he looked genuinely disappointed. Ridiculous of course. He must be relieved, not disappointed. He's made the polite offer but he's off the hook.

We gather together our coats and all the other paraphernalia necessary to protect against autumn elements and head towards the door.

As Craig locks the door behind us, he says, "I meant to ask you, how's the internet dating getting along? Met anyone special yet?"

"The vast majority of them are special needs but that's not what you mean, is it?" I joke.

He turns to look at me and stays absolutely still. The night's blackness falls around us and London seems unusually peaceful. Is he waiting for me to elaborate? The shame.

"I'm becoming a pro. Or at least I'm getting used to feeling like a total witch when I pass over someone's carefully drafted profile," I confess.

"What makes you reject a guy?"

"I dismiss some brave souls because they tell me that in another life they'd have been a cat or a tree. Obviously, I dismiss a fair number that look like serial killers. I dismissed one guy because he claimed to have read Dostoevsky, Tolstoy, Haruki Murakami, Jose Saramago, Don DeLillo, Orhan Pamuk and Marquez."

"Don't you like any of those authors?"

"Yes, the ones I've read, but the guy is either a hermit or a pathological liar. I skipped over a guy's profile because he claimed to be Mr Average looking for someone special to spoil."

"Why?" Craig looks surprised.

"It didn't ring true. No one truly believes they're average, do they? And I didn't like the feeling that he was dangling a carrot. Women can't be wooed with the temptation of being bought things. Least, not all of us." Craig nods and does not call me picky or judgemental the way Daisy and Connie do. Still, I want to explain why I'm being so fastidious. "The thing is, I've done my time with the one who turned out not to be the one and I don't want to waste more time than necessary."

"Quite right," confirms Craig. I'm grateful for his support.

"It's a minefield. The other day I read an article that said one in three of online daters lie about their marital status."

Craig gasps. Like me, he finds dishonesty shocking and disheartening. Connie had simply commented, "So few? I'd have guessed fifty per cent," and Daisy suggested I pay special attention to tan marks on the ring finger.

I grin at him. "Despite all of this, I have been on some dates but nothing has come of any of them."

"So why do you keep trying, Rose?"

"I don't know. I must be a glutton for punishment."

"I think you're hopeful, a true romantic," he says.

I bask in the glow of being thought of so optimistically.

"I've upped the ante. I've tried placing a personal ad in *Time Out*. It's unlikely to bear fruit but it keeps my friends' spirits up."

My God, what is wrong with me? Why do I keep slipping out these terrible admissions to my sons'

278

headmaster? Craig is very easy to talk to and I'd never think of lying to him but do I have to be *this* confessional? I've seen more discreet people on Jerry Springer. Poor Craig looks confused by my outpouring. If he could wave a sign declaring, "Too much information", I'm sure he would.

"Keep me informed about how you get along," he mumbles.

"I think that might be inappropriate, Craig."

"Only if you insist on detailing your progress at school assembly. But maybe we could meet for that drink some other time. I owe you."

"You're too busy," I say dismissively. There's a frost on the ground. I stomp my feet, hoping to stay warm.

"I'd like it. You'd be doing me the favour. I'm trying to meet someone special too. You could point me in the right direction. Give me tips on which sites are best, etiquette for blind dates, etc."

He's single. Craig is *single*. The news makes me want to smile. And laugh. And grab his arm and accept the glass of wine.

Whoa, hang on cowgirl, why do I care? Even if he hasn't got a girlfriend, what difference does it make? He's my boys' headmaster, not a man. Well, obviously he is a man but he's not a man in the way the internet-date men are men. For a start he listens. And he doesn't have BO. But, and it's a big but, he is still my boys' headmaster and as such not at all appropriate or available. I can't believe I'm even thinking of him in that way; not even for a nano-second.

"I couldn't interfere with your love-life like that."
Why do I use phrases like "love-life"? No one says
"love-life" except my mother.

"Oh really, that's not a problem. Anything you could
say would be a light touch in comparison to my pals. I
really don't think I can stomach another Saturday night
on the pull with them."

I laugh at the expression on his face when he uses
the term "on the pull"; he simply could not look more
aghast. I wish I hadn't made up such a convincing lie
about Daisy needing to go on some place tonight, I'd
really like to spend some more time with Craig.

No I wouldn't. That's a ridiculous idea.

And a wonderful idea. Ridiculously wonderful.
Wonderfully ridiculous.

Of course, we'd be nothing more than friends. If we
did find ourselves spending time together. Not that I'm
expecting we will.

This internal battle is still raging three hours later
when I am tucked up in bed with a mug of hot
chocolate. I always treat myself to a hot chocolate after
a particularly pleasant day. My last waking thought is of
Craig and then I fall to sleep and dream of him too.

In my dream, he's spanking me. I wake up too
ashamed to look at myself in the bathroom mirror.

CHAPTER
TWENTY-EIGHT

Friday 20 October

John

It wasn't tricky to get her into bed. But then, as soon as I saw her at the school gate, weeks back, I knew it wouldn't be much of a challenge. There's a type of woman that wants her fun whenever and wherever she can find it, and they are transparent. Of course, there had to be the obligatory protests about her husband and children. That's the modern woman's stab at respectability; they remind a man that they have a family just before they lose all memory of the said family themselves.

Technically the sex was fine. As I mentioned, she's in good shape for her age and she was enthusiastic, confident and practised. We went back to my apartment, the one the firm have rented for me. She was thrilled with it. It's in a huge Georgian terrace in a good part of town. The white façade, original wooden floors, high ceilings and long sash windows all create a fairly romantic setting. That's what she was looking for, a bit of disposable romance. Most women are. And it suited me, taking her back, as I have no privacy issues.

281

Some blokes prefer not to bring women back to their own gaff; it's usually a hygiene issue (their lack of it) or a commitment issue (their lack of it). But I didn't think it was worth splashing out on a hotel. This lay wasn't worth that much to me. Nor did I fancy doing her back at her family home. Even I can be put off my stride if there are wedding pictures and school photographs on the bedstands. Poor innocent little kids smiling down at their mother as she wraps her legs around a strange man's neck. It's not right. So back to my place it was.

The encounter had a perfunctory air to it. As we walked into my apartment I offered her a coffee but she said not now, she'd have one after. I went to the bog and by the time I came out she was standing in the bedroom, wearing nothing but her bra and pants, carefully folding her tracksuit. She unclipped her bra and turned to me, treating me to an unobstructed view of her surgically enhanced, very lovely orbs.

I did make an effort. If word gets back I want it to be known that my performance is still up to scratch. She certainly seemed satisfied. But it was a bit one-sided, if you know what I mean. Put it this way, she was more of a receiver than a giver. Too worried it would mess up her hair no doubt, hubby might just notice that. Still, I'm not complaining, sex is sex and there's no such thing as bad sex, at least not in my book.

After she showered we stood in the kitchen and had a quick coffee. It seemed rude not to make conversation.

"I take it you've done this before?" I asked.

"Once or twice. My husband works away a lot and I married him when I was very young. He's never been very young." I shifted uncomfortably. I hate it when they start telling me their life stories. How can they possibly think I have an interest? She noted my discomfort and added, "I'm not making excuses or expecting sympathy. I'm simply laying out the facts. The old goat wanted a young piece of arm-candy and he got it. He must have known how that would pan out twelve years down the line. I do love him, in my own way. And of course, there's the children. We have an agreement. It's unspoken but we're both aware of it."

"Well, whatever makes you happy," I said as I lit a fag.

She stared at me for a long time and then turned the subject. "I was rather surprised when you asked for my number. I thought you'd been hanging around the school gates to catch the attention of Constance Baker."

Hearing Diane say her name gave me a jolt.

"Did you?" In those situations it's always best to say as little as possible. Even a denial can make you look as guilty as sin. I pulled Diane close to me and gave her a long, slow kiss. It had the required effect, it silenced her.

As she dressed she asked, "Do you want to do this again some time?"

"Of course, babe."

As she left the flat the door banged behind her and I deleted her number from my phone. I'm not one for closing down options under normal circumstances and she'd made it clear that she was keen for uncomplicated, no-strings-attached sex, normally my favourite type. Normally.

But when I was humping away, the strangest thing had happened. The act started to feel like a duty shag, the sort you have with a long-term girlfriend, just to prove to her that you love her at the point when you probably don't. It didn't have the buzz that sex with someone new is supposed to have. Odd, but I just couldn't gather the required enthusiasm. Gutting. I guess my lack of gusto did answer the one question I hoped would be answered by shagging a married mother.

I'm not chasing Connie just because she's a married mother.

I know it sounds weird but I did wonder. The shag was an experiment. Is it the mum thing that's turning me on? Or the unavailable thing? Or the Connie thing? So I thought I'd try another mum. The experiment was conclusive. I'm pursuing Connie because I want Connie.

It's been ten days since we spent the whole day together. A day I'd planned with strategic precision and that she threw out of kilter in a matter of moments. I am not used to her opposition, but oddly her sparky defiance just strengthens my resolve and I find myself wanting her more. We breakfasted together and then she agreed to ditch work and have a laugh. So far so good. I suggested that we could go to Brighton. I'd even made a booking at Hotel Pelirocco. Funny that less than two weeks ago an afternoon session hadn't seemed completely unreasonable. Now it seems as distant a possibility as a trip to the moon. I'd thought that getting her out of town would work very nicely. It's easier to abandon responsibilities on new turf but she wouldn't go for it, she insisted that she had to stay in London. She said she couldn't risk getting snarled up in bad traffic as her kid would be devastated if she was late for pick-up. Still, I wasn't disheartened; a certain amount of discouragement was to be expected.

I had to think on my feet then. I needed somewhere far enough away from her stomping ground for her to forget St Luke for a few hours. I had to be careful not to pick somewhere too significant, somewhere we'd visited together before for instance. It's best to start a fresh set of memories rather than risk old issues kicking off. I had a bit of a problem there, mind you, in so much as I couldn't remember exactly where we used to hang out. The whole relationship is blurred into a mass of dodgy pubs and alley walls.

So we settled on Tate Modern. I am absolutely certain that we've never visited a gallery together and she said there was an installation that she wanted to see. She commented, "That way I won't feel bad about skiving. Seeing the installation is work of sorts." Her need to justify spending time with me was irritating but I took a deep breath and accepted that it was to be expected. I guess I'd used up her resource of wild abandon. I'd squandered it.

We had a laugh. The aspect I couldn't plan or bank on, but that I hoped for, that just sort of happened. Connie and I clicked. We still have that spark. I know she knows it's there too. It thrills me. I think it worries her.

We had a great time. It's official. It was a bright, fresh day. The sky was a solid block of blue and a winter sun reflected off the river, giving the impression that the sludgy Thames was a ribbon of silver. We walked and talked all day. Nothing heavy, neither of us really wanted that, but we never stopped gassing on to one another. There wasn't a single awkward moment. She liked it. I know she did.

But no action. We occasionally banged hands and I had to lean across her a couple of times to open doors or pass the salt, and when there was accidental body contact we were both more than aware. I felt a slight quiver in my cock; she shuddered and then jumped a foot away from me as though she was tangled on an electric fence.

I dropped her back in Holland Park at 3.15, in time for the pick-up. She told me she'd had a great time and then she scrambled out of the car, desperate to avoid the embarrassment of how to say cheers and bye for now. We're northerners and although we've got used to air-kissing southerners we just can't be that phony with each other. We're all or nothing kind of people. A full-on snog or a rush for the door handle. Connie made the call.

So why am I thinking of her? Am I so immature that because a woman says no, I want her more? Probably. I resorted to my usual course of action. Distraction. But nothing doing there either. Humping Diane was like doing a sack of potatoes. Have I lost my appetite? Fuck, that would be a disaster. For me and womankind.

Since my taste for women is well and truly doused right now, I'm spending lots of time with Craig. This is a good thing, as his pathetic attempts with the women make me feel more like the Casanova I know I am. Connie has left me feeling like I have the sex appeal of Homer Simpson.

Despite my own concerns I've tried not to let Craig flounder. Besides instructing him in what to wear, what to listen to, where to hang out and giving him the name of a decent barber, I have been by his side — time after time — as he attempts to get his end away. I've dragged him out with me nearly every Saturday night. I've introduced him to lots of lovely girlies, I've sung his praises, I've plied everyone with alcohol and then I've left him alone with various lasses. Every single time, the same result. No score. It's astounding. Even when the bird is clearly interested, practically gagging for it, he still manages to pop her in a taxi and then go home alone. Other than force-feeding him Viagra, stripping both him and the interested girlie, then turning the lights out in a hope that he'll trip up and just accidentally fall on her and spear her, I don't know what else I can do.

I ask him to come for a beer so we can discuss the problem. He's an intelligent guy — he must know that there are issues and I bet he's aware of how to solve them too. I choose a pub with inviting globe lanterns hanging outside. Inside there's a colourful, warm and friendly atmosphere; it's the sort of place people spill the beans.

I start subtle.

"If you are a bender, mate, it's all right by me."

Craig grins at me. "That's nice to know, John, thank you, but I'm straight."

"Really." I take a long drink of my beer. "Not getting much though, are you?" I point out.

"No, I suppose not by your standards. But it's different for me." He looks me in the eye as he says this. I see a challenge.

"How so?" I ask.

"Well, your end game is sex," he says flatly.

"And yours isn't?" I struggle to keep the incredibility out of my voice.

"You've been married, John, and it's clear that you are once bitten twice shy. You're not after any sort of emotional complexity from your relationship but I still require that."

I stare at Craig and fight the urge to thump him. What the fuck is he bringing Andrea into the conversation for? What does he mean about my not being after any emotional complexity? If he knew about Connie he'd know that currently I'm chasing the embodiment of emotional complexity. Anyway this isn't about my fuckedupness, it's about his.

He continues, "You are just out of a divorce and it's clear that you need to prove . . . well . . . something to yourself or . . . or others. God knows who." He knows he's on quicksand and his voice cracks with uncertainty. He rushes to reassure me. "Not us, mate. If you are doing all this womanizing stuff to prove a point to Tom and me, then you really don't have to. We know you are 'the man' and all that."

"What the fuck are you talking about?" I ask angrily. I'm grateful we've known each other long enough that I'm not required to hide my irritation.

He blanches at my use of expletive. He doesn't like cussing. "I'm just saying if you want to chill out a bit, that's fine. You don't have to be sleeping with someone new every week or so, just to . . . you know."

No, I don't know. But saying as much would mean we were having a discussion about my sex life and we're *not*. We're having a discussion about his sex life or rather lack of it.

"We're not talking about me, mate." I pick up a beermat and start tapping it on the table.

"Well, we are a bit. I was just comparing. I'm trying to say to you that while I understand what you're doing, and why you need to act like you do, I'm just saying I'm coming at it from a different perspective."

I'm bored of the beermat. I fish a coin out of my pocket and practise threading it through my fingers; a neat little trick I saw in a film.

"I've no idea what you are on about, mate. For the record — and this is all I'll say on the matter — I'm not acting any differently now than I used to before I got married."

"Or indeed while you were married," says Craig.

Ah ha. So he's just using the opportunity to take a pop. Craig has always assumed that I womanized throughout my marriage and that was why it broke down. Most people think the same. I sigh and wonder if it's worth trying to explain that nothing is ever that black and white. I decide against it. I've never talked about my marriage to Andrea to anyone and I see no reason to start now.

"Mate, we're talking about you here. Am I to understand that you are looking for someone to marry and that somehow, in your naïve little version of how the world operates, you think you both need to go to your wedding bed as mysteries to one another?"

I largely avoid being sarcastic with Craig; he's too decent to take the piss out of but he's wound me up.

"No, I'm not stupid or that green, I realize that if I meet someone special I will want to . . . you know . . . very much."

"Shag her."

"Yes, make love. I'm just not keen to have sex with anyone I don't care for."

"You could learn to care for them." Even I do that.

"Very possibly, but you expect me to shag them just after I've shaken hands with them and before I even know their full names. It's just not my style."

I could be a bastard and make a quick derisive comment about him not having a style, but instead I take a deep breath and consider what he's saying. It's not all stupid. Getting to know a woman before I shag her has never been a prerequisite that I recommend but on the other hand it probably does have some merit, especially for someone like Craig. In retrospect I see that shagging Diane was a complete waste of time. I've had worse, but nothing quite so meaningless.

290

Craig looks nervous; he doesn't want to offend me and he's one of the few people in this world who realizes I can take offence. "It's not that I'm not grateful for your efforts, mate. I am," he insists. "You know that girl you got chatting to last Saturday on my behalf?"

"I can't remember her."

"Josie."

"Did she have a mole, just there?" I point to my top lip.

"Yes, that's her. Well, I met up with her. We had a drink."

"Good on you, mate. Those moles can be really sexy."

Craig stares at me as though I'm missing the point and continues, "I also had lunch with that student slash barmaid that we chatted to in the Hind a couple of weeks ago."

"Really?"

"Do you remember her?"

"No, but I bet she was a honey." I'm proud of him. "I can't believe you haven't told me this before. You dark horse." I playfully punch Craig on the arm. That's my man. That's really cheered me up. Given me a sense of purpose. I was beginning to think I was wasting my time with Craig and the thought was quite a shocker. I waste enough time.

"She was lovely. A bit too hung up on her ex-boyfriend and a tad too young for me to want to take her on another date but it was a very pleasant lunch," says Craig.

"That's the spirit — nothing ventured, nothing gained." Although I would have shagged her. Women on the rebound are easy targets and he needs the practice. "I hope you went Dutch, mate."

"No, I paid."

"But you said you didn't want to see her again."

"I also said it was a lovely lunch."

Sucker.

CHAPTER
TWENTY-NINE

Wednesday 25 October

Lucy

I am without voice. Peter, Auriol, Sebastian and Henry overrule me. I never thought I'd see the day when a man and a bunch of kids became more vocal, vibrant and vital than me. We are going to Center Parcs.

I've always been grateful that I was born a woman. A beautiful, brilliant, wealthy woman living in the western world has very little to complain about. I had my complex, interesting friends to talk to, handsome men to fawn over me and, for long train journeys — I had my own, quite sensational, thoughts to entertain me. I had it all, and having to wear shoes that cut and mangle my feet seemed a small price to pay for the privileges and excitement of being a woman. I've always rather pitied men because they are so simplistic. Their phone conversations are over in thirty seconds flat and they buy underwear in three-packs for five pounds. But suddenly I am living in a world where they have the upper hand. Now I see that there are lots of advantages to being male. Clearly, the less work more pay issue is an advantage for them, as is the fact that they never have to suffer the indignity of asking for help to open a jam jar, but that's just scratching the surface.

It appears that a holiday for five requires planning with military precision, and in fact I could do with an army to help me. Eva started her holiday on Thursday and it transpires that Friday is washing day so when I start to pack, on Saturday morning, I discover that very few of Auriol's clothes are clean and none of them are ironed. I resort to pulling ill-fitting (or worse — ugly) clothes out from the depths of the closet and I retrieve items from the laundry basket, sniff them and spray on perfume in a desperate attempt to freshen them up. I cobble together enough outfits for the week; providing Auriol makes an effort to stay mud- and paint-free, we'll manage. Despite my extensive wardrobe I discover that I own very little that one would describe as casual and therefore appropriate. Still, I can't regret my lack of nylon. Eventually, I find a couple of pairs of Diesel jeans and dig out my Roxy hoodies that I wear when skiing. It hardly matters anyway; Peter rarely notices what I'm wearing these days and I'll keep away from mirrors.

While I whiz around the house frantically trying to find clean and suitable clothes for us all, Peter chooses to stroll to the newsagent and buy a paper. He then sits in the drawing room and reads it. Rose arrives at 10a.m. on the dot with both the boys in tow. She hands over two carefully packed children's suitcases.

"I've included a change of clothes for each day. I'm probably being excessive but it's bound to be very muddy at this time of year and the boys will get into a mess; no doubt Auriol's the same." Oh, bugger. "Besides, it's better to have too many than too few. I've packed swimwear, goggles and towels. They probably provide towels but Henry is allergic to some washing powders so I've packed sheets for him too." I take the two cases off her as the boys speed past me without so much as saying hi. "And here are their sleeping bags in case Peter wants to sleep under the stars. He used to enjoy camping. This bag is full of games, pens, paper, favourite toys, etc." I take the sleeping bags and the huge rucksack off her and wonder how it will all fit into the car. Like Paul Daniels she produces another bag from nowhere. "This bag contains their spare pairs of trainers, Wellington boots, pool shoes and walking boots. I think that should cover it."

Rose calls to the boys and they reappear instantly. I know I have to call them five times, minimum, before they so much as grunt a response. They fling their arms around her and bestow dozens of kisses. She doles out instructions that they have to be good for their daddy (no mention of being good for me). They assure her they will be and then she turns to leave. "I didn't pack any car snacks because I was sure you would have that under control," she says.

Damn. Car snacks. Friday must be grocery shopping day, as well as laundry day, because the cupboards and the fridge are empty. I send Peter back to the newsagents to buy some snacks; he grumbles and asks why I couldn't have noticed that we were without resources earlier on when he went for the paper. I don't say that food supplies had failed to cross my mind until

Rose mentioned them. I don't do food; that's why capsule vitamins and restaurants were invented. I resist pointing out that as far as I am aware there is no law against him independently thinking of buying car snacks. He returns with pockets full of sweets, crisps and chocolate; the children will be bouncing off the roof by the time we arrive. Surely he could have bought the odd packet of raisins or an apple.

I can't fault the resort for being anything other than exactly what it claims it will be. Center Parcs is perfect for people with children and therefore attracts lots of people with children. It's hellish. Auriol and the boys are in the upper quartile of good behaviour, which is a relief and a horror at once. Wherever I go I can smell nappy sacks, a hideous, synthetic flowery scent that fails to mask the odious stench of child waste, and I hear screaming and crying, as spiteful, unruly children abuse their parents or siblings. I bump into women who have nothing in their lives other than their abusive children and therefore enthuse about the availability of salsa lessons and nature walks. It is so depressing. There is a spa but I discover that all the therapists are fully booked for the entire week. Every single appointment has been snapped up by the mothers who don't work and have no issues with making personal calls between 8a.m. and 6.30p.m. No amount of cash in a brown envelope can convince the receptionist to "find" me a space for a treatment. Without the spa I am devoid of escape routes.

I'd read, but this would mean I'd have to spend time in the chalet. I think I may have a diagnosable allergy towards Aztec designs, certainly when there are several different ones (sofa, cushions and walls) in a small confined area; I can feel a migraine coming on. I am suspicious of every eatery in the resort, as the marketing literature describes them as "elegant" and "sophisticated"; yet the guest is assured that high chairs and handbag clips are available. I know there will be an eat-as-much-as-you-like salad bar.

I sign up the children for as many activities as possible. Kid camps are an absolute brainwave. By enrolling Auriol for horse-riding, swimming and tennis lessons and arranging for the boys to ride quad bikes, scale walls and learn to walk on stilts, I am able to secure child-free time *and* consider myself a good mother. I will be able to return to London and crow about how the children enjoyed themselves learning new skills and Rose will have nothing to grumble about. Although it is only day three, the kids are averaging three activities a day (guarantees exhaustion at bedtime — sod the expense) so I will be out of fresh options by 10a.m. tomorrow.

Peter suggests we could have a family round of golf.

"The children will hack up the greens. They need lessons first," I argue.

"Private lessons for the three of them will cost an arm and a leg. We could teach them," he suggests rather unrealistically. I shake my head.

"We could hire a boat and row on the lake."

"In October? I don't think so."

"Well, we could hike. If we keep moving we'll stay warm." I don't take his suggestion seriously enough to answer. I don't "do" hiking boots and I'm not going to "do" hiking boots until Jimmy Choo does hiking boots.

At least Peter and I are alone, even if we are alone in the Center Parcs chalet, which is sadly lacking in style and space. I look around the tiny kitchenette, which has pine cupboards and a minuscule fridge, two sins in my book. The couch transforms into a sofa bed and, predictably, is grossly uncomfortable as a place of rest in either capacity. I can't sit at the dining table, the laminate is coming unstuck at the edges and I can't fight the urge to pick at it. I prowl around the room watching the rain race down the windows. I sigh. Peter ignores me. I sigh again; this time I ensure it's such a meaningful and voluble sigh that his newspaper shivers.

"Anything wrong?" The question is asked in a way which convinces me that Peter couldn't care less if anything is wrong. Still, I choose to interpret his enquiry as genuine.

"This holiday does not express my personality," I state.

"You'll have to elaborate, I'm a mere male."

"Look, pine doors." I point at the offending items and think that the issue is self-explanatory. How can I be happy amid such ugliness?

"What's wrong with them?" asks Peter. It is times like this when I understand how he came to be married to Rose.

"Nothing, if we were on holiday in a log cabin in Canada, but we're not. Besides, they are not even real wood, they are some sort of plastic or painted MDF. These doors don't say 'me'."

"What sort of doors would say spoilt witch?" asks Peter.

I could kill him. I consider battering Peter to death with my vanity case. Instead I opt to torture him slowly. The weapon of choice is my tongue.

"I long for the life where I holidayed in the Sanderson in LA or Chiva-Som in Thailand. The places I went when I was single. I miss that life. I hate it that I'm now supposed to be grateful for Center Parcs with its poxy Mediterranean café with lakeside views — it's hardly the same as a rooftop terrace overlooking LA, is it?"

We both know that I am saying I miss more than the holidays. I miss my apartment in Soho and I don't really like the stultifying, grown-up home in Holland Park. It may be stylish, but whose style? Not mine. I don't like our people-carrier, even if it is a BMW X5. I liked my Merc SLK. Sometimes I wish I'd stayed in my single life. I wish I hadn't married Peter. I wish I'd stayed his mistress. What good does it do marrying a man you are having an affair with? It simply means you stop receiving flowers. What was it my mother always used to say about a man marrying his mistress? I know, she said it created a vacancy. Is that something else I should be worrying about? Will there be another mistress along in time? Is there one already? Hell, I'm reminding myself of Rose. Oh, horror of horrors. Do I remind Peter of her?

"Have sex with me, Lucy."

Hmmm. Seems unlikely if he's still making that sort of request in the middle of the afternoon. But I don't want to get messy. I've just spent over an hour applying my make-up and doing my hair.

"I hate it when you call it sex," I reply glumly. I'm buying time.

"Make love to me."

I glare at him. The last time we had sex I ended up agreeing to come on this holiday. Can I risk doing it ever again? I might find myself agreeing to buy a caravan and spending a week in the Lakes next. Besides, I loathe it when he requests sex. If he wants me why can't he just take me and be a man about the business?

"I love you, Lucy." He moves his paper to one side as he says this. It's the first time he's shown me his face throughout this entire exchange. His is a disarmingly handsome face but I refuse to be moved.

"Hey, isn't that the name of an old TV show?"

"No, that's *I Love Lucy*. I added the 'you' myself. A personal touch, which distinguishes my emotion from that of millions of viewers of 1950s sitcoms."

I love him too but I cannot say so. I won't say so. Nor will I make love to him.

"I need to make a telephone call to the office." I grab my phone, handbag and cigarettes and leave the chalet.

Talking to Mick cheers me up. He doesn't ask about the holiday, which is tactful of him; he knows how much I was dreading it and we don't like to talk about upsetting issues. Mostly we avoid talking about families (we agree that they are exhausting) or his girlfriends (he tells me they are tiresome) and we limit ourselves to talking about work, travel, restaurants or bars.

Delightful adult subjects. I'd begged Ralph to put me on a pitch or send me on a business trip, rather than sign my holiday form, but Ralph insisted it would be a great idea for me to spend time with my family. Easy for him to say. He's probably never had to be up close and personal with people who think the funniest things on earth are whoopee cushions.

I ask Mick for news from the office. I miss it. Center Parcs is claustrophobic and isolated at the same time. I long to be jostling with other commuters on crowded tubes (it's that desperate) and competing with other traders in the markets. Mick tells me we've had confirmation that he and I did secure the New York business. He says he wishes we could celebrate together. At that moment I want to be celebrating with Mick so much that it hurts. I realize that the best I can hope for is a warm glass of Asti Spumante in the noisy family bar.

"Cheer up, Princess; we'll have a night on the tiles when you get back to civilization," says Mick.

"That thought might be the single thing that gets me through this week," I tell him.

"Ralph's talking about splashing out and throwing a company-wide party to celebrate."

"Must be a tax thing. I bet he needs to spend a chunk of cash on staff training or motivation."

"He might just want to reward the teams for our excellent performances of late. You are so sceptical."

"Who the hell cares why he's throwing it, the important thing is I get to dust off my party frock." Or have the excuse to buy something new.

301

"You're coming?"

"Yes."

"I bet you pull out at the last minute."

"Do you want me to party with you?" I can't help but lift the tone of my voice in a flirtatious way at the end of the sentence.

"Forever, Princess." And then he has to ring off quite suddenly as something of note is happening in the US markets. I long to know what.

When I get back to the chalet the children have returned from their day of activities. It appears that the chalet has shrunk and the smidgen of available space is now jammed with steaming coats and muddy boots. The boys are having a duel. Henry's using a mop and Sebastian the broom. They thwack one another's weapons and narrowly miss decapitating one another or, at least, bringing down the ugly net curtains. Even though neither situation would be a genuine catastrophe in my book, I feel duty bound to yell at them and tell them to settle down. They ignore me. Auriol is crying. Actually, crying suggests a level of mediocrity which she is incapable of. Auriol is in fact, weeping and wailing with all the anguish of an Italian mamma who has just been told her firstborn son has married the town whore. I ask her why and it transpires that she feels left out. It is notable that Peter is still reading his newspaper.

I suffer in silence throughout two games of Tumblin' Monkeys, several hands of cards (complicated by the fact that Auriol has difficulty in picking up the rules) and a game of snakes and ladders, which we are unable

302

to complete because Sebastian turns the board upside down when he has to slide down the longest snake. I tell the children that they all need baths and we ought to be getting ready for supper. Suddenly, the ghastly restaurant which serves Vienetta as a dessert appears inviting. I turn to Peter to tell him it's his turn to oversee bathtime but realize he's vanished. The children tell me that he left for the bar an hour ago, I simply hadn't noticed.

Auriol is the first in and out of the bath, as it is agreed that she takes the longest to select her outfit for the evening. Astounding when one considers I only brought a limited choice with us and the boys have an entire wardrobe pressed and packed.

Auriol emerges from her bedroom in a pink cord skirt and an orange jumper; she's wearing multicoloured stripy tights. The jumper has dozens of yellow daisies embroidered on to it and despite the clash of colours she looks divine. Auriol can carry off pretty much any ensemble; she gets that from my side of the family.

"I haven't seen that jumper before," I say.

"Sebastian and Henry gave it to me."

Rose does this from time to time; she buys an unexpected gift for Auriol. Of course everyone sees this as another demonstration of Rose's generosity of spirit — I see it as a criticism. Did she know that I wouldn't have enough clean clothes for the week? I flash a smile that fails to make it to my eyes and say, "How thoughtful of Rose. We must write a thank-you note."

"Lucy."

"Call me Mummy, Auriol."

"The boys don't."

"Well, I'm not their mummy. Rose is. You know that." I try not to sound impatient with her but really! We have gone through this about a hundred times. I hold my breath and wait for her to say that she wishes Rose was her mummy, the next logical step in the conversation, but instead she says, "Mummy, will you make my hair into a French plait?"

I put down the newspaper and consider it. I am reading an interesting article. But, that said, she does look adorable with her hair in a French plait and besides, she didn't express a preference for Rose to be her mother, as I'd expected.

She never has.

She seems reasonably content with me most of the time, despite my obvious inadequacies. I suddenly find that very compelling. Her acceptance of me is in harsh contrast to my own views. I pick up the brush and start to brush her silky blonde hair. Its glossiness feels soothing under my hand.

"Are you having a lovely holiday, Mummy?"

"I'd prefer it if we were somewhere sunny," I reply. I won't lie to her but I don't want to break the moment by telling her my true thoughts on this living nightmare.

"Do you think that's what's bothering Daddy?"

"What do you mean?"

"I'm not sure he's having a very good time, even though there is a swimmingpool and three restaurants." She shakes her head with bewilderment.

Auriol clearly doesn't understand why her parents insist on complicating things. Nor do I. It bothers me that a four-year-old can identify my husband's discontent, despite spending a matter of a few short hours per day in her parents' company. I recap. So far, we have bickered about the accommodation: I am resolute that it is too cramped for what it costs — Peter described it as spacious. I think he must have had a blow to the head; it will be the only blow he's getting if I have to exist in these hideous conditions. We've argued about the food: I think it is bland and full of additives, Peter thinks it's ideal for the kids. We've rowed about the weather: we agree that it's miserable but Peter's point is that I'm unreasonable to have expected anything other. We've exchanged cross words about the hygiene levels of the changingrooms: in my view totally frightful and I intend to write to the management; Peter is of the belief that what doesn't kill one makes one stronger. I stop the mental tally, as these disagreements all took place before supper on Saturday. The atmosphere is considerably less jovial than that of a number of wakes I have attended.

I consider calling Julia, my PA. I could get her to ring me with a fake emergency that demands my immediate return to London. Surely it would be better if I took myself away from here, from Peter. There's no point in staying and allowing our mutual disgruntlement to fester. I sigh and accept a situation which seems remarkably like defeat.

CHAPTER
THIRTY

Friday 27 October

John

Craig is not often what you'd describe as a bundle of laughs but this evening he is especially withdrawn. He seems distracted and disinterested even in my very funny jokes — I'm left chortling to myself. I wonder if I should ask him what's on his mind. I know that he would ask me if the tables were turned, but I dismiss the idea as a little touchy-feely and try my best to bring him round in my own inimitable way: I take the piss out of his new shoes, tell him he's acting like a boring moron and point out a couple of women at the bar who have been eyeing me up all night. None of which gets any sort of reaction at all.

"Mate, we could at least say hello to them, it's only friendly," I plead. I don't tell him but I could do with a diversion myself.

"They won't be interested in me," he moans.

I can't win. If I point out a hottie who has a slightly more pug mate, Craig takes offence because he rightly assumes I've earmarked the hottie for myself and he thinks that I'm implying he can't pull a beauty. If I point out two lovely ladies he goes all self-conscious on me and says I'm shooting out of his league. To be honest, I'm getting a little bored with my self-appointed task of trying to find a match for Craigy. His selection process is a complete mystery to me. I mean, if he gave me a clear brief I could crack this problem, but he hasn't. He hasn't said whether he's after a blonde or a brunette, whether he likes them curvy or androgynous. He's not even given me a list of things to avoid (like women who chew gum, or go to the loo in pairs, or never carry any cash). Even that sort of pickiness would be a start of sorts. He maintains that the woman he's looking for will have a certain *je ne sais quoi* and he'll know it when he sees it.

Bollocks, frankly.

"Can't we just have a quiet drink?" he asks.

I'm about to say no, definitely not, but then I take a moment to think about the question. In fact, a quiet drink might be OK. I can see the appeal. I'm not sure if I want to cop off with anyone tonight either. Not *anyone*.

Oh crap, I'm not saying I want to cop off with *someone*, am I? A specific and significant someone? Oh disaster. Bloody, bloody Connie. How the fuck has that stuff kicked off again? It was maddening enough the first time round.

"OK, mate," I agree. "A quiet night it is." He looks relieved.

I go to the bar and buy in the drinks. I even order him the orange juice he asks for and I don't think about spiking it. When I return to our table I notice that despite being a wet blanket in terms of chatting up babes at the bar, Craig isn't down or depressed. He is distracted, yes, but he's not crying into his beer; he is in fact bright, agitated and excited.

"What's up?" I ask finally.

"Nothing." Craig blushes, which, sadly for him, clearly indicates that something or other certainly is up. My money is that it's a bird. If it was work that was concerning him he'd let me know. He's no shame about boring me rigid about school and yet he's being coy, there has to be a lady involved. It's only fair that he spills.

"You can tell me." I smile, wanting him to trust me.

"No, I probably can't."

"I'm the soul of discretion."

"No, you are a foghorn."

"I'll understand."

"Get real."

"Mate, I'm offended." I try to look very wounded. I am in fact a tiny bit wounded. It's not like I'm a total emotional cripple, is it? I might be able to relate. "Who is she?"

He relents a fraction, as he's an utter soft touch and can't bear offending anyone, even a worthless bastard like me.

"She's nobody to me, yet. But I just think there is the tiniest possibility that she might be someone quite special and I don't want to tell you anything for now."

"You think I'll jinx it?"

"No, but you'll spoil it."

"Have you shagged her?"

"No!"

"Snogged her?"

"No."

"Been out with her?"

"No."

"Well, in truth, mate, there's not much to tell, is there?" Craig glares at me. I take a sip of my pint and then call his bluff. "Oh, I get it. She's married."

"No!" He nearly chokes on his orange juice and indignation.

"But unavailable, am I right?"

"Yes, sort of."

"Has she slapped you back?"

"No, it's not like that."

"Why not?"

"Because."

"Because?" I wait, but Craig refuses to illuminate. I nurse my pint for an indeterminate amount of time until he splutters.

"She hasn't slapped me back because I haven't made my feelings clear. You wouldn't understand. It's nothing concrete. It's someone I've known for a while and long since admired. It just struck me recently that maybe there might be something there. You know? She might be open to . . . Well, she might not think that it's a completely ridiculous idea . . . Oh, but it's impossible."

I try not to laugh at the fact that my mate sounds like a teenage girl.

"Why is it impossible?"

"She's a mum at school. A single mum," he adds hastily. "But if I get it wrong and she doesn't, you know . . ."

"Fancy you?" I prompt.

Craig splits hairs. "If she doesn't respond kindly, then I'm going to look like a total idiot. An unprofessional total idiot."

Craig downs his orange juice in an attempt to hide his blush. I'm unsure whether he's turned scarlet through agitation, frustration or embarrassment. I know he's expecting me to take a pop but I can't. There's something quite endearing about his shy foray through life. I wish I could be so ingenuous.

We sit silently once again. I'm nursing my pint and Craig is nursing his empty glass. Suddenly, it strikes me that we are a bit fucking sad, two studs like us and we can't get any decent action between us. I mean decent. Obviously I get a fair amount of sex, as much as I want. But somehow that in itself has turned into a problem. Getting a shag is not an issue for me, the way it is for Craig. I'm not hampered by restrictive moral codes. Every hole is a goal. Problem is, recently, I've noticed that the instant the woman makes herself available, the thrill bursts. The thrill is in the chase and no one is running any more. Well, almost no one.

Who would have thought there was such a thing as too many willing ladies? Well, Andrea, my ex, said that on a number of occasions, I suppose. And Connie might have said it too. But who'd have thought that *I'd* consider there being such a thing as too many lovely ladies?

Then there's Craig; out there in the same market but can't get any. He's quite handsome in a boyish way. You can look at him and know for a fact that nothing illegal or foreign has ever been shoved up a single orifice. With the new clothes and haircut he's very marketable. And God love him, here comes the crux, he's decent. You know, that should count for something. If there was any sense in this world he should be doing better than I am. He deserves to, but of course he's not. And the reason is — he has no confidence.

Women are harsh, and they can't see past his glasses and his obsessive interest in antique Royal Doulton matchstick pots. They can't forgive the fact that Elton John and Diana Ross feature in his CD collection. Christ, what am I talking about? That is his CD collection. Women see his nervous ways and think he'll fumble with their bra clasp. They watch him carefully chew his food and they assume he lacks the relevant appetites. They judge, dismiss and discard. They miss his decency, his intelligence and his thoughtfulness. They are so bloody stupid — they like bastards. They prefer men like me to men like Craig. If ever there was evidence for female fuckedupness, then that's it.

I thought it was going to be fairly straightforward — women are always moaning about lack of decent blokes, but they don't mean *decent*. I've watched it, time and time again, over the past few weeks. Women accept the drinks he offers but not the conversation. They slash him down with a curt glance when he asks them to dance. They shred him up with a smug giggle if he offers to share a cab. And with every sneer, indifferent shrug, rude dismissal, I see Craig's embryonic confidence shrivel. He's all but given up. I've been doing my best. I've tried to introduce him to the ways of treat them mean and keep them keen but I'm beginning to see that it will never work for Craig.

I look at him and his goodness assaults me. In some ways it's awful being up close to raw goodness if you are a bit of a shit and in other ways it's quite uplifting and compels you to do the decent thing.

"But what if she does like you?" I ask.

Craig stays silent. It's probable that he's never given any serious consideration to this side of the argument. It's pitiful really. I probe further. "What's she like?" No man can resist talking about the object of his desire. Not even me, certainly not Craig.

"She's caring, honest, sincere and practical."

I'm desperate to know if she's a looker but I know it's not the sort of thing Craig cares about; he might not have noticed.

"She sounds perfect, mate." I say this slowly and deliberately so that Craig knows I'm not taking the piss or being glib.

"You think so?" Craig looks at me and grins hopefully. His whole face is awash with expectancy. It beats me why he still rates my opinion but I'm chuffed that he does.

"Just your cup of tea. I think you should give it a go. Why not ask her along to Tom's wedding? She'll see you in your posh suit. Women love that."

"Maybe. I was thinking that I might try and spend some more time with her as a friend first, you know.

312

Take things slowly. She's been through quite a lot and I don't want to scare her off."

The thought of Craig scaring anyone or anything is highly improbable, but I nod, slap him on the back and say, "Sounds like a plan to me, mate. Good luck. Keep me informed."

And somehow I get the feeling my lessons in love for Craig are at an end.

CHAPTER
THIRTY-ONE

Tuesday 31 October

Lucy

Neither Hallowe'en nor Guy Fawkes night stand up to close moral inspection. One is a tradition derived from heathen superstition, centred on the premise that ghosts, ghouls and monsters are somehow amusing, rather than morbid or petrifying. The other is celebrating the cruel torture of a man who was simply exercising his democratic right to protest, albeit in a rather dramatic way. Personally, I could live without either event. Auriol, however, is bouncing with excitement about the treasures lying in store for her this week.

Eva has made the sweetest little costume for Auriol. She's wearing purple and black tights and a purple and orange witch's dress. It's covered in sequins and netting so that it looks more fairy-like than witchy. I'd been instructed to buy her a witch's hat. I've seen exquisite ones selling in a card shop in the city, near my office. They cost an astronomical forty-five pounds. Clearly marketed at time-poor/cash-rich parents, but they were made of felt and were covered in hand-stitched silk stars and crescent moons. I spotted them weeks ago and described them to Eva and Auriol. The cardboard hats sold in most retail outlets were immediately dismissed; Auriol wanted the hand-stitched one. I like it that she recognizes quality and promised to pick one up. Except I forgot. I've forgotten every day on the trot since late September, despite frequent reminders. I've explained that it's frightfully busy at work at the moment, it always is. Today was my last chance, as it is actually Hallowe'en. Eva reminded me of the importance of the purchase as I left the house this morning. I promised I'd buy it at lunchtime. Except Mick suggested we try the new sushi restaurant and the hat went out of my head.

Auriol was not so much disappointed as furious — there are times when I can see myself in her. She hasn't forgiven me for deserting her at the ghastly Center Parcs place, despite the fact that I hung in there until Thursday lunchtime. She angrily flung herself on to the settee and told me in no uncertain terms that I was a useless mummy and that I never did anything right and what was the point of a promise if I couldn't keep to it. All thoughts or observations I've had or made, so I didn't bother arguing. Instead, I left her to Eva and went upstairs to change. I now wish I'd never suggested having a blasted Hallowe'en party. I only did so because it is the sort of thing that Peter expects mothers to do. Bloody Rose setting unworkable precedents again.

I go to my room to shower and change into my Missoni cardi, DKNY jeans and Westwood boots and by the time I come downstairs calm has been restored. Eva has fashioned a hat out of cardboard and stuck gold stars on to it. It's a lucky thing that she always keeps the art box full to brimming. The hat is rather quaint and fetching. Aren't home crafts the new black this year? Connie was excited to receive a knit-your-own scarf kit from M&S, last Christmas.

The table looks wonderful. Eva, Peter and Auriol have carved a plethora of pumpkins. There are at least ten outside, near the door, and ten more artfully arranged around the kitchen. Eva's made pumpkin soup and pumpkin pie. She's also made purple jellies with green jelly worms hidden inside them and tiny chocolate cakes shaped like cat faces. Plus, she's mixed an enormous vat of rather strong punch (under my instruction). I've ordered two dozen adorable witch cup-cakes from a chi-chi bakery around the corner. They arrive in an enormous wicker basket and while £120 seems a little steep for twenty-four cup cakes, their arrival enchants Auriol. She forgives my forgetfulness over the hat and therefore I consider the cakes priceless. The last thing I want is her moaning to her father about my inadequacies, he's all too well aware of them as is.

I have the distinct feeling that he didn't buy into the authenticity of my urgent recall to the office. I sense his disapproval of me, it simmers dangerously. It's very important that this party goes well. Although I don't regret my decision to bale out of the holiday, I know that I need to claw back some ground with Peter. All my old tricks involved skimpy knickers. That thought is as alien as my attending the Parents' Association fund-raising Tupperware party. Hopefully, the party will be seen as an act of reconciliation.

Three or four little girls are deposited by their mothers. I can't quite remember all the names of the girls, or the mothers. The girls all look alike. They are children of our time — pretty but sulky and demanding. The mothers are all similar too, initially harassed until the drop-off is achieved and then the tension melts from their faces as they anticipate the delight of grabbing a sprog-free coffee. None of us ever thought that such a thing would become a treat.

Eva has agreed to stay to help with the party. I'm paying her double time. She's invited two of her nanny friends, both of whom have arrived with three more children apiece. Eva informs me that I'll have to pay her friends for their professional services too. She insists she can't manage without them. I want to point out that without them, there would be a damn sight less to manage but I can't risk it. If she takes offence and goes home I'll have to cancel the party. Instead I usher the three nannies and the three million children into the playroom, where Eva earns her weight in gold by organizing a game of ghostly musical chairs, which is exactly the same as traditional musical chairs except the children get to howl as they run around waiting to claim their seats.

Peter arrives at about the same time as Connie, Luke and the girls. I realize that for him to do this he must have left the office at about four-thirty. I'm grateful that he's made the effort, and I do know it will have been an effort — after all, I left at three-thirty and to do so I had to suck my boss's dick. Just kidding. But I did have to promise to be in the office before 6 a.m. tomorrow.

"My God, the table looks fantastic!" says Connie. "Look at those cakes! They are amazing." Unfortunately Connie is not pointing to the ones in the wicker basket but rather the cat-shaped ones, which Fran and Auriol have already started to gobble.

"I can't take all the credit," I say, which is no word of a lie but gives the impression that I could perhaps take some of the credit and I'm just being modest. I begin to dole out healthy-sized beakers of punch to the adults. "Is that the doorbell? Do you think it is likely to be kids trick or treating already?"

I'm mildly irritated. I haven't had time to arrange the treats on the pumpkin plate that I bought last year especially for said purpose. Why don't I have the time to do anything properly and elegantly any more?

"It's not trick or treaters," calls Peter from the hall. "It's just the twins."

"The twins?" I didn't invite them. Last week I saw just about enough of them to last me a lifetime.

Peter bustles the boys down into the kitchen. Henry is dressed as a wizard, Sebastian as a little devil. It suits him. I can see in an instant that the costumes are handmade and not by the au pair; they don't have an au pair. Rose is right behind them. Oh God, he didn't invite her too, did he?

It's always an awkward moment when we find ourselves in confined spaces, particularly with people we have in common. Luke and Connie are overly nice to Rose so that she doesn't feel betrayed that they are still friends with me, which I find irritating and unnecessary after all this time. They fling their arms around her and comment that she looks wonderful. It's a trifle nauseating, although, it pains me to admit it, she does look reasonable. New haircut and new clothes are in evidence. Has she lost weight? Is she wearing make-up?

"I can't stay," says Rose. I hadn't heard anyone ask her to. "It's very nice of you to invite the boys over mid-week," she adds.

She's making a point. She doesn't think Peter sees enough of them considering we all live very close to one another, despite the fact that we took them on a week's holiday just last week. We never get any credit for the things we do manage. Just criticism for the occasional lapse.

I beam broadly. "They are always welcome. After all, it's their home too," I say to annoy her.

"No, it's not." She looks directly at me for the first time. Normally she prefers to avoid my eye. I'm not too sure as to why. I don't have the power to turn her into stone. Believe me, if I had, she'd know it by now.

Luke picks up the wicker basket of cakes and offers her one.

"No, thank you. I'm not a fan of shop-bought cakes," she says. How did the she-devil know they were shop-bought? "Besides, I'm in a bit of a hurry."

"No doubt you have somewhere special to go," I comment. Under my breath I add, "after all, it *is* Hallowe'en."

She hears me, which isn't a bad thing. But from the filthy look that Peter fires in my direction I fear he did too, which is a bad thing. I really would be more magnanimous in my victory, if only I felt victorious.

"I've a date, actually," says Rose, and then like the witch that she surely is, she turns on her heel and vanishes.

With her she takes quite a lot of the party spirit.

The children stuff themselves on fizzy drinks and cakes and become hyper. I don't bother to try to get Auriol to stick with water. I haven't the energy for the battle, and besides, Connie won't gossip about my failing. The children scream and behave daftly, as expected, but the adults are much more subdued. We munch our way through the soup and pie and it's all delicious; compliments are duly given to Eva but the atmosphere is tainted. Although we make reasonable headway into the punch, none of us appears the least bit merry. It's amazing that Rose can ruin a party even when she's not at it.

Connie and I escape the hot house by offering to drag the kids to two or three neighbouring houses to trick or treat. We leave Luke in charge of Flora and Peter in charge of the bag of jelly lollypops (bought from Harrods, delivered to my office by courier). I haven't bothered to put them on the pumpkin plate. There's not much point, everyone knows I'm not perfect.

As the door slams behind us the kids dash ahead and straight up the path of our neighbour.

"That was a million laughs," I comment to Connie.

"Well, you didn't help get the evening off to a glorious start, did you?" she points out with best-friend killer honesty. "Why can't you be more pleasant to Rose? She's never done anything to hurt you."

"Hasn't she?"

"No, she hasn't, Lucy. She's lovely. Everyone knows she is."

And that's why I can't be more pleasant to her.

"You could just try being polite. Peter would appreciate it. Why do you complicate things?"

"Some things are just irresistible, Connie. You know that," I reply.

I feel chastised by Connie's appeal and worse, I know that once all the guests have gone, I am going to hear more of the same from Peter.

"So who is her date with?"

"A guy called Rob, I think."

"Where did she meet him? Stamp club?"

"No."

"Did she place an advert?" I ask meanly. Well, honestly, Connie can't expect me to believe that after six barren years men have suddenly started to beat a path to her door, not without some provocation.

"What do you care, Lucy," says Connie. And by her tone it's clear she isn't going to say any more on the subject. She's fiercely loyal to Rose. I feel very alone.

It's after ten by the time we manage to get Auriol and the boys to bed. They are jacked up on sweets and I don't have the energy to stem the flow, so when I notice Henry smuggle a tube of Smarties under his pillow all I say is, "Don't forget to clean your teeth." I close the door on them, take a deep breath and go in search of Peter. I might as well face the music.

He's sitting in his study; he has a large tumbler of whisky in his hand and his eyes are closed. I watch him from the doorway and my chest tightens with love. I still adore him. Even though nowadays we are cross with one another more often than not and even though I know he's about to scold me as though I am a child, I still worship him. Always have. Always will. So why isn't it simpler?

"I know you're there," he says without opening his eyes.

"I can't deny it."

"Did you have a good night?" he asks. His tone is flat.

"Not really."

"No. I thought not."

"You?"

"No."

"Still, the children seemed to enjoy themselves and that was the point," I say with forced joviality.

"Yes, I think they did. Although the boys are not babies any more. They'll soon pick up on your antagonism towards their mother unless you can find a way to keep it in check. For that matter Auriol will too. You were hardly a shining example of generosity of spirit tonight, were you?"

I remain silent. I hate it when he behaves like a schoolteacher, my father or God. Especially when he has a point.

"Why can't you be nicer to her?" he asks.

How long has he got? "It's not personal. It's my sense of humour," I lie. "You know I have a wicked streak."

"Yes, I do," he confirms.

How can I tell him that the reason I find it hard to be nice to Rose is because I think she is always judging me and finding me lacking. She saps my confidence as no other soul on this earth has ever been able to do. Everything about her is a condemnation of me. Her flat, sensible shoes chastise my strappy Manolo Blahniks. Her untrammelled hair reprimands my carefully coiffured look — she might as well wear a sign around her neck declaring that spending £250 on highlighting every month is a mortal sin. Her home-cooked organic meals declare that the convenience foods that I have to resort to on occasion are practically poisonous. Besides, everybody is nice to Rose. She doesn't need me to be nice to her too.

"Poor Lucy," says Peter. His tone is full of genuine concern and a little bit of sadness. He knows why I can't be nice to her. I have to keep making the snide comments about her weight and her tediously dull nature, lest he forgets. Peter loved her once. It is possible that he could love her again. No doubt if the entire situation was reversed Rose would be nice to me. Of course she would, and that irritates me too. I'm not as good a person as she is.

I fling myself on top of Peter. He opens his eyes and stares at me. The intensity is a little overwhelming when he brushes a strand of hair behind my ear and asks, "What are you scared of, Luce?"

"Me? Nothing. I'm never scared," I reply automatically.

"No, seriously. What are you scared of?" he pursues.

Before Peter I feared very little in this world, virtually nothing. But now I have all sorts of fears. I fear how much I love him and I fear that he doesn't love me as much as I love him, or as much as the day he met me, or as much as he loved Rose. But my biggest fear is that I might stop loving him. If I ever stop loving him the world has no purpose, no sense. We stay silent for many minutes. Peter gently strokes my back and continues to stare into my eyes. I begin to feel self-conscious. I haven't checked my make-up since applying it this morning. And when I weighed myself yesterday I was two pounds heavier than last time I checked. I wonder if I feel heavier to Peter. Am I going to give him a dead leg by sitting on his knee?

"You're crying," he says.

I am? The shame.

"Peter, please don't stop loving me," I blurt, answering his question, albeit indirectly. "Even when I'm horrible."

"I won't. We're forever, Lucy. You know that."

But he probably once said forever to Rose too, didn't he? Talk's cheap. I must look unconvinced because Peter adds, "I'll always love you, even though you are the most malicious bitch in town and you don't deserve it."

He grins as he says this; his wide, sexy, usually irresistible grin. I know he's trying to make a joke. It's the kind of thing I used to say about myself. But right now I consider his ugly comments offensive in the extreme. I could rip his head off with my bare hands or bite off his bollocks and spit them in his eye. It takes every ounce of self-control I have for me to stand up and walk away without kicking him.

"I have to be up very early tomorrow. I think it makes sense for me to sleep in the spare room. I don't want to disturb you," I say calmly.

"Oh, don't be like that," he says, seeing through my transparent excuse as I'd wanted him to. I want to reject him but I don't want to have to be above board about it. It's complicated.

"I'm not being like anything," I reply. I make a dignified exit.

"What about a goodnight kiss?" he calls after me.

I pretend not to hear him. If I kiss him and he uses his tongue, I'm not sure I'd resist the temptation to bite it off and then swallow it. A consequence he should have considered before making those ill-advised comments.

CHAPTER
THIRTY-TWO

Saturday 4 November

John

"I'm sure it's not your sort of thing," said Craig. Underselling his offer even while he was trying to tempt us. "You probably have cooler places to go but I could do with the extra pairs of hands, if you could spare the time."

Tom shrugged and said he'd check with Jenny but he imagined it would be all right, they'd both go along.

"Count me in," I said immediately.

"Really?" Craig couldn't hide his surprise.

"Too right, mate. I love fireworks night, always have."

I love the smell of hot dogs and onions in buns, I love drunken kids messing around on waltzers at the dodgy fairs that erupt from nowhere. I love the smell of burning. It's an exciting night, dangerous and colourful.

"Our school bonfire night will be a relatively small affair. A number of local schools share a sports ground and we normally all chip in together to build a bonfire in the field. There will be a couple of fairground attractions but no death wheel or rollercoaster."

"I get it. It will be more coconut shies and hook-a-duck," I said.

"Yes."

"Sounds great." Tom gave me a sly wink over the top of his pint glass. He hadn't forgotten about Connie. Craig, who has a more innocent mind, had.

As we walk to the school sports ground I can't deny a definite feeling of excitement and anticipation and it isn't the bangers that I'm getting worked up about. It's freezing cold and drizzling, but that's traditional. It's only 6p.m. but fireworks belonging to the impatient occasionally flash in the sky, bloom and disappear. As a kid I thought fireworks were like little spells, tiny shots of magic exploding into the air, and I get a similar sense now.

The crowd, as expected, is predominantly families. I start to scan the masses for her face. There are dads carrying kids on their shoulders. There are grandparents fussing over the cost of the neon antennae and flashing wands that the touts are enticing the children with. There's quite a show of teenagers. The girls are dressed inappropriately for the season, wearing short skirts and low-cut shirts; they refuse to fasten their coats no matter how much their mams nag. The lads stand around smoking, sharing a can or two and cussing in loud voices. It's familiar.

Jenny, Tom and I check in with Craig. His school is not in charge of anything too grand, at his own insistence. He's worked behind the scenes for months now but he didn't want to light the first firework. His staff is in charge of the various toffee-apple stores that are dotted around the field.

Having asked us to lend a hand, he's now insisting that everything is under control. It's easy to doubt him, as he's looking extremely harassed and kids are nicking toffee-apples whenever his back is turned. Tom, Jen and I agree to see him later and we kill some time in the funfair. We make ourselves dizzy on the waltzers and I prove that I'm a dab hand at arcade games and shooting ranges, which just goes to show my youth wasn't wasted.

I keep a constant eye out for Connie and am rewarded when I spot her in the queue for cups of tea.

"I'll go and get us all a cuppa. Leave you two lovebirds alone for a while," I tell Tom and Jen, then I quickly disappear into the crowd before they can offer to come with me.

"Hello, Connie." I join her in the queue.

"What are you doing here, John?" She sounds annoyed and panicked in roughly equal proportions, which surprises me — we'd left it friendly enough after our day out. Connie is wearing a pair of the neon disco boppers, which makes me smile. Sometimes she's so uncool she almost circles back in on herself and becomes cool again.

"Nice look," I say with a grin. She can't be humoured — she glares at me and then snatches them off her head.

"Fran wanted me to wear them." She won't be side-tracked. "What are you doing here?"

"I'm here with Tom, my mate and his girlfriend — I should say fiancée or else she'll get arsey. We're here to support Craig. This is quite a big event for him."

"Yes, it is for *everyone* at the school, headmaster, teachers, children and *parents*," she hisses, as she stealthily takes a guilty look around.

"I thought you might be here." I don't see the point in lying. I'm here for her.

Now she looks furious. "Luke's here too." Ah. I hadn't given that much thought. "If he sees you . . ." She lets the sentence trail away because we both know what the consequences might be.

I try to distract her. "Have you been in the funfair?"

"No."

"Not even to hook-a-duck?"

"Luke's over there now, with the girls."

"Have you tried the hot dogs?"

"Generally I avoid them, they're a health hazard."

"Bought candyfloss?"

"No."

"But you like candyfloss."

I have no idea whether she likes candyfloss or not. It's a punt. Suddenly, she looks exhausted. I hope she's tired of resisting me.

"How come you remember things like that? It's unfair. You being here is unfair."

She stares at her feet. The grass has been trodden to mud, she's in heels and her boots are caked. I find her inappropriate footwear pleasing. She's not übersensible, despite what she wants me to believe.

We are at the front of the queue now. "Can I buy your tea?"

"I have money."

I ignore her and order. "Two of your finest polystyrene cups, mate."

The spotty teenager who is serving scalds my hand as he passes me the tea. I offer one to Connie. She hesitates.

"Come on Con, it's freezing. It will taste like cat's piss but you can wrap your fingers around it at least and get a bit of warmth."

She looks over her shoulder and finally takes one from me. Then she allows me to splash in some whisky from my hip flask.

"Do not let a member of the PA see you doing that," she giggles, relaxing slightly after only a sip. She's such a lightweight when it comes to boozing.

"Good turnout," I say, looking over towards the crowd around the bonfire.

"Yes, but I haven't seen your special friend, *Diane*."

I keep my eyes in front of me and consider the situation. Ah, so Diane is a gossip. I knew she had a big mouth, a fact I appreciated when she was giving head, but it may prove to be a nuisance now. She's clearly told people of our interlude. It might not be a bad thing, it has at least piqued Connie's interest *and* it's introduced the topic of sex. Sex is something neither of us has alluded to since we re-met. Before, we shared the most explicit relationship ever. Now, I pretend to be as interested in sex as a spayed dog but the truth is, whenever I look at Connie, I envisage her with her legs or her mouth wide open.

"Is it true? Did you have sex with Diane?"

"Yes."

"Why? Why did you do that?" she demands.

Connie sucks on her top lip when she's angry. Oh crap, the session with the yummy mummy might make her bounce. Jealousy is useful, disappointment is not. I lead her away from the crowds and the caravan selling tea and move towards the thickets of trees that surround the field. She follows me with no resistance. It's not in her interest to be seen with me.

"I thought we were supposed to be being friends," she says.

"We are."

"Sleeping with someone under my nose isn't exactly friendly, is it?"

"As we are just friends, why does it matter who I sleep with?"

"Were you trying to make me jealous?"

"No, I never thought about that, although I'm thrilled to see that you are."

"I am not," she cries loudly, a little like a hammy pantomime dame. "Were you trying to humiliate me? Was this about getting a reaction from me?"

"No. It was nothing to do with you."

"You like her?" I hear panic and maybe even tears in Connie's voice. I turn to her and catch her in the full intensity of a straight-on stare.

"When I say it was nothing to do with you, I'm not being accurate. I needed to have sex with her to understand something about myself, but in a way it was all about you." She's all ears. "I needed to see if it was you I wanted or the challenge of a married mother."

She looks away. She's speechless. A first. That's the problem with being honest, so few people can deal with it. The rain falls like a mist between us. I watch her digest what I've said.

Eventually she steels her courage. "And?"

"And it's you. Just you I want."

She sighs and stays silent for about a week. Dragging her eyes to mine, she says finally, "You are talking yourself into this. It's not real."

"I don't agree." I hold her gaze. I need to force us both to face this.

"We'd be like the millennium eve."

"You've lost me."

"Too much expectation, too much anticipation."

"So you are expecting me."

"I didn't mean that."

"And anticipating me."

She shakes her head, trying to clear the confusion. She never will. "Do you get some sort of kick out of destroying my peace of mind?"

"Oh, Greenie."

I wonder if I should tell her that she didn't used to be special, every piece of skirt was a challenge and nothing more, her included. But now the stakes are much higher, and yes, I do get a kick out of chasing her and tempting her. But the most enormous kick would be having her. Perhaps even keeping her. When did that happen? How the hell did that happen? I'm poacher turned gamekeeper. It's a fucking disaster.

The firework display is about to start, so people amble towards the cordoned-off area. There's quite a crowd gathered. Connie is scanning it, probably looking for her family, but she doesn't leave me. There's a small brass band, which is predictably amateurish but the crowd cheer encouragingly. The English are good at encouraging mediocrity. Then there's a moment's hush when the fairground music, screaming tots, loud teens and shoddy tinny music seem to cease as we wait for the first firework.

Whoosh. The children scatter and then recollect themselves; there's the sound of applause and embarrassed half-hearted oohs and ahs as the sky is momentarily illuminated by rockets and fountains that billow and vanish and flashgun flares that zoom and pop. It's magical.

"Was Diane a good shag?"

She knows it's beneath her dignity to ask but she can't help herself. I love her weakness and vulnerability. Her hair has curled in the rain and she looks a lot like she has looked before. When before? I try to remember and slowly it dawns on me. Oh God, the first time. In the park, wherever the hell that was. I'm having flashbacks to the first time we had sex. That's serious.

"No," I assure her. We both watch the fireworks, comfortably at one another's side.

I remember that time in the park. She rolled off me and said it was a great fuck. *She* set the tone. She told me she didn't want to fall in love and all I did was follow her lead. Yeah, it was convenient for me. I probably didn't want to be tied down but if she hadn't said that . . . If she hadn't called it a fuck. Maybe things might have been different, mightn't they? Because there is a moment where we choose. There always is. And she chose to stomp out our possibility. She might have wanted more from me later on, but it was too late. That first moment, as she rolled off, was the pivotal one.

The fireworks crash and zoom around us. The black sky is alive with blue, pink, white and red showers. The colours zap and are then followed by smoke trails that languidly float into nothingness. The crowds become more confident in their encouragement and enthusiastically yell out their delight.

"We never talk about it," she says. She makes the comment and then lets it float with the smoke into the blackness. I can't be certain but I get the sense that she was thinking about our first time too. I feign ignorance.

"What do you mean?"

"We never talk about *us*. About what I did. What *we* did. How cruel and terrible I was. Or how exciting it was. Or even how sad it was." I shrug. What can I say? "I don't know how you felt about it. *You* don't know how you felt about it. Don't you think that's a bit odd?"

She calls us "it" because it's easier if things are impersonalized. She doesn't need to tell me that.

"We were together for hours the other week and we talked about Big Brother, tiles in your bathroom, the best place to eat jellied eels and I hate jellied eels but we did not talk about Andrea, or Luke, or you or me."

Or love.

Of course we didn't. I might have done if we'd got into the sack. I might have managed to answer some of her questions then, fill in the odd gap. I have been giving it some thought and I have questions of my own.

For example, could we have fallen in love? Might I have married her and not Andrea? Yeah, all right, it wouldn't have been straightforward. What is? She'd have had to have left St Luke and all, but that was a possibility, wasn't it? At one point, I'm sure it was. Could there have been a world where we'd have stood together, with a couple of sprogs of our own, and watched fireworks? Would I have liked that world?

Is she thinking what I'm thinking?

They keep the best till last, a bouquet of colourful rockets, fountains and spinning wheels that make the night look starry when in fact the clouds and rain dominate. I roar with the rest of the crowd. I like my thrills cheap and I don't mind illusions. Applause patters across the field.

"I think we need to talk," she says. She sounds breathless. Nervous. She stares at me. Her mouth is inviting.

I lean closer. A little closer. A fraction nearer still. Our lips are an inch away. I wait. She'll have to come to me. She'll have to choose when because if I get it wrong she'll never forgive me. This is a one-shot game.

"Well, well, well. You two look very cosy. I hope I'm not interrupting anything."

Connie and I jump apart and land with a crash face to face with Diane. I don't hesitate. In a seamless swerve I turn, I lean forward and kiss Diane on the cheek. The move is so swift that everyone could choose to believe that was always the direction I was heading. If they need to believe that.

"You're not interrupting anything at all," says Connie. "He's all yours."

She turns and stalks off, instantly dissolving back into the crowds.

The fireworks are over. Fuck it. I turn to Diane.

"Are you having fun?"

"Not really. Muddy fields aren't my thing but who knows? The night is young," she says with a smile. She really needs to see a decent dentist.

CHAPTER
THIRTY-THREE

Saturday 4 November

Rose

The fireworks were splendid. There was nothing amateur about the show at all. Craig and the headteachers from the other schools must be really pleased with themselves. The vast majority of the crowds are now contentedly shuffling towards the gate. Some teenagers are heading back towards the funfair stalls.

I did an early shift on the toffee-apple stall and so am now free to enjoy the festivities with the twins, Daisy and Simon and Connie, Luke and the girls. Connie and Luke have also brought along Auriol and she's a welcome addition. I'd rather she join us than I bump into Lucy and Peter. Although it's unlikely they'd bring Auriol here, a family bonfire is not Lucy or Peter's idea of a good way to spend a Saturday night. More fool them. I buy candyfloss for all the kids and present them with a flourish.

"What about sugar content?" asks Daisy.

She's having a gentle pop because normally I'm pretty fascist when it comes to the children's eating habits. Daisy finds this particularly amusing, as we were brought up on a diet of pick-and-mix penny sweets and she reasons it never did us any harm — besides the cavities and my lifelong membership of Weight Watchers, that is.

I grin at her. "It's firework night — even I accept that treats are in order."

"You seem in really good spirits."

"I am."

"Dating is really working out for you, isn't it?" she says as she links my arm. She's joyful.

In fact, it's not, but why burst her bubble? The reason I'm so happy tonight is that I'm surrounded by my family and friends and I'm doing a traditional family and friends activity. Just like a normal, non-divorced mother. Dating is more or less something I'm doing so that my friends and family don't despair of me.

I avoid answering her question. "There's Mr Walker, the headmaster. I think I'll go and congratulate him on such a successful evening. Don't lose me."

"OK, we'll be around the bonfire. I think Luke and Simon want to try the toasted marshmallows."

Craig beams at me as he sees me approach.

"Hello, Rose. Are you having a good evening?"

"Very much so."

"Here with your family?"

"Yes and some friends, everyone's having a super night."

"Wonderful." Craig's beam is so wide, it's almost painful. I fear his skin might tear. It's rather special to come across someone who gets so much from creating pleasure for others. I can't help but beam back at him.

"How are the takings?"

"We've done splendidly, Rose. In fact, all but sold out. I was thinking of shutting up shop and finding my friends."

"Yes, you should take the rest of the night off. Have some fun," I enthuse. "You could come and meet my sister, if you like."

The offer is out before I think what I'm doing. Unintentionally I've put Craig in an awkward position. He probably wanted to catch up with his own pals. Now his good manners will dictate that he has to spend time with me. I blush. Craig is unperturbed, in fact he is so polite he manages to appear delighted and agrees at once.

He leaves the toffee-apple store in the charge of Wendy Pickering, a dubious decision in my opinion, but Craig doesn't seem unduly worried and we set off together to find my gang.

"The sports masters are not going to be happy with this churned field," I comment as we make our way across the mud.

"Mr Shaw is rarely cross," comments Craig.

"True, he's lovely," I comment.

Craig shoots me an inquisitive glance. I realize he's probably aware of Mr Shaw's heart-throb status and I don't want to leave the wrong impression. Mr Walker probably has my name down as some sort of nympho after my inappropriate confessions regarding internet dating. I have to clarify that I don't fancy Mr Shaw, even at the risk of sounding a little overly familiar *again*.

"It's such a shame he's blond, I prefer dark-haired men," I add, and then I stare at Craig's thick black hair. I start to blush. What in the world am I thinking of? I'm flirting with the headmaster. Has Daisy been spiking my hot chocolate?

It's peculiar that on a conscious level I know all the reasons Craig is unsuitable as an object of my, shall we say, affection or interest? But if ever I were to have feelings for a man then it would be a man like Mr Walker. No, in truth it would be Craig. I know that he's the boys' headmaster and it would be terrible to have a relationship with him for about a gazillion reasons (as Henry would say). If it didn't work out I'd have to drag the boys out of Holland House and start them at another school. The boys would be devastated to leave Holland House and if it went well the consequences would be just as upsetting for them. They are mortified if a teacher nods to us in Tesco's; they'd be spun straight into therapy if they ever had to deal with seeing Craig eating cornflakes at our breakfast bar. Besides, he's younger than me. And it's not as though he's even hinted that he has any interest in me at all beyond the purely platonic. He wants me to help him find someone on the internet, he sees me as a facilitating cupid. Once he registers, I bet he'll be beating off women with a stick; he's attractive, very interesting, moral, decent, kind. I enjoy chatting with Craig.

Oh, OK, I admit it; I fancy the pants off him.

On and off, for the past sixteen nights, I've had erotic dreams about Craig. Me! Erotic dreams! I was so sure that my libido had shrivelled up and turned to dust. Apparently it's just been hibernating. Since I've discovered that he's single I've started to think of him as something other than a headmaster. Something quite other. Last Saturday I dreamt that we were picnicking on alpine mountains (innocent enough). One moment I was admiring the view, the next I was butt naked and he was eating strawberries off my body. I had to wake myself up. It is so inappropriate to have thoughts like that, even unconscious ones. The thing that disturbed me the most was that I was still a size sixteen, even in my dream, and neither Craig nor I seemed to mind.

On Tuesday I dreamt that we were both in a classroom, discussing the boys' school work (with particular emphasis on the space topic that Sebastian is so excited about right now). One moment we are sitting on those silly classroom chairs that are designed for diddy men and the next we are rolling around on the story carpet, butt naked. In reality, sitting on those chairs is one of the most fearful moments of my life and the main reason I dread parents' meetings. For a start, as I ease into the chair, I always fear I'll break it. Then, once I am in it, there is no way to get out. Even Houdini would struggle. When I stand up the chair is always clasped to my bottom and I have to back out of the classroom. But in my dream there was no sign of that potential embarrassment and humiliation. I felt comfortable.

On Wednesday I dreamt we were climbing trees, butt naked. On Thursday I dreamt we were swimming in a lagoon, butt naked. Do you see a theme? Last night I wasn't bothering to wake myself up. I reasoned that yes, the dreams are inappropriate but what harm? No one knows what I'm thinking — I keep my silly fantasies to myself. I might as well enjoy them and they are so very, very enjoyable.

I look at Craig. The fine mist of drizzle has settled all over his coat, glasses and hair. But instead of looking gloomy and damp he looks iridescent. He's staring at me with mild amusement and a slightly quizzical grin. I don't believe he is laughing at me — he's not the sort to do that. I always feel very secure and snug in Craig's company, as my butt-naked dreams testify. I lock those thoughts away in a big treasure chest and then mentally bury them under fifty foot of sand. I search for something neutral to say.

"Wasn't it glorious weather yesterday? Who would have thought it would turn out so cold today? I love bright autumnal days like yesterday, don't you?"

"It's my favourite kind of weather," agrees Craig.

"I mowed the lawn. I hope that tides me over for the winter now. Although it's a job I rather enjoy, especially when it's bright."

"There's nothing like the smell of fresh air combined with newly cut grass, is there?" he says.

"Absolutely delicious. Makes me feel young. Foolish thought, although not an illusion I rush to push away." Craig smiles, but he can't fully understand; after all, he *is* young. "Make believe, now and again, is a marvellous thing. Isn't it?" I add. I grin to myself. If only he knew.

I spot my family and quicken my pace, as I'm always in a hurry to be with them. However, while I'm delighted to see them, they are not all similarly pleased to see Craig and me. The boys are mortified that I've brought the headmaster over to socialize and glare at me for a minute or two. Luckily, Auriol and Fran are too young to be intimidated and after a short time they encourage the boys to concentrate on twirling sparklers. Connie also seems somewhat abashed by Craig joining us. I put this down to new-mum-at-school syndrome. She'll be desperate to give the right impression (interested, proactive parent but not too pushy). She stays very quiet and holds Luke's hand throughout. Daisy doesn't see anything other than a fellow professional and someone to talk curriculums with, and so manages to desist from asking Craig if he has any designs on me. We write our names with sparklers, visit the hall of mirrors and have a go at knocking the coconuts off their perches. All too quickly, time speeds by; Connie and Luke say they have to get the girls home and Daisy offers to take the boys home for me and put them to bed so I can stay behind and help with the clear-up. Craig and I find ourselves paired off, dismantling the toffee-apple carts so that they can go into the van conveniently. It's notable that most of the other committee members have scuttled home, skiving off the heavy work.

"I'd have put money on the fact that it would be you and me left with the clean-up," comments Craig. He's

343

smiling as he says it and doesn't seem to mind too much, although his nose is red with cold and he isn't wearing gloves so his fingers must be raw with the bitter temperatures.

"At least we know that the equipment will be returned to the hire company clean and in good condition. We'll be entitled to a return of our deposit," I say.

"You're very conscientious, aren't you, Rose?"

"Yes, always have been. We're made the way we're made, don't you think?"

"I'm not sure. That sounds quite fatalistic. I believe in choice. Don't you think we make our own choices?"

"Yes, but usually in ignorance," I laugh. "The thing is I'm a swot, can't help myself. I'm programmed that way. I always impressed the teachers at school."

"I bet you did."

"To avoid alienating my classmates I would sometimes throw the odd question, and while I desisted from sleeping with boys to curry favour, I was prepared to let them copy my homework."

"Very sensible," laughs Craig. "I was just the same. Well, not that I considered sleeping with boys to curry favour." He blushes as he makes the joke. "I just hung out with the cool guys and did their homework for them. I was first-generation university."

"Me too, a dubious honour. Parents so proud —"

"Lecturers so unimpressed."

We laugh at the shared experience. I don't know if it's because there is smoke in the air (that is somehow intoxicating) or whether it is the belief, real or

344

imagined, that Craig understands me which prompts me to add, "Sometimes I wish I could rewrite my youth." Craig looks alarmed. I rush to reassure him. "Not major decisions. I'd still marry Peter and have the twins but I'd do some things a little differently."

"Like what?"

"I'd have been cooler, less eager to please. There are at least half a dozen major occasions when I'd have worn something different, including my wedding day. I'd have worked a bit harder at learning to swim."

Craig empathizes. "I'd have faked an interest in football at school. That would have saved me a lot of hardship."

"I'd have told Phil Hawood I loved him."

"Who's Phil Hawood?"

"My childhood sweetheart. He was a rare soul, someone who knew what he wanted from a very early age. He wanted to settle down, have a family, be happy. I wasn't a very decent girlfriend to him. I was too immature to deal with his foresight."

"What happened to him?"

"He settled down with someone else, had a family and is happy," I say with an accepting shrug.

"Oh."

"Well, there are certain men who are the falling in love type and the woman they fall in love with is largely irrelevant."

Craig chuckles. "I wish I was one of those types."

"Still, Phil Hawood was my hope throughout my divorce. Not that I thought I'd meet him and tear him away from his wife and family or anything crazy like that, you understand — I know when a ship has sailed. It was just that knowing that once upon a time someone loved me very much, well, it was comforting. It seemed reasonable to believe that one day someone would love me in that way again."

"I'm sure they will, Rose," Craig says with an encouraging smile.

I grin back at him. "Oh, I hope so, because if my sister has her way I'm likely to die trying."

Craig checks his watch. "Damn." He glances around the field.

"What's up?"

"I wanted you to meet my friends and I think they might have gone. They've probably sloped off to a pub."

I grin like a helpless teenager, thrilled with the thought that Craig wanted to introduce me to his friends.

"I particularly wanted you to meet Tom and Jen. The thing is, they are getting married next weekend and I wondered —" Craig breaks off mid-sentence and looks to the sky. I follow his gaze. Has a final lone firework caught his eye? I can't see anything. "And I wondered if you'd like to come with me. To the wedding. I'm best man, you see, and I haven't got a date. I think it should be a lovely wedding. It's in a sixteenth-century chapel, right in the heart of the City. Beautiful building, very interesting structurally, and the reception is at . . ."

"Yes."

"Sorry?"

"Yes, I'd love to accompany you," I say with a grin.

"Oh good, I wasn't sure . . ."

346

"What time?"

"I'll pick you up at 10 a.m."

"Hats?"

"Sorry?"

"What's the dress code?"

"Yes, hats, I think. I'll be in a morning suit."

"Lovely. It's a date then."

"A date," Craig confirms.

The thing is, I can list a thousand reasons why it's a terrible idea for me to date my sons' headmaster and they are all rational, reasonable, logical thoughts. But the counter-argument for why I should date him is overwhelming.

He's lovely.

Fireworks *are* magical.

CHAPTER
THIRTY-FOUR

Thursday 9 November

Lucy

"So, Lucy, what's your excuse tonight?"

"Excuse?" I beam at Mick and pretend I don't catch his drift.

"Well, you are unlikely to be gracing us with your presence at the fabulous office party, even though there will be free champagne and it's being held at the oh-so-tomorrow, miserably hip Wasp bar. So I just wondered what excuse you are going to plead. Lack of babysitter? Headache? Tired?"

"I'm coming," I say with a smile.

He can't hide his surprise. "You're coming?"

"Certainly am. Said I would, didn't I? Anyway, the vast majority of the profits that Ralph is celebrating are thanks to me. I deserve a glass of champagne."

"I have to disagree about the *vast* majority."

I stare at Mick and then concede. "True. You've done your share. But the point is, rest assured, I'm coming."

"Good news," says Mick with his cheeky grin.

I need some sort of distraction, and although I have no intention of having a quick grope in the stationery cupboard, making photocopies of my ass, drunkenly insulting my boss or any other traditional office party antics, I cannot spend another night alone in that house in Holland Park. When I say alone, I mean with Auriol, but being with a child is just like being alone but with the misery of having to play Buckaroo. Peter is as busy as ever. I'm trying not to be paranoid; I'm resisting the thought that he's avoiding me. He's been out every night since the disastrous Hallowe'en party. Annoyingly, he's just called to say that his dinner tonight has been cancelled and he is now free. He asked me to give my office party a miss. He even suggested we go to Nobu, my favourite haunt. While I was tempted, I felt unable to agree to his proposal. I don't want to turn into one of those women who makes herself available at the drop of a hat. Such behaviour didn't do Rose any favours, did it?

"I'm glad you're coming, we can get silly on the dance floor," says Mick with a smile.

"I don't do silly on the dance floor," I remind him.

"Only kids care about being cool, Princess." Mick flings out the comment with flippancy but it feels like he's punched me. He winks at me and walks away.

I'm too old to be cool. He thinks I'm old, he said so. He pretty much told me to start dancing to the Agadoo at parties. I seethe.

I catch sight of the box of six bottles of champagne that are secreted under my desk, a client thank-you for the tens of thousands of pounds I've helped make his company this year. It arrived last week and I stashed it away, all but forgetting about it. I could do with some

349

instant cheer. It's only 4p.m., but the atmosphere is unusually flippant. Many traders are still enjoying lunch and the majority of PAs have spent the last hour or so in the bathrooms trying on new outfits. Others have spent the entire afternoon at the hairdresser's — it depends on their level of seniority. It's accepted that an office party in November signals the start of Christmas festivities. The hunting season has begun. Most PAs in the City only put up with the year-round arrogance and the crippling work schedules because their long-term aim is to marry their boss. The office party is a very risky occasion for wives sitting at home and a mass of opportunities for the next crop of bright young beauties.

My PA, Julia, is not at the hairdresser's or preening in the loo. She does not want to marry me. In truth she rarely wants to look at me; she got the short straw when HR were dealing out the roles. I demand a lot from my team, but not as much as I demand from myself, so I'm not unreasonable; still, I think she'd prefer to be working for a fat guy. Yet it is a party to say thank-you to staff and Julia is quietly efficient; she deserves a thank-you. I instruct her to dig out the champagne flutes and I pop open a bottle of champagne.

"Julia, you know, you can be really funny."

I drape my arm around Julia's neck. We are both finding our high heels a little trickier to walk in than usual. We stumble down the corridors and towards the lift. Luckily, we are late for the party and no one is around to witness the spectacle we are making. I really don't know where the time's gone, we were having such a giggle. The floor is empty now, except for Vic, the Puerto Rican guy who vacs the carpets. I give him the three remaining bottles of champagne because I can't be bothered to carry them home. I warn Julia that if she tells anyone else I'll sack her. I can't have people speculating that I have a soft underbelly.

"You can be nice *and* funny, Lucy. How come I've never noticed before?" Julia starts to giggle. "Normally I think you are so scary. But you're a sweetheart."

Even though we've drunk over a bottle of champagne each and I'm close to getting off my face, I'm not off the planet. I'm no sweetheart. Still, if it makes Julia happier coming into work thinking that perhaps I'm not a Class A bitch, then who am I to burst her bubble? We are not the first to discover that a couple of bottles of Bolly can forge a convincing, if short-term, friendship. Besides, we're both learning new things about one another. Julia *is* hilarious. She can do amazing impressions of just about anyone on the trading floor.

"Your impressions are really, really witty and really, really amusing and really, really cutting." My God, I think I just slurred that sentence. Disaster, I'm drunk. I must be. I'm not being at all articulate. I think I said *really* about a zillion times in that last sentence and really there are other words I could have used, really impressive ones like . . . especially. Now that's a really, really good word.

"Do your impression of me."

"I don't have one of you, Lucy," says Julia.

"Liar."

She bursts into giggles as we finally stumble into the lift. I prop myself up on the back wall and Julia stabs around the button that will take us to the ground floor and our waiting taxi. She seems to be having trouble with her aim.

"You'll sack me, if you see my impression of you," she laughs.

"It must be good then," I comment. We both collapse into fits of giggles again, but Julia knows that I may be friendly tonight but I'll be sober in the morning. I'll never get to see the impression.

We arrive at Wasp at about 9p.m. I can't believe this place has been open six months and this is my first visit. I remember a time when I used to go to the opening-night party of every trendy bar and delicious eatery in London. I was a face the columnists expected and wanted to see.

The walls and floor are mirrored so I keep stumbling into myself. I grope my way around as discreetly as possible until I find somewhere to sit down. There are no individual chairs, only massive leather daybeds the size of four coffee tables joined together. People are lying on them; chatting, smoking, drinking and laughing. I recognize most faces but still feel uncomfortable lying down next to colleagues. I'm not one for speedy intimacy, as a rule. However, after I've knocked back a glass of whatever it is Julia hands me, I decide I'd better sit down before I fall down.

I should have eaten lunch. I'm out of the habit of getting trolleyed on Bolly. I remember the days when sloshing back a couple of bottles of bubbly was what I did as a chaser to several Cosmopolitan cocktails and I still felt relatively unaffected. I don't do drunk. Or I didn't do drunk. I like to be in control.

It's another sign of bloody ageing, isn't it? I can no longer handle my drink. Soon it will be thin bones, leather skin, floppy boobs, incontinence, meals-on-wheels. Will I ever feel the thrill of a stranger catching my eye and holding it a little longer than necessary? The fact is, for the last five years or so, since Auriol was born, I don't believe I've lived my life in a true or full way anyhow. It's a half life. A step closer to nothingness, to death. I've travelled less. I've eaten out less. I've missed out on promotions and bonuses. I rarely orgasm. I'm always tired. People promise that motherhood expands horizons in unimaginable ways but that has not been my experience. Motherhood has wrapped me in chains.

I should go home. I don't want people to see me slurring, or dribbling or passing out. I've enjoyed a rather unique position at Gordon Webster Handle in that I've seen just about every one of my colleagues plastered and pathetic but no one has seen me behave with anything other than decorum.

Ever.

Even Peter.

I mean, of course, I get a little squiffy with him sometimes. We have been known to knock back a couple of bottles of wine at dinner but I feel totally different now. Not squiffy, more splattered. Not that what I'm feeling is actually bad, rather it's unknown and as such, a little disconcerting.

"Go with it, Lucy," yells Julia, as though she's read my mind.

She's lying on the red leather daybed, next to me, and staring at the ceiling. I look up. Fantastic images of incredibly beautiful clubbers are being projected on to the ceiling. As the floor and walls are mirrored it becomes almost impossible to work out what's up and what's down. Reality begins to lift and float with something more dreamlike and a little easier to handle: illusion. I wonder what Peter's doing right now? Sitting with his feet up probably. He'll be balancing the remote control and a bottle of beer on his stomach. Feet up on the coffee table, even though I'm always telling him not to do that.

I flop on to my back and watch the images flitter and flutter above me. Julia passes me a cigarette and I take a drag. For the first time in months I start to feel a little relaxed.

"Hey look, Lucy. Ralph is snogging Mick's PA," says Julia.

I try to sit up but find the movement too taxing. I take her word for it.

"I thought he fancied me," I comment.

"He fancies everybody. He's totally indiscriminate," she says. I see. "He tried it on with me when I was working late one night. Very clumsy attempt. Embarrassing all round, to be honest. What about you? When did he take a pop?"

"Well, he's never actually moved in on me," I confess. "I'm too senior for him to risk that," I add.

"Right," says Julia but she sounds unimpressed.

I thought Ralph fancied *me*. I've been giving him a gentle cold shoulder since he joined, as I was sure if he made a pass our working relationship would be destroyed, but it looks like I needn't have worried myself. I didn't realize he was indiscriminate. I normally pick up on that sort of thing. Not that I fancy him in the slightest, but. Well. I just thought.

The evening seems to be being played on a faulty video recorder. One moment everything is happening at double speed and life rushes by in a series of vibrant, disjointed images, loud noises and spicy smells. The next everything is slowed right down and it seems to me that the people dancing look exactly like footage of the guys landing on the moon. Sushi is being served but I can't be bothered to sit up to eat any; I do however accept two, or perhaps three, funny-coloured cocktails from beautiful girls who want to be writing novels; most of the liquid makes it to my mouth.

The noise around me is deafening; laughter and lasciviousness bash against one another. Unassuming people who usually limit themselves to the odd decent glass of port after dinner are suddenly downing fluorescent liquids and challenging one another to break-dancing competitions. The loos are already packed with sobbing girls trying to fix their rivers of mascara and there are groups of guys from accounts wearing paper hats and acting "wacky". Their desperate show of merriment puts me in mind of the presenters of the programmes that Auriol likes to watch.

Suddenly, I notice the presence of someone sitting on the daybed next to me. I'm still lying flat and can't summon the energy to turn and see who it is. It's not Julia — she disappeared to snog one of the traders some time ago. She's a thoughtful girl, though; she left me with two drinks lined up so I haven't had to go to the bar.

"Hi-ya, Princess."

"Mick!" I beam at him. "Lie back, lie down flat," I instruct. "It's sensational. Look at what's on the ceiling." There are no longer images of sexy clubbers strutting their stuff; there's now a montage of fabulous street scenes. One minute I'm in Venice, then Miami and then Barcelona.

"Sit up, Princess," says Mick. He gently grasps my shoulders and pulls me to a sitting position. I am a floppy dead weight and don't help him. "Has someone been spiking your drinks?" he asks.

"Nooooooo. I did all this on my own," I slur back with a smile. "I've eaten very little for three days now. And tonight I have drunk lots and lots. It's wonderful." I fling my arms wide to illustrate my exuberance. Nothing spills out of my glass because it's empty. I look around for my next one.

"Why aren't you eating?"

"Don't want to get fat." I can't believe I've said this. Never in my life have I ever admitted to dieting, although I've dieted since I was an adolescent. I no longer regard the way I eat, or rather what I don't eat, as a matter of dieting, it's simply being sensible. I never eat processed food, saturated fats, crisps, chips, sweets, biscuits, cakes or ice cream. It's a fact that a moment on the lips is a month on the hips. I also regard alcohol as prohibitively fattening and since my thirty-third birthday, when I noted a considerable slow-down in my metabolism, I've made it my rule to limit my alcohol consumption considerably. It's stupid to break my own policy. Even as I accept this in a part of my subconsciousness, I take a large gulp of champagne. Why aren't I more bothered?

"I've never seen you this drunk, Luce."

"I've never been this drunk, Mick. Do you like my dress?"

"Sorry?"

"My dress. It's new. Do you think it suits me?" All at once I need a compliment specifically from Mick, and I need it *now*.

"Very nice."

"Really?"

"It's great," he says.

Even three sheets to the wind I note the lack of enthusiasm in his voice. Since NY Mick and I have settled into a relationship that is sprinkled with friendly banter, more friendly than before we went away and less flirtatious. Of course I'm delighted to have a buddy and I acknowledge that the relationship couldn't have gone any other way, I'm married, but.

But. A small part of me thinks that this new safe relationship is just a teensy bit dull. By opting to be "just good friends", I've agreed to don the invisibility cloak. Why do all grown-up decisions have to be so dull? What to do? What to do? I am unused to having relationships with men unless they are sexual. I don't have a precedent for a male friend. In the past I had lovers, admirers, exes and men I flirt with, and those relationships were fun.

"Look, look, up there!" I catch Mick off-guard and am able to push him flat on his back on the enormous daybed. I lie down next to him; our arms are touching and we both watch the images flicker above us. "See, it's New York." I beam at him. "I had a fabulous time in New York," I comment, trying to sound casual. "Did you?"

Mick smiles. "It was a laugh, Princess."

"I didn't get this drunk ever in New York," I state. I'm aware that my voice sounds a little like Auriol's when she's telling me of one of her achievements about which she is particularly proud, arranging her soft toys in size order, perhaps.

"No, Lucy, you didn't."

"I wonder what would have happened if I had."

Mick shrugs and sits up. The movement is swift and decisive, which just goes to show he's got great stomach muscles. "Now come on, I'm going to get you a big glass of water and you are going to stop drinking."

This just goes to show he doesn't know me very well at all.

Noise, constant noise, clamours and tears around the room at full volume now. People are shouting, chatting, laughing, singing. No one is listening. Music is blaring and the clink of bottles hitting the rim of glasses sounds like a chorus of *Jingle Bells*. Despite this I'm almost asleep when Mick arrives back moments, or maybe ten minutes, later. He brings with him a bottle of water and Joe Whitehead. Since meeting Joe in September my initial impression of him (that he is an incompetent nuisance) has only deteriorated. He is spotty, sweaty and sneaky. All of which I might forgive if he was good at his job, but he's not. I'm too drunk to bother being polite to him. When he asks me if I'm having a good time I mouth, "I can't hear you, the music is so loud," and then I turn my attention back to Mick.

Annoyingly Mick won't lie back down on the enormous daybed, although Joe has no qualms about flinging himself flat. He's flapping his arms and legs up and down, the way one does in the snow to make snow angels. I notice that everyone clears off our daybed, driven away by his BO.

"I lurve the feel of leather on my skin," he shouts with a leer.

Idiot.

Mick insists I stay upright so I can drink the water he's brought me. I take sulky sips. I'm not sure I want to be sober. I'm having quite a lot of fun being drunk and I'm short on fun these days. Admittedly, I haven't actually spoken to anyone at the party. I haven't had the chance to network or impress and clearly I'm not in a fit state to try to do so now. I haven't had a dance or even investigated the terrace, which, apparently, is heated and has great views of London. Perhaps I'm not using my night of freedom to the optimum but I am having fun and I don't want to be sober. Whenever

Mick looks away I sneak a quick slurp of whatever glass is to hand. As the bill for the evening is being footed by GWH there are a large number of unfinished, discarded drinks littering the tables. This way I mix vodka, gin, champagne, beer and wine. A Russian roulette cocktail game: with each sip I wonder if this is the one that will make me keel over.

I move closer to Mick. "What do you think of kids?" I ask him.

He looks at me quizzically but accepts the nonsequential nature of the conversation.

"I like them but I couldn't eat a whole one," he quips with a grin. A peal of laughter explodes from somewhere. It's crazy and disproportionate. Oh God, it's me laughing.

"I don't understand kids," I confide. "Got one, don't know what to do with her." He's a guy, so he doesn't ask me what I mean. I don't care, I take his silence as encouragement enough. "I mean all that endless zoo visiting and play-date arranging and the smells." Mick blanches so I don't go into detail about the offensive odours that kids seem to emit on a more or less continuous basis from the moment they burst into your life. "I don't know my own daughter. I don't know the person I created."

Suddenly, the truth and sadness of this sentence slams me to the floor. I think I'm in danger of crying. Bloody alcohol. I've seen this happen to other people a million times, how the hell have I let myself get into this position? I decide to change the subject.

360

I glance around the party room. It seems that everyone has now drunk enough to be freed from the restraints of recognized, civil small talk or even the affable chat owed to closer colleagues; the room oozes unreserved, barefaced disorderliness. I remember this exciting recklessness from years ago and I like it. I feel great.

I move closer to Mick's ear, he must be able to feel my breath on his lobe. I can see the hairs on the back of his neck rise. I wonder if that's the only part of his anatomy that's starting to stand to attention. I drape one hand around his neck and let the other rest on his thigh.

"Then again, I've got a husband and I don't know what to do with him either," I admit in a whisper. "I don't think he knows what to do with me any more. He's forgotten."

I let the words sit between us. Mick does not look at me but stares straight ahead; his stillness proves I have his attention. The rest of the room, so noisy and powerful a second ago, disappears. The world is silent while I wait for Mick's response. I know what I've done — I've opened a can of worms. I want ideas to creep in and out of his head. Inappropriate, dangerous ideas. I want Mick to pick up on my discontent and I want him to act on it. More, I need him to. He looks sexy tonight and he's here, right? Available. Right? And I really could do with being desired.

It seems that several light years pass while I allow Mick to fully comprehend the situation. I'm drunker than I've ever been and I'm expressing frustration with my family life, I'm sitting next to him on a large leather daybed — if there is ever going to be one, then this would be his moment to up the stakes.

"You never said anything like that in New York," he replies, carefully.

I'd actually been expecting him to suggest we move somewhere quieter, so I reply without thought or guile, "I was never this drunk in New York, Mick."

He quickly turns to me. "It's not my style to seduce drunken women, Princess. Thanks for the offer and all." With that he stands up and calls to Joe, "Mate, I have to go. See to it that Lucy drinks lots of water and get her into a cab within the hour. She needs to get home too."

"I'm on it, captain," says Joe, putting his fingers to his forehead in a salute.

Then Mick walks out of the room, without so much as a glance my way.

He's gone. I feel stupid, angry, disgusted. Disgusted at him and myself. I can't believe that I've just served myself up on a platter and he said no. No. He wanted it well enough in New York. I'm sure he did. What's gone wrong between then and now? Am I so repulsive? So decrepit? No doubt he's gone to find a woman who still has puppy fat and has no idea who Spandau Ballet are.

Joe sits up.

"Fuck water. Who does he think he is?"

It takes me a minute to understand Joe. I feel lost and displaced. Peter doesn't want me. He can hardly bear to come home any more and when he does we do nothing but row. Auriol wants me too much and I am a

362

failure as a mother. Connie doesn't understand me — she loves the whole mother thing. Bloody, bloody Rose. I bet she's at home right now making chocolate brownies and fruit pies from scratch. I drop my head into my hands and fight tears. My hands look gnarled and grey. It might just be the lighting of the club but I don't think so. I'm old. Mick didn't want me. I feel confused and self-conscious. Even fucking indiscriminate Ralph didn't want me. I'm washed up. I'm over.

Joe sits back beside me. I hadn't realized he'd gone but apparently he's been to the bar. He slams down a silver bucket. I see a bottle of Crystal peeping out.

"Mick can be such a bossy wanker. You can handle your drink, can't you, Lucy?"

"Usually," I slur.

"That cheeky bastard has no right to tell you when to stop drinking."

"No right," I agree. I shake my head and as I do so I feel my brain rattle around painfully. I think I might vomit. "Feel sick," I mumble.

"Best thing for that, Lucy, is to drink more," advises Joe.

"Really?"

"Always."

The champagne kicks the back of my throat, a frosty addictive liquid. A thousand startling bubbles dance frantically on my tongue and for a moment I do feel better. I hold out my glass for a refill and smile at Jack-ass Joe.

CHAPTER
THIRTY-FIVE

Thursday 9 November

John

There are two days left until Tom takes the jump. I've been drinking pretty solidly since the (highly successful) stag weekend at the end of October, but I think my liver might now look closer to minced offal so I decide to have tonight off the sauce. At 5.30p.m. this evening it seemed a good idea to have a night in, watch a DVD, have a bath, cut my toenails and then turn in before midnight. But it's seven now and I'm bored witless.

Sometimes I have to wonder about my line of work. I get paid shedloads, enough to buy a beauty of a house, but I work all the hours God sends and mostly in places that demand an inconvenient commute from my beauty of a house — so I end up staying somewhere else. As I said, this gaff is quite something, but it's not home. And occasionally I hanker after my creature comforts, like my big fridge, my stereo, cable TV and Andrea. Not necessarily Andrea per se, but you know, company.

My mobile rings into my empty flat and I'm grateful so I pick it up without checking to see who is calling.

"Why did you and Andrea split up?"

"Hello, Connie. How are you?"

She does not return the greeting but waits for an answer to her question. I'd seen it coming. She's been getting pissed off with my avoidance techniques. She wants to talk about the big things. Maybe she's curious. Or vain. Or confused. Or maybe talking is her way of legitimizing shagging and she won't do one without the other. I don't know, but this is the first time she's called me in over five years and I can't see any reason for holding out on her.

"Andrea had an affair."

"No!"

I hear her gasp and I can imagine her face, a study of amazement. Sweet really. I guess she might have chosen to be smug or ecstatic. But I can tell that she's genuinely shocked. It is possible that Connie is one of the few people in the world who really thinks that being unfaithful to me is an inconceivable idea. Would she have been faithful to me? If we'd got together back then, would we have made it through, I wonder?

"I'd assumed . . ." Connie stutters to a stop.

"You assumed that I'd done a bunk," I fill in helpfully.

I wander over to the window and look out on to Kensington High Street. Late-night shoppers are already frantically filling the streets as though it was Christmas Eve rather than early November. I'm not much looking forward to Christmas.

"Well, yes. Why did she have an affair?"

The question allows me to believe that Connie *would* have been faithful to me, if we'd lived the other life, the one where not only did I get the girl but I wanted her at the correct time and so I held on to her. Tightly.

"She thought I was being unfaithful."

"Were you?"

"No, but she said I'd spent a lifetime acting in a way that makes it difficult for anyone to believe in me."

Connie doesn't refute this, not even to be polite.

"Andrea knew about you and . . ." I trail off.

"And all the others," she snaps. I find it encouraging that she's still miffed about the others.

"Not all of them, but some of them," I admit. Even Connie doesn't know about all of them. "Even though I promised her I'd be faithful once we got married she didn't really believe that I was capable of it. She couldn't see why I'd change my ways."

"I can see her point."

"So can I, but I did mean it. I *was* faithful to her. People can change. You have."

Connie is silent for a moment. To date we've both been making a big effort to pretend to believe that our relationship is totally innocent. She's pretending we are just friends. We're not. I'm pretending that I believe she'll resist me. She won't.

"It was a nightmare. If I so much as spoke to another woman, Andrea would have a fit. She was always questioning me. Where was I going? Who with? When would I be back? She started to turn up places just to check if I really was playing football as I'd said I was or if I was playing away. It was miserable for us both."

"But if Andrea was checking up on you and you weren't doing anything wrong, what made her think you were?"

"She thought the sex had gone off the boil."

"Really?"

Connie is clearly made up and then quickly shifts her tone to something more appropriate, something akin to sympathy. She makes little surprised murmuring sounds down the line, but I'm not fooled. She can't help delighting in that confession. She's very competitive.

"But I think it just does, doesn't it? It would have with you and me, given time."

She is silent for about a decade and then, finally, she says, "We'll never know."

"Well, I think it does. Sex comes and goes in a long-term relationship. It's constantly changing and evolving. Things can't stay the same as they are in the first few weeks; we'd all die of exhaustion."

Connie gasps. Once again she is shocked, possibly at my realism. I try to explain.

"I loved her, I really did. But I couldn't manage to keep it dirty and insistent, not once we were married, not all the time. Is it really possible?" Connie is freaking me out now. She's staying silent, not a trivial feat for her. "Don't you agree? What? What is it?"

"My God, I think that is the most mature thing you have ever said to me."

"Don't patronize me, Connie."

"Sorry, sorry." I can almost hear the cogs of Connie's mind whirling, or maybe that's the traffic from outside my window. "Sorry that I sound patronizing. And sorry about Andrea. I wish you'd made it." She coughs.

"Ah well. That's the way the cookie crumbles. I guess we weren't meant to be."

"I thought you were."

I wonder what Connie looks like right now. Where is she sitting? What is she doing? Is she sucking her lip, looking vexed, disappointed or challenging? Is she searching? What more does she want or need to know before she comes to me? She probably wants me to tell her she's the one. That she always was and that Andrea and I were doomed because I couldn't get Connie out of my system. I could tell her this. It wouldn't be true but it would probably do the trick. She is moving closer to me. Mentally, I mean. I can feel it. She's drunk champagne with me, without telling her hubby. She chose to bunk off work to be with me. She chose to watch the fireworks with me, not Luke.

"Andrea is better off with her new bloke. He's good to her. She deserves that," I say with a shrug.

Connie feeling sorry for me might clinch it. She'll note the tinge of regret, the self-effacing tone, and she'll want to remind me that I am a god. At least in her eyes.

"Where are you?" I ask.

"In Diesel, in High Street Ken," she says.

This is no coincidence. She's thinking about me, she's just up the street, not far away. I'm creeping under her skin again. This could be my moment.

"Have you eaten?" I ask.

"No."

"We could eat together."

"Where?"

"Out or in, I don't mind. You choose."

"OK. Out. Meet me at Café Rouge, off Kensington Church Street. Do you know it? I like it there. The manager is a friend of mine. See you in ten." Then she hangs up.

Fuck me. It's worked.

I check my reflection. I'm good to go. I'm not thrilled to hear that the manager is a friend of hers. That might curtail things a little. Even with her taste for danger I can't see her shagging me in full view of an old pal but, no doubt about it, the evening is looking up. Toenail cutting or fucking Connie up against a wall in a back alley like the old days? Hardly a brain-teaser. I'll have to play it carefully though. I've been wanting her too much and too openly of late. It's worked to an extent, drawn her out this far, but Connie isn't keen on open displays of affection. In my experience, she likes it best when men treat her like crap. Now that gets her panting. I might have to play it a bit tonight. I know the routine I'll use.

I'll talk to her about the big stuff. I'll answer more of her questions. I'll even do it honestly — what the hell, she's unshockable and that has always been our way. I'll tell her how she's made me feel recently. How much I've been thinking of her. I might even risk comparing it with the old days when after the first shag or two I barely thought about her at all. I'll move in closer and closer and then I'll pull back from her. Her eyes will flicker with confusion. That's fine. She'll think I'm withdrawing out of respect for her wish to be just friends. She'll be disappointed and delighted at once. But she'll feel safe and in control. If I'm lucky, and I'm judging it right, she'll also be feeling a teensy-weensy bit regretful and questioning. She will come to me. It's only a matter of time. A bit of confusion heightens tension and intensifies everything. I might tell her that she's right and that I should leave her alone. I'll hold her gaze throughout my little speech and —

The phone rings again.

Bugger. I hope Connie hasn't had second thoughts and is calling to say she can't meet after all. I pick up.

"Hi, it's me."

Me being Andrea.

CHAPTER
THIRTY-SIX

Friday 10 November

Lucy

I slept in the spare room again last night. I didn't arrive home until 4a.m. and didn't want to wake Peter or disturb Auriol. This morning I ignored all calls for me to get up and kept my head safely under my pillow until I heard Peter leave for work and Eva and Auriol walk down the street to school. Only when their footsteps pitter-pattered into the distance did I risk moving.

Waves of nausea threatened to overwhelm me. I made it as far as the bathroom before I vomited, but sadly not as far as the loo. My tranquil Philippe Stark minimalist bathroom with ambient lighting and Venetian glass mosaic tiles was instantly transformed into something nasty enough to appear in a Tarantino movie. Carefully, I mopped up the party excess that had split on to my bathroom floor and into my life, and I shook and wept.

I showered, but the odour of last night's foulness clung. I tried to face a glass of wheatgrass but it looked suspiciously like the stuff I'd just regurgitated over the bathroom floor so I couldn't bring myself to swallow more than a mouthful. Instead, I hurriedly ate three rounds of toast and gulped back three large mugs of strong, black coffee. I calculated that Eva would probably be at the supermarket for at least an hour and a half, but what if she veered off plan and came home to pop on a load of whites? I couldn't risk bumping into her. I didn't want to see anyone ever again. I sent a text to Julia and said I was taking a day's holiday; I knew that asking for a sick-day from Ralph would raise questions and eyebrows — both intrusions would be unwelcome. I grabbed my coat, bag and sunglasses and left the house.

It's a grey, drab day and the sunglasses are unnecessary but I need to hide behind them. How could I have done something so stupid? It seems to me that I've spent my entire life being in total control of myself and my surroundings, acting with nothing other than rationale and intelligence. I've never made so much as a single, silly spur-of-the-moment decision and I do not nurse a secret self-destructive impulse but now, all at once, I've fucked it up.

Everything.

My whole life.

No. No that cannot be the case. I won't let it be. The important thing is not to panic. I make the decision to catch the tube. Normally I shun public transport but today I feel it's fitting. I sit sweating alcohol with the other mindless losers of London town, and I fit.

I pay little attention to where I alight and am surprised when I pop up at Bond Street. It has started to rain and I've failed to bring along an umbrella. The drizzle follows me around, suggesting that even the rain gods know of my hideousness.

I spend the morning wandering around London feeling repentant and rebellious at once. I tell myself Peter pushed me to it. I had no choice. He's been ignoring me for months. But even I don't believe me. I know that I always have a choice and no one ever pushes me to do anything. I feel dreadful. Cheap. Used and ruined. Truly spoilt, devastated, wrecked and trashed in a nineteenth-century-heroine way that I've never believed in. Until now.

Inexplicably, with a fated inevitability that I thought was the exclusive domain of the know-no-better-tourist, I find myself walking along Oxford Street towards Tottenham Court Road. An ugly part of town at the best of times, and this is by no means the best of times. Some think that these areas of town represent London's vigour, the thrills and spills of life. I can only see the spills. The homeless, the drunks, the poor and overworked. It's depressingly real, and a contrast to the sleek, shiny streets of the City or the privileged, leafy streets of Holland Park where I usually spend my time. The area is over-illuminated by aggressive, gaudy neon signs that have swallowed the former greatness and grandeur. I think my subconscious is punishing me by trawling me through this vileness. My conscious mind — my instinctive self-preservation — wins out. Within only a few steps it's possible to escape these style atrocities and find the chic, lively parts of town with which I am more familiar. I take a right and hurry towards the wonderfully grand boulevard that is Regent

Street. The saturation of trendy stores and intense retail activity will surely lift my soul.

I discover that London is a series of scenes that have been backdrops for episodes in my life. Like old diaries fluttering open for me to read, I come across a particular set of steps, a certain shop, a statue, where I played out defining moments of my life.

I spot the antique shop in Bond Street where I bought Peter and Rose's wedding gift. The vase is on the windowsill in our downstairs cloakroom. Funnily enough it was not something Rose wanted to hang on to when they were drawing up the settlement — no matter how much it cost, she thought it was worthless. I hate it too.

Then I spy the Vintage House, where I once bought Peter a bottle of single malt worth over £400. I remember his response was a mixture of pleasure at my recklessness, pride at my independent means and mortification that I'd spent that much on a malt which was too complex for him to appreciate. We had great sex that afternoon, though. Astounding. Where did that recklessness seep to?

I stumble across the Anything Left-Handed shop, where we once laughed ourselves hoarse at the quirky stock. He bought me a left-handed clock, even though I'm right-handed. I hung it in my kitchen and thought it was appropriate as time seemed to go backwards, it dragged so, when I wasn't with him. I think the clock is in a cupboard in the spare room now.

Next I pause outside Sotheran's of Sackville Street, the oldest trading antiquarian bookshop in Britain. This place reminds me of Connie. A different Connie from the confident woman she is today. A poor, desperate Connie who was muddled up in an impossible affair. She asked me to help her source a poetry book for her lover there once, a million years ago. I remember her anxious energy and her destructive determination at that time. I can't imagine Connie being unfaithful now. It's as ridiculous as — well, me being unfaithful. I remember that day's shopping with Connie so clearly because that evening I met up with Peter and he promised he'd leave Rose for me.

I trail through Conduit Street and down New Bond Street. I don't pause to look at the beautiful designer labels but find that I turn full circle upon myself and wander back along Piccadilly and towards Leicester Square. Damn my sub-conscious, drawing me towards ugliness I want to avoid.

I look up and see the Piccadilly Lions and I know that from this day on I will associate them with my treachery. Finally, I wander into the National Portrait Gallery.

In December 1999 Peter and I met on the steps of the NPG on Christmas Eve to furtively exchange gifts. He'd bought me diamond earrings. I can't remember what I'd bought him but I know it wasn't an expensive gift. I had purposefully chosen something small because I had expected his gift to be a token and I did not want to embarrass him. Birthdays and Christmases are tricky times for mistresses. For his birthday I had resorted to buying myself beautiful underwear and booking us a room at a quiet hotel. An isolated, discreet gift. That

Christmas he spoilt me and I was left feeling inadequate and inappropriate because I had not quite pitched it properly. I'd undervalued him and myself. I tried to explain that it was hard to buy a married lover a gift that is at once meaningful but will not draw the wife's attention; even the whisky had to be drunk at my house. Mistresses who buy ties or cufflinks are tomcats pissing in a new territory. They want the wife to discover them, which seems especially spiteful at Christmas. I had few scruples about our situation, I wanted him so badly, but I have more class than to force a confrontation during the season of goodwill.

We were actually spending Christmas day together, at his home with Rose. I was one of their many guests. Those terrible days of duplicity were horribly uncomfortable. Sharing him is impossible to be proud of. Having him to myself was all I longed for then. So when did it get more complicated? Why did I complicate matters?

I'd wanted him for so long. Ever since I set eyes on him, when he came with Rose to visit Daisy at university. We were all just kids. How can I have been so stupid as to jeopardize everything I have worked for, for so many years? I am a bloody fool.

I feel a smidgen better once inside the gallery. For a start it's dry, and besides which I adore the clean white lines, the clear signage and the decent gift shop. So many galleries are let down by their gift shops. The NPG is my favourite gallery in London. I like to look important people in the eye. I like to see power, beauty and sex recorded. For seconds at a time I try to block out my own atrocities as I stare dictators, ministers and kings in the eye. It's exhausting, so I scuttle to the café. I need liquids to help the hangover. But what will salve my ravaged soul?

Surrounded by the gently clinking china and the hushed tones of interested gallery visitors I try to make sense of the night before. Random but damning flashbacks assault my consciousness. I struggle to order the events but fail to make sense of them either emotionally or chronologically. His breath smelt of stale food. He needed to shave. His whiskers scratched my neck and face. He had fat fingers. Fingers that grabbed at my stockings and laddered them. I roughly wipe my mouth. I can still feel his attempts at urgent and inexpert kisses on my lips. I want to slice them off. I push the images aside. I can't bear to think of it. I leave the tea. I have to keep busy.

There is a temporary photo exhibition of old movie stars which catches my interest. We live in a culture that gets excited by snapshots of fallen idols. Nothing makes us smile as much as a drunken soap star falling in the gutter, a pop wannabe flashing her bikini line as she inelegantly gets out of a cab or artists who have snorted away their own noses. But, today, I can't stomach anyone else's fallibility; my own inadequacies are repugnant and evident enough. I decide that portraits of great stars, people with style, mystique and charisma, such as Lauren Bacall, David Niven and Virginia McKenna, will be more peaceful and comforting.

In my hungover state I seem to be incapable of reading basic signage and I take the escalator that misses the mezzanine floor, where the exhibition is taking place, and instead find myself transported directly into the Tudor Gallery.

My first thought is, how do I get out? There's no obvious down elevator or stairs. I begin to panic. The clean walls seem to close in on me and the open spaces that I've been luxuriating in vanish in an instant. I have to get out of here. Immediately. No time to linger. I don't want these dead people staring at me. I feel disconcerted, then condemned, as the dour creatures with their beady eyes seem to snigger at my folly. My disloyalty.

I flatten myself against a wall to steady my whirling head and my shallow, panicked breathing. I try to take long, deep breaths. Get a grip, Lucy. The floor is deserted, except for three or four earnest-looking Japanese schoolgirls who are politely ignoring evidence of my mounting disarray.

I look again at the familiar portraits to discover what I thought I already knew. This is a technique I often use at work. The most dangerous traders are those who think they've seen everything before and stop looking properly. I'm always more cautious and careful than that. I always look at everything anew and from fresh angles.

It is said that a sign of a good portrait is that the sitter's eyes follow the viewer around the room. In which case these Tudor portraits should all be judged marvellous, for I begin to believe the sitters are alive and staring at me. I stand for some time in front of a portrait of Henry VIII, arguably the best-known Tudor

— his numerous marriages cementing his infamy if nothing else. Henry VIII's eyes are ferocious slits, quite cold and repulsive. He seems to be sneering at me, as though he knows the dirty secret of my heart and, more specifically, who I allowed between my legs last night.

Well, it takes one to know one.

One by one I study the portraits of his wives. Wives who were betrayed, beheaded, divorced and dispatched. There were wives betraying too, there still are. Where is the progress? I think of Jane Seymour; it might have been a relief to die in childbirth, rather than be married to that scary old bastard. Catherine Parr outlived him, only to die a year or so later, producing a child for another husband. I sigh. I really need more liquids. I'm about to leave the gallery when I catch the eye of Anne Boleyn. She is fixed in a transient moment of glory. She has smug lips and a pretty head that she lost. I swallow hard. Poor Anne, I've always related to her.

I take a moment to search for a portrait of Catherine of Aragon, the first queen. Reputedly she was prudent and good. Not my personal favourite, although popular in her time. I always felt she had too much in common with Rose for me to find the energy to like her. But suddenly and quite strangely I pity her. Dreadful fate to be locked up alone in the tower. After all, her only crime was loving too much and being unable to produce a boy for her STD-ridden husband. I shake my head and acknowledge that I must still be quite drunk to be so sentimental. I wander on.

Noisy schoolchildren jolt me away from a portrait of Henry VIII in which he's pointing at his son from his deathbed. The giant of a man seems small in his final moments. Was he afraid to die after all the killing he had done? Was it worth it? Any of it? The victories, the defeats, the marriages, the mistakes? Our lives are so small in retrospect. If a mighty king, responsible for countries, armies, wars, atrocities and even a new faith, could ultimately be reduced to nothing more than a sick guy in a nightie, then what hope is there for the rest of us?

The schoolchildren are all soaked. It's obviously raining quite hard outside now. By comparison, it's hot in the gallery and so their coats and brightly coloured backpacks steam. They boisterously form energetic caterpillar trails in front of the paintings. Suddenly, there are too many bodies, real, virtual and ghostly.

I take a final glance at the dying king's portrait. Looking again, something previously unobserved hits me. I consider the possibility that Henry VIII might not have died wondering what it was all about. What if he died knowing, *absolutely knowing*, that his son and perhaps even his daughters were unquestionably everything? It's possible. Probable. He might have died believing that his insatiable desire to produce and protect an heir wasn't madness but meaning. The small sickly prince might have been feeble and barely significant to English history but to Henry he was a god. It probably kept him sane.

It must be a great relief to believe in something with such certainty. There are no beheadings in Holland Park nowadays, but on the other hand, belief is rare too. What do I believe in? Myself? Up until yesterday I would have resolutely said yes, yes, but now I see I'm fallible. Peter? Again, until yesterday I would have argued that he was my reason for being, but how can that be if we are snapping and snarling at one another all the time? I don't believe in God but I have to believe in more than Visa cards and designer shoes. *Vogue* can't be my bible forever.

Auriol?

I steal a glance at the gaggles of noisy, drenched kids and for once they do not annoy me. I watch them, with open curiosity, as they play, poke and push one another. But, I do not see disorder and irritants. Instead I'm struck by their energy, their voluble laughter, their candid assassinations and affirmations, and I think that they are marvellous. Each and every one of them. Marvellous.

The kid with the Power Ranger backpack and the runny nose has nice eyes. The girl who keeps scratching her head seems thoughtful. The boys fighting about whether there were more King Henrys or King Georges seem bright. But suddenly it strikes me, however thoughtful or bright or nice-eyed these kids are, these are not the ones that have my answers. These are not the kids that I answer to. I blow a quick kiss of thanks at Henry's portrait and I dash for the door.

I want my daughter. I want to be with Auriol.

CHAPTER
THIRTY-SEVEN

Saturday 11 November

Rose

I love weddings. I love everything about them, from the pretty little ballet slippers the bridesmaids wear to the terrible Abba tribute bands that play at the reception until the early hours. I love the moment the bride steps through the church door, swathed in petticoats and her veil. I love the fact that the congregation always gasps. I love to see women in hats and men in tails. I love the sound of heels clattering on worn enamel tiles in the aisle, as ladies rush to their seats. I love confetti, champagne and even Coronation chicken because it all adds up to something so marvellous. It adds up to a moment of intense possibility and optimism.

Possibility dominating probability for one day at least.

Not that I get the chance to go to many weddings nowadays. So while this wedding is a little peculiar for me, as I don't know either the bride or the groom, I'm delighted to be part of it. I dusted off my hat and splashed out on a new dress for the event. This time I didn't take Daisy or Connie with me when I went shopping. I thought there was every chance that I could be just as productive if I shopped alone, perhaps even more so.

I bought a knee-length ruby red dress and scarf. I tied the scarf around my black hat and teamed the outfit with the jacket from an old work suit. The one I was wearing when Peter first asked me to share a sandwich with him, as it happens. At least the suit has lasted, it's aged very well. Yesterday, I decided that my old black court shoes wouldn't do after all and I bought a pair of knee-high leather boots with killer heels. I've never spent so much on footwear in my life, but Connie assured me they were worth every penny. Last night I dreamt I was having my wicked way with Craig and I was wearing nothing other than the boots, so I'm inclined to agree with her.

At first I feared that because Craig is the Best Man I'd be sitting in the pew on my own, fending off questions about how I know the happy couple. But Craig explained that he was more of a chief usher and that his short pal, who I've met at the school gates, was the real Best Man. So we sat side by side throughout the ceremony and no one suggested I was an imposter and that I had to leave. The ceremony was beautiful. The couple had hit the correct note of simple reverence and evident euphoria.

Unfortunately it's not a bright autumnal day, as they deserve. When we emerge from the church, rain is slapping down on to the pavements and the photos are taken with indecent haste as all the guests are encouraged to get to the reception as quickly as possible. The plan is to drink copious amounts of champagne in an effort to forget the inclement weather.

As we walk through the double glass doors of the reception we are greeted by the sight of hundreds of candles. Candles on tables, candles on chandeliers, candles nestling in flower displays, candles on the bar and huge fat candles, about a metre high, standing on the floor. The entire room is doused with a dreamy, wistful, faraway feeling. It's wonderful.

"Isn't this beautiful?" I comment.

"Yes, it's beautiful, although highly impractical," says Craig. He looks concerned. "They should have had tealights."

"Are you happy for your friends?" I ask.

"I'm violently happy for both of them. What could be finer than finding someone you love so much you want to spend the rest of your life in their company?"

I grin. I'm charmed. Craig might object to the number of candles on health and safety regulations but he is romantic, in a true sense of the word. He's just practical, as am I. I had been concerned that Craig and I might be nervous around one another. I feared we'd flounder once outside familiar boundaries but we haven't. There isn't a single awkward moment where we struggle with small talk. He doesn't reveal a terrible or annoying habit (involving scratching, sniffing or picking) that would make me want to run from him. He doesn't turn out to be a fascist, an addict or an embezzler. He isn't aggressive, shy or dull. He doesn't offend me in any way. The opposite is true: the more I see of him the more I admire him.

384

He is a conscientious usher. He ensures that all the guests are comfortable and mixing with one another. He helps people read the seating plan and find the cloakroom. He notices when the waiters are being a little tardy in refilling glasses and he heads off a crisis when a cousin of Jen's discovers she is wearing the same dress as an aunt of Tom's. He tells the ladies they are fulfilling the male guests' fantasies involving beautiful twins. His manner is flirtatious, confident and yet respectful. Both women melt.

"I'm seeing a whole new side to you, Casanova," I say with a giggle as we slip into our seats.

"I'm not normally this confident, Rose," says Craig. He stares directly at me and adds simply, "It's being around you. I feel a million dollars. You make me a better man than I normally am. Still or sparkling?"

He drops the enormous compliment and the trifling question of my preferred choice of water into our conversation as though both sentences are of equal import. The result is, I am bouncing with joy and can barely mumble that I prefer still.

The reception is wonderful. The wine is plentiful, the band is pitched perfectly, both in terms of volume and tone, and the food isn't cold, which is often the best you can hope for when there are one hundred and fifty people to feed. We are amused by a mime act and a magician. Craig is attentive but not overbearing. He compliments me on my dress but isn't slimy. He makes sure my glass is full but I don't get the feeling he's trying to get me drunk. He asks who is looking after the boys but he doesn't let the conversation deteriorate into school talk.

Unusually, the couple have opted to break up the proceedings by hosting an afternoon tea dance before the speeches and dessert. This gives the old rellies the chance to twirl around the dance floor before the disco music starts up in earnest this evening. I think the idea of a tea dance is truly wonderful and my approval rises further when Craig asks me to join him on the floor.

"I can't waltz," I confess.

"Nor can I. But how hard can it be? Tom's Auntie Madge is managing to do it with a Zimmer frame."

I decide that it will be nice to be held by Craig and so I agree.

We shuffle across the dance floor and repeatedly murmur, "One, two, three. One, two, three" — I doubt we are fooling anyone. After a few moments we settle into swaying in one another's arms and the effect isn't completely ludicrous. It is lovely to be held again. I'm not sure when a man last deliberately put his hands on my body. Can it be as long ago as six years? The thought is nauseating, unless of course you are a nun. Craig has large hands and he grasps me firmly around the place where my waist ought to be. He doesn't seem to be in the slightest bit embarrassed by my lumps and swellings, nor does he crucify me by saying something obvious, like, "I luuurvve your curves." He appears to accept my shape, seemingly without thought, and his acceptance makes me feel calm, relaxed and comfy. I allow my body to smudge a little closer to his.

"Are you enjoying yourself, Rose?"

"Do you need to ask? I've been smiling since the moment you picked me up this morning. I'm having a wonderful day."

"I'm so glad. I'd really like to be part of what makes you happy."

I stare at Craig, stunned and unsure how to best respond. Can he be for real? Is he saying he wants to do this again, maybe more than once? I think he must be. I allow the thought to drift into my consciousness and I examine the idea carefully. I do not find the concept horrifying. Far from it. I like Craig — very much.

For the first time we are a little embarrassed with one another but the embarrassment is exciting. It's not the mortification of two awkward strangers — it is the discomfiture of two lovers who are verbally and physically skirting one another, unsure of their next move, desperate that there is a next move. Craig coughs and changes the subject.

"Tell me about yourself, Rose."

"There's not much to tell," I point out. He knows I am the divorced mother of twins, what can I add?

"I don't believe that. You must have exciting parts of your past that you want to tell me to impress me," he says with a grin. "And you must have thrilling plans for your future, however deeply you are keeping them hidden."

I'm rather flattered that he thinks I might once have done something, *anything*, exciting and of note, although I don't think he's right about my future. I really don't have secret gripping plans. For the first time I wish I had, if only to impress Craig.

I start falteringly, a little like our dance steps.

"I studied Maths at Bristol University. I managed to scramble up to the dizzy heights of a 2:1 grade, although I was more of a 2:2 sort of girl really. I'd forgone a number of dates and parties and spent long hours in the library. Accountancy was a very natural choice for me after I left uni, and actually I was very good at it. Not that I'm saying I'm dull," I add hastily.

"I know you're not dull, Rose," he says with assurance.

An old couple glide past us. I think they are foxtrotting. They manage to look wonderfully elegant, even though they are eighty plus and their faces are creased like yesterday's sheets. The old couple are gazing at one another, their expressions the same — they radiate awe and devotion. Mesmerized, I watch them sashay and my chest tightens. They are only aware of one another, oblivious to anyone or anything else. And as they slip over the aged and grooved wooden floor I wonder how many romances have blossomed on this same floor, how many women have glided with hope and men danced with pride. And I wonder if I've drunk too much?

For six years I have kept my heart hidden behind indestructible barricades that repel any sort of intimacy. I've accepted my life for what it is and learnt to love it for being just that, and I have not allowed myself to hanker for more. It wouldn't have been sensible. More always ends up being less. Loving Peter more than I thought possible left me feeling less of a person in the end. I did not want to risk that searing agony again, as I was afraid that my brittle soul would not be able to endure another, similar disappointment. I'd shatter and then what use would I be to the boys? The boys, always the boys to think of. Thank God.

And, after all, a life full of children, recipes, friends and family *is* a full life and I can't complain.

But, as I watch the old lovers rapt in one another, suddenly it is impossible for me to ignore the fact that my life is full, but not brimming, and the distinction matters. My life is not a life overflowing, ebullient and fluid and I want it to be. I know what is missing. I've always known — I just haven't wanted to admit it. I don't believe a woman needs a man to have a complete life but I do admit that having a soulmate can be a cornucopia. I glance at Craig and wonder how deep and strong a possibility he might represent. None of my recent dates have ignited a spark of interest but unexpectedly I can feel real heat right now. The idea of entertaining possibility makes my heart soar. I become brave and almost tap my toes as I hop from one foot to the other in an inexpert but enthusiastic step.

"It's just that people think accountants are dull and we're not, actually. I am chatty and I know how to get drunk, although it's not a skill I've been honing of late. I even did karaoke in a bar once."

"What did you sing?" asks Craig with a smile.

"Err. *Like a Virgin*," I admit.

"I can well imagine the scene." Craig's smile broadens but he has the good grace not to laugh out loud.

"Have you ever done karaoke?" I challenge.

"Often. *My Way, Go West, Let Me Entertain You.* I have quite a repertoire. Karaoke is great fun. It ought to be available on prescription."

I am excited by how much I have to learn about Craig. I realize that he might be a still water that runs deep and the thought is thrilling.

"So what do you mean when you say accountancy was a natural choice?" he pursues.

"Well, I'm good at exams. I think people ought to pay their taxes. I don't like breaking laws. Or rules, diets or hearts come to that. I am better at being good than bad."

"What else are you good at, Rose?" Craig sends me twirling gently under his arm.

I consider the question. "I'm good at gardening, cheering people up, making jam." I know it doesn't sound glamorous but it is at least honest. I sigh and admit, "I am the epitome of a nice girl. Or at least I was before —"

"Before?"

"Before the divorce."

"Is Peter nice?"

"He's dashing, which was the nearest I could find to nice at the time."

Craig laughs. "Would you like to have a rest?"

Seriously? I'd like to stay in his arms until Cadbury's discover a recipe for calorie-free Dairy Milk, but I understand that the answer required is that I would like to sit down for a breather. He releases me and I feel bereft. At night-time I sometimes sneak into the twins' room and, from the doorway, I watch them sleeping. I derive an unimaginable amount of solace and joy from those secret midnight moments of watching them breathe. It's such an honour to bring life on to the planet and I can spend hours simply appreciating their lives. I always find it difficult to close the door and walk back to my room. A similar feeling sweeps me when Craig drops my hand and walks from the dance floor back to our seats. I don't want to let go.

I need to fill the temporary void so I keep talking. What was I chatting about? Oh yes, Peter.

"I had him fooled. Or maybe I was just a fool."

"What do you mean?" asks Craig. It's admirable that he's not shying away from the sore topic of my ex.

"Peter thought he'd bought nice. He thought I was *nice*."

"You are nice, Rose. So I assume you're saying that was *all* he thought you were. He missed all the other bits." Craig pours us both another glass of wine and we clink glasses.

"Exactly," I murmur.

"Didn't he see that the quirky thing about you, the big, well-guarded secret that stays hidden under all your obedience, and your sincerity and your ferocious work ethic, the fact that there is a heart that beats at a rate of knots, a head that is full of dreams and hopes and an unquashable sense of optimism and joy? You are not dull, Rose."

I do not know what to say. I stare at Craig and I'm amazed. Not only because he's really never looked more gorgeous, and commanding and adult, but because I want to know how he could possibly have guessed? I'm not sure my own sister knows I think of myself that way. How does Craig know? It appears he can read my mind too, because he goes on to answer my unarticulated question.

"If anyone ever took the time to scratch the surface they'd discover Rose the comedian, Rose the idealist, Rose the believer in true and everlasting love. Rose who privately, and rightly, holds the belief that she is rather thrillingly special. So special in fact that she never felt the need to parade her uniqueness, her intelligence or her depth the way so many lesser mortals feel inclined."

I realize that Craig's glass is empty, which might explain his vociferous compliments. But does it explain his insight? How long has this man been thinking about me? How carefully has he been listening to me? Is there a hint that he agrees with me? No doubt Connie would scream "stalker" and run a mile, but I am delighted. Craig has just articulated things that I've barely acknowledged to myself.

"I guess the thing was, you didn't need outside acclamation because you only needed Peter to recognize your talents and strengths," said Craig.

I stare at him warily. How much do I want to say about Peter? He is, after all, a parent at the school that Craig heads. Is it fair of me to prejudice Craig's views? On the other hand, if Craig is going to become my friend then it might be reasonable to expect that I won't be singing Peter's praises day and night.

"Peter didn't see any of my talents, well, at least not beyond jam-making. When I tried to show him that I was anything more than efficient or reliable, he didn't want to know. Passions aren't his thing. He likes cold. He felt he had been duped by me. He thought he had married a pleasant, nice lady who would be no trouble, in the way that his father had married a pleasant lady and had enjoyed a life free of squabbling, noise or strong feelings. But I turned out to be more trouble than he imagined. I expected rather more of him than he was prepared to give when the boys were born. And besides, by then he'd fallen in love with Lucy."

"So it wasn't as clear cut as that he left you for another woman?"

"Not really, although it's the story I feel most comfortable with. There was another woman and he did leave."

"The marriage was already over?"

"The truth is somewhere in between."

Craig nods as though he understands the complexities and nuances of a marriage that was dead years ago. I think it's impossible for him to do so, but I appreciate his effort for trying at least.

"We're having the conversation that we're supposed to have six months down the line, not on a first date," I point out. I wonder if I ought to be more reticent.

"That's weddings for you. They make you think about the big stuff, or at least they ought to."

"What will we talk about in six months?" I make the joke in an effort to break the all but overwhelming tension. I don't consider that my question might appear pushy.

"We'll probably be picking out wallpaper," says Craig, not showing any signs of being shoved.

I wonder if I ought to be scared, very scared or delighted, extremely delighted by this comment. With other men I would comfort and torture myself by believing it was an off-the-cuff and meaningless remark. But I know Craig doesn't do off-the-cuff and meaningless.

I glug back more wine and observe, "It's nearly speech time. Are you giving one?"

"I'm just reading telegrams. John is the funny man."

I scan the room and my eyes settle on John; he is supposed to be sitting on the top table but he's alone at a side table.

"He doesn't look that funny right now," I point out.

Craig follows my gaze. John is slumped almost face down on to the table. His weary demeanour is in stark contrast to the other guests. Everyone else in the room appears animated and exhilarated.

"Oh God, he must have drunk too much. He tends to when he's emotional. Jen will kill him if he messes up the speech. Can you excuse me?"

This mini crisis is rather timely. I need a little bit of thinking space for a minute or two. Craig leaves our table and heads over to drooping John. I watch as Craig gently shakes his friend, they swap a couple of sentences and Craig pours John a glass of water. I think the rescue mission may take some time, so I turn to the man next to me and start to make conversation.

CHAPTER
THIRTY-EIGHT

Saturday 11 November

John

Craig's nose is almost touching mine. I wish he'd stop shaking me. If he doesn't I might throw up, and he won't want vomit in his face, no matter how good mates we are. I've drunk enough to throw. Fuck it, I haven't drunk enough. It's not possible to drink enough. I need to keep on and on and on and . . .

"John, drink some water." Craig firmly pushes a glass towards my hand. I try to grasp it but it slips through my fingers. He guides it to my mouth. "Mate, I've never seen you this wasted."

I can't decide if Craig is in awe or shock. My tongue feels fat in my mouth and I'm struggling to move it in the directions necessary to articulate a response. This must be how those people with nut allergies feel. Poor sods. I stare at Craig. I'm trying to convey the fact that I'm going to be just fine, and the speech and everything, well, that's going to be just fine too. Except I doubt I'm doing much in the way of reassuring, considering I can't actually speak right now.

"Jussneedafewminutes. Itsabloodysilly time forspeeshes. Aferdinner. No one canssstaysober."

Craig tuts and holds the water glass to my mouth so that I can gulp from it. I'm grateful, and too wasted to care that we must look like a couple of benders or a special care patient with hospital staff.

"Sorry."

Then everything turns black.

When I come round I am sat on a chair in the bog. Craig is stood next to me; he has his hand on my shoulder, presumably to stop me slouching forward and knocking myself out as I fall on to the tiled floor. I wonder if I managed to crawl in here on my own or whether he had to drag me.

"Must be something I've eaten," I mumble.

Craig tuts; it's a very articulate tut. It's rammed full of disapproval and despair.

"Drink this," he instructs.

This time I successfully take hold of the glass and even manage to glug back the water without spilling too much of it down my suit. As soon as I finish Craig refills the glass from the faucet and hands me it once again.

"I'll be sick if I glug too much water too quickly." Craig points to the floor. Both our shoes and trousers are splattered with puke. "Mine, I presume?"

"You presume correctly."

"Sorry, mate."

"Yes. You should be."

The chunder, although clearly a pity for our shiny shoes, has helped to make me feel considerably better. I stagger to my feet and while the room is swaying, it's not doing a breakneck-speed spin, which was the case when I was sitting at the table in the reception room. It's a posh gig, so the bogs aren't gross, but there are always nicer places to hang than next to the urinals. I want out of here. I splash some cold water on my face, and Craig and I move on.

The bogs spill out on to a carpeted foyer. The carpet is red and heavily patterned; it's a little threadbare in places but you'd only notice if you were crippled with shame and insisting on staring at the floor rather than meeting your mate's eye. I force myself to look up and notice that the chandeliers are stunning. The echoes of elegance, a tribute to more graceful and sophisticated eras, mock me. I'm too shabby to be here. At least, I'm too shabby to be here like this. Fuck, I'm Tom's best man. He's expecting me to do a speech.

"John, you are Tom's best man, he's expecting you to do a speech," says Craig. He's scowling. Normally temperate, he doesn't bother to hide the fact that he's naffed off.

"I know that, mate."

"I can't do it." He sounds panicked. "I haven't prepared anything."

"I know that, mate. Don't worry, I'll be fine. I've been worse."

Craig looks doubtful. "How much have you had to drink?"

I don't know the exact answer. I started this morning. A couple of jars before the ceremony, with Tom, to calm his nerves and that. And he gave me a hip flask, with my initials on, by way of marking the occasion. Bit over if you ask me, but Jen had read about it being the thing to do in one of her girly wedding magazines, and she wanted him to give me a gift so give me a gift he did. Came in useful. We filled it with whisky and I had the odd nip while we were waiting for the photographer to wrap up the "watch the birdie" bit. Hell, that seemed to take an age. Ended up draining the flask. Then on to the reception, where I've been steadily drinking ever since. Or maybe not so steadily. I think I've gone through a couple of bottles. Thing is, I don't normally do grape, I'm more of a grain man myself, so I switched again when the beef arrived. Big mistake mixing the two.

"You should have brought a date," says Craig. "Then you wouldn't have got so plastered."

"Wouldn't have helped with my chances of pulling the bridesmaids though, would it?" I joke.

"One of the bridesmaids is married, another is a lesbian and the remaining four are pre-schoolers. You were never really in with a chance," Craig points out, tetchily.

"I know, mate. Just joshing."

"I thought you'd bring a date. You've gone on at me for long enough to do so."

"Yeah, well." I don't want to comment on this so I distract him. "She looks happy enough, your Rose. You're in there, mate."

Craig smiles and nods. "She is lovely. It's going really well."

"Good on you." I gently punch his arm. I can't help myself. I'm half cut and my old mate is in line for breaking his celibacy vows. It's an emotional moment. The pungent stench of puke wafts over me when I move my head. "Oh, sorry, mate. You have a bit of" — I point to the splatters — "on your lapel."

Craig scowls at me and marches back into the bathroom. He can't return to his lady friend smelling of odour de puke — it's a known passion-killer. I find a seat and light up. I'm not in a rush to get back to the reception so I might as well wait for Craig, even if his reappearance with a damp suit will be accompanied by a bollocking or at the very least, stern looks of censure.

"There you are, Hardie. I've been looking for you everywhere."

"Oh, Tom. Hello." I'm pretty sure my demeanour suggests that I haven't been searching him out. Luckily, Tom is too hyped to pay me much attention. "I'm just waiting for Craig." I wave in the direction of the bogs. Tom doesn't sit down. He's almost on tiptoes, he's practically bouncing.

"Good do, isn't it, eh? Having a good time, are you?" he asks.

"Fucking brilliant. Best wedding I've been to," I declare.

"Really?"

"Really." It would crucify him to answer in any other way. In truth, I'm having a bloody miserable time and even I can see that Jen has got a bit carried away. Jordan and Peter Andre's do was subtle in comparison to this.

"Except for your own, presumably," he says. "I mean, even though things didn't work out between you and Andrea, you must still have fond memories of, you know, the early days."

As he makes this intimate observation Tom stops bouncing. He decelerates so much he seems to be doing a farcical impression of someone acting in slow motion. He doesn't know how to handle something so private and delicate. Who does?

I have to help him out. It's his day. I don't want to be responsible for putting a downer on it.

"Ah well, all turned out for the best, mate. Did I tell you she's up the duff?"

"No."

"Yup, she rang me the other night to let me know the happy news. With her new bloke. So that's good for them, eh?"

"You all right with that, mate?"

"Too right, mate. Better man than me for the job. I'm not ready for all that crap." I think about what I've just said and I do mean it literally and metaphorically. Nappies, yuk. Tom looks nervous and I see that I have a responsibility to move the conversation back on to something we're both more comfortable with. "You're right though, mate, my wedding day was a monumental occasion. Do you remember we watched the big game?"

"Jesus, yes!" Tom, a lifelong Liverpool supporter, can't resist reliving the moment; he's instantly buoyant again. "We looked beaten as Freddie Ljungberg put

Arsenal ahead. I was beginning to think that Cardiff's Millennium Stadium was an unlucky place."

"Yeah, but Owen's dramatic double in the closing minutes gave Liverpool vic-tor-eee." I punch the air.

"Good thing, Hardie, it would have ruined the wedding if we'd lost, especially after you'd gone to all the trouble of hiring a flat screen TV for the reception."

We sit in reverence for a moment and would perhaps have stayed like that all night except that Craig re-emerges from the loo.

"Is it time for the speeches?" he asks.

"Jesus. Fuck. That's why Jen sent me to find you. Come on lads."

CHAPTER
THIRTY-NINE

Saturday 11 November

Rose

I turn to the guy on my left.

"Hello, my name is Rose Phillips. How do you do?"

I hold out my hand. The guy looks at it lazily. He isn't focusing as he's clearly had quite a lot to drink but I can't be tetchy about that, I've ignored him for most of the day because I've only had eyes for Craig. After a pointed pause he takes my hand and shakes it, limply. His palm is clammy.

"Phillips, eh? Fancy that? I'm Joe Whitehead."

"Bride or groom?"

"I'm neither, baby." Joe Whitehead starts to laugh, clearly delighted with his own joke. "I'm a cousin, once removed, of the bride. Haven't seen her since I was six. But not one to turn down a free drink." He chuckles again and I'm not sure whether I'm supposed to take him seriously.

"Jenny seems a lovely girl," I comment, resorting to approved wedding small talk.

"I can tell you about a lovely girl," he says with a leer.

Inwardly I groan, as I realize that Joe Whitehead is about to launch into a story about his own romantic affairs. I really couldn't care less. My recent foray into dating has given me enough experience to nose out a rejected soul. Joe Whitehead is one. He's drinking too much, he doesn't appear to have a date with him and he wants to talk to a complete stranger about another girl. While I like to behave nicely on all occasions, the truth is, right now, I don't give a damn about Joe Whitehead's tragic love affairs. I'm as high as a kite and I don't want to be brought down. I feel excited, ecstatic, appreciated, grateful and delightful. I wave to the waitress and ask for a refill of my coffee, and as I take a sip and nibble on a mint I think I'm eating food fit for the gods. My senses are zinging. Everything is suddenly sharper and brighter. I'm packed full of anticipation. All of a sudden, my future (at least my immediate future) seems dazzling. The last thing I want is to hear a sad tale. Sorry, selfish I may be, but there it is.

"The speeches are expected to begin any moment," I say, deflecting the opportunity for shared confidences. No doubt the off-the-blocks time depends on John's sobriety. I saw Craig practically carrying him out of the reception a few moments ago.

"Your bloke seems to have ditched you." Joe seems to find his observation funny; he laughs like a jackal. I remain silent. "You've just got it together too, haven't you?"

"We've known each other a long time but yes, this is our first date." I hate myself for sharing this with this coarse stranger, it wasn't my intention, but good manners dictate that I can't lie.

"You can tell. He's being very attentive. That never lasts."

I tune out. Cynicism and spite are not what I want to choose from today's menu.

Jenny's mum and the bridesmaids look agitated, they are clustered around Jenny and are all talking at once. Clearly there is some small wedding crisis. Maybe it is to do with John's drunkenness or maybe it's something else. Yet Jen stands in the middle of the jabbering women and she looks unconcerned. Craig has been entertaining me with stories about how Jen has organized this wedding with military precision and dictatorial intolerance. According to Craig she has bossed, yelled, ripped and cried her way through the last six months — normal bridal behaviour. Yet she is now standing in the vortex of the day and she is calm.

If there is a crisis, she accepts that in reality it will be minor and likely to pass unnoticed by all the guests other than the groom's mother. She's suddenly unconcerned about the fact that the priest wavered from the previously agreed order of service, and she's not fretful that Tom's dad insisted on wearing flashing heart cufflinks.

She is serene. The full implication of her wedding day has occurred to her. Love, commitment and loyalty billow around her and she's cosseted and insulated from the world's irritations and mishaps, at least for a while.

I understand. I catch her eye and beam; she smiles back.

"She's called Mrs Phillips too. Isn't that the weirdest?"

This comment comes from Joe What's-his-name. He has been chatting on since I introduced myself but I haven't taken in a word that he has spoken. He hasn't noticed my lack of participation. The man is a mix of morbidity and arrogance. I gleaned this much from the first couple of sentences we exchanged. But I realize I'm being horribly rude. After all, I was the one who spoke first. Besides, maybe I'm being overly judgemental. Daisy and Connie think that I always am. Maybe I should give this man a chance to improve, like a wine that's left to breathe. Having spent such a delightful day with Craig my tolerance stores are replete.

"I'm sorry, you were saying?"

"I was telling you about the most fabulous shag on this planet."

Stunned, I'm not sure how to respond. What is it that makes him think this is an acceptable conversation to have with a stranger?

"I was saying, funny coincidence. She has the same surname as you. She's a Mrs Phillips too. What do you make of that?"

Very little. I stare at the horrible Joe and downgrade my first impression (boorish) to a more damning condemnation (despicably uncouth).

"Not that she calls herself Mrs Phillips. She's too independent, a career girl."

He grins at me and I feel an all too familiar sense of not coming up to scratch. I hate the other Mrs Phillips, without even knowing her. I take a deep breath and think about Craig. I don't want the fabulousness of our day so far to be smeared and tarnished by this man's sorry stories. I try to excuse myself.

"I'm sorry, I need to —"

"You're nothing alike, physically," says Joe, rudely cutting across me. "She's a . . ." He looks me up and down and just manages to rein in the sneer that was playing on his lips. He has enough sense to shut the hell up. Clearly, he was going to say that the other Mrs Phillips, the *adulterous* Mrs Phillips, does not have to wear reinforced tummy-tuck knickers. No doubt her knees are not bruised when she releases her boobs from her bra; they do not shudder and scatter in an unwieldy fashion, they probably sit proudly pointing forwards. I scan the room and hope to spot Craig.

"She's bloody gorgeous. She's got a fierce intellect too. Although, you know, whatever. I don't need my women to be brilliant, just bendy." He starts to snort with laughter and drains his glass of red. "Really, it was the best night of my life. I think I showed her a trick or two as well. I honestly think she'll be banging on my door begging for more in the not too distant future."

Life really is too short for me to have to put up with this. I begin to gather my thoughts and my bag and make to leave the table. I'll wait for Craig somewhere else. I don't care if I appear bad-mannered, the man is insufferable. I can't stay a moment longer.

406

"I'm sure you and the other Mrs Phillips will be very happy together, Mr Whitehouse." I'm not sure if that's his name but he doesn't correct me. Frankly I couldn't care less. I push back my chair and stand up.

"Don't call her Mrs Phillips, she suits her maiden name best. That's what she prefers to be known as. Lucy Hewitt-Jones — it's got more class."

The room morphs. My legs, robust — sturdy even under normal circumstances — fail me. I collapse back into my chair.

"Lucy Hewitt-Jones? Blonde, leggy?" I wish I could add vacant.

"You know her?" Joe's face is flushed with excitement.

"Works for Gordon Webster Handle?" I need to be certain there's no mistake. But of course there isn't. Lucy Hewitt-Jones is a distinctive enough name.

"Yes," Joe smiles. Or rather leers. "I do too. That's how we met. So how do you know her?"

There's horrible buzzing in my ears. I watch Joe Thingy's mouth move but I can't hear the words he's stringing together. I'm suddenly icy cold and there's a boxing match being hosted in my gut.

"She's married to my husband, I mean my ex-husband." He looks traumatized. The arrogance floods from him in an instant. I look down as I half expect to see his arrogance in a puddle on the floor. Shaming and smelly, like the urine of a small child unable to hold it till they get to the loo. But adult "accidents" are never so easily detectable. Neither of us knows what to say next. "If you'll excuse me."

I lurch as I try to find my feet. I move incredibly slowly because I know to try to rush now would surely end in my tripping or fainting. The drama of which would be unforgivable. Very slowly I gather together my bag and my jacket. My fingers have turned to mush and fail me by not being able to smartly button up the jacket. As I walk from the room, the sound of wailing children and the screech of the mic being called into action pierce my body like arrows. Once out of sight I start to run. The corridors close in on me as I rush like a desperate criminal from a bloody scene.

CHAPTER
FORTY

Monday 20 November

Lucy

The day of my epiphany in the National Portrait Gallery didn't pan out exactly as I'd imagined, which I'm already beginning to realize is a fundamental consequence of involving oneself with children. Things rarely pan out as one imagines. I ran out of the gallery, frantically trying to flag a cab. It was still raining and so they were scarce. Never in my life have I struggled to hail a taxi, they normally risk a pile-up to pick me up. But then, never in my life have I behaved frantically; I am sure the two facts correlate. Cabbies probably steer well away from anyone looking desperate. In the end I dashed towards the underground and endured that atrocity for the second time in one day. I ran from the tube station to home and flung open the front door only to be greeted by a fairly bemused Eva. Auriol was nowhere to be seen, she was still at school. It was only two-twenty. Which seemed peculiar to me: the day already felt as though it was a month long.

I smoked a cigarette, drank a black coffee and paced the kitchen until I alighted on the idea of popping to

Connie's. We could walk to the school gate together. That way I'd kill some time and with her at my side I was less likely to break any invisible (but all important) school gate etiquette that I was unaware of.

Connie was delighted to see me and was thrilled with my decision to attempt to bond with Auriol.

"I need her. I need to know that there is a reason, and progress, and a point," I rambled to Connie. I didn't say that I also needed Auriol to glue me to Peter and I didn't mention why my hangover was quite so vicious and shaming.

Connie is rather dreamy and impractical much of the time. She indulges in "why are we here" thoughts far more than the average grown-up. Her insistence on remaining eternally studenty is largely annoying but that day I found it a comfort.

Connie was happy for me to accompany her to the school gates. Once there I became the object of more attention than I desired. Half the mums made a big thing about introducing themselves to me and saying how nice it was to meet me *at last* — the other half pointedly ignored me. I'd failed in their eyes by not sacrificing myself at the altar of motherhood. I tried smiling at them and conveying that I pledged to do just that, from that day forward, but I was strung out and I'm pretty sure my weak grin looked more like a hostile grimace.

Auriol was thrilled to see me at the gate and after she'd established that no, Eva was not ill, she relaxed and took hold of my hand.

"Come and see my classroom, Mummy," she insisted.

410

"We could go to Connie's and play with Fran if you like," I offered, keen to escape the confines of the school grounds as quickly as possible. It was hardly my scene.

"No. I want you to see my firework picture. It's on the wall. You said we could do anything I wanted."

Had I? In those brief seconds when she flung herself into my arms and I said hello and garbled other bits, had I already relinquished all power? We said goodbye to Connie and her girls and then I allowed Auriol to tug at my coat sleeve and drag me into her classroom.

Of course I'd visited the classroom before Auriol was offered a place at the school. I knew what to expect. Tiny tables and chairs, disorder, odd scribbled pictures hung on the wall, illegible writing proudly displayed as if it were ancient calligraphy, Lego crunching underfoot and a scruffy mat in the corner where the children listen to stories. As I entered the room Miss Gibbon, Auriol's teacher, rushed towards me with an outstretched hand and a wide beam.

"Is it OK if we take a poke around?" I asked, suddenly self-conscious. A fish out of water, I didn't know what was allowed or expected.

"It's wonderful to see you, Mrs Phillips. Most of the mums have had an unofficial tour by now. The children love it if their parents are involved and know what they've achieved in their first couple of months."

The young teacher blushed as soon as the words were out of her mouth. She hadn't meant to charge me with neglect but had done so anyway.

"This is mine," said Auriol as she proudly pointed to a coat peg. There was a passport-size photo of her,

Blu-tacked above the peg. I hadn't seen the photo before. I peered at it. "Eva took me to a box to get that photo," Auriol explained. She looked anxious on the shot. Her smile was forced and lopsided.

"When?" I asked.

"Day before school started. I didn't know I'd like school then. But I know now," said Auriol, explaining her strained smirk. Miss Gibbon, who was hovering in the background and doing a lousy impression of not eavesdropping, smiled with satisfaction. "Come on."

Auriol moved me around the classroom. She proudly showed me her tray, her pictures that had been deemed good enough to be pinned on the wall, the reading books, the flash cards, the weighing scales, the measuring jugs and the games cupboard. Some of it was familiar because it was the same equipment they used in schools when I was an infant. The rest of it was new in a startling sense. I felt like Peter's mother had said she felt the first time she ventured into a shop selling mobile phones. Wasn't this equipment marvellous but what was it all for?

"I have twenty words," said Auriol. Her tone was triumphant but I had no idea what she was talking about. She pointed to a poster pinned on the wall. Upon which simple words were written: "I", "am", "you", "was", etc. She put her tiny finger under each word and started to read to me.

"If, in, what, and."

I didn't interrupt her and when she finished I said, "That was twenty-four words — you have twenty-four words, more than you thought." I smiled.

412

Proud, she grinned back at me. "I can read whole books." She rushed over to the library corner and picked up a book.

"This is Mum. This is Dad. This is a dog. This is a cat." Placing her tiny finger under each word as she said it, she carefully completed the simple book. Of course I'd heard her attempts to read before, as she often read with Eva, but I hadn't realized she was so advanced. Mortification and pride fought for my attention. Since that afternoon I've realized that this conflict is one I might be living with for quite some time. Mortification at all I've missed, pride in what she's achieved even though she's been largely neglected by me.

I knew she was bright.

"Auriol is very good at reading," said Miss Gibbon. "One of the best in the class."

"I can see that," I commented, and then I had to rush Auriol out of the class before I was further exposed.

I took Auriol out for tea that night. We did not go home so that I could change clothes because she was starving and we agreed that reading was "hungry-making work".

The next day Peter, Auriol and I went to the movies and I let her sit on my knee throughout the allegedly scary bits, even though my shirt got creased and the movie was a Disney cartoon and we both knew that really she wasn't in the least bit scared.

On Sunday the twins came to visit as usual, and we all went rollerblading in Kensington Gardens, which was unusual. I can't say I enjoyed myself. Sebastian knocked me over four times and I'm pretty sure none of the collisions were accidents, but Peter and Auriol were glowing with happiness, despite the drizzle and the cold. As I lowered myself into a hot bath that night I examined my grazed knees and palms and fat tears slid down my face. I brushed them away impatiently. I told myself I was crying at my injuries, or even at the fact that, in my rush to leave the house today, I'd left my gloves behind so that my fingers had stung with cold all day and now looked about as attractive as defrosting fish fingers, economy brand. It would be dreadful to think the tears were tears of regret at my actions, or grief for the time I'd squandered, or terror at being discovered for what I really am. Although any of these things is enough to make me cry.

The idyllic little scenes I've just described turned out not to be wholly representative. Over the course of the week Auriol became less cooperative, not more. The novelty of my appearing at the school gate wore off with indecent haste and by day three she asked, "Aren't you supposed to be making money? Where's Eva? Eva knows that I go to the library on Tuesdays."

I had imagined that the moment I decided I was ready to embrace my daughter, family life and all the associated that I would be welcomed with literal and metaphorical open arms. I was wrong. Auriol is finding my sudden interest in her whereabouts rather claustrophobic. She behaved like a stroppy teenager when I suggested we limit the number of play-dates she can accept in a week. But she is so tired after school, I do believe she needs down time. On Wednesday I asked her where she'd picked up the expression "fart-head". She informed me that it was none of my business and went on to assure me that I am the only, only, only Mummy that doesn't allow sleepovers, and for that she hates me.

We don't know one another. It is as I suspected, except worse. I was aware that I didn't have any real understanding of my daughter's nature but I hadn't imagined her to be particularly complex. She's four years old, for God's sake, I hadn't realized there had been enough time for her to develop mysterious and elusive intricacies. Over the last ten days I've struggled to find common ground but I'm exposed, as I don't know the names of her friends, or her favourite TV shows, or which books she's already had read to her as bedtime stories. I realize that playing with her would be a "good thing" but I have no patience for threading beads, hosting imaginary tea parties for her soft toys or dressing and undressing Barbie dolls as though they were stuck in a Ground Hog Day nightmare. Instead, I try to encourage her to play Connect 4 and noughts and crosses. After initial objections, yesterday she agreed, and it turns out that she has a very logical mind. I shared with her my tip for both games, which is to insist on going first and always to take the centre position. It might not be the most philanthropic motherly advice but it's a start and she did enjoy winning.

It transpires that we are rather alike, which I'm pleased about, but our being similar does have its issues. We are both strong-willed, independent and self-sufficient. We have clear ideas (often conflicting) on how and when things should be done. We disagree about what Auriol should eat, when she should practise her flash cards and at what time she ought to go to bed. As I haven't ever given motherhood much thought, a number of bad habits have been allowed to develop. It used to be that Auriol would switch off her own bedside light at any time she liked at night. Providing she stayed in her room after Eva put her there, I didn't much care. Having given it some thought, I've decided that lights ought to be out by 7p.m. on a week-night bedtime. My suggestion was greeted with contempt.

"I'm not a baby, Mummy," she insisted.

But it's just occurring to both of us that actually, she is. She's my baby.

I've stretched bedtime to 8p.m. at weekends, at great personal sacrifice. After a full day of entertaining her I quite often want to hurl her into bed at around five. I had no idea how hard it was to spend an entire day encouraging a child to eat fruit and vegetables, limit the hours on the computer or in front of the TV and disallow sweet snacks. I often ache with holding my body in a form of protest. I fall into my bed exhausted, but as I am erect with tension sleep often eludes me.

Connie has taken a great interest in my progress. I think she's enjoying being the one to offer advice and assurance. Over the last week there have been times that I wanted to throttle her as her patronizing chorus of "I told you so" and "You'll get the hang of it" sallied forth. There are days when I want to yell at her that she was part of my downfall. If she had not embraced motherhood quite so fully then I would still have had someone to drink cocktails with, and then I would have stayed in practice and not got plastered at Wasp bar, and then I would not have allowed Joe Whitehead to . . . At this point my argument disintegrates. I haven't got the stomach for blame. It's never been my style. I take responsibility for my own disasters. Besides, I realize that Connie has taken the natural path. Loving your kids and adapting your life to accommodate the life you've created is the proper way. It must be because it feels right to me now. Even when I'm getting it wrong, it feels right.

Yes. Because this week I'm already discovering that even when I do fall into bed exhausted but stiff with tension, I can identify a smidgen of pride hidden deep inside and I know that what I'm trying to achieve is a good thing. On Thursday I felt a glow when Auriol chose for me to bath her, rather than Eva, and that glow was fanned when I won a smile of pleasure from Auriol for remembering her favourite Girls Aloud song on Saturday. Something very deep inside me has stirred, resentment has been dislodged and something more positive, that I can't quite identify yet, is growing in its place. It's worthwhile.

That said, I'm no saint, and after ten days of trying to qualify for a mother of the year award I ring Connie and demand she meets me for a cocktail after our kids are in bed.

I arrive at the bar first and I order us both a Cosmopolitan. When Connie arrives soon after me, she pounces on it gleefully.

"I'm finding this mothering thing is often bloody, but why am I surprised? That's what I'd expected. Auriol told me she hated me again today."

"Oh, that. They all say that from time to time." She waves her hand dismissively and the sense of rejection I've been carrying around since teatime dissolves. "The books say that you have to reply with some crap like, 'Well, I still love you.'"

"Really?" I'm shocked.

"Yes, but I usually say, 'That's a horrible word, Fran, and you should think very carefully before being so mean to your mum. I feed you.'" We both laugh. "There's no such thing as a perfect mum. Whatever I do she'll blame me when she grows up and she's in therapy. How's work?"

"It's fine. Actually, no, it isn't. I'll probably be sacked soon. The word on the street is that I've taken my eye off the ball and I'm yesterday's hero."

"Rubbish. You'll be there when you're contemplating Saga holidays and need a hearing aid to listen to the gossip."

"Connie, please don't be gross."

But I find myself laughing and something in the pit of my stomach moves again. More resentment is dissolving, the contentment is growing. OK, maybe growing old isn't totally horrifying. It's not great, but there's always surgery — and consider the alternative to growing old.

I'm not joking about the problems at work though. A week is a long time in the City. Last week I turned down all invitations to lunch, drinks or dinner. I used

418

the excuse that I haven't time for a lunch-break because I want to leave the office in time to read to Auriol, which is half of the truth. The other half of the equation is that I have to ask, after the office party, how can I ever trust myself to socialize with a colleague again? My commitment to Auriol is seen as a betrayal at work. Today, a sizeable new client, who I was sure was winging his way towards me, was given to Joe Whitehead to care-take. The irony isn't lost on me. I feel passed over but can't prove that the client was ever intended to come into my pasture. I did not take this news lying down and marched into Ralph's office and demanded that he offer an explanation. He said that Joe had more experience in that particular field. Maybe he has.

Maybe.

Or maybe word of my indiscretion at the party has leaked into the boardroom.

Or maybe my femininity, and therefore frailty, is exposed now that I've admitted, in my heart, that I am a mother. I don't know which is worse.

"Do you still see much of that Mick?" asks Connie.

"No," I reply shortly.

Connie keeps her eyes on me — she's waiting for me to elaborate. I want to, I'm just not sure where to start. Mick and I have been avoiding one another. I can't decide if it's because I propositioned him when I was drunk or because he turned me down. Either alternative would be better than the possibility that he has heard about Joe. I look at Connie and wonder if she could cope with me confessing to having sex with a man other than Peter. Before I married Peter, Connie used to be thrilled with stories about my exploits, but I'm not sure she'd see tight, drunken, regretful adultery with a nasty loner as source for titilation. What possessed me? Even while I ask the question, I know the answer. I've never been into self-delusion. Alcohol and loneliness were the catalysts and culprits. A fatal cocktail.

I decide I don't want to hang my filthy linen in Connie's backyard. I won't tell her about my horrid indiscretion. Joe is *not* important. No one need ever know. He was nothing more than a wake-up call. He meant *nothing*. Speaking of him would give him import that he doesn't deserve. I push him to the back of my mind, the way I have had to on countless occasions this week. If I think of the moment when he kissed me and I could smell stale, old food on his teeth, I might start to heave. Peter never smells of anything other than Listerine mouthwash and Colgate toothpaste. Joe Whitehead's mouth, full of metal and rotting meat, made me pull back. We had sex without kissing. Prostitutes do the same thing, I understand.

I've stayed silent long enough for Connie to realize I'm not in the mood to swap confidences about Mick or any other aspect of GWH. She moves on to a topic nearer to her heart.

"So will you be volunteering to help sew costumes for the nativity play?" I stare at her horrified. "Or sell tickets?" I shake my head. "Serve coffee at the interval?"

"Get real, Connie. No. I'm doing my best but I'm not PA material, we both know that."

"You could be, if you wanted to be."

"Now there's a truth. Don't expect to see me at those hideous children's group coffee mornings any time soon, either."

"Why?"

"Everyone sits on their fat arses and eats cake all morning in some depressing town hall. I cannot stand those ghastly places. They always smell of child crap."

Connie laughs and orders us each another cocktail.

"I'll have a bottle of mineral water instead. I'm still hungover from the office party."

My hangover is moral rather than physical but it's very real. Connie eyes me with curiosity but doesn't probe.

"How's Eva accepting your recent bonding with Auriol?" she asks.

"I thought that at least Eva would see my interest as a positive thing. I know I must be lessening her workload because mine seems to have increased tenfold. But instead of being pleased for my positive contribution she's chosen to interpret my actions as 'unnecessary interference'. She believes I'm rushing home from work early to check up on her and she sees any suggestion I make regarding the structure of Auriol's day as a direct criticism."

"Oh dear."

"She's resigned twice in the last ten days. I don't know how to manage the situation. I am not willing to see less of Auriol just to placate the nanny."

"So?"

"I've decided to do what I always do — I've thrown cash at the problem. So far I have managed to persuade her to stay by offering to pay for her gym membership and driving lessons. I wonder what will happen first, our bankruptcy or her final resignation. It'll be a close call."

Connie laughs. "And how's Peter?"

"Really good," I beam. "We're good."

There is an upside to my new approach to mothering. The overwhelming positive outcome, which far outweights the slights at work and the battles with Auriol and Eva, is that Peter has noticed I'm trying. He sees me hold my temper when Auriol won't hold my hand and he sees me bite my lip when she bites my leg. I think I am slowly forging new connections between us and I hope to weave enough strands of common ground and understanding to patch up the holes in our relationship. I see now that Joe Whitehead was indeed a wake-up call. Not a threat. Not a problem. I like to think of him as a relationship aid.

If I have to think of him at all.

My mobile starts to ring.

"I bet that's him now," I say, smiling at Connie. "Do you mind if I take it?"

"Go ahead."

"Hello Lucy, it's Joe here." Fuck. My insides turn to liquid.

"Who?" I ask, to buy time.

I signal to Connie that it's too noisy to take the call in the bar and I walk outside and out of earshot.

All the while I'm praying that the call is business related.

"I was wondering if you wanted to meet up some time soon. We could do Thursday night all over again," says Joe. In my mind's eye I can see his grey skin and feel his damp palms. I shudder.

"I'm sorry, I have no idea what you are talking about." I hope my voice sounds calm. I don't want to be drawn. There must be no discussion about that night. To admit that it happened would give it a dignity that it is miles below.

"Come on, Lucy. It's a bit late to play hard to get."

"I'm not playing anything." I shiver. I've left my coat inside the bar, although even if I was wearing a ski-suit I think I'd be chilled.

"I'm going on a date tomorrow. How do you feel about that?"

"I have no feelings on the matter."

"Lucy, baby, I know you are jealous. Why don't you just say so? One word from you and I'd blow her out."

"Which wouldn't be hard because no doubt she's a figment of your imagination," I snap. Damn. That's hardly neutral.

Joe laughs. "I love your sense of humour. We should go out, spend a little more time together. We didn't get much chance to chat to one another the other night, did we? Too much animal attraction." He laughs to himself. I'm closer to screaming. How deluded is this lunatic? "You want me, don't you? You just can't admit as much because you are married."

"How did you get my number?"

"Julia gave it to me."

"If you ever call me again I'll —"

"What, Lucy? Tell your husband that your lover called."

Without notice tears prickle my eyes and the hairs on my arms stand up as goosebumps take hold.

"You are not my lover," I hiss into the phone.

"I was last week."

"I was drunk. You were a mistake."

"My mother says the same thing. She doesn't mean it either."

I suspect she does. "Don't call me again, ever." I hang up.

The sound of laughter, clinking glasses and chatter drifts out of the bar as the door swings open. Outside on the street, where I am standing, everything seems much more depressing.

CHAPTER
FORTY-ONE

Wednesday 22 November

Rose

Since Lucy-gate I've barely slept or eaten. I struggle to hold a thought in my head, let alone expel a coherent sentence into the big, bad world. I am floored. Literally. Since that Joe Whatshisname (oh, how I wish I'd paid more attention to his introduction) revealed his nasty secret I've laboured to keep on my feet. It was with enormous effort that I placed left foot in front of right and managed to walk out of the reception and on to the street, where I was able to hail a cab. Once home I crawled into bed. The children were at Peter's and he would not be returning them for twenty-four hours. I tried to stay calm. Breathe deeply. Order my thoughts. It was important not to jump to conclusions or make rash judgements.

What was the treacherous, home-wrecking, despicable bitch thinking of?

Sorry, sorry. What was Lucy Hewitt-Jones, aka Mrs Phillips the second, thinking of?

I stayed under the duvet for the twenty-four child-free hours and I pored over the information Joe had given me. I considered the possibility that, quite simply, he was a liar — that Lucy was no more having an affair with him than I was. This was possible. He was clearly a low and repulsive sort; maybe he was harbouring some warped sexual fantasy about her that had absolutely no truth at its root. He wasn't at all funny or particularly good-looking. He wasn't anywhere near as attractive as Peter. Why would she? For all Lucy's faults, the one thing I can say about her is that she's got impeccable taste. If she did . . . go with Joe, then she was certainly slumming it.

But why would he make it up? What would possess a man to name a co-worker and say that they had a thing going, if they didn't? It would be too risky to do such a thing, especially in the City where lawsuits for sexual harassment and defamation are rife.

And she does have form. Even before Peter, Lucy had a record of seducing men who were already in relationships or allowing herself a little extracurricular activity while she was supposed to be seeing someone. She used to insist that monogamy was as unnatural as a polystyrene cup of instant noodles.

But I thought she'd changed.

I feel like a load of washing on a spin cycle. One moment I am delighted, the next distraught. One moment I'm certain and confident, the next I feel I'm wading through an indelible fog. It's ignoble of me but I am delighted that all is not well between Peter and Lucy, doesn't that serve them right? Since the day he packed his bags, well-meaning friends and family have assured me that no good would come of their relationship. It's generally agreed (although not statistically proven) that relationships which start through adultery will ultimately find themselves back in the same messy gloop sooner or later — a different cast to be sure, but in the end it's the same horrifying lying, cheating and betraying.

But I never wanted it to be so.

The fact of Lucy's infidelity leaves me distraught and more at sea than I have ever been — even when Peter left me. I thought Lucy loved Peter. To say that her loving him, choosing him above all other men, was a horrific inconvenience to me is a laughable understatement. Her love for Peter was a death blow for my marriage. The devastating and shattering effects cannot be exaggerated. I could perhaps have fought off a lesser mortal but Lucy's love was too great an opponent.

But perversely, the enormity and certainty of their love has always been a peculiar comfort to me.

Yes, it hurt. My God, the treachery and duplicity that they had practised upon me was life-seizing. I used to wonder if I would ever be able to breathe in a world so dramatically altered after he left. But, as the months passed, I began to find solace in their unflinching, selfish certainty. I reasoned that if Lucy and Peter loved one another to the extent that Peter was prepared to leave his children and me and they were prepared to blast apart our happy society, forcing friends to scuttle to opposing trenches, then maybe they knew something I didn't.

Maybe they knew that "it" existed — "The One", a soulmate, call it what you will. Maybe they were privy to a certainty that eluded most of us, most of the time. It seemed to me that Lucy and Peter's horrible selfishness had a cold beauty, because they believed that they were one another's "someone". The someone who made life bearable and gave existence meaning. Not such a depressing thought, if you follow it through to its ultimate conclusion. Luke and Connie were meant for one another. They were one another's "it". Daisy and Simon had "it" too. I took comfort that if this was so, then maybe, just maybe, all my suffering had a reason. Sometimes, on my very best days, I daydreamed and wondered if there was still an "it" out there for me. Last Saturday, at the wedding, I began irresponsibly to imagine that Craig might have a bit of "it" about him. Maybe he had potential. Of course Joe's revelation put paid to that.

Lucy is sleeping with *someone else* now. Not only is it now impossible to believe in anything beautiful, or permanent, or meaningful, but any potential I had with Craig is well and truly splattered since I ran from the reception without so much as nodding in his direction.

Lucy has robbed me all over again.

I hate her.

I manage to function in a lacklustre way. I feed, wash clothes, iron, clean and argue about teeth-brushing as usual but I don't have the energy to double- and treble-check their homework or music scales. The boys are taking advantage of my distraction and last Tuesday they "forgot" to stay behind for auditions for the school nativity play. They are both delighted to have sunk into the obscurity of being given catch-all roles as villagers.

I've been preening them for the roles of narrator or kings since reception class, but it seems I missed my moment. I took my eye off the ball for a second and that's all it took. It's the story of my life. In a way this suits me. Bigger parts might have required after-school rehearsals and the risk of running into Craig, something I dread. When I drop off or pick up the boys from school I don't walk them right up to the gate any more. The boys interpret this as a response to their bid for independence and are delighted.

Thinking about Craig fills me with disappointment and remorse. What must he think of me? Well, it's obvious, isn't it? He must think I'm quite mad, totally insane. We were having such a good time. The memory punches me and leaves me gasping. But what does it matter? How could I trust him or anyone, ever again? This world is soiled and fetid. I'll probably have to pull the kids out of Holland House. But I can't think about that right now. I'm dizzy with trying to decide what to think about what.

Paralysed with indecision and shock, I am unsure as to what my next move should be. Do I want to tell Peter what I know of Lucy's latest torrid affair? There would undoubtedly be some sweet satisfaction as I watched him receive the news, the same news he once so haplessly delivered to me. I could expose her and no one would blame me. The generous would assume that I had a latent but long-standing loyalty to my ex-husband. The less generous would be delighted in my ugly revenge and insist he had it coming. But do I want to be the one to bring all that woe into his life? Do

I want to spill my news on to his living-room floor and watch the poison seep into everything he treasures? He did it to me! But still, I am unsure.

Should I confront Lucy? It would be delightful to see her squirm. To show her that she's not so clever and that I have the upper hand for once. I could bully and threaten and frighten her. Except it's not my style to bully and it's not hers to be frightened. She might even tell me that Peter already knows that she has sex with other men. They might have an *arrangement*. The thought is hideous and I shy away from involving myself in their business at all.

Connie and Daisy sense that I'm not myself. They assume I must be coming down with a flu bug and reason that it must be fairly bad as I don't reject or resist their offers to help out. Connie has done the school run for me on more than one occasion and Daisy keeps me company on Sunday when the boys are at Peter's. Not that I am much company. I'm maudlin and secretive. We watch re-runs of *Little House on the Prairie*, as we did when we were kids. If she notices that I'm crying by the time the credits come up on screen, she chooses to believe that I'm moved by the storyline.

My friends are stunned by my ready acceptance of their offers of help, as I rarely agree to the need for support. Even when the twins were very young and Peter first left, I preferred to manage on my own. I liked being self-sufficient. The twins gave me a purpose and I enjoyed their company. And, I suppose, I rather enjoyed being a martyr, but to be a martyr you have to believe in a cause and now I'm not so sure.

430

I hear Daisy and Connie whispering in the kitchen, asking one another if they know the nature of my ailment or why I seem so listless. I refuse to comment on whether I had fun with Craig at the wedding. I had anticipated sharing my exuberance with them but that now seems light years away. I've yet to decide if I want to share the revelation of Lucy's latest infidelity with them. It's tricky: Daisy will be furious and will insist that I expose Lucy instantly and as nastily as possible. I'm not sure I have the stomach for her anger on top of my own. Connie will be miserably confused. Lucy is her friend.

Oh my God, that is assuming Connie is ignorant of Lucy's affair.

It is possible that she is Lucy's confidante. The thought is horrific but it's not impossible. Connie has a history of secrecy herself. They say a leopard never changes its spots. I want to trust her but it's not easy. It's odd that Lucy's latest crime has eroded my belief in human nature so thoroughly. Why on earth I should ever have hung any hopes on Lucy is a mystery. But who would have thought she was able to inflict any more damage, more pain? Is there no limit? I start to scrutinize every sentence Connie utters and, as discreetly as possible, I cross-examine her as to whether Lucy is happy at work and with Peter. She is as discreet as she has been for the last five years. Gently, but firmly, she makes it clear that she's uncomfortable talking about Lucy. Her consistency heartens me. If she'd been more insistent and offered too many assurances of domestic bliss then I would have had reason to suspect that she knows of Lucy's affair. I conclude she's probably ignorant of it.

Each night I fall asleep ravaged by the day's endless churning of facts, rumour and conjecture. The hardest part to swallow is that I would put money on it that Lucy is sleeping soundly. In my experience there is rest for the wicked. It's those with a conscience who toss and turn.

CHAPTER
FORTY-TWO

Thursday 23 November

John

Craig calls me to say that he doesn't want to meet in a pub. He's actually stated that he doesn't want to go to a pub *at all* tonight.

"Why?" I can't imagine.

"I want to talk."

Doesn't everyone? "What?" He hears the panic in my voice and tries to reassure me.

"Nothing big. I'm just saying that you can't hear yourself think in some of those pubs we go to. I'll get some tins in. I'll do a spag bol."

Craig knows how to get his way with me. I thought Andrea was the only person who knew that the way to my heart is through beer and bolognese. I agree.

Craig lives in a small two-bedroom ex-council flat in Notting Hill. He bought it as soon as he started earning, with the help of an inheritance from his old nan. It was a smart investment. Nationally, house prices have rocketed; teachers can rarely afford to buy anything, anywhere, nowadays and in Notting Hill, in particular, prices have gone cosmic. After *the film* everyone wanted to live there. I think people believed they'd end up being a neighbour to Julia Roberts.

But his flat, while worth a bob or two, is nothing special. It's barely distinguishable from just about every other boy flat I've ever been in. The walls are blue, there's lots of IKEA furniture, the kitchen is an 80s horror and the towels in the bathroom smell a bit musty. I feel quite at home, as I used to live in just the same way, well, worse actually, until I married and Andrea brought wood floors, shaggy rugs and cushions into my life. While I have regressed back to eating takeaways practically every night, I have hung on to her sartorial influence, not least because having a cool and/or comfortable pad helps when pulling women. Craig's place is discernibly different from most men's in one way; there are lots of books, photos and postcards, which, generally speaking, men avoid.

When I arrive at Craig's a smell of fried onions and mince is drifting on to the communal landing. Good as his word. He opens the door to me and we greet one another in our usual way.

"All right."

"All right."

Both enquiry and reply. No one would guess I'm chuffed to see him or him me. We eat in relative silence. A DVD of *Blade Runner* is playing in the background. It's Craig's favourite movie so it's usually playing when he's home. At my house it's *Butch Cassidy and the Sundance Kid*. When the credits roll I take charge of the remote and flick from channel to channel until I settle on *Jackass*.

434

"Nice bol, by the way. Cheers."

"No problem."

I've taken the chair and Craig is flopped on to the sofa. We watch *Jackass* and laugh our heads off if anyone gets seriously hurt or humiliated, not just me, but Craig too — proving that he does have the Y-chromosome.

"What did you think of her?"

I have no idea what Craig is talking about. Johnnie Knoxville is on screen when he asks this so he can't mean a TV hottie. Craig sees my confusion.

"Rose? What did you think of her? The girl I took to Tom's wedding — she was the one I was telling you about."

Despite the fact that Craig said he wanted to talk tonight, I'd hoped he didn't mean he wanted to talk *talk*. We talk *talked* last month, I'm not sure I'd be comfortable if it became a habit. Still, there is no such thing as a free lunch. I decide to help myself to another tinnie — if I'm going to have to do deep and meaningful then I'm going to need a little lubrication.

"Your special someone?" I conclude, quickly getting with the programme.

"Well, hardly. Well, no. Well, yes. But."

"Which is it?"

"I think she's special," he says finally.

I'm not into redheads and I thought she was a bit lardy but then lots of men really go for that, they like something to get hold of. Craig looks bloody miserable, which is odd. Now he's found his "special someone" he

435

can have a profound and intense relationship and finally get his leg over — conscience fully satiated.

"She ran away," he says.

"What?"

"At the wedding. We were getting on so well. Or at least I thought we were. No. Yes. We really were. I don't understand it."

Craig is staring at me in exactly the same way he used to when he was a kid and some hard bastard off our estate had robbed his dinner money or deliberately run over his bike to bend the front wheel.

I mute the TV volume and say, "Talk me through it, mate."

He doesn't need to be asked twice. "We were having a great time, chatting, getting to know each other a bit better. She seemed very relaxed and happy. We even danced."

I know this. I watched them through my alcoholic blur and yes, from where I was swaying, they were having a great time. She was definitely into him. She was laughing at his jokes, gazing into his eyes, the full monty. Frankly, I was jealous. Not that the Rose bird is my type, not anywhere near, but anyone could see that whatever they were cooking up between them was pretty *special*, to use Craig's word.

It was that honest and straightforward even I saw it.

I remember looking from them to Tom and Jen and back again. Frankly, it was a bit fucking depressing. It was Craig and this woman's promising start that led me to drink so much. Not that I begrudge Craig a bit of happiness. Honestly, I want him to be heaped with happiness. And the same for Tom and Jen. If I ever won the lottery I'd buy Craig a new gaff and I'd do the same for Tom too. They are like brothers. I think that's why seeing them both operate so damned functionally drove me to drink. I'm not a cretin, and I'm the best-looking of the three of us, so the question had to be asked, why was I the one sitting on my own with no one other than Aunt Madge for company?

Look, I'm digressing. My point is that Craig and his girl seemed to be getting on just fine.

"What happened? Step on her toe? Women can be very funny about their shoes."

Craig refuses to let me lighten up the evening.

"You happened, you idiot. Rose noticed that you were catatonic and so I went to try to sober you up, which took a while."

"Sorry."

"And then there were the speeches. I kept looking for her. At first I thought she must be in the loo or at the bar but no, she'd gone, vanished without a trace."

"A regular Cinderella."

"I thought that perhaps she'd got a call from home. She has twin boys. Maybe something was wrong with one of them. So I called her mobile and left messages but she's never got back to me. I called all the next day, too. It was a relief when the boys turned up to school on Monday as usual but she wasn't at the gate, a friend of hers had dropped them off. I made casual enquiries. The boys said their mother was fine but because they are seven years old they didn't offer any details and I could hardly probe."

True, what is the etiquette when it comes to the headmaster talking to a couple of lads about the potential of boning their mother?

"I can't talk to her friends to see what's wrong because they're all mums at my school, it would be unprofessional. I wonder if I should call round. But when? I can't visit when the boys are at home but I can hardly dip out of school to see to my personal business. What do you think?" asks Craig.

"I think you're insane to involve yourself with a woman with two seven-year-old lads."

"For God's sake, John."

"OK. Sorry. Did you tell her she's fat?"

"No! Of course not. For one thing she isn't." Craig looks exasperated.

"You didn't say that she looked 'well'? Because women think you mean fat if you say that."

"Do they?"

"Always."

"No, I think I said she looked beautiful."

"Did you comment positively on any other woman in the room, including the bride?"

"I said that Jen looked relaxed."

"That's OK. Did you cut across her sentence?"

"No."

"Did you disagree with her? Suggest that women only vote for the vaguely sexy political candidates? Criticize her driving? Talk about *Star Trek*?"

"No, no, no. John, I honestly don't think I said anything to offend her."

438

"Well, someone must have, mate. You need to find out who and what."

"You think I should talk to her."

"It helps, in a relationship, and I should know."

"You don't talk much then."

I grin at my clever friend, "No, mate, not if I can avoid it."

"Should I go round to see her and ask her why she ran away?"

"Yes."

"You think so?"

"Yes."

Craig sits up and punches my arm. "It's good to have you on side, mate. You're a real buddy."

"Can we just watch the rest of *Jackass* now?" I ask and turn the volume back up.

Craig stares at the screen for about four minutes and then he says, "Tom told me that Andrea got in touch to say that she's expecting a baby with her new bloke."

"Did he?"

"How do you feel about that?"

"Pleased for her." I don't take my eyes off the TV.

"Really?"

"Yes."

"Didn't you two ever fancy having kids?"

I press the mute button again. The hilarious antics carry on silently. Without the cries of agony or the screams and crashes the programme loses something. It puts me in mind of an old Charlie Chaplin movie, which I never found that funny.

"I think Andrea thought I was a kid."

"Bit unfair," says Craig loyally. Then more honestly he adds, "But just a bit."

"We did try at one point but timing was all wrong."

"Girl stuff?" he asks, misunderstanding me.

I can't bring myself to explain that I don't mean her lunar-driven cycle and all that, more *our* timing. We only tried for a baby to stick us together but we were already shattered. It was a good thing that the fertility gods weren't paying us much attention.

"Can I ask you something really personal?" Craig has no idea about what level of probing is acceptable conversation between blokes. I consider it a sweet eccentricity and privately, I don't mind indulging him.

"Fire."

"Was Andrea your One?"

"No mate, Cameron Diaz is my One. She just doesn't know it yet."

"Seriously."

He won't be budged. He stares at me earnestly. His face is twitching with concern and a real desire to understand me. It suddenly dawns on me that I might have been duped. Of course Craig knows that he has to go round to see this Rose bird if he wants to make a go of it. He's not an idiot. He probably only asked for my opinion so that he could bring up the subject of women and lure me into exchanging confidences.

I watch the silent screen and tell him, I don't believe in The One. There are loads of people out there who could make me happy.

"Why don't they then?"

"I'm happy."

440

"You didn't seem it at Tom's wedding." It's not a question, so I'm not obliged to comment. Craig works with little kids all the time, so he rephrases. "I hadn't seen you that drunk for a long time, mate, and I wondered why you wanted to get wasted."

"Nervous about giving the speech."

"No. You were excited about giving the speech."

Craig is kind enough not to point out that while I stumbled through the speech it wasn't as good as it perhaps could have been. I still got the laughs but the humour wasn't as fast and sophisticated as I'd planned. I couldn't read my prompt cards and had to ad-lib a fair amount. Still, not to worry, if Craig cracks it with this Rose bird I'll dust off my speech and try again in a few years.

I don't take my eyes off the TV but I know that Craig is still staring at me with the full intensity of a concerned best mate. The heat is making me itch. I give in.

"It does mean something to me that Andrea is up the duff. I'm not jealous," I hasten to add this and turn to him so that he can read my face and know I'm being as honest as I know how to be. "She's a good lass. I'm happy for her. She's clearly moved on and that's good. But it sort of brought home to me that I haven't. I haven't really moved since the divorce."

"You bought your new house in Marlow."

"Yes."

I can't believe that the one time I want Craig to understand that I'm not talking literally, I'm talking figuratively, he's turned all man on me. I mean I haven't moved on emotionally but I'd wax my ass and chest before I say so straight out.

"In some ways I feel that I'm right back where I was ten years ago, except in those days I listened to Oasis and Blur when I was fucking and now it's the Arctic Monkeys and Kaiser Chiefs. I keep running over old scenarios and wondering what I could have done differently to change the outcome."

"With Andrea?"

"Among others. I'm sort of conducting an experiment at the moment."

"An experiment?"

"Yes. Do you remember I once talked to you about that woman whose kid goes to your school?"

"Mrs Baker?"

"Yes, Connie. She meant a lot to me at one point."

"And then nothing at all. You said so."

"I just wonder if I've got that last bit wrong."

"What?" Craig leaps off the sofa and starts to pace the room. He's melodramatically running his hands through his hair. "Are you having an affair with her?"

"No."

"Are you planning on doing so? Are you trying to seduce her?"

I don't answer directly. "She's aged well. She's looking great and she's got this new indefinable aura, a sort of confidence that she didn't have when we were together."

"It's called happiness. She's a happily married woman. She's a mother."

Craig is furious. When he gets really angry a small muscle in his cheek flickers and he looks like a psycho. When we were kids I used to encourage him to use this party trick to freak out the bullies, but he can't do it on demand. I've only seen it appear about a dozen times.

"I really want her."

"No, you don't, John. You don't know what you want and you are going to mess with her head. It's not on."

"She's a big girl, she'll be able to decide for herself if I'm going to mess with her head or not," I point out.

Craig flops back into his chair and looks defeated. I know he wants to grapple together a compelling argument for me to leave Connie alone.

"Why are you suddenly interested in her after all these years?" he asks. His voice is always soft but today I can barely hear him.

"I'm not sure."

"Do you think it might be rebound from the divorce? Or an ego boost? If she used to be mad about you, do you see her as an easy target?"

"Not at all," I say with a wry grin.

"A challenge, then? You like a challenge."

"I don't know." I wish he'd shut up. Why isn't he suggesting she's my One? He's normally so keen on the sentiment. Why is he insistent that any feelings I have for Connie have to be shallow and have a deviant motive?

"Is she interested in you?"

"Of course —" I falter. Craig hears the catch in my voice.

"What if she isn't interested in you?" asks Craig, in his quiet, steady voice.

I'm a bit irritated with him for even suggesting this. Normally, he has one hundred per cent certainty in my pulling power.

"She is or, at least, she will be," I assure him.

"She's married," he repeats.

"I'm aware of that," I say dryly. I don't want to have to tell Craig that Connie was married the first time we met and that proved to be nothing more than an initial stumbling-block. I think the revelation would damage his view of the world.

"And they seem a really happy couple. Quite especially so," he adds. "Has she given you any encouragement?"

"Sort of," I say carefully. In fact our conversations have been littered with polite but consistent rebuffs but still, I'm confident. I'm sure she's just playing with me. "She will see things from my point of view, sooner or later," I assert.

"I just mention it because you're my pal and if she doesn't want you and you're knocked back — well, I just don't want to see you hurt."

I'm shocked. I don't like Craig's insight, or sympathy or warnings. When I think I've heard as much as I can bear from Craig, he adds something yet more traumatizing than his compassion or counsel. "I don't want to see you hurt, *again*."

CHAPTER
FORTY-THREE

Sunday 3 December

Lucy

"Put your finger right there, Auriol." Obediently Auriol pushes her tiny forefinger on to the ribbon and I'm able to tighten the bow around the parcel. I step back and view my work with triumph. "What do you think?"

"They look excellent!" says Auriol brightly as she surveys the two huge boxes wrapped in blue metallic paper, presents for Sebastian and Henry.

Inside one is an Xbox 360 and inside the second there are six games for them to play. I had considered buying them a console each but Peter said that would be too much and that it would be good for the boys to practise sharing. I doubted their ability to do this but understood the principle. In addition I've bought them each a new bike. They have bikes at their mother's but I thought the ones I'd purchased for their birthday (with fifteen gears) could stay at our home for them to use when they are here. Despite mildly chastising me that I was spoiling the boys, I knew Peter was thrilled with my efforts. I hadn't realized that gift-buying for kids is an aphrodisiac. But, at the moment, pretty much everything I do seems to have Peter simmering. I hadn't realized that he thought the Mary Poppins type was so hot. I notice that I am singing under my breath. I stop, stare at Auriol and throw her a return wide smile.

Without any warning the smile Auriol was wearing collapses, her brightness and breeziness vanishes and suddenly she is sobbing.

"I want an Xbox."

I take a deep breath and summon my now oft-drawn-upon supplies of patience. No one ever said this was going to be easy. But no one ever said it would be this hard either. I reach for a tissue and wipe her eyes and nose (it always seems to be in need of a tissue even when she doesn't have a cold — is that something I just have to get used to?).

"But it's not your birthday, sweetie," I say reasonably.

"I want, want, want one," she says as she slams her foot on the kitchen tiles. The vulnerable sobbing has disappeared as quickly as it arrived and in its place a tempest is stirring.

Sometimes, I still find it very hard to like her; loving her is a given but liking is occasionally still a test. Until very recently, whenever Auriol threw a tantrum I employed the policy of giving in to her immediately. Whatever it was she demanded I'd find a way to provide it. It was not because I was besotted and wanted to fulfil her every whim — the truth is, I don't like scenes. If I said yes she could have another ice cream/Barbie doll/TV in her room/friend to play then I avoided a scene. As I averaged seven hours a week contact with her, it didn't really matter to me if she was spoilt to the point of being delinquent. Now, however, I try to get home most nights for bathtime or at least in time to read her a story. I don't go to the gym on Saturdays and I now have my manicure on Sunday morning, when she's at horse riding. Previously I had always timed my beautician appointments to coincide with Auriol being at home. With the increase in contact I realize that I cannot allow her tantrums to continue because I have to live with the consequences. Occasionally, of late, I've discovered that I have to bite the bullet and say no.

"When it's your birthday Mummy and Daddy will buy you whatever you want and wrap it in a big box just like this one," I tell her.

"No!"

For a moment I'm puzzled. "Except with pink paper," I assure her.

"And?"

I try to think. "A purple ribbon?"

"No. No. I want a bigger box." Auriol flounces out of the room and I follow her progress through the house, tracking her by which doors she's banging closed. As she exits dramatically, Peter comes into the kitchen. He is much more serene.

"Hello, darling, what are you up to?"

I stand away from the beautifully wrapped gifts so that Peter can get the full benefit of my efforts with the bows.

"Just finishing wrapping up the boys' gifts," I say with a beam. "Are you going to take them round now?"

"Yes, I thought so. Would you like to come?"

A month ago I could have answered that question in a heartbeat. No, I would not like to visit Rose's home and I do not want to have to endure watching her brats greedily open their gifts. I would have told him that I had no interest in whether they delighted in the presents or hated them, the result was normally the same — the twins would dismiss the gifts in moments and move on to the next parcel. It always sickened me. Besides, not a birthday had gone by without Rose alluding to the fact that she gave birth with nothing more than gas and air and that both the twins weighed over 8lb. I hate the way she tries to collude with Peter and constantly prompts him with "do you remember" stories. However, now, I take a deep breath and I wonder what to say for the best. The best for everyone.

"Would you like me to come?" I ask.

"Yes," says Peter firmly.

My heart sinks. "I think Rose prefers it if I don't," I comment. I'm pretty sure that if I attend the twins' party she'll surmise I'm there just to spite her. She'll end up annoyed, I'll end up frustrated. A lose/lose situation. All my good work of the last few weeks could be blasted apart in one hasty sentence.

"Auriol would love it if we went as a family," says Peter.

It's a low trick. In the past I've followed a strict policy of limiting the time Auriol spends with Rose and the boys. I maintained that the only things Auriol could learn from Rose were pastry-making and cross stitch, not skills I felt Auriol necessarily needed. Once, when

448

Peter was in an especially grumpy mood, he'd pointed out that maybe she'd learn respect and the ability to be pleasant from Rose. The insult was implicit but marked and I was furious. Now, I concede it might not be a bad thing for Rose to have some influence on Auriol. I'd never admit it aloud, but Sebastian and Henry aren't absolute little snots the *entire* time. They can be quite decent company when she's not inciting them to rebel against me.

"OK, I'll come."

Peter looks thrilled. He cups my face in his hands and kisses me. "You really are wonderful."

"I know."

For reasons which are beyond me, it takes us about another forty minutes to get ready to leave the house. I have noticed that it's impossible to go anywhere on the spur of the moment with a child or even to leave one destination smartly in order to arrive at another promptly. I'm slowly accepting this to be a life truism, but I am still uncomfortable with it. Lateness is laziness. While Peter and Auriol run around the house collecting car keys and essential favourite dolls, I utilize the few spare moments by attending to some of the e-mail which is backing up in my inbox. Shortening the hours in my day has led to a backlog of e-mails, so I systematically work through them at home, adding another three or four hours on to my day after Auriol is asleep. On Thursday the unthinkable happened — I couldn't be bothered. I spent the evening shopping online for toys for Auriol instead and then on Friday Peter and I went to Nobu. It was an overdue trip. I am aware that I probably have over two hundred e-mails waiting for my attention and I can't put off attending to them beyond this weekend.

I see his notes immediately. His name jumps out like a vivid scab. **Joe Whitehead.** I'm tempted to press delete without even reading them, but there is always the slim chance that he's contacting me about a work issue. I'm being disparaged and overlooked at work enough at the moment as it is, so it would be professional suicide to ignore e-mails.

The first one is a round robin to the entire floor. It's a grumble that people congregating at the water-cooler chat too loudly and apparently he finds this distracting. Moron. I never go near the water-cooler as it is right next to his desk. I press delete, with a sense of relief.

The second note is one of those ridiculous chain letters. This one is about confidence and individuality. The instruction at the end of the note is to pass it on to ten people you admire for having those two qualities. I see from the address list that Joe has only sent the note to six people, two of whom must be relatives as they share his surname. He doesn't have ten friends, let alone ten confident and individual friends. I'm so not surprised. Maybe a nicer person would pity him. I'm just ashamed that my name has found its way into his e-mail address book. I press delete.

The third note is more worrying. I'm the only addressee.

Beautiful Lucy, you look hot in your blue suit. Is it new? Are you trying to impress me?

Yours, duly impressed, Joe
xxx

I press delete.
The fourth note is similar.

Hey Stunner, have you been working out? Your legs are looking fab. I'd like to get hot and sweaty with you again some time soon.
Yours, panting, Joe
xxx

I press delete. Notes five and six are on a similar line. The subject matter being my hair and my mouth. We have firewalls at GWH, so Joe cannot use any expletives, but the notes feel dangerous and threatening. The volume screams desperation. The fact that he has sent me so many e-mails without receiving any encouragement through a reply makes me as fearful as if the man had laid a shotgun on my desk. I delete six more notes without reading them. I doubt they are work related. As I press refresh, two more notes come into my inbox and then messenger pings on to my screen.

Hey, Sweetheart, you are online, me too, want to chat or more?!
xxxx

I slam down the screen of my laptop. For Joe to have a messenger link he must have tampered with my computer. The thought is horrifying. I look around, as I half expect him to be standing in the kitchen with me. I've noticed that he's always encroaching on my space at work. I'm reluctant to call him a stalker because I want to believe he is too ridiculous to warrant such a threatening label. But the fact is if I venture to the bathroom or the photocopier he always seems to pop up from nowhere, right by my side. More than once I've spotted him in the queue at the deli when I've been buying my sandwiches. He seems to be in an increasing number of the same think-tank groups as I am. I try to tell myself it is just coincidence and I find ways to avoid him — I hold my pee and send Julia out to buy my lunch. After receiving an insufferable number of text messages and phone calls, I reported my mobile lost and changed my telephone number. This has been hugely inconvenient but has meant that Joe can't call me. I've avoided his gaze, I've rebuffed his conversation and I've never found his jokes funny so it's been easy to refuse to laugh at his gags. I thought he'd get the message. He's had his moment. There is not going to be a repeat performance.

Why doesn't he go away?

"Everything all right, darling?"

I look up and Peter and Auriol are standing in the doorway. They have their coats on and look ready to leave. They both look beautiful and the kitchen appears to glimmer in their presence. Joe's messages seem so dark by contrast. Shame scratches at my throat.

"Yes, fine," I say hastily. And I force a smile.

"Problem at work?"

"No. Why would you think that?"

"Because you look worried."

I kiss Peter and hurry them both out of the door. "Nothing I can't handle," I assure him.

CHAPTER
FORTY-FOUR

Sunday 3 December

Rose

I have no idea why Peter insists on torturing me on an ongoing basis. I wonder at the depth of his cruelty when I open the door and see that he has brought Lucy to the twins' birthday party. I accept that Auriol must be a guest but why is he so insistent on ruining everything?

Of course Lucy looks absolutely wonderful. She is wearing white trousers and a white shirt, for a children's party! It's madness. Or at least it would be for mere mortals; she'll probably leave the party looking immaculate. I am wearing my cerise cardigan from Monsoon and had been rather pleased with the effect until I opened the door and was faced with the combined effects of years and years of self-absorption, iron willpower (when it comes to carbs or saturated-fat intake), a platinum American Express and several hours' grooming in front of a mirror. I study Lucy very closely and note that she's wearing her latest adultery rather well. But then, it always was a look that suited her. She looks unchanged from last time I saw her and yet *my* whole world has altered.

454

Lucy presents the boys with two enormous boxes. She tells them that these presents are just the little gifts and that their real presents are waiting for them at home and they can open them next time they visit. I balk at her use of the word "home" but as the boys' real home is full of their guests I resist pulling her up.

The boys tear off the wrapping paper while we are standing in the hall. I'm irrationally irritated by their obvious excitement. I remind myself they are just kids, they know their dad's pockets are deep and are anticipating something especially "cool"; it's not disloyal for them to be so clearly keyed up by Peter and Lucy's gifts. I try not to mind that my more modest, but very thoughtful presents did not attract such a frenzy of attention. I'm grateful that their desire to open the gifts as quickly as possible at least means that they are opened in the hall and Lucy is denied the theatre of all our guests looking on and appreciating her generosity.

"Wicked, a 360!" yells Sebastian.

"Look at all these games!" cries Henry. Both boys bounce up and down and, unprompted, they lavish a number of "thank-yous" and "just what I wanteds" on the smug and self-satisfied-looking Peter and Lucy.

The boys pick up their spoils and run through to the sitting room so that they can show off to their friends. All thoughts of the zoologist I've hired are forgotten. The boys came across Mr Mammals and his collection of exotic pets (ranging from tarantulas to pythons) at someone else's party months ago. Since then, they have repeatedly asked if he could come and

455

entertain at their party. They've talked of nothing else all day and we've been waiting for their father to arrive, to let the show begin. Now the lizards and geckos are forgotten. I snatch the Xbox away from the boys, muttering that we can look at it later, after the party is over. I'm pretty certain that Henry and Sebastian are now desperate for the party (which we've planned with minute detail and for several months) to zoom by.

As I pass Peter I mutter, "I battle every day to limit the time they waste on their Game Boys and watching TV. This isn't going to help matters."

"They are kids, Rose. This is the stuff kids like."

As opposed to autumnal displays on the table in the lean-to, I suppose. I wonder if the boys have told him about the conkers. I take a deep breath and consider whether this would be a good moment to blow that haughty, superior look off his face? Would it be fun to see Lucy shrivel with ignominy as I announce the fact that she has a new lover and my husband, ex-husband, is yesterday's story. I bite my tongue. Between them they have ruined enough "special occasions" for the boys and me. They are not having this one.

I remember that the twins' third birthday was the day Peter chose to tell me he and Lucy were expecting a baby. Auriol was a honeymoon baby. Or at least that was the official line. By my calculations she was conceived a few weeks before the vows, not that that sort of thing matters a jot to anyone any more, even me. That's why I think it's pathetic they'd lie about it. It sometimes seems to me that lying is Peter and

Lucy's natural state and they are actually incapable of being straightforward. Lots of women who have secret fears about whether they can or can't get pregnant throw away the pills as soon as. No shame there. The interesting thing is, of course, Lucy would never admit that she had secret fears about anything, but she must have. Despite all the evidence, she's only human.

My take on it is that she was desperate to have a baby, motivation questionable. Probably just to show me that anything I had with Peter she could have too. She no doubt assumed that fifteen years of aggressive dieting, high-stress living, moderate to high alcohol intake and low use of recreational drugs might well hamper her attempts, and therefore she stopped using contraception as soon as Peter moved his shoes out from my understairs cupboard and into hers.

When Peter called to tell me his good news, Lucy was sixteen weeks pregnant, although not showing, naturally. He had known about the upcoming addition to his family for eleven and a half weeks, yet he decided that the twins' birthday was the optimum time to tell me. Sod him.

Obviously, I congratulated him. A baby is something I get excited about, whatever the circumstances — it's a new life. But I was vexed to the extreme when he commented that we'd all need to sit down and discuss the best way to introduce the twins to the subject of a new brother or sister.

"Half brother or sister," I corrected.

"That seems unnecessarily pedantic," he'd replied.

457

He'd never been one for details. Who he slept with while he was married to me was nothing but a detail, apparently. I wanted to point out that Peter had not thought to sit down with either the boys or me to discuss the initial move out of our family home. The destruction of their family life was executed with Ninja silence. Why the sudden keenness for chat? Instead, I sighed, said I'd give it some thought and that I'd come up with an idea on how best to approach the matter — after all, my concern was to save the boys' feelings. I didn't want them to feel rejected or pushed out as Peter started afresh.

Feeling rejected and pushed out must be, exclusively, my territory.

When I first told people about Peter's happy news they were sympathetic but sensibly pointed out that I must have always known it was going to happen. True. I also know that one day I am going to die but I don't like to dwell on that fact either.

It's simply another biological fact in favour of chaps, isn't it? They get to pick themselves up, dust themselves down and start all over again with incredible — in fact indecent — ease. I'm of course delighted that the boys live with me and are my responsibility. I would die rather than have it any other way. But occasionally it crosses my mind that Peter ought to have had a single restless night because Henry hasn't quite got the hang of long division (will he ever get to university?) or a sleepless night because Sebastian is in trouble for being too rough on the rugby pitch (do I have a thug in the making?). It seems unfair that the only necessary qualification for starting up a second family is destroying the first one.

Following the ill-timed announcement of the pregnancy, Peter chose Christmas day to text me with the news that the baby Lucy was carrying was a "healthy baby girl", although I can't believe they got their scan results on that particular day. In the text he also asked if I would "hug the boys for him". While texting these good tidings and good wishes it appears that he didn't think to use the phone to actually speak to his sons. He's not what I would describe as a traditionalist. He asked me to sign divorce papers on Mothers' day and every Easter I fight to keep the children at home with me. Whether his actions are malicious or thoughtless I am unsure. It hardly matters. In addition, birthdays, anniversaries and holidays are spoilt because like an amputee I ache in the place where my limb once was.

All the children are now agog watching spiders scuttle and frogs leap so I leave the room, partly because I have to take the clingfilm off the sandwiches and partly because since Joe Whatshisface's revelation I am continually angry and irrational, which is not a great mindset at a kids' birthday party.

Connie follows me through to the dining room.

"Do you think there's enough food?" I ask her. She gazes at the table.

"Yes, even if you open your doors and call in the homeless of London. Please tell me this stuff is shop-bought."

"Certainly not. All home-baked."

She groans dramatically. "Can I do anything to help?"

"You can make some juice. I have cordial in the top left-hand cupboard, it's —"

"Organic?" she interrupts with a grin.

"Am I very predictable?" I ask.

"No, actually, Rose, you are not." Her tone is suddenly serious and I get the sense that Connie followed me out of the sitting room with a mission. "I'm quite relieved that you've put on such an elaborate home-baked, organic, tooth-kind spread, in fact."

"Are you?"

Normally she gently teases me about my party spreads. Her style is to stuff as many E-numbers down a child as possible and hope they don't throw before they get home. In fairness her attitude to adult entertainment is similar, except she's more likely to ply her adult guests with champagne than Jelly-tots.

"Recently, you haven't been yourself at all, Rose. I've been worried about you."

"Don't worry about me. I'll be fine," I say.

I count the paper plates, we're one short. I bustle through to the kitchen to unearth the wayward plate; I know I bought enough. Connie trails behind me.

"You *will be* fine. So, you are saying that there is something wrong."

"Bit out of sorts," I admit.

"Have you seen a doctor?"

"It's not physical." I bend down and bury my head by rummaging in a cupboard; this way I can avoid meeting her eye.

460

"Is it something to do with Mr Walker? I mean Craig. Did something happen when you went to that wedding with him?"

I consider the question and decide to start with the easy bit. I keep my head in the cupboard and mumble. "The wedding was wonderful. Craig and I were getting on beautifully but —"

"Can I do anything to help?" Lucy's imperious tones are instantly recognizable. Hastily I pull my head out of the cupboard and, naturally, I bang it while doing so. I yelp but try to hide my discomfort. Why is it that I am always clumsier, uglier and sillier in her company?

"Everything is under control," I inform her. "You can go and watch the entertainer if you want to." Or go to hell, I don't mind.

"Creepy crawlies are not my thing," she says.

That's not what I hear.

I have found the missing plate, so I push past her and go back into the dining room to set it down. They both follow me. My house isn't large at the best of times. I'm beginning to feel awfully claustrophobic.

I watch Lucy cast a disparaging eye over the table. The food had appeared wholesome and appetizing only a moment ago, but under her gaze my offerings look dull and basic. Lucy always hires outside professionals to cater for Auriol's parties. They are triumphant social events.

"Eight years old. I can hardly believe it. They grow up so quickly. It seems only minutes ago they were in nappies. Thank God that's all over, hey?" she says.

I would consider this comment innocuous if it had been issued from anyone else and as such would not have caused me much discomfort, but, like all of Lucy's trite conversational fillers, I find it insulting and dishonest.

"Frankly, I wish Peter had left me with more children. People say how do you manage with twins? I can't explain that I wanted four."

Lucy and Connie stare at me in astonishment. I've never uttered this thought before. How would Daisy respond? My two to her none, how could I be so selfish? But the truth is I feel incomplete and I would love to still be changing nappies. When Peter first left I had fantasies about having more children with him. Not through sex of course. I could never knowingly have sex with the man after he'd enjoyed Lucy's body but I did consider approaching him for a sperm donation. Madness, I realize. But at the time it seemed quite sane to me — grief confuses everything. Neither Lucy nor Connie know how to follow my confession, so I take up the responsibility of conversation.

"But you are right, Lucy, it's all over for me now, isn't it? That part of my life. It will surprise you to know that it was only last week that I finally sorted through the boys' clothes and at last parted with sacks full of baby garments. Ultimately, I had to ask myself, why do I hoard this junk?"

"You might meet someone new and have more children," says Connie, weakly. She's mortified and sad for me. I can see it in her eyes.

462

I stare her down. "No I won't. Not now. I worry that I hurried the boys through their babyhood. It's certainly flown by. I look at baby socks and can't imagine, let alone remember, them fitting into such dinky delights. The portions of food they eat now are the same size as mine. I threw out eight ice cube trays because the days of my mashing food and freezing it are well behind me."

"For which you should be grateful. I am," says Lucy.

"But we're not alike, are we, Lucy? I think that much, at least, is established."

Daisy wanders through to the dining room. The increase in volume from the lounge indicates that the show is over and the kids are ready for their tea. Daisy has probably come to announce as much. Seeing the three of us gathered around the party food stops her in her tracks.

"How cosy. Just like old times," she snipes as she glares at Lucy.

Daisy has never forgiven her friend for stealing my husband. She says she respects my tolerance towards Lucy and can understand that I have to be civil to the woman because of the boys, but she maintains that such a courtesy is not required from her. I envy her open hostility.

At that moment the children start to file, noisily, into the dining room. With sixteen guests it's an extremely tight squeeze, so Lucy and Connie sensibly opt to leave the serving to Daisy and me. Peter is nowhere to be seen — situation normal. I imagine he's watching a football match on the portable and doubt that he'll

463

emerge until the cake has to be cut. He rarely misses a photo opportunity.

The party is a great success. The children happily munch through my healthy goodies and defy the cynicism of our time by being entirely charmed with games of pass-the-parcel and pin-the-tail-on-the-donkey. However, managing a party that is devoid of incident (such as a broken limb or all-out fisticuffs) demands great energy and by the time I hand out the final party bag to the last remaining small guest, I am fit to drop.

Connie, Luke and the girls leave promptly because Fran hasn't practised her reading. It's typical of Connie's planning, or rather lack of it, that the homework has been left until Sunday night. I can't imagine much is going to be achieved after a party. Daisy and Simon make a swift exit too. Daisy cannot bear to be in the same room as Lucy and Peter longer than absolutely necessary, and as Peter and the boys are in the middle of one of the new Xbox 360 games it's clear they are not going to go any time soon.

"I'll stay if you need me to," says Daisy. I note that the offer is made while she pushes her hands into her gloves.

"I'm fine," I tell her as I kiss her goodbye.

I hear her mutter to Simon, "The cheek of Lucy and Peter, they —" I close the door. There's nothing she can tell me that I don't already know.

I'm very conscientious about recycling so I spend a moment or two wondering if the waxy cardboard party plates can be recycled or if they will contaminate a whole container of painstakingly gathered paper.

Lucy interrupts my thoughts.

"Do you need a hand with clearing up?"

The novelty of this question stuns me. Why is she trying to be helpful? It's not her style.

"No thank you. You and Auriol can go home if you want. I'm sure Peter will be finished playing soon and then he'll follow you."

I realize I'm as good as evicting her and this comment is borderline rude. So shoot me.

"Oh, it's OK. I don't mind hanging around. Auriol is playing with the Xbox too. She loves being here with the boys."

I stare at Lucy suspiciously. What *is* her game?

She takes me at my word when I say that I don't need her help and she flops on to a stool at the breakfast bar. She is about to light up but I inform her that we have a no smoking policy in our house, a fact that she must be aware of — I can only surmise that my rules mean nothing to her. I dance around her, scooping up discarded cake and used napkins, I mop up previously undetected spillages and fold away the deckchairs that I dragged out of the shed earlier today. There are some women who clean up and others that make mess. It's just a fact.

"The boys seemed to enjoy the party. You're very good at all of this, Rose. You are marvellous at keeping children focused. You get their interest but maintain discipline. You have such a knack. I do wonder how you do it."

I think this is the first time Lucy has bestowed a compliment on me, ever, although I'm often complimentary about something Lucy is wearing, or her hair colour. I even found it in me to be nice about her exquisite engagement ring. I stare at her and she meets my gaze, uncompromisingly. I'm not sure whether she means I am good at mopping up after young boys, or throwing parties or being a mother, and anyway I'm unsure whether she meant it as a genuine accolade. The way she waved her hand around my kitchen as she spoke was characteristically elegant, almost majestic and therefore seemed dismissive. I can't deduce if she's being facetious. Possibly. Probably. Since when has she had any interest in stimulating and managing children?

"Discipline isn't a knack." I manage to inject the word with the original derision that she had mustered. "It's a skill and it's hard work."

"Have you ever had days when it just goes wrong, however hard you try?"

Oh yes. There have been times, when the boys were younger, when all efforts of persuasion, bribe or threat proved useless. When the children hit one another once too often, broke things through deliberate malice and relentlessly spat their food on to the table then, once or twice, I found myself losing all sense of perspective and dignity.

There were moments when I wondered whether I was any good at being a mother and whether, if Peter was still around, the boys would continue to behave so dreadfully. With him, maybe I'd have had the strength

466

to battle, or at the very least I'd have had someone to curl up on the settee with, at the end of the day; someone who would congratulate me for getting through the day.

I'd rather eat ground glass than confess as much to Lucy.

"Mostly I try to reason with them, although twin boys aren't always especially reasonable beings. I had no choice: by the time the twins were four years old they were physically unmanageable, they weighed over three stone apiece, and I found that the only way to get them to do anything or go anywhere was to solicit their cooperation. I don't slap and I find that I spend rather more time on the time-out step than either of the boys but at least it's peaceful there. Yelling has never worked with the twins. They are too confident in my love to take my anger for anything more than an elaborate pantomime. If I ranted they would laugh, which was often the defuse we needed."

Other times they would simply ignore me, driving my fury up a notch. I'm not generous enough to share this bit with Lucy.

When I pause I fully expect her to launch into her own monologue. Lucy has advice on everything. I'm surprised when she remains mute. I can't believe that *Lucy* is so thoroughly rapt by something *I* have to say. I can only deduce that Auriol is being a monster at home and Lucy has finally understood that she can't simply address the problem by hiring nanny after nanny after nanny. Funny, because I've always found Auriol to be rather biddable — certainly by comparison to my boys.

"Sometimes I try everything and nothing seems to work. I run out of ideas and don't know where to find the answers," says Lucy.

I stare at Lucy and see something that in any other woman I would identify as desperation or vulnerability. I must be mistaken. I look closer and try to see frustration or a lack of patience, things I can more comfortably attribute to Lucy.

I continue, "Motherhood is enormous. It's an endless outpouring of love. Children want, demand and need every single ounce of your energy, enthusiasm, imagination and patience. Then, when you are completely and utterly wrung dry and out of resource, they want some more. The miracle is ninety-nine times out of a hundred we find more to give."

Lucy's face sinks. I fight the urge to mop it up with the other party spillages. She looks devastated. No doubt she realizes that whatever I say next, whatever secret I'm about to share on good discipline methods for children, she lacks the raw materials.

"Do you want a glass of wine?" I offer. She nods.

I pour us one each. I've been totally miserable since the wedding reception. I've felt unfairly burdened by yet another of Lucy's mess-ups. Seeing her spirits dampened as she sits at my breakfast bar has perked me up. Suddenly, I feel quite cheerful.

"You think there's a secret, don't you, Lucy? Something that you haven't been clued into just yet? But you assume that once you are clued in the whole mother-thing will be a piece of cake. That's why you are bothering to talk to me." Lucy doesn't deny it. She's too brazen. "Well, you're right," I add.

Lucy leans closer to me. She looks excited. She's desperate for a solution. No doubt she thinks I'm about to tell her that you can buy discipline in a pot, just as she buys her expensive face cream that wards off old age.

"The secret is that most of the time, most of us like being needed in that all-consuming way. Most of the time, most of us wouldn't change a thing. I often hear people say that kids can be cruel or hideous, which is true. But usually given the correct circumstances kids are loving, funny, honest and kind. And they have soft skin, which feels indescribably delicious when they wrap you in a careless hug. On balance motherhood works for me."

Lucy looks as though she is swallowing something very distasteful; cold sprouts and mouldy bread come to mind.

"But there are bad days, Lucy. There are times when it seems that motherhood is just another name for failure. I remember when they were about four, old enough to know better, and they didn't want to walk home from the library. I had no stroller by then and no car with me. There was an unexpected downpour and suddenly we were surrounded by inches-deep puddles, but there was no sign of a cab. The boys lay, like dead weights, in the wet high street and no amount of reasonable discussion, or coercion or sweeteners, could move them. Just that once I resorted to pretty much dragging them along the street. Both of them wailing and kicking. Henry biting me, Sebastian punching me. All of us screaming, insanely. The boys forgot the incident once we were home and they were furnished with milk and biscuits. I cried all night."

"You allow things to affect you too deeply, Rose," says the Ice Queen.

I shoot her a look which I hope communicates that I don't want her opinion. I continue.

"I cried because I hated you and I hated Peter but most of all I hated myself. I've never hated the boys. I still loved them. I pitied them their inability to express themselves reasonably. I pitied their tired bodies. Do you understand what I'm saying, Lucy? It's not easy. Motherhood is not easy. You have to accept that. That's the secret. That's what makes it worthwhile."

We sit in silence listening to the kitchen clock ticking and the sound effects from the boys' Xbox game drifting through from the sitting room. I stare at my glass of wine and wonder if it was my licence to tell her I sometimes hated her. I sometimes hate her. The strangest thing is I hardly care. Eventually, it is Lucy who breaks the quiet.

"You think I'm a terrible mother, don't you, Rose?"

"Since when have you cared what I think?"

"Some of the things you've just said make sense. I've been coming to the same conclusions myself lately."

She sounds self-righteous and conceited. I can't stand it a moment longer.

"Is that while you are smoking a post-coital cigarette with Joe?"

470

Lucy doesn't get the chance to reply because at that moment Peter walks into the kitchen. He and Auriol already have their coats on. He's holding Lucy's open so she can slip into it.

"Sorry to break up the chat, ladies, but I think it's time we ought to be getting Auriol home to bed. Thanks for the party. I think everybody has had a great time."

I wouldn't say that, exactly.

CHAPTER
FORTY-FIVE

Tuesday 5 December

John

Bless Craig. He's the most trusting man on the planet. When I offered to come into school with him, to help to make scenery for the school nativity play, he almost kissed my feet and didn't suspect, for an instant, that I might have an ulterior motive.

"Are you sure, John?"

"Well, you said that you're short of volunteers and time. My project at the Beeb is almost wrapped up — I can get to the school by about three-thirty, if it helps." I shrugged, to give the impression that I didn't mind either way.

"Normally the parents are very forthcoming with their time," he assured me. "It's just that December is a busy time and although we've got a number of volunteers to sew costumes and paint scenery, no one with any experience with a saw has come forward."

The fathers are clearly lazy bastards. I don't blame them. I wouldn't normally give up an evening in the pub to make the backdrop for a nativity scene, but I've seen the list of volunteers, neatly pinned to

472

Craig's office noticeboard. I figure it will be worth my while.

I know Connie is the photographer and all, but God, do I wish I'd had a camera to snap her face when she first clapped eyes on me in the school hall.

I couldn't have planned the moment better. She arrived at about four, so it was already dark outside but the streetlight was streaming in through the large glass windows. It's a wet night but I don't feel the cold so I've stripped down to my T-shirt (which shows off my muscles). I'm standing in the centre of a light shaft, holding a toolbox (which looks pretty manly) and I'm surrounded by about four mums. All of whom have previously shunned the idea of picking up anything heavier than a cotton reel but are now vying to become budding carpenters.

Connie spots me and is aghast.

I realize that I have a bit of ground to make up, since I never made it to Café Rouge. But I'm not unduly worried. As I've mentioned, Connie responds well to a bit of messing around. My standing her up might be the thing that convinces her she wants to be back in my bed.

"Ah, Mrs Baker," I yell, cutting across the gaggle of would-be assistants. "I understand you are pretty good with a saw and hammer. I wonder if you'd mind giving me a hand."

Connie scowls, carefully unwraps her scarf from around her neck and then says, "I wouldn't say I was any sort of expert. I'd rather paint scenery."

"Only possible after it's made, I'm afraid," interjects one of the other mums. "It would be extremely useful if you could help Mr Harding."

This woman is oblivious to Connie's pleading stares, which is peculiar because I can see them as clearly as a nun in a brothel.

Connie can't make a fuss, so she follows me as I lead her to the far end of the hall where I've previously laid out the wood and tools. I've strategically chosen to set up camp as far away as possible from the other helpers. As soon as we are out of earshot Connie demands, "Are you trying to embarrass me?"

"No, I'm helping out," I answer plainly.

"Since when have you been the milk of human kindness?"

"Connie, that's not fair. You know I always help out a mate if I can."

Connie looks mildly chastised but then seems to remember something.

"Well, you clearly don't count me in with your friends or else you'd have turned up at Café Rouge."

"Oh, I'm sorry about that. Something came up."

Connie glares at me and then seems to lose interest in arguing. All at once her body relaxes. I watch as she appears to melt. In the old days she was often rigid with tension, now she seems fluid.

"Not to worry. I was only half expecting you to show. It didn't matter. I still had a drink with my friend who manages the place. He thought it was funny that I'd been stood up."

474

I'm stunned. I don't know how to take this. She's told a friend of hers about me and they joked about her being stood up. Clearly Connie did not see our agreement to meet as anything like a date. If she had believed that we were on a date and I'd stood her up, wild horses wouldn't have dragged that confession from her. She turns to look at the wood at our feet.

"I really am hopeless with any kind of woodwork. I only volunteer for these things so that the staff think highly of me. I wouldn't have had you down as a handy man either."

"I'm not especially, but Craig was desperate," I confess. Connie smiles. She seems genuinely friendly. I had been expecting anger, tension and accusations. I don't know how to behave in light of her reasonableness. She is being so level-headed that it's possible to mistake her attitude for indifference. The thought chills me.

"Well, let's just get on with this then. We should be as professional as possible. Don't be overly friendly, OK?" she adds.

"OK."

Connie lowers her voice, "If I went home now people might think I was acting peculiarly."

"They might."

"And as you already have a reputation at the school gate, I don't want to fuel any gossip about us. Although, in retrospect, that thing you did with Diane, since it's not going anywhere, it's been quite a master stroke. At least it's not my name that they are linking with yours."

"Would you have minded if I wanted it to go somewhere with Diane?"

"Only in so much as I didn't want to be a casualty of your pillow talk."

She shoots me a cagey look and then picks up a large piece of wood. She waves it around elaborately, as though studying it, and then lays it on the floor and walks around it a couple of times. I realize this is for the benefit of the other mum-helpers, who may be watching. When she's satisfied that they aren't interested anyway, she sits down again and says, "I really appreciate you opening up to me on the phone the other night. Telling me that stuff about your marriage helped me understand things a little more."

"What things?"

"You. Why you are bothering with me again. It's been confusing. You turning up at the school gate all the time and then firework night, it forced me to think about things that I hadn't thought about for a long while. But now I get it."

"Do you?" I'm not sure I do. I have no idea where she's going with this and I don't like the feeling that I'm at sea.

"I'm a grasp at the past, aren't I? This isn't really about me at all. You don't feel anything for *me*. You just want to be reminded of a time before your heart was broken."

"What?" I must yell this. Because Connie shoots a fretful look at the other mums and urges me to keep my voice down. I stare at her, amazed that she could

476

have got it so wrong. Because she is wrong. Isn't she?

"It's OK," she whispers. "It's nothing to be ashamed of. You've been through a divorce, of course you're not thinking clearly. I'd have preferred it if I hadn't been the woman you alighted on to try to recapture something so elusive. You have no idea how difficult this has been for me, but in a way I accept that it had to be me and I'm sorry that I can't help you in any other way than by proving that what's gone is gone."

Connie holds my gaze. She's searching my face for an acknowledgement and appreciation of her understanding, I'm searching hers for signs that she's been brainwashed. Is she saying that she thinks I'm on the rebound? Has she been talking to Craig? Impossible, but they said the same thing. Connie thinks I'm struggling to deal with Andrea and my divorce and all that and that's why I'm paying her attention. Connie doesn't think this is about her? That's a first.

"This *is* about you Connie. About us."

"No, it's not," she grins. "Answer me this, John: before bumping into me at the school gate, when did you last think of me?"

I don't answer. She nods and looks self-satisfied; my silence has proven her point.

"Plus, over the last few months I've been begging you to sit down and talk to me but you won't. If you were really interested in *me* you'd have the good grace to do that. What you are doing is avoiding a chat because you don't want to stumble around your subconscious. Don't worry, I get it. I get you."

"You're just saying this because you're peeved that I didn't show up the other night. This is an honourable exit for you."

She solemnly shakes her head.

"In that case you are just scared shitless about how you feel about me. You want me but you haven't got the nerve any more. You're trying to talk your way out of this."

Connie looks sad. For me. Her pity is nauseating.

"You think I lack the nerve to shag you again, John?" she whispers. "Well, you're wrong. I dare do it. I dare do it now as I did then." She pauses to great effect. "I dare shag you, but I won't because I don't want to. I'm absolutely certain. I don't want to. I don't want to betray Luke and I don't want to risk hurting my family, not for a nanosecond, but most of all, I. Don't. Want. You. Have I said anything other? Even once, since we met up?"

For a moment I am too stunned to move. She sounds serious and convincing. But I don't believe her. I don't want to believe her.

"Well, why did you agree to meet up with me the other night?"

"I've been wondering if you've ever told Mr Walker about us."

"He knows we had a thing."

She gasps and snaps her neck around to stare at Craig, who is standing only a few metres away.

"How could you? He's my daughter's headmaster. You stupid —"

478

Craig saves my skin because at that moment he butts in. He introduces us to Mrs Someone-or-Other who is director of the nativity and we all discuss the scenic needs. Connie says very little. She stares at the floor and refuses to meet anyone's eye. Even so, she's so scarlet she's giving off a light that could safely draw a ship into harbour. Matters are settled relatively quickly and Mrs Something-or-Other and Craig leave us to get on.

"You have let me down so often, John. Time, after time, after time. In fact, thinking about it, that's all you've ever done from the first moment I met you."

Although Connie is clearly vexed, her calm has not vanished. I'm used to Connie the tempest, and I don't know this Connie. She's not wild, passionate or furious in the way that she used to be just before she agreed to brutish or fanatical sex. She's frustrated, exasperated and maybe even disappointed. Her tone reminds me of my old schoolteachers.

"Don't you get it? This school isn't just a building with lots of Lego and sticky-back plastic. It's my daughter's life. And my daughter's life cannot be part of your game. Plus, I wanted to ask you, how long are you planning on hanging around for? Because, if it's much longer, I'm going to have to talk to Luke. I really didn't want to bring up your name to him, it's going to be difficult and painful, but if you are settling here then I don't think I have a choice. I'm so ashamed that my actions keep hurting him."

This last sentence was said more to herself than to me, but it was the one I heard loud and clear.

I'm stunned. There is something about Connie's calm that is far more final than her rants or threats of yesteryear. She's ashamed. She's really sorry that she might hurt Luke again by just mentioning my name.

I consider the possibility that truly she didn't agree to meet me the other night because she wanted to rake over old coals and perhaps start up a new fire, as I'd imagined. I get it. Honestly, I get it. She really has changed. It's not just an act. It's not a complicated game of hard-to-get.

I run through all our conversations since September and consider that she really never had any intention of resuming her affair with me. Maybe I've heard what I wanted to hear. What I needed to hear. It is possible that all she wanted was reassurances about protecting her family and her future.

I stare out of the hall window. It's still raining and the droplets of water that are clinging to the pane are illuminated by the street lamps. The thousands of tiny particles make up a picture that reminds me of once when I was at a meeting in the Chrysler Building, New York. The meeting was going badly. We couldn't solve the clients' issues and several of us had snarled at one another around a meeting table for hours on end. It was a cold wet February day, and as time got on it drew dark outside. The client had just asked me a difficult question. To buy time I'd stood up and walked around the meeting table and then paused to look out of the window. It was a technique I was taught on some management training programme. The idea is you don't say the first thing that comes into your head.

I remember noting the view for the first time, although surely I'd glanced out of the window hundreds of times just that afternoon, let alone on previous visits. I didn't answer the client's question (because I couldn't) but said something like, "Whenever I'm faced with views of cities I am stunned by a sense of opportunity. So many lives. So much possibility." My comment resonated because of its incongruous nature and maybe because of its truth and simplicity. The client thought I'd said something profound about his business choices and he was delighted.

Afterwards my buddies and my boss congratulated me on my genius bullshitting but I hadn't been bullshitting. I *had* been struck by a sense of possibility as I looked out of that window, and if that happened to be what the client wanted to hear, then all well and good, but in fact what was important to me was that I'd said what I wanted to say. It was my truth of the moment.

The December raindrops on the school window glisten, putting me in mind of hosts of lit windows in skyscrapers. I am overcome with a sense of possibility once again.

Suddenly it's clear to me that Connie does know me well. She does have insight into my mind and we do have a brief section of time that is common to us and us alone. But that's all we have. Connie is slamming shut a door but it's a door in the past and, by doing so, she's unlocked all the portals to my future. I'm suddenly grateful.

"Craig knows that we were once an item but he thinks it was before you married. He likes you and your family a lot, by the way. You are making a good impression. I know that's important to you. And as it happens I'm pretty much finished up with my project here and I found out today that I'm about to be posted elsewhere. Perhaps Manchester."

"Oh," says Connie. What else is there to say?

As relief floods her face I am once again struck by her beauty. Connie is yummy. That's one thing I haven't been deceiving myself about. She is slim, with high enough tits and ass; kid-bearing hasn't plundered her body as it does so many. Her eyes are clearer than I remembered — less anguished. Her skin is, what's that word they use? It's an old-fashioned word. I know, radiant. That's it. She's luminous. Because she's happy.

I look at her and see possibility. But she's not my possibility. And Andrea is not my possibility. Not any more. But I know it's out there. Somewhere.

"I can manage this on my own if you want to take off," I offer. There really is no point in her staying with me. "The damage you might cause with the saw will only serve to ruin all the good work you've done with Craig, thus far," I joke.

Connie understands, "Oh, OK. If you think you can cope. Maybe I'll go and see how the others are getting on with making the crowns. Even I can glue glitter on to cardboard."

I nod.

Connie walks away. She wanders back to the gaggle of mums at the far end of the hall. They are crouching

482

around a roll of gold material and debating how best to get three wise men costumes out of the modest piece of cloth. Connie can't resist, she peeks over her shoulder to check if I'm watching her. I am. We catch one another's gaze and I smile. She beams at me. And I almost love her.

CHAPTER
FORTY-SIX

Wednesday 6 December

Lucy

I am at my desk by 7.45 a.m. I check the Dow, the FTSE and the Nikkei. I linger on the Bloomberg site to get a measure of what the markets have been doing overnight. I keep wondering if I heard her correctly. She did say Joe, didn't she? A post-coital cigarette with Joe . . . *Spurred traders to scale back bets on how far the Federal Reserve will raise interest rates this year . . .* But how could she know? What possible connection could Joe and Rose have? I take a gulp of coffee. *The advance sent the yield on the 10-year note down to its lowest this month. Speculation mounted in the US . . .* Bloody London, everyone knows everyone. It's a lousy village . . . *central bank will not lift borrowing costs as far as . . .* he has a mouth the size of Bush's arms programme . . .

"Lucy, Lucy, are you OK?"

I look up and realize that Mick is leaning over my desk and is talking to me.

"Sorry, I was just reading about the markets."

"You seemed miles away."

"It's fascinating stuff."

"Why, what's happened?" Mick, ever the professional, assumes something major has happened in the markets. Not unreasonably he thinks that would be the only thing to work me up into such a state.

"Nothing much, actually," I sigh.

Mick looks confused. A crease appears above his nose.

"Are you OK, Lucy?"

"I'm —" I'm about to say I'm fine. I'm about to issue the statement of contentment that I use to ward off all personal questions and that I have used repeatedly to Mick in the past month. But at that moment a messenger pops on to my screen. It's from Joe.

Sweetheart, I don't want to appear stuffy but I'm watching you flirt with Mick Harrison and I don't like it. I'm your man.

xxx

I slam my laptop closed and look across the floor to Joe's desk. Normally I avoid his gaze, although I can feel his eyes on me pretty much constantly. Joe issues what he probably considers a sexy smile — it's one hundred per cent creepy.

"Have you got time for a coffee?"

"For you Princess, I'll make time."

There are about a thousand coffee houses within spitting distance of GWH but I lead Mick at least half a mile away from the office because I'm becoming paranoid about who knows who, who's listening in to my conversations and who they are going to repeat those conversations to. I'm beginning to get a hint of the fear that must have prevailed during the McCarthy era.

Mick waits until we are seated in the corner of the quietest, dingiest café I can find and then says, "I'm glad you've agreed we need to talk."

I start to empty sachets of sugar into my double espresso. When I've emptied a fourth packet Mick puts his hand on mine and says, "You don't take sugar."

We sit in silence for a few more moments. There's so much I want to say to Mick but at the same time I don't want to say anything at all. If I apologize for my clumsy attempt at seducing him at the party, we will have to discuss the fact that we've nurtured a low-grade flirtation for many months now — a flirtation that I took seriously and he didn't.

If I tell him that Joe is stalking me and making my working life impossible I will have to confess to having had sex with Joe. It's too horrible. Too demeaning. I can't imagine Mick ever calling me Princess again. Besides, do I trust him? He might run straight back to the office, take all the men out for lunch so he can spread the gossip and by close of play today my reputation around the City's financial markets will be in tatters.

If I tell him that my husband's ex-wife is threatening me, possibly about to blackmail me, I'll have to allude to the fact that my marriage is in trouble. Although

486

arguably points one and two say that much, fairly clearly, anyway.

"Lucy, I would like to apologize for my behaviour at the office party. I was wondering if we could put it behind us. To be honest my recollections of the evening are fairly vague. I was quite drunk too. So if either of us said anything or did anything that either of us is embarrassed about, we needn't be because I don't remember it."

Mick has clearly practised that speech. The speed with which he delivered it suggests he is keen to plummet through his rehearsed apology as efficiently as possible. It is very brave of him to deliver it in the first place. I'm sure he doesn't want to have to linger or repeat himself.

I smile at him with a true sense of gratitude. Mick was not drunk at the party. He was as sober as a judge. His claim that he can't remember much is undermined by the fact that he *can* remember I was drunk. He said that he was drunk *too*. However, I can see that Mick has given our situation a lot of thought and decided that sweeping the incident under the shagpile is the kindest option. I'm grateful. It shows that he is a genuine friend. I beam at him.

"Oh, Mick, we both know that it's not you who owes me an apology. It's the other way round. I was the one who was totally out of order. I'm sorry that I put you in an awkward position."

Even though his apology has made me feel I'm sloshing about in the milk of human kindness, I struggle to be too much more explicit. It's degrading.

487

"I was very drunk and not thinking clearly. I am sorry that I —"

"Tried to get me into the sack."

"Mick!" I glance hastily around the café. He's grinning. I guess it's better if we can laugh about it.

"That's what I'm offended about, Lucy. You had to have your beer goggles on before you'd make a move on me."

He's still grinning but we both know that there is an element of truth in what he's saying. I'd never have tried to seduce Mick if I hadn't gotten so blinding. My drunkenness is at once the get-out clause and the insult. It's a complicated situation. Luckily, Mick is a simple man and defuses the potential intricacies of hurt feelings, loose morals and tricky consequences by laughing at me.

"It's me who should be offended you turned me down," I joke back.

"I like you too much to shag you. I rarely shag women I actually like."

And with that compliment and testament to our friendship we agree to let the matter lie.

"So, we're good now, hey?" asks Mick.

"We're good," I assure him.

"You can get back to being ball-breaking Lucy and cutting thrusting deals and earning big bonuses for us all. All of that. Hey? Because to be straight, Lucy, people are beginning to notice that you're not quite yourself, right now. Your eye is so far off the ball, you seem to be playing a totally different game. I mean I respect your family thing and I know that you've said you want to spend more time with Auriol. That's cool. However, if you're planning on spending less time in the office you're going to have to be more efficient when you are there."

"How serious is the gossip? I'm asking you because you are my friend and I think you'll be honest with me."

"Sorry. It's serious. The other day Ralph asked me if everything was OK in your world."

We stare at one another, aware that this is an issue. Ralph should not have reason to discuss me with other members of staff and even if he does do so then why has he chosen Mick? The answer is transparent. Everyone assumes we are shagging, or have been shagging and that we've now broken up. I realize that I've compromised us both.

"I'm so sorry, Mick. Point noted."

"It's not like it's all your fault. My reputation doesn't help," admits Mick gallantly.

Mick reaches for his coat. His work is done and he's conscious that we both need to get back to work. I put my hand on his arm.

"You're a good mate, Mick."

"I am, Princess."

"So I have to tell you something." Mick flops back into the plastic seat and settles at the ugly Formica table.

"Do you need more coffee?"

I shake my head; if I have a distraction I might lose my nerve.

"It's a shame that people are gossiping about you but I deserve it. I did shag someone."

Mick actually gasps. I've shocked him, or disappointed him, or maybe he's scared for me.

"Things had been pretty gloomy at home, between Peter and me. Well, you know that much. I was feeling old and used."

"Used?"

"Used by the whole maternal and wifey bit. I'm not a natural at self-sacrifice. I was bored and I felt neglected. The whole formula."

I'm lucky that I'm justifying myself to Mick; he's pretty egocentric too and tries to sympathize with me. Some would be livid with my miserable little excuses.

"So you did it to shake things up a bit?"

"I did it because I was absolutely pissed. It was the night of the party. After you left."

"I see."

Mick's lips disappear as he sucks them into invisibility. He stays absolutely still and silent for an age. I realize that I've hurt him. Perhaps only his pride is wounded, but maybe evidence of my indiscriminate sexual offers that evening are genuinely distasteful to him.

"Who was the lucky man?" he asks at length. His tone betrays irritation and curiosity.

For the first time I can't bring myself to hold his gaze. I drop my head into my hands and mutter.

"Joe Whitehead."

"What? Did you just say Joe Whitehead?"

I nod and drag my eyes back to Mick. I might as well look at his disgust square on — I face mine in the mirror every morning.

"That snivelling, stupid, sneaky shit?"

"Yeah, you've got him."

Mick pushes his chair back and for a moment I think he's going to storm out of the café like a jilted lover. Instead he goes to the counter and orders more coffee.

He slams the tiny cups on the table. "I wish there was whisky in these," he says. "Joe Whitehead is so beneath you, Lucy."

"Apparently not," I comment.

I have the decency to face the fact that we are as low as those we lie with. And while Joe has got a terrible and fast-depreciating record at work for being irresponsible, a brown-noser, a loner, a shirk and a fool, I do not believe I can take any moral high ground.

"Best put it behind you, Luce. Just forget it," says Mick.

It's obvious from his expression that he wishes to put the thought right out of his mind. I understand. I almost balk when I think of Joe Whitehead's fat little hands grabbing, inexpertly, at my flesh.

The sex was the worst I have ever known. A grunting, derisory grapple punctuated with pungent whiffs of stale sweat and the sound of his excited panting. It was all over in a few minutes. Almost not long enough for me to realize what was happening. Not that I'm suggesting I was forced, I wasn't. I didn't say no, but then nor did I say yes.

After Mick had left, Joe and I had several more drinks in Wasp bar. Joe suggested we go on somewhere else. I said no, I needed to get home. I was in a hideous state, wobbling and slurring, I did not want to be seen that way. Joe agreed to get my coat and rushed off quite helpfully. He was gone for ages. When he finally returned, he dragged me up from the daybed and led me out of the main room.

"Aren't we going the wrong way?" I slurred. I wasn't sure. The mirrors were disorientating and I could hardly stand, let alone navigate.

"I know a back door, it leads to the main road. It will be easier to get a cab." Then Joe put my coat over my head. He thought he was being funny and he kept saying, "No one can see you are with me now, Lucy, so don't worry." Which, even at the time, struck me as peculiar. He knew I didn't want to be with him.

I didn't like having the coat over my head, I felt claustrophobic and vulnerable. I never liked wearing a blindfold, not for pin-the-tail-on-the-donkey as a kid or even in bed with Peter. I like to see where I'm going. I grabbed at the coat and tried to put it on properly but Joe just laughed and held it tightly over my head. I told him to stop it, that he was messing up my hair, but I didn't make too much of a fuss, I didn't want to draw attention to our departure. He was right, I didn't want to be seen with him. The exchange took just a minute or so but when he took the coat off my head we weren't outside, we were in a tiny private room.

I knew exactly what the room was normally used for. It was the sort of room I would probably have looked for with Mick if he had taken up my hint. The sort of room that the management let at great cost and with great discretion. It was decently decorated, if not a little obvious. There were no mirrors like in the main bar but there were lashings of red velvet. Red-velvet cushioned walls, red-velvet flowing curtains and a red-velvet daybed. The room said sex. And hell.

There was one lone bucket in which rested a cold bottle of champagne, not Crystal now but a bottle of house. There were no glasses. In his haste to arrange this seduction, Joe must have forgotten to specify. I assumed that he'd screamed instructions and passed wedges of cash across the counter as he collected our coats.

I groaned, told him I really didn't want anything more to drink, just wanted to go home. He asked me to relax, suggested I needed to lie down and sleep off the excess. I stayed standing. Joe tried to get me to drink the champagne from the bottle but I clamped my mouth closed and the sticky bubbles ran down my chin and shirt. He licked up the mess and I didn't stop him.

In that moment I thought the quickest way to get home was to give in to it.

Mick waits for me to respond to his suggestion. I pull out a box of cigarettes from my bag. I offer him one. He refuses but helps me to light up; my hands are shaking, and I can't see the damn lighter because tears are threatening. I blink furiously and take a deep breath.

"I would put it behind me. I had. But there's a problem. He has not."

"He's fallen for you?"

"Inevitably." I flash Mick a grin but it's entirely fake. I've never felt worse. "He's turned into a bit of a stalker, actually." I try to laugh but the effort breaks me. The tears can no longer be kept in check. Mick's kindness is a fatal blow. I start to sob. "He contacts me all the time, text, e-mail and on messenger."

"How's he managed that?"

"He's tampered with my laptop. He got my mobile number from Julia. I've had to change phones but last night he rang me at home. He thinks we have something going. He won't accept that I was drunk and that he was a mistake. He hounds me, asking when we can meet again. Mick, he's scaring me. I don't want to lose my family or my job but I definitely don't ever want to have to do that with him again."

"It's OK, Princess, it's OK." Mick is around my side of the table and he's kneeling on the floor next to me. He's rubbing his hand on my back. "I'll sort this out. We'll sort it out together. Don't worry. We'll have the bastard fired by this afternoon."

I have never before believed in the need for, or the existence of, a knight in shining armour. But right now I think I can hear Mick's horse gallop towards me and I'm enormously grateful.

Mick establishes that I have kept some of the e-mails but none of the texts. I show him my BlackBerry and he seems confident that we have a case of sexual harassment. Depressingly he says that there will be no disagreement that Joe has affected my performance at work in the past month.

"But I had sex with him."

"So what? You don't want to have sex with him again. He needs to know that no is no. Besides, morally he's behaved hideously. He took advantage of you when you were plastered."

"But it's going to be so embarrassing if Ralph knows what I've done. And anyway, even if Ralph does fire Joe, mud sticks. I'll be marked out as a troublemaker."

Mick can't deny that I have a point. My career in the City will only survive until the next set of culling and then I'll probably be offered a hearty redundancy package and shown the door too. The City doesn't like squealers.

"Well, before we try the official channels, we can confront him together, if you prefer."

"And say what?"

"Say that we will go to Ralph if he doesn't resign." Neither of us considers the possibility of just asking Joe to stop pestering me — it's gone too far for that. "This isn't just about his inappropriate behaviour in terms of harassing a co-worker. These e-mails suggest the man's bonkers. He needs help. We'll put that to him. If he has a shred of sanity or dignity left he'll get out sharpish. He won't want a blot in his copybook either."

"It might work," I admit.

For the first time in a month I allow myself to feel hopeful. I lean across and hug Mick. "You really are a friend. Thank you."

"No. A true friend would have shagged you when you offered and saved you from Joe," says Mick with a sheepish grin. After seeing me cry he's unsure how much joshing I can take.

"Yes, this is all your fault." I try to smile through my snot and tears. "Seriously though, some good has come out of this debacle," I add.

"What's that then?"

"Something's changed for me. I've started to appreciate what I have now it's all at risk. I know I'm so lucky to have my husband, my daughter, my friends." I squeeze Mick's hand affectionately. Suddenly, the relief that Mick's support has afforded disappears. "Oh shit. *Peter.*"

"Are you going to tell him?"

"Do you think I should?"

"I wouldn't. But then I've never been married, so I don't know."

"Peter's ex-wife knows about Joe," I confess.

"What?" Mick can't believe my life can get any more tragic or farcical. Neither can I. "How?"

"I have no idea, but she does. She made reference to it when I saw her last Sunday. I've hardly slept since."

"Do you think she'll tell your husband?"

"I don't know. She doesn't owe me any favours. Oh God, I'm so ashamed. What have I done? You see, Mick, in my book having sex with a hideous little man was terrible but I had managed to compartmentalize the disaster in my brain. I had done a lousy thing. But it was over and I'll never do it again."

"There were mitigating circumstances and no pre-calculation," adds Mick supportively.

"Exactly. But the consequences are foul. I saw that when I looked into Rose's face on Sunday. I destroyed her family because I loved Peter so much and I had to

496

have him for myself. It's complex to explain, but Rose glared at me as though I'd destroyed her all over again. You'd expect her to be joyful or vengeful but she looked devastated. For the first time in my life I felt like a thoroughly bad person."

"You said you loved Peter. Do you still?"

"Yes. More than ever. But as Rose knows, loving a person sometimes isn't enough. She loved Peter and they still separated and Rose hadn't even done anything wrong."

"But he loved you."

"Yes, he did."

"Does he still?"

"Yes."

"Enough?"

"I don't know."

"Well, there's only one way to find out."

"Who says I want to find out?"

"I can't help you with that, I'm afraid, Princess. Work, yes, but home is so much more —"

"Personal?"

"Just so much more. Full stop."

Mick and I know that we have to get back to the office. We need to face Joe, and Ralph will be wondering where the hell we are. Mick tries to pay but I stop him. These coffees really must be on me. I leave the money on the table. The coins roll into my slops and spillages. It seems I can't do anything right any more.

CHAPTER
FORTY-SEVEN

Wednesday 6 December

Rose

Time marches on and waits for no man, let alone a slightly harassed single mum who is approximately fifteen minutes late for her final night class on car maintenance. I try to sneak into the back of the class, unnoticed, but the tutor is too polite to allow this and insists on interrupting his instruction to welcome me and to sympathize about the unreliability of public transport. Helen grins at me and Susanne throws a small wave. They both look slightly more glamorous than they usually do, which in Helen's case means she looks as though she's just stepped out of the pages of a glossy magazine and in Susanne's case means she's wearing lipstick. I am in shoes with a three-inch heel (which I am unused to, hence my being late for the bus and, in turn, the class). None of us are appropriately dressed for playing around with engines but tonight we are celebrating surviving the course.

We're going to a local Italian restaurant straight after class and I, for one, am extremely excited about the prospect of sitting with a glass of Chianti and munching a pizza. Since Lucy-gate I have mostly lived in my own head, with nothing other than my confusion and anger for company. The idea of sitting still for a few hours, chatting about cheery girl-stuff, is just what I need.

The moment the class is over Helen, Susanne and I charge out of the musty room. I'm not sorry to leave behind the smell of oil and creosote. We thank the tutor and nod goodbye to the various spotty boys but firmly refuse their generous invite to join them in the pub to talk sparkplugs.

We each hold on to our gossip until we are shown to our seats, have ordered our food and have a glass of wine in our hands.

"Cheers," says Susanne. "To Christmas."

"Christmas?" yells Helen in disbelief. "How can you be thinking about Christmas now? It's weeks away"

How can she not be thinking about Christmas yet? Helen is clearly one of those people who buys her gifts on Christmas Eve, probably from the 7 – 11. In our house Christmas becomes a hot topic just after bonfire night. The boys have written, rewritten and then rewritten the rewrites of their letters to Santa, several times. They are not especially committed believers. Sebastian purports to be atheist, having declared, when he was six, that Santa, Rudolf and Mrs Christmas, etc. are all bogus; although he did concede that the North Pole was real but only after I'd shown him our Reader's Digest world atlas. Henry hedges his bets a little more. He sets the table from time to time in December and tries to keep his room tidyish, just in case there is a naughty and nice book. I guess he's more of an agnostic. However, as Christmas nears they both like to cover themselves and drop Santa a line detailing their plastic desires. They are a little like lapsed Catholics popping to confession once every year or so.

"I feel I've just taken down the sodding tinsel from last year," groans Helen.

"I know. Time flies," I agree.

The first school term is always the busiest. I have held it together throughout harvest festival, jeans day, character from a book day, the fitting of sports mouth-guards, school photos, Hallowe'en, bonfire night and suddenly, here we are two weeks away from nativity. Two villagers' costumes to go and I'm in the clear. Well, besides embarking on the mammoth amount of work that is necessary to make sure Christmas runs smoothly.

Daisy, Simon, Mum and Dad are coming to my house this year, as they do every year. For some reason, unaccountable to me, this has caused Daisy to throw a mini strop.

"I was wondering if we could have Christmas at my house this year?" she said at the beginning of November.

"We never do," I stated flatly.

"That's my point," she muttered.

"You don't like cooking," I added reasonably.

"You could cook at mine." She didn't look hopeful. I've been hosting Christmas for over a decade. It's traditional. Why would we do it differently this year?

"Oh, I prefer my own oven. Besides, you haven't got as much space," I argued.

"I have a spare room for Mum and Dad. There's the bed settee, we'd manage."

"I don't think so," I said firmly and finally. "The boys like to stay in their own home on Christmas day."

Daisy shot me a murderous glance. "The boys couldn't care less. It's you," she muttered.

I chose not to say anything else. I didn't want a row but I certainly didn't want to give way. I have ambiguous feelings towards Christmas and only manage to get through it if I follow a set and strict agenda. My agenda.

Until Peter left, I loved Christmas with an unadulterated passion. His departure has complicated this, like everything else.

I loved Christmas throughout my twenties. When friends were becoming weary and viewed it as nothing other than an excuse to get drunk and have sex with inappropriate strangers, I still saw it as a gloriously magical time. I liked choosing oh-so-perfect gifts. I liked spending evenings writing cards and carefully wrapping pressies with copious amounts of tissue and ribbons. I liked the full churches and I did not resent once-a-year-Christians appearing at midnight mass, slightly the worse for wear but well-intentioned. I loved being a great hostess and, throughout the season, I threw my doors open for several parties and gatherings besides the big day itself. I prided myself on producing delicious, distinguished, unparalleled lunches. My pheasant and pork with crackling and roast apples, seasoned delicately with thyme and parsley, served with caramelized fennel and spiced red cabbage and cranberries, is an unsurpassable feast, even if I say so myself.

Until Peter left.

Then I noticed that Christmas came with overwhelming expectations. Suddenly it was chilling to notice families sitting around hearths, to watch couples drag home Christmas trees and to know that tear-jerking nativity plays were being performed in every school hall up and down the country. My coping strategy was to carry on as I did before and then some. Now I invest more, not less, time into selecting thoughtful gifts. Wrapping them has become an art form. I now have two Christmas trees, one in the hall, the other in the lounge. I practise recipes for roast parsnip and honey weeks in advance of Christmas day.

Yet at Christmas I still notice the enormous black hole in my life. However many car maintenance courses or blind dates I fit in, no matter how many committees I sit on or hours I spend reading to the children or managing their health, education and emotional needs, there is a hole. A gap. A void. Secretly, I find that I've started to look forward to January, when things get back to normal. Tacky tinsel is put away and over-eating and binge drinking is seen for what it was, ruinous on one's health.

Helen and Susanne start to talk about work. Helen has been offered a promotion but she's unsure whether to take it. She says she sees little enough of her partner, Mike, as it is.

"Besides, Mike got promoted about two months ago so it's not as if we need the money," she says.

She looks embarrassed, because Susanne and I know that Mike will not have sat in the pub with his mates discussing whether the promotion would have a detrimental effect on their relationship. No doubt he took the private car parking space and the bigger office without a moment's hesitation. She doesn't need us to point this out to her.

"I'd take it, girl. See how you get along," says Susanne. I nod encouragingly.

Susanne is rushed off her feet in the salon at the moment. Despite Helen's reluctance to embrace the onslaught of Christmas, the rest of the western world are very aware that the geese are getting fat, which has a direct correlation to their hair needing to be trimmed, permed, lightened or straightened.

"It's my busiest time of year. If I'm unsociable and don't resurface until January, don't write me off," says Susanne with a smile.

"We won't. I'm sure that we'll keep in touch. You two are the best thing about the course," I say. We all grin reassuringly at one another and luxuriate in a moment of female friendship. "I also liked the bit about changing tyres, I think that will be useful," I add with a smirk.

Susanne nudges me playfully and then asks, "So what next?" Next? Why do people keep asking me that? "I'm going to have a go at a fine art course. There's one starting in the spring. It's not expensive and you sketch live models in the first modular. They might have male models. It will be the first bit of naked flesh I've seen since —" Susanne stops talking and starts to count on her fingers.

"Not for me," I state firmly. "I was never any good at art and couldn't bring myself to stare at naked bodies for hours on end. Flesh, I've always thought, ought to be covered up."

They both laugh even though I'm not trying to be funny.

Helen says, "I thought I might join a sociology class."

Both ladies turn to me. I shrug. I haven't thought about it at all. All I've been thinking about is Lucy and Peter. Susanne lets me off the hook.

"You've been too busy dating to give it any thought, haven't you? How's it going?"

"Frankly, I'm wondering when I can quit the search for Mr Right. As I don't think he exists, my task is a little like looking for an invisible needle in a haystack."

"He exists," chorus Susanne and Helen at once.

I stare at them both, mystified. I can understand that Helen might believe in Mr Right. After all, she has Mike, and while I might think he's a little selfish when it comes to his career progression versus life balance, it doesn't seem to bother her. But Susanne is alone and has been for more months than she has fingers and toes. Where do they find their optimism?

"How did it go with the headmaster? We haven't seen you since the wedding date. You've cut so many classes and when you do show up you rush off before we can chat," observes Susanne.

I stare at my pizza and wonder how honest I can be with Helen and Susanne. I'm desperate to tell someone about the revelation I uncovered at the wedding and it can't be Connie or Daisy, not until I've worked out what to do about Lucy.

"I had a great time," I admit.

"You liked him?" There is surprise in Helen's voice.

"Very much," I confess with a shy smile. "He's kind, thoughtful and funny. Plus, he looked great in his suit."

"Wow," the girls chorus. They beam at one another and heartily tuck into their bowls of steaming pasta.

"So when are you seeing him again?" asks Helen.

"Oh, I'm not." The girls drop their forks and jaws. I explain. "Well, I was at the wedding and I got talking to this man on our table, horrible character actually, a complete bore. And, you'll never guess, it turns out he is Lucy's lover." Confused, Helen and Susanne stare at me. "You know, Lucy who is married to my — to Peter. Well, after that, I couldn't think of anything else and I was in such a state that I ran out of the reception without saying goodbye to Craig."

As I admit this, I recognize the sensation of embarrassment creeping down from my scalp, covering my face, neck and chest in a scarlet blush. What must Craig think of me?

"I don't understand," says Helen. "You were having a good time with Craig?"

"Wonderful."

"But you left him, without any explanation, because you heard some gossip about your ex's wife. That poor man."

Helen and Susanne exchange looks of bewilderment.

I try to justify my actions. "But Lucy is having an affair, it's monumental."

"Why?" asks Susanne. Which I think is pretty dim of her.

"Well, it's karma, isn't it? I mean this is what everyone said would happen. But it's terrible that it has, because what was it all for? My husband left me for her."

I think the issue at stake is clear but from the look on my friends' faces they'd disagree.

"But what has Lucy's affair got to do with yours?" probes Susanne.

I answer her question with a question. "Isn't it just typical that she ruins something else for me? I was having such a fabulous time with Craig. You know what? For the first time since Peter, I was actually enjoying being held by another man. I enjoyed Craig's conversation, his manners, his jokes. But since I left him in the lurch, Lucy has ruined that potential relationship."

"She didn't ruin anything for you," says Helen. She puts down her fork and watches me carefully. Her eyes are full of concern.

"You did that," adds Susanne. "You didn't have to leave."

I look from one to the other of my friends and I'm bemused by their reaction. What are they talking about?

"Of course I had to leave. I was confused and shocked."

506

"You could at least have said goodbye. Explained you had something to work through. You didn't have to abandon the man," says Helen. "For one thing, it's rude."

"Maybe," I concede guiltily.

I don't like it that Susanne and Helen are accusing me of having terrible manners or worse, especially as part of me agrees with them. With the benefit of hindsight, I realize that I could have made up an excuse for my sudden departure. It would have caused less disruption in the long run. At pick-up and drop-off I still have to duck and dive behind trees to avoid Craig, although recently I've noticed he no longer shows his face at the school gate. I think he's avoiding me too. Some of the mothers have started to grumble about his absence; they are accusing him of being inaccessible and remote. I feel badly for him. And I've missed not being involved in the school nativity this year. Usually I help paint scenery and I volunteer to practise lines with the kids. It's fun, but rehearsals are out of the question this year, which is a shame. I realize that I ought to try to explain myself to my friends, at a minimum.

"But this news of Lucy's affair is just another example of how true love doesn't exist and this whole search for the perfect man is just pointless," I mutter, resentfully.

"How come?"

"When Peter left I justified his actions by telling myself that Lucy and Peter were one another's soulmates and oddly that helped me make sense of the hurt."

"You'd have been better cutting up his suits," comments Susanne casually, as she takes a big gulp of the house white.

"Do you think so?"

"It seems more natural." She leans across the table and fills up my wine glass.

"Did you ever show Peter how angry you were with him?" asks Helen. She makes her enquiry sound nonchalant but I catch her eye and identify a steely determination. I wonder where this is leading. I think about her question.

"No, I don't think so. There were the boys to consider. Arguing in front of them wouldn't have done them any good."

"I agree with you there. But perhaps having a good old barney when they were safely tucked up in bed, or better yet, staying with grandparents, well . . . you might have found that helpful," she suggests.

I'm shocked. "In what way?"

"It would have been therapeutic," replies Helen.

"Help you put things behind you," adds Susanne.

"Get a few things off your chest."

"Stop you feeling like a doormat."

"Help you let things go."

They are a great double act. I'm lost for words. My friends think I need therapy. They think I'm a doormat. They think I haven't let the past go, which is ridiculous because Peter and I broke up six years ago. Of course I've let go. OK, occasionally I refer to him as my husband, that's just a slip of the tongue. Sometimes I do find myself wondering what they are up to on a Sunday without me. But that's natural. I don't want him back. It's just that —

"You need some closure with Peter."

I'm not sure whether it's Helen or Susanne that says this. It hardly matters, it's clear they speak as one. In fact they sound very like Connie and Daisy, Luke and Simon, my mother and the man at the corner shop. I consider how best to phrase my indignant response but Susanne doesn't allow me the time to gather my thoughts or argument, she charges on.

"Everyone can see it, Rose. It's such a shame you are wasting so much time." I want to object but she disarms me with a compliment. "Rose, you have so much love to give. It breaks my heart seeing it wasted."

"That's why your sister and your friends put so much effort into trying to find you a new man or at least a new hobby. Something you could get passionate about, other than the past."

"But the men I dated were all hopeless," I point out.

"OK, so you met some dull guys, tight guys, guys with thin lips. Sadly there is a lot of flotsam and jetsam on the beach but then you met Craig and he was a pearl."

"Yes, but —"

"I bet subconsciously you were quite pleased when in the middle of your successful date with Craig you discovered this news about your ex and his wife. It gave you an excuse to cut and run."

"My subconscious is not that complicated. *I'm* not that complicated," I object.

"We are all complicated, Rose."

"I'm homely and straightforward. I'm not self-destructive or complex."

Helen and Susanne stare at me. I think I see pity in their faces.

We fall silent and sip our wine. I hope to God that is the conversation closed. I frantically search for something else to talk about but all I can think of is the scary possibility that they might be right.

"Answer me one thing," says Susanne. "If you hadn't found out about Lucy's affair that day at the wedding, would you have seen Craig again?"

"Yes," I reply hotly, then I pause and add, "probably."

"Maybe," says Susanne; she looks sceptical. "Or maybe you'd have decided that the boys didn't like you dating the headmaster, or perhaps you found it awkward at the school gate, or feasibly — on closer intimacy — you'd have found his laugh to be irritating. I'd bet my bottom dollar, Rose, you'd have found some excuse to finish it."

"Why would I do that?"

"You tell me. Because you like being alone? Because you still want Peter? Because you hate yourself so much that you think allowing your youth to seep away in an endless stream of missed possibilities is acceptable? I don't know. I'm stumped."

Her words are brutal, all the more so because the thoughts she's articulating are ones that I have had. In the dead of night when thoughts become fears and reason becomes elusive I have wondered the same things.

"Maybe you secretly think the news of Lucy's affair was pretty convenient for you. The first favour she's done you," concludes Susanne. She probably realizes that she's said as much as I can take, because within the same breath she asks, "Now who wants pudding? The tiramisù is fabulous here."

While Helen and Susanne think about which dessert they'd prefer I chew on their words. I feel sick with the possibility that Susanne has offered an insight so accurate that it feels like a violation. Is it unnatural to divorce in silence? I do often feel used or overlooked but have I ever said so? Even once? No, I haven't. I always wear a cheery demeanour. Does Peter have any idea how much damage he caused? I doubt it. He's unlikely to have given the situation much thought; besides, I do my best to reassure him constantly that everything is fine. I tell him that the boys are fine, that I'm fine, that him living round the corner to us is fine, that sending his daughter to my kids' school is fine. Well, it's not fine. Not all of it. Not all of the time. It's not my fault that Peter left but perhaps it is my fault that he doesn't know how much suffering has occurred as a consequence.

Is it in my power to put a stop to my feelings of hurt and anger?

I'm amazed that my friends don't want to know what I am going to do with my choice piece of gossip. They don't seem to care whether I plan to expose Lucy or not. It's obvious that they don't care about Peter and his domestics. They care about me. And Peter and his domestics have nothing to do with me. They haven't for a long time.

Since the wedding reception I have been frantic and resentful. I have done nothing other than churn over the past and imagine glorious showdowns where I expose Lucy and devastate Peter. But in reality I have done nothing other than make a single snide comment to Lucy, in order to let her know that I know her torrid secret. Even then, I'm not certain she heard me. The truth is I am not sure what I want to do with this knowledge. Even in my wildest fantasies I never imagine my breaking up Peter and Lucy will mean that Peter will return to me. That would be ridiculous. A step too far and not what I want. So what do I want? As I spoon delicious light and creamy tiramisù into my mouth I consider everything Susanne and Helen have said. They are right about many, many things, but it strikes me that there's one thing Susanne got completely wrong.

I could never imagine Craig's laugh becoming irritating.

CHAPTER
FORTY-EIGHT

Tuesday 12 December

John

Barefoot children with teatowels on their heads scuttle past me at breakneck speed. I am tempted to yell, "No running in the corridors," which terrifies me as it's such a sensible and grown-up thought for me to have.

I pop my head around a classroom door and spot Mrs Foster, the teacher who directed me to Craig's office back in September. She's surrounded by a group of little girls wearing pillowcases tied at the waist with tinsel. She's attaching wings and haloes and it's clearly a tricky job, because the girls are phenomenally excited. They bounce and fidget; it's a miracle there are not more casualties of safety-pin pricks. I wave to her across the sea of blonde heads and she beams back, recognizing me in an instant.

"Ah, Mr Harding, Mr Walker's pal. How lovely to see you again. Have you come to watch the nativity?" I nod. "You made a splendid job of the scenery. We've never had a more authentic backdrop."

"Glad to help. Have you seen Mr Walker?"

We are both doing that thing that adults do around kids. We're using titles and surnames in an attempt to trick the kids into thinking we command respect and might be in control.

"He's probably in the hall, greeting parents. We're serving mince pies and mulled wine before the performance this year. We used to leave it until afterwards but we've discovered that if the parents have a little seasonal spirit inside them they are less likely to punch one another as they grapple for front row seats."

I smile and turn to set out to find Craig. I call over my shoulder. "Break a leg, Mrs Foster."

The school hall is heaving. It's frosty outside so the parents are all insulated with large coats, but the mums are keen to disrobe and reveal their new outfits, bought especially for the nativity performance. The fathers, therefore, are left balancing bulky coats, gloves, hats and scarves while the mothers daintily concentrate on balancing a paper plate with a mince pie and a paper cup of mulled wine. The parents are possibly even more excited than the tiny angels. The mothers are gleaming, chatty and slightly manic. They cannot wait to see their budding Robert De Niros and Nicole Kidmans pace the boards. The fathers catch each other's glance and roll their eyes at one another in mock despair at their wives' enthusiasm but each one is armed with a camera and camcorder.

I can't see Craig but I do spot Connie, almost instantly.

It's like it always has been for the two of us. We are in a crowded room and somehow we pick one another

514

out, we are drawn to one another — maybe it's an animal instinct that identifies attraction or danger. She turns to me in slow motion and then at comedy double speed she pushes through the crowd to stand face to face.

She launches in. "Well, I wish I could call this a nice surprise. I thought things were settled. I really didn't expect to see you here. I didn't really expect to see you *again*. You said you were going away. Well, there's no alternative, I'm going to introduce you to Luke. I'm fed up of this skulking about. He's right over there."

I scan the crowd in the direction she is pointing. I am a little bit curious and interested in meeting Luke. If I had time I'd study the man, understand him and maybe even learn from him. But I don't have time and there's no point in upsetting his day by pushing my way into his consciousness this late in the game.

"I've come to say goodbye."

"We've said goodbye."

We have, not in so many words, but what's not said is often valuable.

"To Craig," I add.

"Oh, I see." Connie is still and silent for a moment. "So you are going to Manchester?"

"Yes, I'm looking forward to it."

"Good shops."

"Clean start." I smile at her. She nods. She knows that besides saying see ya to Craig, I'm saying goodbye to us, it, whatever and all that.

"Mr Walker was meeting and greeting the parents at the gate. I'm not sure if you'll get to see him now until after the play. You should stay and watch it. Fran is Mary." She beams at me with unapologetic pride.

"That's only because I pulled strings," I tell her.

"You didn't." She looks aghast.

"No, I didn't. She got the part on the strength of her audition." I can't pee on the proud mum's parade. It's obvious that Connie is already imagining gracefully acknowledging her daughter's thanks, as her daughter delivers her Oscar acceptance speech.

"So when are you off?"

"This afternoon. My work here is done."

"Was it a successful project?" she asks politely.

I wanted to get you to fall in love with me again but you didn't, so no, not especially. I say this in my head. To Connie I reply, "Yes, unexpected outcome but very educational."

She nods. Somebody jolts Connie's arm and she nearly spills her mulled wine. We're being squeezed closer and closer together, as more parents arrive and space is at a premium.

"We never talked," she says.

"We never did anything other," I reply.

She grins. "No. I mean really talked about the old days."

I give in to the awful inevitability. I've been playing dodgeball for too long. I'm tired. "What is it you want to know?"

We fall silent, it seems like hours pass. I begin to wonder if I was right all along and talking between men and women is impossible. After an age Connie says, "It doesn't matter any more." But she's not accusing me.

516

She's not angry with me. She's peaceful. We both know that the past is for learning from and letting go. You can't revisit it. It vanishes.

"Oh, except one thing. Do you know what went on between my friend Rose and Mr Walker? He must have done something really awful to upset her. She's been acting so peculiarly since their date."

"She *is* peculiar," I confirm. "She ditched him at the wedding. Without a word of warning. Just ran off."

"She did?"

"She did. He was gutted."

"He was?"

"Yes, he's really into her. I don't know, women." I shrug.

"We're a mystery, aren't we?" says Connie with a graceful smile. I can see that she's no longer thinking about me, but she's consumed with curiosity and concern for her pal. "I'd better go. I want a good seat." She leans towards me and kisses me on the cheek. "'Bye, John. Look after yourself."

Then she melts into the crowd of twitchy, excited parents before I even have a chance to wink.

CHAPTER
FORTY-NINE

Tuesday 12 December

Lucy

He left my life as easily and unobtrusively as he entered it, but he has had a profound effect on how I will choose to live from now onwards, and he'll never have any idea how much he affected me.

Joe Whitehead was laughingly easy to scare off. When Mick and I returned to the office, Mick called Joe into the boardroom and we faced him together. Coolly, calmly and courageously Mick stood in my corner and explained to Joe why we thought it would be better for Joe to resign that afternoon, rather than to force our hand and make us bring the whole sorry mess to Ralph's attention, the attention of the HR department and perhaps the courts. Joe was brazen for only a minute or so. He insisted I'd enjoyed myself at the time.

"I find that hard to believe," said Mick. "And you are even more insane than I thought if you really believe it to be so."

Mick pointed out that it wasn't just Joe's conduct with me that was unprofessional. He listed at least half a dozen incidents where Joe had gone completely berserk with a junior member of his team and blamed them for problems that he ought to have resolved personally. Mick highlighted incidents where clients had expressed dissatisfaction or suffered financial losses. Mick made it clear that if he reported this latest incident to Ralph, Ralph no doubt would see it as the perfect excuse to fire Joe.

Joe must have recognized the non-negotiable sense in what Mick said because he quietly agreed to resign with immediate effect. No doubt he reasoned that it was better to search for new employment without a filthy black smudge of scandal hanging over his head. I understood that. I watched as he packed up his belongings and I thought, there but for the grace of God go I, or more specifically in this case, there but for the grace of Mick.

Without the continuous threat of exposure from the psycho stalker hanging over me, I quickly started to perform efficiently once again at GWH. I hadn't realized how much mindspace I've been giving to worrying about Joe Whitehead. Now I've stopped jumping when my phone beeps to indicate an incoming text message. I no longer dread logging on to my e-mail account, I know I won't be faced with dozens of messages from him, and when messenger pops up on my screen, I know it will be a sweet tiding from Peter. It's an enormous relief.

Ralph has noticed that my performance and attitude have picked up and has had no reason to call anyone into his office to discuss my output, not me or Mick. I still managed to get out of the office pretty sharpish this week, three nights out of five, and intend to go on doing so. I'm also planning to limit travel and will be relying heavily on video conferencing in the new year. But when I'm at the office, I'm working harder than I ever did. I don't want to have to give up my career. I am finding a balance. Balance, by its very definition, will mean that I have to forgo the largest bonuses and the heartiest pats on the back so that I can spend more time with Auriol and Peter. But that's OK. After all these years trading commodities I've finally realized money comes and goes, time just goes, therefore the most valuable commodity is time and I want to spend as much of that as I can with my family. Simple really.

So I have Joe Whitehead to thank for my redefining my priorities and the notable increase in domestic harmony, albeit indirectly.

Of course, I'm not out of the woods yet. While my work life is less tremulous and stressful I am living on a knife-edge at home. The more time and effort I put into understanding and relating to Auriol (and therefore, among other things, winning the praise and respect of Peter), the more keenly aware I am that the stakes I'm playing with are frighteningly high. Rose could blow my world apart in one easy move. A few months ago I did not believe that my world was centred round my home life. I thought my world was wherever I happened to be; be that GWH, a spa, a cocktail bar or a five-star hotel somewhere hot. I used to rush out of the house gratefully, away from the cloying domesticity, at every opportunity. Now, I wonder how I'd manage if I lost

Peter and Auriol so soon after finding them, really finding them.

I called Rose with the intention of pleading my case and begging her to keep my secret. She was out when I rang and it's not the sort of message one can leave on the answering machine. She didn't call back and maybe that was for the best; I'm not sure throwing myself on her mercy is my most sensible option. It's unlikely she'll consider me a credible case for her charity and understanding. I consider whether it's worth my denying everything. I could head off the threat of her spilling the beans by telling Peter that there have been some tiresome rumours circulating at GWH, all completely unfounded. He'd believe me. He trusts me. It is his trust that makes that option impossible. I've always played the affairs of the heart and loins by my own incomparable rules, not the same moral standards that the majority profess to follow, but there have always been rules. Rule number one, I can't lie to Peter.

So, I am at Rose's mercy. Nine days have passed since she let me know that she is aware of my infidelity. Every time the doorbell has rung since, I've wondered if it is Rose, just popping round to reclaim what is hers by telling my love that I had sex with an ugly man. Her silence, to date, does not reassure me. Perhaps she's waiting for the ultimate humiliating moment to expose me. The school nativity play, when her revelation could be savoured by our children and friends? Christmas day? Or perhaps she's playing a long game and is waiting until Auriol's wedding day.

I spot her straight away in the throng of parents milling around the school hall, munching unnecessary calories and sipping cheap mulled wine. She's wearing her hair in an up-do. I wouldn't have expected it to suit her (they can be very ageing) but it does, she looks modern and confident. My vulnerability obviously suits her. She's carrying a plate of mince pies and is offering them around. No doubt they are home-made. I did donate mince pies for today's event but they were shop-bought. Still, Auriol was pleased, because I forgot all about the contribution for the harvest festival. Small steps.

Peter sees Luke already seated on the skinny benches set up for the audience. Luke is surrounded by coats and bags spread to guard a bunch of places, no doubt at Connie's instruction. Peter heads over to chat to him and keep him company. I tell him I'll catch up and push in the opposite direction and head towards Rose.

"Hello, Rose."

"Hello, Lucy, you are looking marvellous as usual," she says as her eyes quickly scan my chocolate brown velvet trousers and rollneck jumper from Joseph.

I wonder if I'll sound sincere if I tell her that I think her hair suits her. The moment is lost when Rose adds, "You seem to become lovelier with every misdeed you commit. You are a regular Dorian Gray, aren't you, Lucy?"

I smile coolly. "I'd rather not have to live with your jibes from now until eternity, Rose. Do you think we ought to talk about what you know?"

522

"What's there to talk about? You are committing adultery. Situation normal."

While Rose's talk is fighting talk, I notice she has lowered her voice and she glances apprehensively to left and right as she delivers her barbed comment. She doesn't want the other parents to know of my disgrace; after all, I am associated with her. I take comfort in her conventionality. Rose smiles at a kid who helps himself to the last mince pie and then puts the plate to one side.

She folds her arms across her mammoth chest. "The power balance has changed, hasn't it, Lucy?" she says. I stare at her. I don't see how. "I am in control for once. I am top dog and you are waiting to see what *I'll* do."

I *am* waiting to see what she'll do, but nothing has changed. I've lived my life under Rose's shadow. Will Peter propose to Rose? Will he leave Rose? Will Peter propose to me, after Rose? Will we buy a house near Rose? Will we send our daughter to the school Rose chose? And so on.

"I'll be frank, I'm enjoying this," she says.

"I'm sure you are," I concede.

"You've never given me a second thought, Lucy, and I feel rather wonderful, rather powerful, now that you *have* to think about me. I bet you've thought of nothing much besides me for several days now."

Rose is understandably excited but despite her protestations that she's enjoying this situation she seems rather more manic than thrilled. Being nasty doesn't suit her. Dullness is her worst offence.

"Is that what you believe? That I rarely think of you?" I ask. "I've rarely thought of anything else for years."

She holds my gaze, trying to ascertain my level of honesty. I meet her eye. I'm telling the truth. For all of Rose's faults she's not stupid. She warily weighs up what I have just said.

"You're a horror. You've ruined everything with your greedy, relentlessly selfish ways. You stole my husband and broke up my family and it appears even that wasn't enough for you." She hisses this angry statement. I rather admire her bluntness.

We are both aware that this is the shoot-out at the old chaparral. It's been a long time coming. I'm rather looking forward to a bit of honest mud-slinging; I've always resented Rose's pious acceptance of Peter's and my betrayal. Her seemingly timid, obliging nature has never rung true. Surely she must have been angry with us; it seems gutless not to say so.

I glance at the clock. The nativity is due to start in fifteen minutes. As much as we fear and loathe one another, as much as we are desperate to "have it out", neither of us is willing to miss a moment of the nativity. The twins are villagers, Auriol is a tree, we both think our children have been miscast and they demand our support all the more because of that.

Rose is probably making the same calculation. She must decide that she has less than fifteen minutes worth of rant in her, or that she can't wait a moment longer to blow my life apart, because she orders me to follow her to one of the classrooms where we'll be undisturbed.

Once we are quietly ensconced among mini table and chairs, powder paint and plasticine, I announce, "I'm not having an affair with Joe, if that's what you think."

"I don't know what to think. He said you were," she replies.

I could take advantage of Rose's frank confession. Clearly, she has her doubts about whether Joe told her the truth. I haven't time to ascertain how well they know one another and under what circumstances his confidence occurred. None of that matters right now. I could flat-out deny him. I might even be doing her a favour. But there's something so hideously low about denying your wrong-doings, it's almost like committing the crime twice. I can't do that.

Besides, I'm not given much of a chance. Rose apparently has six years of grievances to dump at my door and only fifteen minutes to do it in. She doesn't waste a second.

"Do you have any idea what you've done, Lucy?"

I stare at the rows of trays that secrete away the children's work books, tins of crayons and snacks for breaktimes. I wonder if she's really expecting an answer.

"I think so."

"I doubt it. You stole my husband and therefore, indirectly, my best years. I wasted my twenties, my youth, on Peter. You stole my memories and a significant part of my future. You deprived my children of their birthright — an involved, on the spot, father. You deprived me of my enormous family, and I wanted to live in the country, among wild flowers, birds, even grass snakes. But I'm locked here in London in the smog and shoddiness."

"Rose, you live in Holland Park, you can't complain."

"We live very comfortably, and if living in London had been what I wanted, then I'd have nothing to complain about, but it wasn't. I wanted their childhood to be about adventure, discovery and wonderment, not piano lessons and SAT results."

I'm shocked by this. I've always thought that Rose loved the rigidity of being an Alpha mum in central London. I thought she enjoyed being defined by the amount of after-school activities she could cram into her kids' day.

"I hate it that you have chosen how and where my boys live," she adds.

"I don't see it that way. It's the other way round."

"I have to stay near Peter but Peter isn't in the same house because he left us for you. We can't just up sticks to Australia or even North Yorkshire. I'm responsible for maintaining that relationship between them, a relationship that you did your best to destroy. I don't suppose you stopped to give that much thought when you were whipping off your knickers for my husband, did you?"

Her anger is mounting. I scrabble around for a consolation to offer up.

526

"At least you get to stay at home enjoying your kids. I have to go out to work and we can't afford four kids either because we are maintaining you."

"You're not doing me any favours, just the minimum legal requirement. Besides, there are times when I'd like to buy posh suits and hang out at the coffee machine."

"My work involves rather more than that and you know it."

"Yes, and you love your job, you'd hate staying at home with Auriol. You don't even like children but you still insisted on having the daughter that should have been mine."

This accusation was true up until very recently. I can't expect Rose to believe in or understand my recent change of heart, so I don't contradict her. Besides, there isn't opportunity, she's in full flow.

"And what you did to me isn't a thing of the past, you know, Lucy. I'm still being hurt by it. Do you know, Sebastian once asked if he could live with his dad? My heart broke, shattered into a million little pieces, but I said he could if he really wanted to and I asked him why he wanted to. He said it was because you and his father allowed him to play on Game Boy all day and never made him do his homework." Rose looks at me with contempt.

"I hated Peter, quite decisively, in that moment. He's often stooped to the lowest trick in the book, allowing the twins to do as they please, watch TV and eat ice cream, never insisting on a regular bedtime or brushed teeth. In some ways that seems like a bigger betrayal than shagging you. I've seen your parenting skills. I know that both of you opt for the line of least resistance. An army of nannies, endless treats, never as much as a hint of discipline. You don't care enough to engage with Auriol. You don't care enough to say no and I'm left mopping it up. But all of this I could accept, if you had loved him."

Rose is quivering. It's cold in the classroom but I think she's shaking with frustration, rage or disappointment — a storm of emotion — rather than the low temperatures. But she is not weeping or yelling and suddenly I am struck by the dignity of her silent enduring. She no longer seems gutless or timid. I do not think her quivering upper arms are ridiculous, they are almost noble. I respect her. I know why my love was married to her. I know why my best friend sings her praises. I know why my child likes being in her company.

I've always known. That has been my problem.

"I do love Peter," I tell her. It sounds silly saying something so big among endless Topsy and Tim books and multiplication tables. "I love him as much as you did, perhaps even more. Who knows? How can you measure and compare love?"

"Then why did you sleep with someone else?"

Rose looks me in the eye and her question is delivered without malice or anger, she's simply bewildered. No doubt when Peter was hers she never had so much as a moment's discontent. She never wavered, or made mistakes or felt frustrations. She made cakes and other sweet things.

528

Listening to her tirade against me was painful. Not because I felt unjustifiably vilified but because being so close to broken dreams is entirely miserable. Her list of inconvenient consequences, affronts, insults and pain that my pursuit of love has caused her is sickening. I want to apologize to her that she had to go through so much misery so that I could have Peter and I want to apologize that I didn't appreciate Peter and Auriol enough to stop myself having meaningless sex with a stranger and bringing this new heap of trouble to her feet, but I can't. I can't tell her about my frustrations, jealousies and discontent that led me to such an extreme measure, because all I was kicking back from is, clearly, all that she wants. If I tell her that domesticity was beating the very life out of me I will simply be hurting her more.

I'm not that evil.

Any explanation for my actions that I give must not appear to be a justification, because nothing can justify my betraying Peter. I cannot expect this woman's pity or sympathy but I do owe her something.

"I've struggled with being a second wife," I admit. "You're a tough act to follow." I steal a glance at Rose and see that she's astonished that I've confessed as much. "I did try my best."

"And your best has always been so damned sensational, hasn't it, Lucy?"

"Not when it came to being a mother, it seems. I'm really trying now, Rose. I want to be a better mum and wife. I really do. I'm never going to do it the way you do." Rose shoots me an agitated look. I rush to reassure her. "Not because there's anything at all wrong with the way you mother, actually the opposite. I was — I am — jealous of you. I'll never be as good in the same way. But I'm trying to find my way. I *am* trying, I'm turning over a new leaf. And this is not the moment to bring my family down like a card house. I had sex with someone else. It's over. He's gone. It meant nothing."

"It might mean everything."

"Only if you tell Peter. Otherwise it still means nothing. Please don't tell him, Rose."

"And that's it, is it, Lucy? Your new leaf is going to be based on more secrets and lies. If I keep quiet the problem hasn't gone away, it's just hibernating."

"I don't think I have any choice, Rose."

"Yes, you do. You know you do. You, more than most, always have a choice."

The bell rings, signalling that the play is about to start. We both bolt for the door. I don't know whether she's going to talk to Peter about Joe or not, but right this second there's a little girl dressed in a green rollneck jumper, brown tights and carrying two prickly branches who needs to see me in the audience, so we can't discuss this for another moment.

CHAPTER
FIFTY

Tuesday 12 December

Rose

Of course I cry. The boys' performances as villagers are
fairly perfunctory but that does not stop great big fat
tears sliding down my cheeks and splashing into my
lap. I take some comfort from the fact that there are
few dry eyes in the house. Not many parents can steel
themselves against the sight of earnest children belting
out *Oh Little Town of Bethlehem*.

In the last month or so I feel I have been doused and
wrung out more often than an old sock on washing day.
I have felt despondency, hope, elation, love, anger and
just ten minutes ago something nudging up towards
pity. I pity Lucy. How extraordinary is that? *She* is
jealous of *me*. What a revelation. This knowledge drifts
into my consciousness and cushions me in a way much
finer emotions have not been able to. I never took so
much comfort from biting my tongue and holding on
to my self-respect. I never felt consoled as I scrambled
on to the moral high ground. Isn't it strange that
something as base as Lucy's jealousy can placate me. It
goes to show I'm not as purely delightful as I've always

thought I was. Pitying her is a bonus. I feel quite light-headed.

But even while I pity her, I do not like her. And I owe her nothing at all. My emotions are a jumble and so it is unsurprising that the squishy red lips lisping out the well-rehearsed lines that "There's no room in the inn," Fran's (rather good) enactment of a weary Mary and the terrified shepherds facing the angel Gabriel cause me to blub.

The surprise is I've forgotten my tissues. Darn. I always carry a small packet, how could I have been so careless? I quietly sniffle and snuffle, hoping I'm not attracting too much attention. It transpires I am, when suddenly not one but two handkerchiefs are proffered at the same time.

Peter is sitting in front of me. He turns and holds out a handkerchief. It would be symbolic if it was one that I had given him on behalf of the boys on their first Fathers' day, but it is not. I bought his handkerchiefs from BHS; the one he's offering is Paul Smith. The other handkerchief is offered from my right. I look to see who is making the donation. Craig.

I hadn't noticed that I'd slipped into a seat right next to him. Because Lucy and I were battling out our differences in Year Two's classroom we nearly missed the beginning of the show. Flustered, I rushed into the hall and flung myself into the first available seat I spotted. I wonder if he thinks I did it on purpose. I have no idea whose handkerchief I should take. There's no etiquette for this particular situation. I grab both and blow my nose noisily, on each, in turn.

532

When the performance is over the children file in untidy lines back to their classrooms. A few brave kids break rank to rush into the audience to soak up their parents' praise, and to get and give an excited hug. I'm stunned when Henry and Sebastian are among this number. They fling themselves at me and tuck under an arm each.

"Well done, boys. Stellar performances," I gush.

I hope they can't see I've been crying. They'll be embarrassed and this spontaneous show of affection will be retracted instantly.

"Oh, Mum, we didn't have to do nothing," says Henry.

"Didn't have to do *anything*," I correct.

"Hi Dad," says Sebastian casually, as he spots Peter.

"Your mum is right, you were great villagers. Lots of realism when you were pretending to be asleep," says Peter with a wink. "Good costumes," he adds.

"Mum made them," says Sebastian. "Even the sandals. They're way past cool, aren't they?"

"Way past," confirms Peter.

I feel uncomfortable with all this sudden and vocal appreciation. The boys really must be pinning their Christmas gift hopes on me and ditching the possibility of Santa bringing the latest Hot Wheels contraption. I shoo them away and tell them to go back to their classroom to get changed. I turn to Peter.

"Can I have a word, Peter? It won't take long." I don't meet Lucy's eye.

We wander along the corridor, away from the noise of the hall. Many of the parents are tucking into their second round of mince pies and mulled wine; others are dashing for the door, keen to get back to the office before their bosses notice their absence.

As I walk along the corridor, decorated with hand-made paper chains and snowflakes, I consider how best I should phrase what I have to say.

People think it's hard when you are left with a couple of screaming babies that have barely settled into a night-time routine, let alone started potty training. That wasn't the hard bit — Peter hadn't been around much from the moment they were born anyway. He'd huffed and puffed if he had to do the least little thing. If he bathed them twice a week, he'd expect a medal. The hard bit wasn't the fact that he didn't want me — even that I learnt to live with. The hard bit was explaining to the boys why Peter left. They first started asking that tricky question when they were four. Auriol's age. They came home from school, gobsmacked to discover that most mothers and fathers lived in the same home. They asked, over and over again, why did Daddy leave?

I look at Peter, who is carefully examining a painting of a robin redbreast. I wonder how he would answer that one. What is the correct answer? Because he couldn't keep it in his trousers? A little explicit for four-year-olds, I fear.

I told them it was because he fell in love with Lucy and Lucy had fallen in love with their daddy. I even went so far as to list Lucy's many attributes so that it seemed like a natural thing, and they wouldn't think of their father as abhorrent. But even though I tried to be careful I couldn't stop the hurt and fear.

"He must not like me," said Henry, in alarm. His little face twisted with pain and confusion.

"No, darling, he just didn't like Mummy enough." This was the most sanitized response I could come up with.

Sebastian started to laugh. "Now, you're joking me, Mummy."

Henry turned to me, face awash with incredulity and astonishment, "But that's impossible."

That's love.

There was weekend after weekend when they begged me not to have to go to Peter's. It's boring, they complained. I'd pack up their favourite toys and insist they went. I'd call Peter and tell him to take them to the circus or the fair because I knew they desperately wanted to do these things. And I'd sit alone while Peter and Lucy played happy families, using my sons as a supporting cast. I kept reminding myself of the importance of the boys building a relationship with their daddy.

That's love.

There are lots of things that nobody ever tells you about having kids. Many new mothers resent the lack of warnings and wander around their homes with a mewing infant in arms, dressed in a spew-spattered dressing-gown and resentfully bewailing that they weren't forewarned.

Some new mums make up conspiracy theories about existing parents begrudging the freedom childless couples enjoy and assume parents deliberately withhold information, so as to trick others into joining their frazzled ranks. I don't buy that.

My theory is that the people with kids simply don't have the time to tell the people without them *everything*. On days when their child has slept, eaten and cooed appropriately they wear a glazed expression akin to a Stepford wife and murmur, "It's wonderful." But they fail to offer any real insight into the wonderfulness.

On days when babies have refused to sleep, toddlers have peed on carpets and broken neighbours' china, when schoolchildren have sworn, spat or simply refused to acknowledge any rules or guidelines, parents shake their weary heads and mutter, "It changes everything, you'll see."

But as most days mums really don't have time to run a comb through their hair, they cannot be expected to carve out the hours required to fully brief expectant parents about the exact nature and extent of that life change.

Indeed, no one warns you that for about five years after giving birth, finding time to go to the bathroom *alone* will rank among life's greatest luxuries. No one tells you that reliable babysitters are like gold dust. Or that you will dutifully run up and down stairs thirty times a night to nurse a child with a fever, although you are the sort of woman who would struggle to drag themselves to a step class, even one run by George Clooney.

Being a mother means a life of contradictions. No one tells you that children have tiny foibles. A little bop or way of handling a watering can that will reduce you to tears of happiness.

No one tells you that you will vanish. That you've never been more important. That you will feel sticky, scruffy and be used as a human trampoline, but that your arms will feel empty if you ever do escape to the shops or an office. You would die for them. You live for them. They take up every moment of your conscious and unconscious mind and more than that.

What is Peter saying now? "The boys' costumes are great. Maybe next year you could help out with Auriol's. Lucy isn't a seamstress."

The nerve of him. I stare at this man who was once my be-all and end-all and I almost laugh. He's looking relaxed and affable. He really doesn't think there's anything inappropriate in asking me to help out with making a costume for Auriol, and perhaps there isn't. She did struggle with those enormous prickly branches today. I felt sorry for her; it can't have been comfortable. I would have sewn material leaves on to her rollneck jumper.

"OK," I nod. And it doesn't hurt. Helping Auriol — therefore Lucy — doesn't hurt. In fact, it feels OK. I hand him back his designer handkerchief.

"Keep it," he says.

At least until I wash it, is what he means. I smile to myself. Peter could always be a bit overly fussy. This doesn't hurt me; it amuses me. And I think it's a bit of a relief that I'm no longer caught up in a world where BHS handkerchiefs were considered below par.

Frankly, there were times when Peter's snobbery was a little irritating.

He brushes his hair out of his eyes. It's a familiar gesture. I'm fond of him. I'm mildly irritated by him and fond of him in the same breath. I am not furious with him and I don't love him. I feel the chains of resentment that I've hampered myself with fall from my ankles and arms. I feel weightless.

"What did you want to talk to me about?" he asks.

"I was just wondering if it was OK with you for me to take the boys up to north London for Christmas day. Daisy wants to be hostess this year."

"Wow, quite a break with tradition for you guys. I know you love Christmas day at your house."

"Yes, but Daisy really wants this. I think she's sick of feeling like the baby and wants to show Mum and Dad that she can cook a great lunch too. Change can be a good thing."

"Well, I've no problem with the boys going there. They'll have a great day."

"You could stop by in the afternoon if you like, to see them."

"I don't think that's a good idea. Daisy won't like Lucy in her house."

"I'd make sure Daisy is polite." He looks unconvinced. "I'd make sure Lucy got a warm welcome, as opposed to the one she deserves," I add with a giggle.

Peter smiles and appreciates my joke. "We'll think about it. Thanks."

"I think it's time we all moved on," I say. This time there's not a hint of a giggle in my voice. I'm deadly serious.

"That's great to hear, Rose."

"The past is a foreign country; the future seems more like home."

"Have you been on the mulled wine?"

Peter is very English and always struggled with my amateur philosophizing. That's why I didn't do too much thinking for a long time. But he smiles at me and I see enough respect and warmth for me not to feel silly.

"Well, you'd better be getting back to Lucy, she'll be wondering where you are."

At that second Lucy appears in the corridor.

"Hello, darling, we're just making plans for Christmas day," says Peter, casually putting his arm around her shoulder. He kisses her cheek. I check. Do I feel anything? No resentment. No pain. No, nothing at all. "Rose invited us to join them at Daisy's for an hour in the afternoon."

Lucy eyes me nervously. "That's nice," she mutters.

"We're just talking about some things being in the past and all the better for that," I say to her.

We share a moment. We exchange the glance of conspirators and I think she understands that she has my silence, which is why it's somewhat peculiar that she turns to Peter and says, "Sweetheart, have you got time to come home for lunch, rather than go back to the office, there's something important I need to tell you. We need to talk."

"I'll leave you to it," I mutter and I walk back to the hall, anticipating a mince pie and a well-earned glass of mulled wine.

I have no idea whether Lucy and Peter will go home and have a heart to heart or whether she will bottle and go home for frantic, diverting sex instead. The important thing is, I don't mind. It's none of my business. I imagine they'll be OK. And not just because I think they are the type to always be OK, but because I think they are meant for one another and I think they know that too. And love is quite extraordinary in its capacity to forgive. As Sebastian and Henry would say, whatever.

I have more important things to do. First I have to call Daisy and tell her that we're all coming to hers for Christmas lunch and then I have to hunt out my future.

Epilogue

Tuesday 12 December

Craig

Rose is holding out my handkerchief. She looks apprehensive but excited. She's shiny. I don't mean her cheeks and forehead, although they are shiny (for once it is hot in the school hall and the place is heaving with frantic parents), I mean her eyes are shiny. I think Rose has many attributes, both physical and mental. I love her kindness, her laugh and her red hair, but her eyes are possibly my favourite. Her eyes are so beautiful. They are clever, glittering and mischievous. It's easy to miss the mischievousness because Rose wants everyone to believe she's so eminently sensible. But I'm not fooled. I know she once enjoyed karaoke.

I take the handkerchief off her and push it into my jacket pocket.

She's apologetic. "Sorry, it's a bit of a mess. Lipstick and snot, pretty hideous combination, but if you wash it on a hot wash, then —"

"I might never wash it, Rose. I might keep it under my pillow." She looks startled. "I'm just joking," I add hastily.

She smiles back, relieved. Rose and I have not spoken since Tom's wedding. The last thing I said to her was that in six months' time we'd probably be picking out wallpaper together. My God, how I've agonized over that comment. I hadn't meant to scare her off and sound stalker-ish. I just thought she needed to be reassured that I wasn't a flighty, fly-by-night type. I wanted her to know that I thought we had a future or at least the possibility of one. For the last month I've spent my time reconsidering the entire date — at length — and in particular that remark. I reasoned that Rose must have thought I was mad and over-keen or, at the very least, a shallow, silly and glib man. But I wasn't lying or even exaggerating. At the wedding I felt so close to Rose. I thought that there was genuine respect between us and the chat was amusing and interesting. I thought we were doing well. But then she vanished.

For the last month I have wondered how best to sort out this mess. It's terrible that she is so horribly embarrassed that she no longer dares show her face at school. It's clear that she's avoiding me, which is one better than reporting me to the Board of Governors for inappropriate behaviour I suppose, but I can barely take consolation from that. At least if she did report me I'd get the chance to put my side to her. I'd get the chance to tell her just how great I think she is and how much I've missed her in this last month. I hadn't realized how far she'd crept under my skin.

I noticed Rose long before John started his campaign to find me a woman. Since the boys started school I've been struck by her cheerful nature and her can-do attitude. I liked the way she mothered. She's quite old-fashioned in her approach but not out of touch. Her boys clearly adore her. She's popular with the other mums and the teachers too, because while she's involved in every committee the school has set up, she manages to be discreet and helpful and not pushy or overbearing.

It was at last summer's sports day that I began to realize that my interest in Rose was not purely platonic. I found myself craning my neck, searching her out at every opportunity. I felt a genuine pinch of disappointment in my gut when she didn't win the mothers' race and a genuine stir somewhere a little bit lower when she lay on the grass panting and laughing trying to recover from the exertion of the race.

I found myself lingering at the school gate in the hope of exchanging a word or two with her. I was always thrilled to see her at the Parents' Association meetings, which I looked forward to much more than the nights trawling around pubs and bars with John.

I am mortified that I've stepped over the mark at the wedding and ruined our friendship. I've spent the last month wishing I'd just let things be as they were. Being her friend forever would have been better than losing her altogether. But then she sat next to me at the nativity play and I began to wonder. To hope.

Mrs Baker came to see me the moment the play was over. I accepted her beams and congratulations on the production along with those from all the other mothers.

"Are you taking Rose to the Christmas dance on Friday?" she asked me.

"Erm, well, no. I wasn't planning on asking her," I mumbled, totally mortified that Mrs Baker would address this subject so publicly.

"Why not?" she demanded.

"I don't think Rose would like it," I admitted.

"Rose sometimes doesn't know what's good for her," said Mrs Baker with a hint of impatience. "Our mutual friend, John, told me that she ditched you at the wedding. Is that right?"

I felt the heat of my blush but managed to nod.

"He said you were gutted. Is that right?" she demanded.

Cheers, John, what a mate. Again I nodded.

"Well, I can't begin to explain why," said Mrs Baker. "But I do know that you're the only man she's shown any interest in for *six* years. Faint heart never wins fair maid, and all that. I'd suggest you ask her out again."

"You do?"

"Yes, and not just because John and I are determined matchmakers." She grinned at me.

"Well, thank you, Mrs Baker, for bothering to talk to me about this. I'll think about what you said."

"You do that." And then she added, "Call me Connie."

Connie Baker might have it wrong. After all, how can I trust the judgement of a woman who was once crazy about John Harding? But she seemed genuine and there's always the possibility that she might have it right.

Might is a word and concept that is largely undervalued but I think might is a powerful word.

Rose is staring at the ceiling. She's probably trying to avoid my eye.

"Nice decorations," she comments.

"Do you think so? I think they missed your touch."

She looks at me and smiles shyly. "I owe you an apology and an explanation."

"Not at all. I assume you don't like wedding cake," I grin. What else can I do but make a joke about the most humiliating moment of my life.

She smiles back. Rose is doing a lot of smiling today. She doesn't look like a woman who is scared of the headmaster turning into a stalker. She doesn't look like a woman who might want to report me, or reject me, or run from me.

"Were you worried that the boys wouldn't approve of our dating?" I hazard this guess. It is one of many theories I've had a chance to form. I have approximately thirty-seven others to try, if this doesn't prove to be correct.

"Yes, but that wasn't why I left. I had some stuff that I needed to work through. I had some things that I had to let go before I could grab on to anything new. Do you understand?"

I nod. I think I do. I want to. "Have you done that, now?" I ask.

I push my glasses up on to the bridge of my nose. It's important to establish where we stand, just so I can prepare myself for the possibility of another vanishing act.

"Yes." She smiles again. Each one is a delight.

"Perhaps you could tell me all about it, over a coffee?" I carefully lay my offer before her. I hold my breath.

"No, I don't think so." The disappointment floors me. I'd thought she was going to accept. Or at least I'd hoped it. I gasp and scramble around my brain for a dignified and hasty exit from this conversation. "I think I should explain it over cocktails, in a bar. A really trendy bar. Ideally over-priced and very busy. I want to feel life again. My treat. Are you free tonight?" says Rose with a wide and cheerful beam.

"Tonight, erm, I can be. Will you be able to get someone to sit for the boys at such short notice?" I ask.

"I imagine so. Let's get on with it, Craig, I've wasted enough time."

And so we shall.

Get on with it.

Little Children

Tom Perrotta

Beneath the placid surface of suburbia, the adults are kicking their toys out of their prams . . .

In this brilliantly perceptive novel, a group of parents, trapped in middle-class stability, deal with marriage, kids and their suburban life in very different ways . . .

There's Mary Ann, a super-mom who is already preparing her 4-year-old son for Harvard. Then there's Todd, the handsome stay-at-home dad. He's trying (for his wife's sake) to pass his bar exam although he doesn't want to be a lawyer. Sarah is a lapsed feminist who isn't quite sure how she ended up being a traditional wife.

They all raise their kids in the kind of quiet suburb where nothing ever seems to happen, until one eventful summer when a convicted criminal moves into the neighbourhood and two parents begin an affair, which will take them further than they could ever have imagined . . .

ISBN 978-0-7531-7926-0 (hb)
ISBN 978-0-7531-7927-7 (pb)

Any Way You Want Me

Lucy Diamond

On paper, Sadie's got it all — the partner, the children, the house. But Sadie can't help harking back to the time when she was a career woman by day and a party animal by night. The only sleepless nights she's getting now are due to the baby. Maybe a little reinvention is the answer . . .

Sadie can't resist creating a fictitious online identity for herself as a hot TV producer. It's only a bit of harmless fun . . . until truth and fantasy become dangerously tangled. It isn't long before she's wondering if the exciting alter ego she has dreamed up really is the kind of person she wants to be after all . . .

ISBN 978-0-7531-7922-2 (hb)
ISBN 978-0-7531-7923-9 (pb)

The Betrayal of Grace Mulcahy

Colette Caddle

The life and marriage of Grace and Michael Mulcahy
has all the signs of being a successful and fulfilled one:
a daughter, rewarding jobs and plenty of friends. But
when Grace discovers that her partner in her interior
design business, 52-year-old Miriam, is embezzling her,
the seeds are sown for Grace's bind.

When confronted with her betrayal, Miriam begs Grace
not to tell anyone in order to preserve Miriam's
marriage, which will fall apart if the truth outs. Grace
agrees to keep quiet but finds it leads to all sorts of
complications and misunderstandings that put a strain
on all of her relationships both professional and
personal. By the time she notices how close things are
to crumbling, it could be too late to piece together the
ties that bind her to those she loves.

ISBN 978-0-7531-7728-0 (hb)
ISBN 978-0-7531-7729-7 (pb)

Midnight Cactus

Bella Pollen

From the author of *Hunting Unicorns*

On the run from her claustrophobic marriage in London, Alice Coleman moves her two small children to a ghost town in the Arizona desert — and there finds an escape she hadn't thought possible.

But the mythic Southwest has room for more than one fugitive. In the dusty, alien atmosphere, it seems that everyone — from Benjamín, the town's loyal caretaker, to the laconic and mysterious Duval — has something to hide.

And as winter moves to scorching summer, what seemed idyllic turns deadly as Alice is drawn deeper into an obsessive quest for revenge, until finally she must decide how far she is willing to go.

ISBN 978-0-7531-7732-7 (hb)
ISBN 978-0-7531-7733-4 (pb)

Husbands

Adele Parks

Can you have one too many?

Bella secretly married her childhood sweetheart, Stevie, when they were at university, two big kids playing at being grown-ups. When it all unravelled, Bella simply got up and left. And the secret remained a secret.

Years later, Bella meets Philip and, despite her vow never to marry again, she can't resist him. He's funny, charming, interesting and kind. Only hitch is, she's still married to Stevie. Bella, typically, just ignores the problem. And the moment to tell Philip never quite seems to arrive.

So Bella plans never to reveal her secret; she hasn't seen Stevie for years, probably never will again. Except that Bella's best friend Laura has fallen in love, and when she introduces her new man to the gang it is none other than Stevie. Could things get any more complicated? Only if Bella and Stevie fall in love with each other again . . .

ISBN 978-0-7531-7521-7 (hb)
ISBN 978-0-7531-7522-4 (pb)

ISIS publish a wide range of books in large print, from fiction to biography. Any suggestions for books you would like to see in large print or audio are always welcome. Please send to the Editorial Department at:

ISIS Publishing Limited
7 Centremead
Osney Mead
Oxford OX2 0ES

A full list of titles is available free of charge from:

Ulverscroft Large Print Books Limited

(UK)
The Green
Bradgate Road, Anstey
Leicester LE7 7FU
Tel: (0116) 236 4325

(Australia)
P.O. Box 314
St Leonards
NSW 1590
Tel: (02) 9436 2622

(USA)
P.O. Box 1230
West Seneca
N.Y. 14224-1230
Tel: (716) 674 4270

(Canada)
P.O. Box 80038
Burlington
Ontario L7L 6B1
Tel: (905) 637 8734

(New Zealand)
P.O. Box 456
Feilding
Tel: (06) 323 6828

Details of **ISIS** complete and unabridged audio books are also available from these offices. Alternatively, contact your local library for details of their collection of **ISIS** large print and unabridged audio books.